The Annunciation

Patrick Lynch

THE
ANNUNCIATION

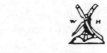

HEINEMANN : LONDON

First published in Great Britain 1993
by William Heinemann Ltd
an imprint of Reed Consumer Books Ltd
Michelin House, 81 Fulham Road, London SW3 6RB
and Auckland, Melbourne, Singapore and Toronto

Copyright © Patrick Lynch 1993
The author has asserted his moral rights

A CIP catalogue record for this book
is available at the British Library

ISBN 0 434 70319 2

Phototypeset by Intype, London
Printed in Great Britain
by St Edmundsbury Press, Bury St Edmunds

For
Peter & Dorothy
Edward & Iris
&
Sylvie

The author would like to thank David Sington and Dr Helena Scott for their invaluable help with the scientific and medical elements of this story.

Contents

Prologue
1

PART ONE
Rise early, work hard, strike oil
9

PART TWO
The Annunciation
221

PART THREE
A sacrifice
415

Epilogue
565

All men dream; but not equally. Those who dream
by night in the dusty recesses of their minds
wake in the day to find it was vanity:
but the dreamers of the day are dangerous men,
for they may act their dream with open eyes,
to make it possible.

T. E. Lawrence

Prologue

The Forest of Fontainebleau, France. August 21st, 1995.

There was a jungle stink after the clean air of the woods. Breathing lightly through her open mouth, the young woman walked between the rows of cabinets in which she knew the cells were breeding. After four months of preparation she knew everything. In this room, one floor down from the data banks, the cultures were kept at a steady thirty-seven degrees centigrade like the nutrient solutions which flowed in and out of the cabinets from the reservoirs hidden behind them. Sweat pricked along her hairline. She touched nothing. To her it was a bad place, a place that would come back to her in her dreams.

It was dark apart from the trembling beam of her flashlight. From all sides came a steady hum from the heating and air purification systems. She listened.

'What are you doing?'

Alain's voice sounded loud in her head. She blinked once and looked down to where he was kneeling.

'I was just thinking.'

'Well don't think. Just give me some light.'

His voice sounded strangled, scared. The air in the room was bad, and the knowledge of what was happening inside the cabinets made it hard to stay calm. After a moment the man looked up from the plan which he had spread on the linoleum floor. He squinted into the flashlight.

'Where's the stuff?'

The woman was held for a moment by his eyes. Filaments of yellow radiated out from the pupil into the blue of the iris. She had never noticed it before.

'*Marie!*'

The sound of her name startled her. She took out a pair of cellophane gloves and kneeling down, unzipped the camera bag she had been carrying. Inside there was a small glass bottle containing a cocktail of sodium phenate and ammonium chloride. Smudged thumbprints showed clearly on the glass.

Everyone in the group had been impressed by the thinking behind the mixture. It had been explained to them by Hans Fleischman, the German newcomer, as they sat around a table in a poorly lit cafe. Powerful antiseptics like sodium phenate would change the acid/alkaline balance of the nutrient solution. This could be detected by sensors which would then automatically shut off the supply of nutrient to the cells. Just the right amount of an acid solution like ammonium chloride would compensate for the alkalinity of the sodium phenate without affecting its killing power. It was Fleischman who had acquired the chemicals and mixed them. It was Fleischman who carried a rifle in spite of what Jean-Christophe had said. He had driven them to the drop-off point with the gun between his knees: a high-velocity model with night sights. Jean-Christophe had said nothing. After all it was Fleischman who had come to them with the plans of the laboratory and the seven-figure codes for passing the secure doors. Without him the whole project, though Jean-Christophe's idea, would have been impossible.

The nutrient solution for the cultures was kept in four sealed reservoirs just behind the row of cabinets. Each of the reservoirs was pressurised with nitrogen gas and the temperature and flow of the liquid controlled by a computerised system of gates and sensors. The man opened the pressure valves on each reservoir in turn and unscrewed the lids. Working close to him, her breath coming and going on the nape of his neck, she poured the poison into each one. Then the reservoirs were re-sealed. On one of the computer terminals at the side of the room a warning message blinked on and off as the temperature of the solution dropped, but only for a few seconds. The heating system soon made up the difference.

'We're done,' said the man.

Guided by her flashlight, they moved back to the staircase. Taking the steps two by two the man went on up to the first floor where other lights moved on the ceiling and on the walls. The woman took a last look back at the room. Nothing appeared to have changed, but she knew that inside the cabinets everything was dying. Terrible violence was being done in complete silence. It was what made the whole business of cellular manipulation so sinister to her. At that level outrage remained voiceless. She looked down at the camera case in which she had deposited the empty bottle. She was still wearing the gloves. She pulled them off and slipped them into the bag. It was then she noticed the big grey metal doors beside her.

In the upper room nobody looked up as the man entered. The room was almost empty except for two parallel rows of white metal cabinets, each one about the size of a small refrigerator. There was also a pair of computer terminals in one corner, with some more machinery beside them. It seemed cold after the culture room. Jean-Christophe was taking a coil of electric cable from his bag. Nobody spoke. He plugged it into a socket beside the computer terminals. The other end he connected to an electromagnet, a U-shaped block of iron bound round with insulated wire. Luc began opening the white cabinets where the data disks were stored in racks. At the press of a button each disk slid out on a tray where it could be picked up by a handle

3

on the top. There were four in each cabinet. Luc lifted them out one by one and Jean-Christophe passed the electromagnet over them. As they worked, the green display lights on the trays lit up their hands and faces. Jean-Christophe's eyes cut from the disk he was holding to Luc's hand and back again.

'Take it easy,' he said as they moved to the second cabinet, 'or you'll drop one of these things.'

Luc didn't respond. It didn't feel good, destroying data that had taken years to compile. It went against the grain.

'What's the time?' he said.

'We're okay.'

'Late aren't we?'

'We're *okay*.'

They worked on in complete silence. It took ten minutes to destroy the data bank, sixty thousand man-hours of compilation, selection, correction, observation.

When he had put the magnet back in the bag Jean-Christophe looked up. He stared at Alain. It was a quarter past midnight. At twenty-five past they had to be at the rendezvous point.

'Where's Marie?' he said.

As the door rode back on well-oiled hinges she knew she was making a mistake. The room before her was pitch black and the smell she had noticed in the culture room was much worse. Heavy and waxy, it clung to the back of the throat. She took a step forward, throwing the beam of the flashlight across the bare walls. She went along a passage and then turned left into a larger room. Then she saw what looked like a cage. Almost as soon as she had seen it the flashlight went out.

'*Merde!*'

She shook the flashlight. Then she struck it against her palm. There was something wrong with the contact. She shook it again. The light flashed feebly and then went dead.

4

She looked around her trying to find something to latch onto in the stinking dark. There was nothing. In her panic she had turned. She didn't know the way back now. The blood was beating in her head. She gripped the dead flashlight trying to think. All she had to do was to walk forward until she reached a wall. Then, by working her way around the room she would eventually come to the door. There might be other doors, but she would know if she were in the right place. Her door opened onto the staircase, and she would see the lights of the others.

The thought that they would soon be finished, might already be looking for her, pushed her forward. But as she extended her hands in the dark, she felt sure something was there, something that would catch hold of her reaching fingers. She snatched back her hands as though she had been bitten. She struggled to control her breath. Then she moved forward.

In three short strides she came up against something cold and metallic. Her foot struck the base of whatever it was. Then there was noise that stopped her dead. Something directly in front of her had moved. It was right in front of her, at the level of her face. *Vivisection* – the words flashed in her head like a razor. *They were doing animal experiments*. This had never occurred to any of them. The assumption had been that the only living things in the Fontainebleau laboratory were the cell cultures. *The staff are all dead from the heart down* was what Alain had said.

The darkness was suddenly unbearable. She had seen hundreds of photographs of animals staring out of cages in uncomprehending misery, heads shaven, skin covered in sores, bodies covered with electrodes. She squeezed her eyes shut, as though the darkness could be squeezed out from under the lids. Then, gripping the flashlight with both hands, she stepped back from the noise.

'Marie!'

It was Alain's voice. It sounded far away. It seemed

5

to be coming from her right. She turned and blundered forward, her hands reaching out in front of her.

'Marie, where are you?'

She came hard against another metal panel. There was a sudden burst of movement. All around her the darkness was alive with thrashing, twisting, scuffling sounds. She screamed once, biting off the end of the scream in fear of the sound of her own voice. Then, as she stood back from the cage, the flashlight came on.

'She was behind me when I came out of the culture room,' said Alain. Jean-Christophe looked at his watch.

'It's twenty past. If we don't make it to the rendezvous Fleischman will just keep driving.'

'He wouldn't go without us.'

Jean-Christophe looked at Alain's face.

'You don't think so?'

It was a rhesus monkey. It was held upright in a harness, the arms extended, cruciform. The eyes were wild, staring. Marie looked down from the face to the wispy hair curled on the breast bone. Her mouth was suddenly dry. The area of the animal's stomach was covered in dark tumours. They were swollen and purple, like fingers pushing out from the inside. The skin was flaking away around each of them. They had attached its hands and feet so that it couldn't scratch itself. If it had scratched itself, it would have spoilt their experiment.

Marie felt a strange calm come over her. The beam of the flashlight ceased trembling. She looked at the dying animal, her eyes sucking up the detail of its misery. At first she thought it was yawning, or displaying its fangs to warn her away. But now she could see from its squeezing rib cage and the rush of air escaping through its stretched jaws – she could see that it was screaming, howling in agony or fear. *They have cut the vocal chords.* She nodded once,

6

understanding everything. They had cut the vocal chords so as not to be bothered by the screams.

'Marie!'

There was no more time. In another moment the men would find her. A short, crouching run through the thickly growing ferns, and they would be back in the Landcruiser celebrating their success. They wouldn't risk waiting any longer. They were probably behind time already. She had to act. Somewhere to her left she heard the door to the room open. Light was flung along the passage illuminating the wall behind her.

'Marie!'

She reached forward and drew back the bolt of the cage door. The crucified animal strained against its harness, twisting and turning. She worked feverishly, her fingers undoing the straps which held the animal in place. She could hardly see through the tears in her eyes.

'Marie, what are you doing in here?'

The men entered the room just as she undid the last strap. There was a moment of silence, as the animal realised that it could move its limbs. Marie half turned to find Alain's face in the moving shadows of the flashlights. There was a flurry of movement. She turned back just in time to see the monkey explode from the cage, eyes staring, fangs bared. It leapt against her, biting at her face, tearing at her hair with its hands. She tried to draw a breath to scream, but her mouth was suddenly full of blood, and she was choking, toppling backwards. Alain tried to pull the animal off. It was wrenching its head back and forth, tearing at the girl's face. Marie screams were deafening in the confined space. Alain yanked at the animal so hard that he lost his footing. They fell over, the girl falling on top of him, winding him for a second. Alain grabbed a hairy forearm which was tensed and trembling like a steel cable. With a swift bite the animal almost severed his index finger. He let go with a yell, hardly able to believe the pain. The

7

flashlight rolled away across the floor. As he reached out for it he realised that Jean-Christophe was standing over them. Again Marie screamed.

'Hit it, Jean-Christophe! Hit it!'

Alain struggled to get up from under Marie's twisting body.

'Kill it, for Christ's sake!' he screamed, but he could see the other man's face. Jean-Christophe was rooted to the spot, too horrified to move. Then there was a flash of blue flame and a bang so loud that Alain thought his skull had been shattered. Silence followed.

Alain let his head rest against the floor. He could feel the blood flowing from his body. Fleischman was in the room, the rifle by his side, his voice angry but controlled.

'Are you crazy? What are you doing in here?'

Alain tried to find Fleischman's face.

'Marie freed one of the animals. It attacked her.'

'And the cultures?'

Jean-Christophe was somewhere in the shadows. Vomit splashed against the cement floor.

'I think Marie is hurt.' Alain tried to control his voice as he spoke. Fleischman came forward and shone his flashlight into Marie's face, and then down at Alain.

'Yes. She is bitten in the face. It's bad.'

'Jesus, Jesus,' Jean-Christophe was mumbling and spitting.

'We have to get her to a hospital,' said Alain, raising himself on one arm and trying to get a look at Marie's face. The monkey's gaping, bloody jaws blocked his view. With his good hand he pushed the dead animal aside. Marie was still, her face a bloody mass of bites. Through the tear in the thick flesh of her cheek Alain could see her teeth.

PART ONE

Rise early, work hard, strike oil

1

As soon as Mike Varela pushed his security pass into the door he knew something was wrong. In the ten months he had been with Swift and Drew this simple act had become automatic, like the outer door itself which on receiving his card gave a simultaneous subterranean clunk as the vertical bolts retracted.

This time there was no clunk. Mike watched, his mouth twitching as he heard nylon wheels mesh in the brushed steel panel. His card was being read. He stood for a second, hands on hips, the impatient M&A prodigy, glaring through multiple reflections at the bent backs in European Sales. Ted Farmer, someone Mike knew from his loud, wise-cracking mouth, was telling a story from the other side of the desk, his face lit by the green glow of his Reuters screen.

The guys in sales were always having fun – something Mike often remarked to himself as he made his way into the recesses of the twenty-seventh floor. In M&A, particularly in this subsection which handled cross-border LBO business, people tended to be wrapped tighter. There was more riding on each deal was how Mike explained it. That and the fact that Napier Drew, a grandson of one of the founders, was a professional pain-in-the-ass. Napier headed up the LBO operation and kept

11

everyone's noses to the grindstone while he himself spent most of the day talking on the phone about the fishing up in Cape Cod to one or other of his WASP friends.

After a moment of listening to the security panel fizz and grind, Mike hammered on the outside door, one of three, each plated with thick glass which sealed off the offices of Swift and Drew from the vestibule. Nobody could hear him on the other side. There was a hiss of air conditioning as Mike focused on the slot into which his pass had disappeared.

Then a female voice he could not recognise came through on the p.a. system.

'Could Miguel Varela please come down to reception on the fifteenth floor.'

Magically everyone on European sales turned and looked at him. Ted waved and then said something which made several of the other guys look down at their shoes, their shoulders shaking. Mike felt the blood rise to his face. *Miguel!* Nobody in Swift and Drew called him Miguel. It made him sound like a refugee from Spanish Harlem. He punched the lift button, chipping his thumbnail.

He had a five-floor slow-motion fall to think about his summons. It wouldn't make any difference to the outcome, but not knowing what came next, even for a few seconds in the empty lift, was intolerable. Mike held back the glossy black hair from his forehead, his mouth a thin line.

That it concerned the Mendelhaus/Raeburn buy-out was a certainty. Driving down Broadway in the heavy seven o'clock traffic, the cellphone in his new BMW coupé had purred twice, and he'd had Ray Kilczynski on the line from Bond Sales worrying about negative covenant documentation which hadn't arrived. It had to go into the prospectus before they could even think about the issue of bonds due just three days later.

'Time's running out on this, Mike,' he'd said. 'You'd better kick some Ivy League ass in the legal department.'

It was nothing to worry about. This was what he'd told Ray, but as he slipped the phone back into its cradle he couldn't help feeling unsettled. As the BMW – driven from the showroom only the week before in celebration of the Mendelhaus deal – slid into the shadow of Mitsubishi Tower, Mike looked at the clock, counting out the time they had left in hours. The hold-up with the legal documentation might be just an administrative wrinkle, but too much was riding on the deal for him to enjoy the ride in his thermostatically-controlled seat. Also, he reminded himself, Pat Tyler ran a very tight ship in Corporate Law, and a delay like this, especially with such a simple deal, was almost unheard of.

As the elevator lights counted down, twenty-three, twenty-two, twenty-one, Mike ran the deal through his head for the hundredth time – or rather what it meant to him, which, depending on certain variables, looked to be a lot. When the ownership of Raeburn Corporation passed into the hands of Mendelhaus in exchange for $1.4 billion, as was supposed to happen in one week's time, he could look forward to a bonus of at least $200,000 as the originator of the deal. In ten months at Swift and Drew it was the first time Napier had let him take any initiative, the first time he'd got into the commission money.

And the deal had looked so good he'd gone out and bought a flashy car on which he had eleven big payments to meet. Similarly the apartment he'd bought on Park Avenue South in the summer drew down one half of his present salary, which was beginning to get a little uncomfortable the way he lived.

But what worried Mike most as he watched the num-

13

bers tumble was the small but ever-present possibility that he might actually lose his job. Swift and Drew was one of the Street's old blue-blood operations, and he was only there because he didn't mess up, because he made the company money. Napier Drew had him in his sights. One slip up and he was out. Mike, a second generation Mexican immigrant, had heard Napier call him a wetback on the phone one lunch-time when he first joined the company. He hadn't seen that Mike was listening, but when he caught his eye, Napier had just smiled and crossed his Timberland Beef-Roll loafers on the teak desk.

By the time the doors opened on the fifteenth floor, Mike's shoulders were hunched inside his Italian suit and he was smoking one of the cigarettes normally reserved for clients.

'Mr Varela?'

The receptionist was new, Hispanic, or maybe Italian; young and cute.

'Mr Drew senior would like you to go up straight away.'

Mike looked at her eyes. She was the one who had called him Miguel. It was just a linguistic slip. But he didn't see how he could check.

'Drew?'

'That's right, Mr Varela.'

She didn't have to say which floor, everybody knew that. Drew was at the top.

Back in the elevator Mike touched the sixty and leaned back against the wall of the rising car. The elevator carried him silently up to a sunlit landing with a plain marble floor. Opposite him were the doors of two more elevators which served the final five floors where the directors had their suites of offices. You couldn't enter these lifts without a special pass. Those without passes had to ring. Mike felt like a travelling salesman as he reached out his hand.

He touched the buzzer and a panel slid back revealing the cyclops stare of a security camera.

'Mike Varela,' he said, his voice echoing in the marble vestibule. There was no acknowledgement. The panel clicked back into place. There was an interval of thirty seconds and then the lift door opened. Mike went on up. This time to the very top.

What he saw when the lift door slid back was a stone fireplace, and a large Turkish carpet. The windows on either side of the room were hung with transparent drapes. A tall brunette was waiting for him. She smiled moistly as he stepped out of the lift and then turned with a swish of silk stocking and walked away. Mike followed her. Nothing was said. They walked along a corridor which was lit naturally from above. There were engravings of hunting scenes on the plum-coloured walls. There was a heavy oak door, another corridor, some steps and double doors leading into a large dimly-lit room. As silently as she had appeared, the brunette left, closing the doors behind her.

'Michael.'

Mike turned and saw, not the old man himself, but Harvey Swift, one of the senior partners, a distinguished grey-haired man in a tweed suit. Sunlight lancing in through the drawn curtains lit his manicured left hand. He was holding a dead cigar. Mike noticed that beyond Swift's head there was an open door. The colder light in the doorway suggested utility. A bathroom maybe or a kitchen. Mike refocused on the smiling man's face, his heart thumping in his chest.

'Sit down, Mike.'

'I thought it was Mr Drew who wanted to see me,' said Mike, pointlessly.

A barely perceptible ripple of anger crossed Swift's face. Mike noticed he was very pale.

15

'Drew is indisposed,' he said shortly, and then, adjusting himself in the leather armchair, he went on: 'This deal, Michael. Mendelhaus, Raeburn. You think it makes good sense?'

Mike noticed a movement of shadow on the open door. He was sure Drew was behind it. He tried to concentrate.

'Yes, sir. Raeburn has been steadily losing market share. It's a tired company pushing dated, mass-market products. Much of the capital is in the hands of institutions who are known to be unhappy with the earnings performance, and the remaining family stockholders show all the signs of being ready to sell. It's a textbook target. Mendelhaus is a – '

Swift held up a trembling hand. Mike sat back in his chair as though he had been pushed. When Swift spoke his voice was almost a whisper.

'People from UBG, Mendelhaus's main shareholder as you know, they called this morning, asking us to go no further with the transaction. I succeeded in contacting the chairman of Mendelhaus, Oswald Hunziker – briefly – but he had no information to give me, except to confirm that our services *are no longer required*.'

He waited for a long time for the younger man to say something, but Mike was too stunned to speak.

'I couldn't insist on an explanation, but then they had paid their fee, and were under no obligation to explain anything. Obviously for one reason or another the deal no longer made sense.'

This time the man's white hand stopped Mike's words on his lips.

'It may have something to do with this.'

He picked up a slim black box, about the size of a cigarette lighter and touched a button. A panel in the wall slid back to reveal a Reuters screen. Swift pressed another button, the screen blinked and Mike was reading a split screen, on the left a stacked series of graphs show-

16

ing share prices of leading European pharmaceuticals stocks and on the right a news report on a speech given by the French minister for science and industry. The speech said that European Community directives banning all human embryo experimentation would hit French industry badly, especially in the face of Japanese and Korean competition. Mike frowned. The graphs on the left all showed five percent declines since the day before.

'I understand Mendelhaus may have had some genetics interests.'

Mike looked at the old man, his lips forming the first word of the tumbling objections which filled his head.

'Swift and Drew has lost a lot of money on this deal, Michael.' Swift's voice had hardened. 'A lot of money. We have also lost face, in some ways more serious. People, people on the board are saying we, you, put Mendelhaus under pressure to make the bid and that it fell apart for the same reason. They don't take into account the present climate in Europe, unfortunately.'

'But that doesn't – '

Swift showed Mike his hand again. 'Arrangements have been made for a cheque to be paid into your account for an amount which I think in the circumstances is more than generous.'

He waited a moment, letting it sink in. Mike felt like he was being lowered through the floor.

'You are no longer an employee of the company, Mr Varela. Unless you are off the premises within a half hour the security people will remove you.'

Swift indicated a box on the floor on the other side of the room. A cardboard box, the flaps still open on top.

'Those are your things, Michael. Now I'm sorry but I have a number of important matters to attend to as you can imagine.'

Mike began to protest, but the old man was struggling to relight his cigar, his mind already on his next meeting.

17

The double doors opened behind them and the brunette reappeared still smiling. Mike looked from her to the old man and then back again. He wanted to say something, but he couldn't think what. He stared one last time at the other door, and left without a word.

The descent to the street carrying the cardboard box seemed to take a long time. Mike felt as though he were being lowered into a different social stratum. Alone in the lift with the cheap smell of cardboard rising from the box which held his jumble of Rolodex, ball-points and directories, a spasm of anger and shame contorted his face. But still he couldn't speak.

It was cool in the subterranean car park. Climbing into the BMW, which looked more like a coffin now, he turned the key. The dials seemed to register his emotions and for a moment he was faced by alarm lights. Then he keyed in the code which started the engine.

He drove around for a couple of hours. At midday, stuck in a jam in the cold shadow of the new Hiraizumi Centre on 8th Avenue, he picked up the cellphone and punched in a number.

'Daily.'

For once Mike did not smile as he usually did at the formal edge to Karen Daily's voice.

'Karen, this is Mike.'

He listened hard in the pause that followed. When Karen spoke again she had lowered her voice and appeared to be speaking close in to the phone.

'Michael, I'm afraid I can't talk right now. I'm in a meeting.'

'Hey! Don't do me any favours.' Mike tried to sound cheerful. 'I just wanted to know if you could make your-self free tonight. I wanted to cook something at home.'

'What time?'

The professional hardness had crept back into her

voice. Mike smiled, glad at least to have got his way. He had expected her to be a little more difficult. It was the first time he had called her in a month.

She strained back, arching her body so that her heavy red hair brushed his legs. Mike felt her shudder deep inside. Then she came slowly forward, until her flushed face was close to his and he could feel her deep drawn breaths. She smiled and licked her lips. His smiling eyes on hers, Mike cupped the full smoothness of her buttocks and felt her lift, rising away from his stomach, drawing herself to the end of his sex. For a moment he had to catch his breath. She smiled. Mike laughed.

'If I come again it's going to be blood.'

'You can't be *serious*.'

Karen eyed him mischievously and moved slowly down on him until he felt the pressure of her muscular loins against his. Her eyes were half closed, the lids trembling as she concentrated on her pleasure. Mike felt her move inside again as she arched away from him, pushing away from his chest with her hands. Slowly and then faster she rode him, her head thrown back. Mike watched, astonished as he always was by her voluptuous intensity. Then her nails dug into his skin and she was saying his name over and over.

They lay in the big bed for a long time half covered by the damp sheets. Mike was smoking another unaccustomed cigarette, looking around at the heavy drapes, the thick pile carpet, wondering how long he would be able to hang on to it all.

'So how come you didn't call, Michael?'

It was a moment before Mike realised she was talking. He turned and looked at her thick, silky, red hair spread on the cinnamon sheets.

'How come you didn't call?'

She reached across and took the cigarette from him,

19

drawing deep and blowing smoke up at the ceiling. Mike shrugged.

'We've been pretty busy on a European deal for the last couple of weeks.'

'So what?'

Mike looked away across the room, realising that what Karen wanted was not an explanation. She wanted a fight. Fuck first then a fight. It was her style.

'You've been busy before now and it didn't stop us meeting up.'

Mike thought about explaining how he had been given a free hand on a big deal for the first time. *It was very important for me, Karen. You understand that.* But he didn't say anything. He wanted to tell her that he had lost his job, but didn't know how to start. Their relationship, going back over a year, had been based on a lot of success. They were always going out to celebrate something; her promotion or his. Now they had to talk about failure, but it was his failure. Karen was still on the up. Mike sighed.

'Hey Michael! Fuck this!'

Karen's voice startled him. She stood up on the mattress, steadying herself against the ceiling with one hand. Light from the bedside lamp was thrown against her pointed breasts, her strong face lit with its prominent nose.

'Karen, I lost my job, okay?'

Mike looked up at her as she towered over him. Her expression changed. She stepped off the bed and walked across to her clothes on the other side of the room.

'I see, I see.'

She slipped on her skirt and turned to face him.

'I see how it is, Michael.' She pointed at him with her varnished finger. 'You get to take a few initiatives and – poof – you disappear on me. Then you lose your job and who do you call? Good old Karen Daily. Good old Karen will understand. Good old Karen will give you her shoulder to cry on. Hey! She'll do better than that, she'll give you a friendly fuck just the way you like it. She'll fuck you asleep and be there in the morning when you wake up, with a steaming cup of coffee.'

She was almost screaming now. Her rages, just like her orgasms, made Mike feel like a spectator.

'Well that's not how it works, Mister Varela. I have problems of my own you know. I have a career of my own.'

She started pulling on her clothes, snagging her stockings with a nail and cursing loudly. Mike stood up, covering himself from her anger with a sheet. He came across the room, but didn't know what to say. All he knew was that everything had gone wrong. Things were falling apart so fast, he didn't know what to grab hold of to keep them together.

She was dressed now and facing him. He was surprised to see tears streaming down her face. He took a step towards her, but was stopped dead in his tracks. Karen had screwed up her small fists and narrowed her eyes. With her red hair everywhere she looked crazy.

'Touch me Michael, and I'll bust you in the mouth.'

Then she was gone. Mike walked through the empty apartment to the door on the landing. He saw the top of Karen's head as she rushed down the stairs.

'Fuck you, Karen,' he said. But he didn't say it loud.

2

Los Angeles. September 8th, 1995.

Harry Waterman hated Sunset Boulevard, and he especially hated phoney little dives like this one, which made out they were something to do with the movie business and stung you an extra couple of bucks per drink for the privilege. The bar called itself The Sierra Madre, and all over the walls were black and white photos of the old-time stars – as if they used to drop by here now and again on their way to the studio. There was Jean Harlow, 'the blonde bombshell', there was Gary Cooper, there was Judy Garland in pigtails, and of course there was old Bogey himself, right over the cash register.

The picture of Bogart made Waterman wince. The star of stars was done up in the private eye gear: the raincoat, the black trilby, the cigarette dangling from his mouth. Ever since *The Maltese Falcon* every investigator in the world, no matter who he worked for, had been haunted by that image. You just had to say the word 'investigation' and you could tell what the other guy was thinking: 'Well you're no Philip Marlowe, are you?' And the other guy was right. Waterman was the wrong side of forty, had lost most of his hair, and was thirty-five pounds over-weight even by his own reckoning. Maybe, Waterman thought, this sleaze-ball reporter he was waiting for had chosen The Sierra Madre just to make him feel bad –

make him feel second class. But no, that was stupid. They'd never actually met before. Micky Harborne was still just a voice on the other end of a phone.

It was just after half past seven and the place was still pretty empty. Over in the far corner a couple of guys in ultra-lightweight suits were drinking cocktails with miniature umbrellas sticking out the top of them. On a TV above them John Robinson, the old head coach of the Rams, was making his tips for the coming season. Waterman had always been a Raiders fan himself. *The silver and black! The skull and crossbones!* But he didn't follow the game much any more. He'd liked the Raiders better when they were the Oakland Raiders, way back in the seventies. Oakland had been his home then. Three years running he'd even bought a season ticket.

Robinson got to the end of his tips with scarcely a mention of his old LA rivals. Waterman turned away and finished off his Johnny Walker. When he looked up again the picture had switched to a demo somewhere in Europe. Strasbourg, the caption said. There were a lot of people carrying crosses and placards being held back by a thin line of policemen in blue uniforms. Behind the policemen a succession of steel grey Mercedes sped by a little too fast for dignity or comfort. One of the placards said: STOP THEM PLAYING GOD.

Waterman picked up his glass and dangled it in front of the barman who was standing a few feet away, enjoying a good joke on the telephone. He had one of those moustaches that were so narrow they could have been drawn by an eyebrow pencil, and his left hand flapped around as he talked as if a bluebottle was bugging him or something. It was a better than even bet that the guy would tell you that he was really an actor or a dancer or something, and that he was just filling in time before his 'big break'. You could still hear that kind of shit on Sunset Boulevard. Waterman tilted his glass slowly one way,

23

then the other, so that the ice-cubes clinked against the sides: *clink . . . clink.* The barman looked at him and stopped laughing. Then he said goodbye and hung up.

'That was scotch,' said Waterman, putting down the glass.

The barman poured another measure without saying a word. Waterman took a ten dollar bill from the top pocket of his navy blue jacket and handed it over.

'That's for the two,' he said. 'Keep the change.'

The barman looked at the bill unsmiling.

'The Johnny Walkers are six dollars each,' he said, 'sir.'

Six dollars! Waterman reached into his trouser pocket, gathered up a fistful of change and emptied it all over the top of the bar. The noise made the other customers look round. The barman pouted weakly, but his face was going the colour of a boiled lobster.

'Help yourself,' said Waterman, and watched as the barman counted off six quarters, four dimes and two nickels with as much dignity as he could manage, which wasn't much. Looking around the room again, an idea occurred to him. Maybe the barman wasn't the only one there on the left hand side of the tracks. Maybe that was the reason Micky Harborne had wanted to meet here. Maybe he was actually gay himself.

He hadn't thought about it before. After all, the journalist had just accused two of Hollywood's – no, *America*'s – most famous tough-guys of being homosexuals in secret. He had even hinted in his story that they had both died of AIDS, not of cancer at all, as the press had been told. Real sleaze-ball stuff. On the other hand, maybe it wasn't so odd. Maybe Harborne was having a laugh at straight America: *Well guess what, Mister Clean, with your white picket fence and your flag pole on the back lawn? Your all-American heroes are really a bunch of fags!* Or maybe you were supposed to

24

feel bad about the fact that the stars had had to keep their homosexuality a secret.

Waterman took his copy of *Exclusive!* magazine and spread it out in front of him. Harborne's article began on page nineteen, opposite an advertisement for mail order lingerie. Half of the first page was taken up with a blurred photo of Bladon and McArthur with their arms around each other's shoulders, grinning at the camera. Ray Bladon wore jeans and a black stetson with silver studs on the band, something he must have used in at least half a dozen of his movies. Matt McArthur wore sunglasses and swimming shorts. By itself nobody could call it an incriminating photograph, but in the context it lent a kind of credibility to Harborne's story: just the fact that it was out of focus made the whole thing seem clandestine.

Waterman skimmed through the story again, just in case he'd missed the real point of it. But no, there was no veiled attack here on American morality, or the hypocrisy of the film industry, just gleeful iconoclasm, just a seedy half-baked 'exposé' of two old movie stars who couldn't answer back. All the same, Bill Miller, Waterman's immediate superior back at the Centre for Disease Control, thought there was something in the story worth checking on. So here he was, drawing his $275-a-day plus expenses, checking.

When he'd first heard about the assignment he'd wondered whether Miller wasn't having one of his little jokes. It was the sort of thing he would do. Harry narrowed his eyes as he pictured Miller talking to one of his flunkeys in the CDC executive dining room. *Here's a nice little story for the Professor.* Miller had it in for Waterman and Waterman knew why. Primo, he resented the fact that Waterman had more qualifications than he did, and since the Rinaldo case two years ago, in which Harry had gone out on a limb on an infected blood plasma imports racket, Miller had been extra-shitty. Harry had filed a report on the plasma and its provenance which Miller had not fully understood. There had been a couple of embarrassing meetings. Then Waterman had received a big slap on the back from someone very high up. Since then Miller had taken to calling him 'Professor', and assignments which Waterman considered perfect for him had been going to other investigators. The Bladon/ McArthur deaths was his first case for nearly three months. *Two faggots die of a broken heart* was the way he had described the problem to his wife. He ordered his third Johnny Walker. It was getting dark outside and Harborne was late.

He was still looking outside when he heard someone sit down on the stool next to him. He turned around and saw a man maybe fifteen years his junior with large round glasses, wavy blond hair and a perfectly cultivated swathe of one-millimetre stubble. The man was looking straight back at him.

'Harry? How you doing?' he said, holding out his hand. There were gold rings on two of his fingers and a little leather bracelet on his wrist. Waterman had expected someone older. He sat up and smiled the best he could.

'Yeah, fine, Micky,' he said. 'Thanks for coming.'

'No problem. Whaddaya drinking?'

'Scotch. Hey, but this is on me.'

'Forget it, Harry,' said Harborne, like they'd been pals for years. 'I'm on a roll. Hey Jeff! A sour for me and a scotch over here. You ever had a sour, Harry? A pisco sour?'

Waterman said no he hadn't, and the next thing he knew he was sitting in front of a stubby little glass full of opaque green liquid with white froth on top. At least there wasn't a goddamn miniature umbrella sticking out of it.

'Well I think maybe we should drink to the man himself, don't you?' said Harborne, and raised his glass towards the wall behind them. There in the middle was a photo of Ray Bladon, dressed as the trapper in *The Frontiersman*, a picture he had made back in the sixties. Waterman hadn't noticed it before. Maybe *that* was the reason Harborne had wanted to meet here.

'To Big Ray!' he said. 'The toughest tough-guy ever to have a perm!'

Waterman raised his glass obligingly, but he didn't like Harborne's little joke. *The Frontiersman* had been a damn good movie. When he was in high school he'd been to see it twice. He took a sip from his little glass. He was afraid the green stuff would be sweet. It was like biting into a lemon.

'So what can I do for you, Harry?' said Harborne. 'What's all the interest?'

'It's probably a load of nothing,' said Waterman. He didn't want Harborne to think there was another story here for him. If a reporter ever thought that, you could be sure he would clam up for the rest of the evening in case you passed on the idea to someone else. 'Like I said on the phone, there's a couple of things you pointed up in your article that the CDC wanted to check on.'

'The CDC in Atlanta?'

Waterman sensed that Harborne *was* interested. He'd already picked up on the fact that the investigation had been initiated by the CDC's national headquarters right over on the other side of the country. But that didn't mean a thing. This really was just a load of nothing.

'Yea,' he said, 'this is their kind of stuff. It's just a bit of statistical research, really, but they have all the hardware over there, the data.'

Harborne nodded in a 'sounds fascinating' kind of way, and didn't say anything. Waterman took another bite of the lemon.

'Anyway, Micky,' he went on. 'You uncovered evidence that Bladon and McArthur were more than just old

27

pals, if I read you right. In fact, you're really saying they were homosexual partners, right?'

'*You* could say that, Harry, if you wanted to,' said Harborne. 'But *I* never said so, not for sure – never. You have to draw your own conclusions, right?'

'Okay, I know what you're saying. But to us it don't mean a thing what they did to each other. It just puts the other thing in a different light.'

'What other thing is that?'

'Well you also pointed out that the two men died within a few weeks of each other. Matt McArthur at some Swiss clinic, and Bladon here in California – both of cancer.'

'Of cancer, *officially*.'

'Yeah, Micky, I know you think this cancer thing is becoming Hollywood's polite word for AIDS, but it's really the *official* cause of death that interests us. If it really does turn out to have been AIDS that killed them – either of them – then that's it, as far as we're concerned. I mean, we've got no special interest. Happens all the time.'

Harborne's face fell. The possibility that Bladon and McArthur had died of the gay plague, as straights used to call it before it got to them too, was the spiciest part of his whole story.

'I don't get it,' he said.

'As you pointed out,' said Waterman, trying to be generous, 'the official cause of death in McArthur's case was *heart* cancer. I haven't had a chance to check that out, because he died in Switzerland, and that's where the papers are. The point is that heart cancer was also Bladon's cause of death. I've already seen the papers from the hospital, and it looks like that's what it really was.'

'You went to the hospital? You got the records?'

'It wasn't easy,' Waterman said, lying in fact because it had been very easy indeed. 'But the CDC's got a lot of friends in this business, you know. It ain't the same story in Switzerland, I'm beginning to find out, but I don't believe the relatives would dream up a thing like heart cancer if they were trying to conceal the real cause of death. I mean a straight heart attack would have been much more convincing. Nobody would have looked at it twice.'

'Nobody did except me, Harry,' said Harborne.

'Sure,' said Waterman, with a show of sincerity the Johnny Walkers and the pisco sour did not make easy. 'And a great piece it was, no doubt about it. A great piece.'

Harborne didn't look happy at all. His arms were folded like he was getting himself ready for a punch-up. Waterman was afraid of this – that was why he hadn't wanted to say too much on the phone. In a couple of days he'd been able to do what Harborne should have done before he ever filed his story: check some of the facts. Maybe Harborne felt that the person really being investigated was him. Waterman ploughed on. They weren't here to discuss Harborne's professionalism, or lack of it.

'The point is, Micky, if McArthur died of the heart cancer too, then we have a real coincidence here. Because heart cancer is one of the rarest kinds around. I could explain why if you want to know.'

Waterman was almost hoping Harborne would say he did want to know. He liked this kind of stuff. It reminded him, and anyone else around, that he wasn't some peeping-tom investigator with a few years as a cop behind him and all the education of a mule. He'd been a biology major at Stanford – yes, Stanford – and he knew a lot about things most investigators had never even heard of. By now he could have been a big shot in one of those bio-tech companies they had out here in California, if he hadn't let the booze take it away from him, the booze and Mrs Waterman. That was why the CDC used him. He knew his stuff.

He took another sip of his pisco sour so that Harborne could give him his cue. But Harborne just said: 'I'll take your word for it.' *Well, what the hell can you expect?*

'It's *so* rare in fact,' said Waterman, 'that if two people who are, one way or another, close to each other, both get it, then we have to check it out.'

Harborne had relaxed a little. It looked like his story was still important after all, though he still didn't understand why.

'Check for what?' he said. 'Cancer's cancer, right?'

Harry bit the lemon.

'What we check for is any evidence of a virus – a virus which caused the cancers. If it's statistically unlikely – and it is – that these men should both develop this kind of cancer independently, there has to be a chance that one of them *gave* it to the other. See what I mean? If that's the case we have a new disease on our hands, a virus we didn't know about. A virus that causes cancer in the heart. That kind of thing could be important, it could even be useful, and, like I say, it could be nothing.'

Harborne nodded slowly. Waterman had a feeling the guy was out of his depth already.

'You said this cancer, heart cancer, is very rare, right?' he said.

'Yes.'

'Then even if this is some new virus, it isn't exactly the end of the world, right? People aren't gonna be dying of heart cancer all over California?'

Waterman laughed reassuringly. 'Hell, no. We dig up this kind of thing all the time. Someone spots a bit of a coincidence. We check it out. It gets stored on a computer somewhere, and if it happens again some place we compare the two cases and see if there's any connection. That's the story. Like I said, it's just statistics.'

Harborne was slowly hauling it in, and Waterman could tell that it didn't interest him very much, at least not professionally. A soap star having a tit cut off was fine because the idea of a single-breasted actress yielded any number of interesting journalistic angles, but *viral cancers?* He couldn't find an angle on that if he looked all night. Besides, was someone like Harborne going to run a story that showed up his own mistakes? Waterman didn't think so – and that was just fine. He didn't want some amateur making things complicated. He took the opportunity to order two more sours just to keep the guy on his stool.

'So what do you want, Harry?' said Harborne. 'You got my story.'

'Sure, and I wouldn't be bothering you normally on something like this. But, you know, these are – were – important people. And trying to get the details about their lives could be pretty tough, especially with the story you wrote and everything. And you know Bladon, he never let the press get near him. He was one hell of a secretive guy.'

Harborne was trying to look attentive but his gaze kept drifting over Waterman's shoulder. There were a couple of girls now a few stools down wearing tight black skirts. Waterman had noticed them come in and he couldn't help glancing round too. They were just close enough to hear what Harborne and he were saying. It looked like Harborne was already straining at the leash. Waterman could just imagine the chat-up lines.

'So what I need, Micky,' he went on, 'is some names and numbers. People who knew about these guys. What they did during their last few months. Where they went. You know, details. If there is a bug out there, where could they have picked it up? That's the sort of stuff we're looking for. You see what I mean?'

'Sure Harry, I got my sources,' said Harborne, 'but there's a lot of leg work involved in that kind of thing. I don't have my own personal deep-throat in Hollywood. I wish I did.'

'Of course, my enquiries will be *very* discreet, Micky, and if anything does come up, I'll be sure to pass it on to you *exclusive*. You have my word.'

Harborne was lighting a Sobrani cigarette. Black paper and a gold filter. He took a drag, let his head roll back and exhaled with one long smooth breath. Waterman knew it wasn't for his benefit. But having the girls there was working to his advantage. Harborne had a chance here to show off his importance.

'Frankly,' said Waterman, as loud as he could without actually shouting, 'for information like that, on the top stars, I don't know who else could possibly help. I mean you're really *in* there, Micky. You *know* them. The others just pretend they do.'

Harborne was pink with pleasure. The girls had stopped talking to each other and were both looking straight at him with glazed, stupid expressions on their faces. One of them, a blonde with big blue eyes, was even biting her lip with the excitement of it all. *Hollywood groupies!* Well, Waterman thought, they fell for The Sierra Madre, didn't they? So they could fall for Micky Harborne.

'I guess you're right Harry,' he said. How could he resist seeming magnanimous with an audience like this? 'And hell, I know it's all in a good cause, right?'

'Sure, Micky.'

'So maybe I can give you a few ideas. You got a pencil on you?'

Waterman reached inside his jacket and took out his note pad and his ball-point. The girls were leaning so far over they were almost falling off their stools. Then Harborne looked at them, put on a quizzical expression and said: 'Tommy Cruise's place, right? Last Saturday? Are you trying out for his new picture?'

3

Manhattan. September 29th, 1995.

It smelled like someone in the elevator had dropped a
bottle of Chanel. Cathy Ryder, pressed back against the
red carpeted wall, tried to pin down a culprit. But there
were so many overdressed women it could have been any
one of eight – and there were only nine of them in the
car, which rose with a faint geriatric trembling to the
reception room on the fifth floor. Cathy raised a gloved
hand to her nose trying to recapture the soft signal of her
own perfume.

Product launches were always crowded with cosmetics
groupies, usually top-drawer wives in search of the product that was going to give them back their lost youth and
their lost husband. Looking around, you had to sympathise. With some of these girls it was difficult to see
where the bags stopped and the double chins started.

As the doors on the fifth floor slid back Cathy moved
quickly out of their sugary slipstream and made her way
over to the buffet. She hadn't eaten since breakfast,
having spent the whole day in Webber Atlantic being
balled out by Michael Paine, head of the research department and established sonofabitch.

Over the last three months Webber's research had
made three disastrous buy recommendations, two of them
on the basis of Cathy's work. Paine wasted no time in

33

pointing out the effect this had on Webber's funds under management. The message was clear. Either Cathy started picking the right stocks or she'd be out on the street. Paine, a thin man with a tight cap of receding curls, had looked down at her battered violin case which was leaning against the desk and said: 'I hope you know how to play that thing!' before stalking off.

For a long time Cathy had sat looking at her old violin. She would have done anything not to draw attention to it, but there was nowhere else to put the thing – nowhere safe – and she needed it with her on Tuesdays and Thursdays for her lunch-time lessons. It was the only thing she had kept from her childhood. To play it was not only satisfying. It also brought back the past, the big house in Maine where she had been raised, and the square of sunlight in the lounge in which she had stood pretending it was the spotlight in a packed Carnegie Hall. Both her parents were dead now. But though the instrument reminded her of the past, it also reminded her of her failure to become the violinist she had dreamed of being. It looked out of place in the teak and plastic of Webber Atlantic. It looked the way she felt.

Paine's anger had shaken her and to show willing she had come along to the Raeburn product launch out of office hours. She hoped she would get to talk to some of the management about their sales projections for the new product range and the effect this might have on revenues – which had certainly been sleepy enough for the last year or so.

The invitation had been pinned to her notice board for a week. It had come from Lindsey Sherman, Raeburn's PR spokesperson. And it was Lindsey that Cathy first saw when she went through into the main reception room which had been lined with chairs for the guests.

Cathy admired Lindsey. She was petite and blonde, unlike Cathy herself who was above average height with thick black hair which she found difficult to control. Her hairdresser referred to the different styles he suggested as 'solutions'. It was fair enough – her hair *was* a problem. But Cathy had her good points too: long black eyes for one, 'Egyptian eyes' as her father used to say; slender athletic legs, and broad shoulders which made her full breasts seem less apparent than they would otherwise have been. Perhaps most appealing of all was her mouth: slightly fuller in the top lip which gave her face a girlish expression at odds with the clear, almost strident message of her body.

Lindsey was introducing an eminent scientist, Walter Iron, a small man, dressed – comically, Cathy thought – in a white lab coat, as if he hadn't had time to change in his rush over from Berkley, where Raeburn had its R&D operations. But the old heads all around her nodded reverentially as he came to the microphone. The fact was, cosmetics had moved up country into big budget science, and products were now sold with text-book diagrams of molecule chains printed on the packaging. If people liked their scientists to dress like scientists that was fine, Cathy reflected.

'. . . improves elasticity in the epidermal collagen network, ensuring greater efficiency in the micro-circulation, and an improvement in the take-up of proteins necessary for optimal cellular regeneration.'

Cathy did her best to suppress a grin as a woman in front of her turned to her partner and smiled as if they had just been treated to a particularly brilliant passage of Mozart.

As far as anyone could tell, wrinkles had been Professor Iron's life's work. This may have accounted for his head being so smooth and hairless with an extra-terrestrial pink glow about it. The talk ran on for about twenty minutes and then the ladies in the audience were invited to go into the next room for the demonstration.

35

As the crowd stood up, Cathy made her way towards Lindsey Sherman.

'Cathy! You're looking fabulous as usual.'

Cathy blushed. She could never quite deal with Lindsey's enthusiasm, her standard ploy being to get onto professional terrain.

'I was hoping for a few figures on the new product,' she said, looking at the smaller woman from under the fine arches of her eyebrows, 'for my report.'

They talked statistics for a while, Cathy making notes in a small notebook. It was standard stuff.

'You look unconvinced,' said Lindsey in mid-stream. Cathy blushed again and began to offer a denial.

'You should come and see the demonstrations. They're what's most impressive.'

Cathy smiled.

'That's what I'm here for.'

She followed Lindsey through to a darkened room which had swallowed up all but a few of the other guests. Under clinical focused light, three models were being treated with Raeburn's new products by technicians, women this time, but still wearing the white coats.

Cathy watched, standing behind the seated audience, Lindsey having gone forward into the lights. The most striking thing about the scene was that the women in the three chairs were all beautiful and obviously in no need of rejuvenation. But a glance around at her at the audience was enough to show that the message Raeburn wanted to give was being received loud and clear.

At first Cathy didn't notice him, but then after a moment his heavy breathing and the faint pressure of his arm against her own, brought her head round. She started and took a step back.

'Excuse me,' said the man. 'I didn't mean to startle you.'

She saw his broad glistening smile in the semi-dark. It

36

was difficult to be precise, but he looked to be in his forties, very tall, with a greying moustache.

'They don't look as if they need too much of that cream, right?'

He nodded towards the stage. Cathy looked back at the models. Her manner was formal, distant. Men bothered her all the time.

'I was just thinking the same thing,' she conceded, if only to demonstrate that she hadn't been startled.

Again the man touched her, this time putting his hand on her sleeve. He smelt of Bourbon. She looked at his hand, and after a moment he removed it.

'I saw you talking to the girl,' he said, and for the first time Cathy realised that he was a foreigner, a German maybe.

'Yes.'

She had drawn herself up to her full height and adopted her coldest Webber Atlantic manner.

'Well, if you're looking for a good story, I've got one to tell you.'

Suddenly it dawned on Cathy that the man assumed she was a journalist. There were a number of people from the leading women's magazines there with their tape recorders and bulging press packs. She was about to put him straight when it occurred to her that his story might have a bearing on her research. She didn't want to talk to the stranger, but after what Mike Paine had said to her she reckoned she should play along just on the off-chance that there was some inside information here.

'We're always interested in genuine sources,' she said in an undertone.

'And that's what you're looking at,' said the man. He paused, stifling a belch.

'Well, go on.'

The man gestured to the door through which they could see the buffet laid out under the bright light of the chandeliers. Cathy followed him through. He swayed slightly as he walked, steadying himself finally against the buffet table, a glass of champagne in his free hand.

'So what's the story?'

Cathy thought directness was her best bet. That's how journalists talked, wasn't it? The man considered her for a while, his eyes flickering over her breasts and throat.

'How much do you know about modern cosmetics?' he said eventually.

Cathy shrugged.

'You know about placenta-based products? Like these?'

He gestured dismissively towards the demonstration room.

'Well, as I understand it, the idea is that organic material found in animal placenta produces substances similar to those which keep the skin healthy, and which are produced less as we get older. Isn't that the idea?'

The man eyed her narrowly. He leaned forward so that their faces were close, and she could smell the booze on his breath.

'To start with, placenta-based products, this pink gel they're squeezing all over themselves. Well you can forget about it. They might as well stick to cold cream. These men in the white coats? They're just fumbling in the dark like everyone has before.'

Cathy was taken aback. The man's manner was authoritative. He seemed to know what he was talking about even through the booze. It wasn't what she had expected. She started to take notes mostly so as to play the journalist.

'But that's the best the industry can do,' she said, looking at him over her note pad and taking in the expensive clothes, trying to get an idea of who he was. But there was time for that later. First the information.

38

'Past tense.' He leaned forward again. 'It *was* the best the industry could do.'

He looked around the room. Cathy felt her heart quicken. 'There are people in Europe who have a product which will make this type of garbage obsolete in a matter of weeks. When they start selling their stuff, all these companies with their big R&D budgets – Raeburn, Melos Pharmaceuticals, Bio Factors – they won't stand a chance.'

'Which people in Europe?'

The man frowned at her and straightened so that she was looking up into his red face.

'Come, come now. You think I don't know how much that kind of information is worth?'

He had become defensive in a moment. Cathy tried to think what a journalist would do in her place. Should she take out her chequebook? How much could she offer? She smiled at the man, showing him her dazzling teeth.

'You don't think I get out my chequebook for any man, do you?'

The man blinked and began to smile himself, mesmerised by her parted lips and the hint of pink tongue resting against the perfect teeth. Such a sweet smile.

'I don't know who you are, what your angle is.' She shrugged. 'I can't just take everything on trust.'

The man looked flustered, congested. Again his eyes flickered over her breasts.

'OK, OK,' he said, wiping a large hand across his mouth. 'I don't need the money anyway.'

Suddenly he sounded bitter. Possibilities flashed through Cathy's mind: a resentful ex-employee, a board member with an axe to grind? People went to the press for all kinds of reasons. The problem was those kind of stories were no good to Webber Atlantic. She needed hard facts.

'Mendelhaus,' said the man after a moment. At first

Cathy didn't understand. She brought her pen to her lips. 'The name is Mendelhaus. That's the company I'm talking about.'

'Mendelhaus?'

'Hey, for a journalist you're not that quick off the mark.'

Cathy squared her shoulders and pushed forward her chin.

'I'm just surprised I've never heard of it.'

The man smiled at her, showing a flash of gold.

'Why should you have heard of it? What are you anyway, some kind of cosmetics expert?'

Cathy felt a blush creep into her cheeks.

'A health care and cosmetics company,' he continued. 'A little jewel.'

'European? You said before it was a European company the big corporations had to fear.'

'That's right. And here's one for the quotes book: anyone buying cosmetics stock in the next few months is in for a big hit.'

He was backing away from her, his finger still raised. A number of heads had turned. The cosmetics groupies were beginning to come out of the demonstration. They squinted in the bright light. They were obviously excited by what they had seen. Several of them were carrying sample packs of products. When Cathy turned back to the door which led to the elevators the man was gone.

'So what did you think?'

Cathy came to herself looking into Lindsey Sherman's brilliant blue eyes.

'I don't know what to think,' was all she could manage.

4

Manhattan. September 28th, 1995.

The traffic was tumbling in waves down Park Avenue, an angry, impatient mass of blazing headlamps and sheet steel. Waiting at a red light, Mike Varela sat staring through the tinted windscreen, trying to ignore the cold, hollow sensation in his chest which seemed to grow with every passing minute. It was a sensation he had been fighting for three weeks, ever since his interview with Harvey Swift, but as he drove back that evening from his father's house in Queens, it felt like it might finally overwhelm him. Anger had kept it at bay before, but anger wouldn't come this time. Only fear. He watched the metallic horde as it roared past him, searching for the faces of the drivers. He couldn't see them.

Nearly three weeks had gone by before he'd told his father what had happened. He'd thought he could fix up another job for himself in no time – just make a few calls around the Street and wait for the offers. He'd wanted to do that first so that he could simply say he'd changed banks – stop the old man worrying. But the offers hadn't come, not one. It was as if Napier Drew had put in a bad word for him at every investment bank in the city. So in the end he'd had to call his father and tell him the news. That had been a couple of days ago, and it had been hard. To him, unemployment was the worst of all possible

41

ills. That was the reason he'd left his home; that was the reason he'd pushed his son through every goddamn exam and scholarship in sight. Mike had told him not to worry about it, but it hadn't done much good. For a moment the anger came back as he thought of Napier and his WASP pals having a good laugh about it all down at the Harvard Club: *could Miguel Varela please come down to reception* . . . Miguel, the wetback! He stabbed the accelerator of the BMW and let the wheels scream against the tarmac.

His father had never really understood what Mike did for a living anyway. Old Joaquin Diaz had made his money, such as it was, selling Mexican champagne whole-sale up and down the East Coast. Mergers and acqui-sitions, leveraged buy-outs, junk bonds, all that meant nothing to him. It was the sort of thing *they* did. *They*, the Americans who ran America, the ones who had it all worked out. He was proud that his son could do that sort of thing too, but he never understood it. And he never knew how determinedly Mike had buried his origins to get there – right down to the family name. Mike's full name was Miguel Diaz Varela. Like all Hispanic people his father's name came after his Christian name and his mother's name last. That way you could go on tacking as many ancestral names onto the end as you liked, because your surname was always in the same place. So to his father, and to the passport office, Mike Varela was really Mike Diaz, which was a pity because Diaz was unmistak-ably Hispanic, whereas Varela could as easily have been Italian. Mike never thought about using his mother's name until he was in business school. There the uniformly Anglo-Saxon administrators had assumed that his last name was his surname, and put him down as Michael Varela. All his mail said Michael Varela, all his bills said Michael Varela, everything said Michael Varela.

At first Mike had been angry, but in spite of his anger

42

he had never gone to the trouble of putting the administrators right on the matter. The truth was he didn't want to go and explain to everyone that Mike was short for Miguel, not Michael, and that his surname was really Diaz. And by the end of his two years, he was putting his name down as Michael Varela too, at least when it suited him. He even had his first Gold Card issued in that name. These days he only held onto the name Diaz because he was afraid of what his father might think if he ever found out about it. As he drove the BMW down into the underground carpark he wished for a moment that he'd stuck with plain old Miguel Diaz. At least that way those creeps in Swift and Drew couldn't have had their little joke.

Mike's apartment lay on the eighth floor of a stout, sand-coloured building, which had originally served as headquarters for the Continental Guardian Insurance Company back in the 1920s. The company had long since disappeared from the corporate map, but its old headquarters still had a heavy corporate feel. There were stone giants in flowing robes either side of the entrance, one a woman, holding a child to her breast, the other a warrior with a sword at his side. Embedded in the floor of the hall was a circle of brass about eight feet in diameter, with the name of the company written around the inside and the same two figures again, this time standing together. Mike had always complained about the impersonal appearance of the place to his friends, but really he liked it. There was something strong and permanent about this building, and the very words *Continental Guardian* gave you a feeling of security. To Mike the building said: *they can't get you in here*. As Mike crossed the hall, the cold hollow sensation in his chest returned, because he knew that very soon he would have to sell. Just two months without work and the payments would wipe him

43

out. And the really stupid part was, he still didn't know *why*.

Inside the apartment Mike picked up the phone and dialled a number at Swift and Drew. There was still some one there he thought he could talk to, but the guy had been in Tokyo most of the past three weeks. His name was Walt Simmonds and he'd been partly responsible for recruiting Mike in the first place. His speciality was Asia.

The phone at the other end rang four times and then a woman's voice said: 'Investment Banking.'

The cold hollow feeling was getting worse. Mike tried to sound business-as-usual.

'Walt Simmonds, please.'

There was a pause. Did she recognise his voice, who-ever she was?

'Er, he's not here right now. Do you want to leave a message?' *A message? How could he leave a message?*

'No,' he said, 'it doesn't . . . do you know if he's coming back at all?'

'Yeah, I think so. He was here a few minutes ago.'

'OK, I'll call again later.'

'OK . . . No, wait, he's here. I'll transfer you. Just a second.'

Mike's pulse was racing. He took a couple of deep breaths.

'Hello, this is Simmonds.' The voice was curt and impatient.

'Walt? This is Mike here. Mike Varela.'

'Mike!' Simmonds's voice was instantly quieter, like he didn't want anyone else to hear. 'How's it going?'

Mike tried to sound humorous.

'Well, could be worse, Walt. You hear about what happened?'

He heard Simmonds talking to someone else in the room. It sounded like he was getting rid of his secretary.

'Yes, of course. Pretty tough going.'

44

Mike decided not to go straight into his problems just yet. He didn't want to sound too anxious.

'How was Tokyo?'

'Well, fine. Getting sorted out. We should see some action before the end of the year. There are some good deals coming up if we can get 'em. We got some high-powered new Japs coming in, and I reckon that should help.'

Mike couldn't wait any longer. 'You got a handle on what happened here?' he asked. 'I mean it just came out of the blue as far as I was concerned.'

'Well, for me too, Mike. I mean I thought that deal of yours was all sewn up.'

'It was. We were just a few days away from the bid. Damn it, the Mendelhaus execs even had their hotels booked over here for the signing.'

'Didn't they say anything upstairs?'

'Harvey Swift said something about genetic research being banned by the EC. But that can't be anything to do with it. I mean Mendelhaus is a Swiss company, for Christ's sake. They're not even *in* the EC. And besides, that kind of bio-tech stuff isn't their field anyway. They're into face cream and health farms.'

'What about the CFO at Mendelhaus – Bruggman, wasn't it?'

'I tried so many times, Walt. The guy just doesn't return my calls. I've tried some of his juniors, too, but I never get beyond the goddamn secretaries. I still don't know why they pulled out.'

'Well, I dunno either, Mike. Maybe they weren't happy about the mezzanine, or something. I mean that kind of leverage is still pretty *avant garde* in a place like that. Maybe they just didn't want all the hassle and the bad publicity they could get from an issue that didn't sell.'

'Believe me, Walt, I had 'em convinced on that one. It was the heart of the whole thing. With all the uncertainty in the EC right now a good Swiss name like Mendelhaus is just what the market's looking for. You only gotta ask the guys in Sales. I'm telling you, the finance on this take-over was watertight.'

'Well, I don't know, Mike. Maybe they weren't serious about the deal in the first place. That happens, you know. You work your ass off on a project and then your client turns around and says yeah, maybe next time. Knowing when they really *are* serious is part of the job.'

Simmonds wasn't sympathising any more. He was giving his one-time junior a lecture.

'So you haven't heard anything else about it?'

'No I haven't, except that to be able to underwrite the bonds we re-organised half our books, and that it cost us a lot of money. That's why they wanted blood, Mike. They took quite a hit going liquid.'

That wasn't Mike's fault and he wanted to say so, but he let it drop. He didn't want to argue with Walt Simmonds. He wanted his help.

'That's too bad,' he said. 'Anyway' – this was the hardest part of all – 'if you hear of anything going on the street, Walt, any recruiting, could you let me know? I mean, I've been scouting around, but you've probably got a better ear for these things than I have.'

He'd wanted to sound casual, but it had been a bad performance. He knew the fear and the need had shown through.

'Of course,' said Simmonds. 'If I hear of anything, I'll give you a call, OK?'

Mike's heart sank. There was nothing in Simmonds's words except *goodbye and good luck*.

'Yeah. Thanks Walt.'

There was a click on the line, followed by a bland electronic hum. Mike replaced the receiver and let his face come to rest against the palms of his hands. He was on his own.

After a minute or two he got up from the leather arm-chair and fixed himself a Jack Daniels on ice, a big one. The liquor momentarily burned away the cold hollow feeling inside. He'd never been much of a drinker. Too much liquor kept him awake, and then he was no good the next day. You couldn't afford to be below par in M&A – how many times had he told himself that? – you had to stay sharp. But then, he wasn't in M&A any more. He wasn't in anything.

He didn't want to go on thinking like that. He took another shot of the whisky and picked up the remote control for the TV. From the middle of the walnut panel-ling opposite the screen came to life. It was CNN. Fine. At least he'd see that he wasn't the only human being in the world with problems. And sure enough, here was a picture of a building somewhere that looked like a bomb had gone off inside it.

'*The laboratory, which lies just outside Joinville, in the north-east of France,*' the female voice-over said, '*was attacked during the early hours of yesterday morning. A member of staff was assaulted and, according to sources inside the company, damage done to the tune of at least two million dollars. This is the second incident of its kind in recent months. Last August a laboratory in Fontaine-bleau was also sabotaged. The likely motive? Growing militancy in the Green movement here over the issue of research on human genetic material.*'

The picture cut to a distinguished looking man, about sixty years old, who was standing in the middle of a great crush of reporters, all thrusting microphones at him and shouting questions.

'*The president of Etienne Louvois, Laurent Cuvillier, visited the Joinville laboratory this morning, and gave his reaction to the press.*'

The man began to speak in French, but there was another voice-over translation into English: '*This type of*

47

research is vital for the advancement of knowledge, and for the future health and prosperity of mankind. The vandals who have committed this outrage, and the fanatics who support them, will only succeed in handing our competitors outside the Community a huge technological advantage. Even worse, they will be driving science underground, where it is accountable to no one but itself and those that pay for it!'

Mike Varela felt a ripple of anger as he watched. This story exactly proved his point. Restrictions on genetic research inside the European Community could only be *good* news for companies outside, like Mendelhaus. Harvey Swift didn't know what the fuck he was talking about. And if science really was going underground, where in the world could it be safer than under the Swiss Alps?

5

Alleinmatt, Switzerland. September 28th, 1995.

Five miles south-east of Alleinmatt, almost out of sight
of the chairlift which carries skiers to the black-graded
pistes around the towering Heulendthorn, a blinding field
of ice and snow surges up nine hundred feet to a craggy
ridge known as the Phönixlager, German for 'Lair of the
Phoenix'. Alleinmatt's exclusive clientele rarely venture
that way, although experts, hooked on the thrills of helicopter skiing, do occasionally gain access to the lower
section, enjoying the heady pleasures of a forty-five
degree drop through deep powder. From there skiers
must negotiate a narrow and treacherous trail which
begins just above the tree-line and ends on the valley
floor, nearly two miles from the village. Most of the
season, however, the danger of avalanches is so acute
below the Phönixlager as to make the trip unthinkable.

The only other people to brave the northern face of
the ridge are climbers who hack their way up the freezing
cliffs in winter or wait for summer when the pale grey
spines turn brown in the sun, and the snow retreats to
reveal the strata of ice beneath, blue like the sky before
dawn. In the most sheltered crevices that ice remains all
year round, a trap for the unwary. Most climbers,
however, prefer the more established challenge of the

Heulendthorn, which provides a longer, if no less difficult, climb to a higher altitude.

For those few climbers who scale the heights of this lonely place, the peculiar nature of the Phönixlager is revealed. The ridge does not, as appears from below the Heulendthorn, follow a straight line, but is in fact shaped like a horseshoe, enclosing a freezing desolate area of almost perpetual shadow. The ridges on the southern side, although marginally lower, seem if anything even more precipitous than those on the north. When the wind is from the right direction, it catches sometimes between the crags, sounding a short but urgent note, like the call of some giant bird of prey, echoing back and forth between the granite walls. Then if you close your eyes, it is easy to imagine that the phoenix itself is circling just above you, looking for its prey among the broken boulders and the icy slopes.

The ridges on the southern side also pose a small puzzle to anyone in a position to study them. Half a mile down the steepest, most unyielding slope of all there appears to be a small door let into the rock. With high-power field-glasses the impression becomes certainty. A thin thread falling away from the door suggests a narrow path of some kind. Questioned about such things, the locals usually mention the Swiss army, which has installations all over the Alps. According to official sources there are certain mountains which contain as much as twelve kilometres of tunnels and galleries, some packed with electronics, some heated for human habitation and maintained by crews of uniformed guards, some simply freezing in the sub-zero darkness, waiting for the time when the Swiss authorities need them – in the event of an invasion for example, or a thermonuclear war.

But about the door in the Phönixlager the locals would be wrong. Pressurised bolts hold the door fast on three sides. A climber, a badly lost one, looking for shelter, would never be able to open it. If he could, he would see nothing, only freezing darkness. The tunnel behind the door runs twenty metres into the solid rock and then stops at the top of a metal staircase which goes down, down and round in tight spirals for another fifty feet until it reaches another gallery, slightly broader this time and heated. The breath still comes in puffs of freezing moisture, but there is a difference of some ten degrees from the blackness of the upper gallery.

Standing silent for a while and waiting for his heart to quieten, the hypothetical climber would hear the sound of generators, deep-throated, sinister in the cold darkness, coming from the end of the gallery which is still dark, although emergency lighting is recessed into the dripping walls. Following the gallery towards the humming he would come to another door, of polished metal this time, behind which the humming is distinct.

Behind this door on the afternoon of September 28th voices could be heard: the voices of two men, one speaking softly and persuasively, the other anxious, older.

The coldness of the place had nothing to do with the alpine microclimate. Their breath froze in air which was maintained at a constant minus five degrees centigrade. Around them, running from floor to ceiling were white metal shelves on which were stacked aluminium boxes, unmarked except for discreet barcodes. A faint blue light trickled down from above.

Dressed in a business suit and a grey overcoat, the older man, a Zurich banker he might have been, shivered and toyed with an unlit cigarette. Standing opposite him, apparently unaffected by the cold, was Egon Kessler. He spoke in the High German of his native Berlin.

'I'm afraid we had to come in here, Karl. It makes me very uncomfortable when members of the board come into the labs to discuss the director's programme. The

51

laboratory is not the board room. Technicians may appear to be concentrating on their work, but they all have ears.'

'But surely they have your confidence?' exclaimed the other man in his slightly comical Sweizerdeutsche. He looked around uneasily at the rows of boxes.

'Of course,' said Kessler, 'but there are certain matters which are better kept to the board – and even there I think the franchise may be a little too extensive.'

The older man straightened up.

'You can say that kind of thing to me, Doctor Kessler, if you like, but you might do well to recall that the decision to support this programme was a collective one. We are not about to change the long-established procedures of the company just to suit Professor . . .'

'I'm sorry,' said Kessler, calm once again. 'I didn't mean to imply that anyone on the board might not be trustworthy. It's just that sometimes they seem unable to *understand*. I mean you saw in there . . .'

'What I saw was genuine concern about a dangerous course of action. Perhaps you don't see it up here, but opposition to this kind of work is growing stronger everywhere. Even in Switzerland. We cannot afford to embarrass our political friends. There is a *quid pro quo*. What do you think would happen if *we* should fall victim to sabotage? There would be publicity. Perhaps even an enquiry. These people have a habit of looking into things the government will obligingly ignore. They are unpredictable.'

Kessler raised a hand, appealing gently for calm.

'Karl, Karl,' he said, 'we all share your concern, but let me assure you all the necessary steps have been taken. The movements you refer to are a problem for our competitors, not for us. They cannot reach us here. They know nothing about us.'

'How can you be so sure?'

Kessler smiled.

'It is easy to win friends in any organisation – not just in governments – when you bring more with you than good intentions. Whether they know it or not, these misguided people work for us, not against us. And if they should ever turn their attention on our activities, we will know about it even before they do.'

The older man reached into his pocket for a gold lighter, turning it over in his hand.

'Nevertheless, there are other sources of unwelcome attention. There is foreign pressure. A higher profile brings higher exposure. Given last year's failures – your department's failure – you cannot be surprised if some members of the board are reluctant to take more risks. We were lucky last time.'

'Karl,' said Kessler. 'It is precisely because of those failures – unforeseeable as they were – that these risks may have to be taken. And I do not see, with the resources we can command, that the risks are really so great. There is a good chance that we will secure voluntary co-operation – the director himself believes so.'

The older man shuddered.

'I have as great a respect for the director as you do,' he said. 'But on that point I doubt his judgement very much. No woman *I* have ever met would agree to such a thing.'

'But she is not like any woman you have ever met. She is the only woman of her kind that has ever been found. As far as we know she may be a true anomaly, unique, a freak of nature. That is why we need her. And that is why we need you to make sure there are no further problems with the board.'

The older man shook his head.

'I have supported you and the director from the beginning. You know that. But I still cannot understand how a method that is supposed to have a universal application, that has been developed over a decade using proven scientific methods, supported by, I think you will admit, massive investment, can depend upon one woman. It isn't logical. The skin product after all . . .'

'The skin products are just a spin-off, a worthless detour in research terms. A commercial necessity perhaps – I can accept that, even if the director is not so patient – but no more than that.'

'Without it, Doctor Kessler, I doubt whether the director would still have his precious programme at all. The costs have been huge, as you well know.'

'All the more reason not to lose sight of the greater goals, now that we have come so far. For those goals, for real progress, we need embryonic material that is universally donable. The use of a patient's own cells is too dangerous: the genetic material has too often become corrupted with time. We have seen that all too clearly. I tell you this girl's childhood cancer, the discovery of the research records, they add up to a gift from Heaven.'

Kessler examined the older man's face for a moment to see if he was making any headway. As a member of the board, he was entitled to any of the services the company could provide, the thousand-and-one devices to hide away the years like so many guilty secrets. And yet here he was, a shivering old man with bags under his eyes, a double chin and broken veins. Kessler admired him for being what he was: old. The other directors all looked like film stars.

'A gift from Heaven? I wonder if she will see it that way,' he said.

'Karl, we are offering her a place in medical history. And we will offer her money besides. Damn it, we are in the process of constructing the third millennium. Everything, *everything* can change. We are looking at a new age. And she will be the mother of that age.'

The older man stuck a cigarette between his lips and lit it hastily. His hands were shaking.

'What if she doesn't co-operate?'

'She will,' said Kessler. 'She will have come so far down the road to meet us that going back will seem impossible.'

'*Seem?*'

'Will *be* impossible.'

6

Manhattan. October 2nd, 1995.

The call had come through on the Friday. An Ernst Krystal introduced himself as the man with whom she had spoken at the Raeburn launch. Cathy felt herself blushing, but her embarrassment at being found out to be an analyst and not a reporter was quickly replaced by puzzlement. How did he know where she was working?

'Lindsey Sherman,' he explained. 'Always very helpful. I wanted to find out which paper you were with and so . . .'

'You must think I'm a terrible liar. To tell you the truth – ' Cathy glanced quickly around the office. It was lunch-time and only a couple of the analysts were still there. 'To tell you the truth I was intrigued by what you said about Mendelhaus so I played along.'

He had wasted no time. If she wanted to know more about the company in question she should come to the Bristol for lunch on Monday. So here she was, dressed up in her smartest charcoal grey suit and a light blue rollneck cashmere sweater.

The maitre d' led her through a maze of brilliant white tables. Sitting on the far side of the room near a window which gave onto a small courtyard with a fountain was the man she had met at the launch. She was surprised to find him quite attractive. He was dressed in a dark suit.

He was slightly tanned and this made the abundant grey hair and the moustache more striking. He was smoking a cigar. Next to his hand there was a leather portfolio.

'Miss Ryder!' He stood up and smiled. She watched her slender hand disappear into his powerful grip.

They ordered lunch. When he started to talk she had taken out her microcassette and placed it under the small spray of flowers in the centre of the table.

'There is no need,' he said. 'All the details are in this dossier.'

When she leafed through the papers he produced from the leather portfolio she was impressed. There was a breakdown of key US companies with cosmetics interests and a comparison with Mendelhaus. Everything seemed to have been worked out to the last ratio, although she couldn't help feeling Mendelhaus's sales projections were wildly optimistic.

'You project Erixil sales of $12 million in the first quarter even though the product hasn't been launched yet. I don't see . . .'

'I can understand your scepticism, Miss Ryder. But as I believe I suggested in our last meeting this is a special case.'

'What makes Erixil so special?'

'It is simply a different approach to the problem, a bolder, more fundamental one. Raeburn, and all the others, have realised that the unfathomable multiplicity of substances – proteins, I'm talking about – needed to keep a complex system like an epidermis behaving at optimal efficiency is always going to be produced better by nature than by a man in a white coat. That is why they have focused on placenta-based products. They take primitive, unspecialised cells from unborn animals and hope that when they meet human skin cells they will pick up and understand the signals they receive and produce

57

enough of the substances the old cells lack to make a difference.'

'But you said that kind of work was dead end. You said they might as well stick to cold cream.'

Krystal emptied his glass.

'That's right. Because the truth is, they're fumbling about in the dark. They can't come up with a real answer because they don't yet understand the problem. They simply don't understand the mechanics of the ageing process.'

'And Mendelhaus do?'

'Better, much better. And the result is that instead of smearing unborn veal on your face, you will soon be able to assist your skin to *help itself*. An epidermis gets thin and dry because the systems that serve it, providing water, oxygen and food, removing waste, break down. Chemical systems exist to repair it, but they are designed to work hardest in youth, when the body is growing. Those systems can be turned up, as it were, if you know how to do it.'

'But why should they ever be allowed to turn down?' said Cathy.

'Well, I'm afraid,' said Krystal with a shrug, 'once we have passed the age at which we can successfully reproduce, we ourselves cease to be a priority. Surely you knew that? The mechanism which has so successfully ensured the survival of our species through the ages has left us no more than the dispensable tools of our genes. This new product is the first step towards reversing that lamentable state of affairs.'

He refilled his glass and hers.

'But how have Mendelhaus been able to do all this? How can they know so much more about the genetics involved?'

Krystal sat back from the table and raised his napkin to his mouth.

'I am afraid I am not in a position to go into details there,' he said. 'Nor am I competent to do so. The research methods are highly – '

'Secret?'

Krystal smiled. 'I was going to say complex. But if you wish it, I could put you in touch with the people concerned. They could explain it better than I could – if they were prepared to.'

Cathy was intrigued, but she couldn't help thinking about Mike Paine and what he would make of a report full of genetic science. *Never mind this shit, just give me the bottom line damn it* was what he would say. She looked back down at the report next to her plate.

'You predict drastic reductions in sales for all the other companies. You predict stock slides of anything up to 50 per cent.'

'In my opinion the prediction is conservative. Remember what happened to sales of typewriters when the word processor became a commercial proposition. And the difference here is that where the change from typewriter to word processor involved an investment of capital and effort – you had to get round people's fear of computers – here, there is only a minor difference in price, at least in the first three months. As for the instructions, they are a lot simpler than a home perm.'

'So you think the beauty-conscious American woman will just rush straight out and buy Erixil?'

'Yes.'

'What about the stock in Mendelhaus? Will our clients be able to buy any?'

'Unfortunately Mendelhaus is wholly owned by Union Bank of Geneva and the company's founding families. There are no shares available on the open market. On the other hand UBG shares are available to your investors in ADR form.'

'So in effect the only advice I could give is to sell the other companies?'

'Or short sell. If you contract to sell Raeburn at a slight discount to present prices in, say, two months' time you will make what I think one could qualify as *very* serious money. You will be able to pick up Raeburn stock at a fraction of current prices by the time it comes to honour your obligations.'

Cathy felt the hair on the back of her neck tingle. She tried to look calm.

'I still don't understand your interest in all this. Are you hoping to pull the same stunt?'

'I mentioned the Union Bank of Geneva and its interest in Mendelhaus. Let us say, what is good for them is good for me. When news of Mendelhaus's advances reaches the market, investors will soon see the connection. Of course my giving you this information in advance will probably make little or no material difference in the end, but – ' he fixed her with a paternal stare – 'I thought it might make a difference *to you*.'

Cathy felt embarrassed. He had been giving her free information and she had been giving him a hard time. She smiled for him as he raised his finger at the approaching *garçon*.

'I hope you can do something with this material,' he said once the waiter had taken their order. 'There will be a Mendelhaus product launch in one month's time. I will send you the details. At that time everyone will know what you know now. If I were you I would produce some research and some recommendations before that happens.'

7

Los Angeles. October 2nd, 1995.

Harry Waterman sat waiting in a leather armchair with his hands around a glass of iced Perrier. Twelve feet above him the blades of a fan – all carved wood and shining brass – went silently round and round, blowing a refreshing draught of air across his damp forehead. Beyond the French windows on his right lay a courtyard with a fountain. In the huge airy Reading Room – that was what they called the waiting room in this place – the antique chairs and tables were arranged in little groups so that no one would have to look at anyone else. Waterman reckoned that there was room for at least twenty-five people, but since only two doctors practised here, it was very unlikely that there would ever be more than five or six patients waiting at any one time. Privacy was thus assured. This afternoon there were just two other people waiting, and both were hidden away behind newspapers in far-off corners of the room. Waterman sipped the Perrier and tried not to think what a check-up would cost in a place like this. He listened to the sound of the fountain and breathed in the scent of the roses and the leather *and the money*.

The two doctors were called Nierman and Fanshawe. Waterman had got their names from one of Micky Harborne's friends, a set designer called Bryan Oplinger.

According to Oplinger, who smoked just a bit too much dope for Waterman's liking, Dr Nierman came from a rich New England family whose lineage went all the way back to the Boston Tea Party and beyond. His mother was a pillar of the Daughters of the American Revolution, and that kind of thing. No one knew much about Fanshawe except that he was a Brit and had a plummy accent. But that was enough. Between the two of them they had almost cornered the market among the ultra-rich of Beverly Hills, and their clientele included half the big names in Hollywood. Some people, it seemed, would pay almost anything to ensure that their excretions were scrutinised and their orifices probed only by the sort of doctor who played polo at week-ends.

All the same, Waterman did not feel comfortable. The moment he'd turned into the driveway in his 1989 Chevrolet, he'd felt a growing sense of embarrassment, of shame. There probably hadn't been a Chevrolet parked out there in twenty years, if ever. And just the way he looked was so . . . so *low budget*. He was glad they had arranged the chairs the way they had in their goddamn Reading Room. He didn't want the other patients, whoever they were, to see his nasty blue jacket, which was going shiny near the cuffs, or his beige trousers which were so creased up around his crutch and the back of his knees, that it looked as if he'd spent the night in them. He picked up a copy of the London *Times*, which was lying on the table in front of him, and tried to read it. That was what everybody else was doing.

The lead story in the *Times* was about Italian car workers laying siege to a railway depot where imports of British-built Japanese cars, Nissans and Toyotas, were coming in. Below this was another big story: *Etienne Louvois – Minister resigns*. The French Minister of Science and Industry, it said, had just resigned over his government's 'halfhearted' defence of the national interest following the Etienne Louvois affair. Waterman remembered the story from the TV: there had been an invasion by Green protesters at a big lab owned by Etienne Louvois, France's biggest pharmaceuticals company. The protesters claimed that Louvois was carrying out experiments on human genetic material which were a violation of European Community Directives, although not of French law itself. The management of Etienne Louvois had vowed to continue their work until ordered to stop by the French authorities, putting the government in an embarrassing position.

'Mr Waterman?'

A young nurse in a crisp white uniform was standing in front of him, a respectful six feet away. Waterman folded up the newspaper very untidily and stood up.

'Dr Fanshawe is ready for you now. Sorry for having kept you waiting.'

She was English too. Pretty, with brown hair, and a smattering of freckles across the bridge of her nose. Waterman could just imagine her horseback-riding across some country estate. He felt shabbier than ever.

The nurse turned with a smile and led him out of the Reading Room, down a wide corridor with watercolours on the walls, and into an office – an outer office, as it turned out. Here a smart middle-aged lady sat behind a desk with what looked like an old-fashioned ledger in front of her. She smiled too and said: 'Good afternoon'. Waterman couldn't tell if she was English or not. Then the pretty nurse opened a pair of double doors and ushered him into another office, a much bigger one.

'Mr Waterman, Doctor,' she said.

Dr Fanshawe stood up from behind his desk and smiled a tight, professional smile. He was in his fifties, with thin silvery hair, half-moon glasses and slightly sunburnt skin. That was one of the things about the Brits, Waterman recalled defensively, they never could manage to get a decent suntan.

'How do you do?' said the doctor as they shook hands.

'Fine, thank you . . . sir,' Waterman replied, and then silently cursed himself for sounding so damned subordinate.

'Call me Bill,' said Fanshawe. 'All my patients do.'

'Okay,' said Waterman, but he couldn't bring himself to say it, he couldn't bring himself to say: 'Okay, *Bill*.'

'Now what can I do for you?'

Fanshawe motioned towards another leather armchair a few feet from the desk and sat down himself.

Waterman cleared his throat. Business at last.

'Well, as I explained to your secretary on the telephone, I just need to know a little bit about one of your ex-patients, Raymond Bladon.' *Why the fuck did I call him Raymond?* Waterman thought.

Fanshawe just nodded slowly.

'You see we're looking into the possibility that Mr Bladon, and a friend of his, Matthew – I mean Matt McArthur may have died from the effects of a viral infection.'

'Yes, my secretary did explain that,' said Fanshawe. 'You'll have to forgive me, but I wasn't *entirely* clear . . . Are you from the CDC yourself?'

Waterman shifted in his chair. Why was that so damned difficult to believe?

'I work freelance,' he said, 'on investigations of this sort. Field research, that kind of thing.' He hoped he wouldn't have to go into details. These days, thanks to Bill Miller, he was being paid for nothing more scientific than delving into people's sexual histories. There were plenty of parents out there who would shell out good money just to be sure that a prospective son-in-law wasn't about to introduce the family to some nasty inheritable disease. He'd got many a doctor to break the Hippocratic

Oath in that line of business. He just hoped that such lowly things were outside Fanshawe's experience. 'You know what they say,' Waterman went on, 'the biggest laboratory of all is the outside world, right?'

Fanshawe was nodding again, but only very slightly.

'Anyway, I can assure you that anything you say will be treated in absolute confidence.'

Fanshawe looked at him in silence for a moment and then glanced at his watch.

'I see. Well fire away then. I'm afraid I have another patient in about ten minutes.'

'Okay then,' he said. *Bill* was out of the question now. 'You were Ray Bladon's doctor for how many years?'

'About six years. I can check that if you want.'

'No need. Were you his only doctor? He didn't see anyone else?'

Fanshawe hesitated. 'Not in general practice, to my knowledge. Of course when he fell ill he was treated in hospital.'

'Of course. And before that, had he suffered from any unusual ailments? How was his health generally?'

Fanshawe put his palms together like he was about to start praying. 'Mr Waterman,' he said, and there was a touch of impatience in his perfect English syllables, 'as you must be aware, Ray Bladon was a man who prided himself on good health. It was a part of his trade mark. But that trade mark was, in my view, exaggerated by the studios and the promoters in the entertainment industry.'

Waterman nodded. Fanshawe was right: they'd decided that Bladon had to be a legend, and legends didn't get sick. They went out in a blaze of glory, maybe. It was amazing that people still wanted to believe in that kind of thing. They still wanted to believe that the humiliation of disease and decay was not inevitable – that the tough-guys had it beat. They wanted to believe it today more than ever.

'I can't deny,' Fanshawe went on, feeling his way it seemed, 'that Ray was . . . unusually concerned not to display any physical weakness. But it is my strong belief that this was primarily because it was expected of him. To be strong, I mean. He believed that his strength was a symbol, a symbol of hope. I think we should respect that. And I think it quite wrong, *quite* wrong, for the newspapers and the media to be trying to make a big thing out of uncovering his . . . his weaknesses, trying to make him look like some kind of fraud. If Ray Bladon was larger than life then it was those same people who made him seem that way.'

So Fanshawe had seen Harborne's article too. And in his staid, English way he was pissed off about it – not just at the homosexual thing, or hints about AIDS, but at the way *Exclusive!* magazine had tried to make Bladon's whole life look like a lie. Part of the article asserted that the guy had undergone cosmetic surgery, and had spent a lot of time at expensive health farms. In particular it pinpointed a three-month period in the spring of 1994 when he had been completely out of circulation. Some other magazines and papers had picked up on the same idea.

'I can tell you,' Fanshawe added, 'that some of his relatives are pretty upset about it all.'

'Believe me, I sympathise,' said Waterman. 'But what are you saying? Are you saying his health had been bad?'

'Not really. His heart did give *some* cause for concern, and I advised him to slow down a bit just to be on the safe side – although I don't think he liked that particular piece of advice. There were irregularities in the beat, you see, although by no means always. Anyway, he had equipment installed in his gym to monitor that, just in case it got worse, which it never did.'

'Did you call in a second opinion?'

Fanshawe looked sharply at Waterman over his half-moon glasses.

'Yes, as a matter of fact I did, although most doctors in that situation would not have done. Dr Walsh concurred with my view that no treatment was necessary.'

'I see.'

'No, overall, for a man of his years – he was nearly seventy when he died – Ray Bladon was in good condition. He exercised regularly and carefully, he ate sensibly and he didn't smoke. He wasn't a hard drinker either, in spite of the rumours. My role was confined to treating the odd ailment.'

'Like what?'

'Well piles, for example.'

'Piles?'

'Yes, piles – haemorrhoids in your parlance. He rode a great deal. It's quite a common problem among people who ride.'

'And there was never anything worse than that? Nothing consistent with a viral infection?'

'Perhaps the odd case of flu. Nothing I couldn't account for. I'm afraid the cancer came as a complete surprise. There was nothing irregular in his heartbeat at all the last time I examined him, you see. His blood pressure was a touch too high, but nothing serious.'

'And when was the last time you saw him?'

'Well, about eighteen months before his death last autumn. I mean, that was the last check-up he had. He was due for another one in the spring, about six months before he died, but he cancelled it. I did see him at the hospital just before . . . the end.'

Waterman began to see that it wasn't just loyalty to Ray Bladon that made Fanshawe angry at the newspapers: he was afraid all this might bring his competence into question. Waterman suddenly felt a lot more confident.

'Dr Fanshawe, my job is to try and isolate possible

sources of infection, so we can establish where a virus might have come from if a virus was indeed involved. So I have to ask you if you believe Bladon was a practising homosexual.'

Fanshawe smiled.

'I don't have any difficulty with that question, Mr Waterman,' he said. 'I'm absolutely convinced that he was not. And believe me, in my current practice, I've had plenty of experience in such matters.'

Waterman could believe that. And he was pleased. Micky Harborne's story had been a cheap shot, and he didn't like cheap shots. He still wanted to be sure, all the same.

'So you give no credence whatever to the suggestion that he and Matt McArthur had any form of physical relationship.'

'None whatever. Let me put it another way, Mr Waterman: it was a pack of bloody lies.'

For a moment there was silence. Then Fanshawe leaned forward and said: 'Tell me, from your researches so far, do you believe a virus *was* involved?'

Waterman felt flattered. Fanshawe wanted his opinion: professional to professional. He would be as candid as the doctor had been.

'I have to say, Bill,' he said, though *Bill* still didn't come easily, 'that I can't find any evidence for it. Looks to me like it was just a coincidence. Sure, the cancers were surprisingly virulent, but then heart cancers are pretty rare things, and people just aren't on the look-out for them. Otherwise they'd have been picked up earlier.'

'Well perhaps McArthur's *was* picked up,' said Fanshawe, 'in a way. I mean there was the irregular heartbeat. The cancer may have had something to do with that, although we'd no way of knowing – '

'Of course. But that doesn't alter the statistical position, which is why I'm here.'

Fanshawe smiled and tapped his hands against his desk. It meant: 'well that's that I guess.'

'Just one other thing,' said Waterman. His ten minutes weren't up yet. 'You said you didn't examine Ray Bladon at any time during the eighteen months before his death, right?'

'Almost eighteen months, yes.'

'And other than the hospital where he died, you have no reason to suppose he saw any other doctor, or any other medical establishment? No one asked you for his records or anything?'

Fanshawe hesitated again.

'Well, nothing like that,' he said. 'But, in the *strictest* confidence – and I can't even verify it – I believe he had seen someone.'

'Who?'

'I have no idea. All I can say is that when I saw Ray at the hospital – he was unconscious at the time – it looked to me as if he had undergone some minor cosmetic surgery.'

'Are you sure?'

'Well it would have been almost impossible to tell for anyone who didn't know him as well as I did. It was superb work, really superb. Just a minor tuck under the chin, to tighten the jaw line.'

To demonstrate the effect he put his thumbs around the very top of his throat and gently pulled back the flesh. The definition of his chin became sharper.

'But the scars were invisible. I used to work in a place in the UK where they did that kind of thing. That's how I was able to spot it. But I can tell you, another few weeks and even I wouldn't have noticed.'

The missing three months! So there it was. Bladon *had* had cosmetic surgery. Maybe Micky Harborne wasn't such a fool after all. Still, it didn't change anything, unless . . .

'And there was something else I noticed, which I must say puzzled me a bit,' said Fanshawe.

69

'Yes?'

'Well I could understand why Ray might go to someone else for cosmetic surgery. I mean we don't do anything like that here – although I would have expected him to ask for a recommendation, I must say. But to have a mole removed or whatever, well, I don't know why he didn't just come here.'

'A mole?'

'I'm sorry, I'm not being very clear. You see when I was in the hospital I noticed another scar on his body that I couldn't account for. It was about two inches or so below his left nipple, between his fifth and sixth rib; less than an inch in length, and slightly curved. Just a little white line, really.'

'You're sure it wasn't just a cut or something?'

'No, I don't think so. The line was too perfect. No, it looked like another piece of minor surgery.'

'And you think he might have had a mole removed?'

'A mole or a cyst or something. I can't think what else it could be. I wanted to ask him, actually, but, as I said, he was unconscious at the time. I suppose he must have had it done at the same time as his tuck. They probably threw it in free of charge. Of course, if a new mole had appeared, and he'd been advised to have it removed, then presumably the doctor concerned wanted to do a biopsy to check for skin cancer. In which case I really should have been informed. But these days, well . . .'

He shrugged and then tapped his fingers on the edge of the desk again. The ten minutes definitely were up this time. Waterman shook the doctor's hand and left. As he passed through the Reading Room on his way out he looked around for the English nurse with the upturned nose and the freckles. Yes, there she was, coming towards him with another patient in tow. For an instant their eyes met as they passed each other, but this time she didn't smile.

70

8

Manhattan. November 2nd, 1995.

The Erixil launch took place on the seventieth floor of the brand new Hiraizumi Centre on 8th Avenue. The Centre, which lay a few blocks to the north of Times Square, was said to be the first building in New York City history to cost over $1 billion. It had only been completed a few weeks earlier, and as yet few New Yorkers, besides builders and decorators, had been inside. For this reason, if for no other, the launch was extremely well attended: outside on the street the taxis and limousines stood three-abreast, disgorging their well-heeled passengers. As she threaded her way between the bumpers, pulling her best cashmere coat close about her so as not to get it dirty, Cathy Ryder wondered just how Mendelhaus had managed to arrange it: the top ten floors of the Centre were supposed to be reserved for the Hiraizumi Corporation itself, or for one or other of its numerous subsidiaries. There were no conference facilities for hire up there. But whatever it had cost them in favours or money, it was an inspired choice, and one that made a welcome change from the mid-town hotels that most companies used for their launches. A visit to the Hiraizumi Centre was an event in itself.

The scale and audacity of the building was as remarkable as its cost. It was nothing less than a colossal rendering of the *torii* gate of a Japanese Shinto temple, consisting of two tall towers, both over nine hundred feet tall, supporting a horizontal top section which curved gently downwards towards the middle and reached out beyond the supporting towers on either side. The exterior of the building was made up of huge rectangular plates of dark tinted glass. In the middle of the top section the Hiraizumi symbol, a crested wave inside a circle, was boldly displayed using another type of glass, this time with a highly reflective golden surface over which arc-lights played. At the bottom, between the two towers, was a covered lobby area half the size of a football field, with batteries of elevators going up and down on either side. Over the entrance to this area was a giant marble gateway, eighty feet high, identical in colour and shape to the building itself. As you approached from the street, the gateway had the effect of amplifying the seeming immensity of the dark building behind it. You couldn't look up to admire the strength and size of the one without realising how much greater was the other.

Cathy found herself sharing the glass elevator with half a dozen other guests, among whom was the exalted Ben Steiner of Salomon Brothers. Steiner was supposed to be the best analyst on Wall Street in what had become known informally as the 'vanity sector'. The vanity sector was made up of companies that produced the almost infinite variety of products that were supposed to improve the outward appearance of the human body: everything from zit cream to lipstick, nail polish to hair-restorer. With the huge sales boom in Eastern Europe still going strong, the manufacture of these products was regarded these days as an industry in its own right, separate from either pharmaceuticals or chemicals and subject to its own laws. Steiner had spotted and evaluated the growth potential of the vanity sector ahead of most of his rivals – the team at Webber Atlantic included – and had been riding high ever since. No one seemed to know how much he got paid, but the word on the street was that Goldman Sachs had offered him $200,000 a year and he'd turned them down. He stood leaning against the side of the elevator with his hands in his raincoat pockets looking bored. He was below average height, with a high forehead, round horn-rimmed glasses and curly black hair – kind of Jewish preppy, Cathy thought. She sensed him looking at her now and again, and wondered if he knew who she was. Half of her hoped he did, and the other half hoped he didn't.

After their lunch together, Cathy had done exactly what Ernst Krystal had suggested. Her professional judgement had told her she should treat everything he said with great caution: after all he was a Mendelhaus man, and he was probably being paid to drum up interest. But Michael Paine, the head of research, had been on everyone's back so much, demanding firm recommendations, that she had decided to go for broke. Using Krystal's figures and Krystal's product descriptions, she had predicted that the Erixil range would prove so effective as to overturn the whole cosmetics industry. She had gone on to recommend that Webber Atlantic clients reduce or liquidate their holdings in Mendelhaus's competitor companies, including Raeburn Corporation whose latest product launch she had attended only a few weeks earlier, and which several other analysts had been tipping following rumours of a take-over bid. She also recommended purchase of stock in Union Bank of Geneva, the majority shareholders of Mendelhaus, although the financial services sector was entirely outside her ambit. Paine had grilled her on her report before allowing it to be sent out, but she had stuck to her guns. Erixil would make Mendelhaus top dog, not only in the crucial European market, but in the US as well. In the end Paine had agreed to release the report – 'we need a little action round here,' he'd said – but not before making it pretty clear that if she were wrong it would mean the end of her career at Webber Atlantic.

Cathy had been prepared for that at the time. There had

73

been a lot of talk in the office about another round of cannings, and she knew she was quite junior enough to be among the likely victims. In effect, she had nothing to lose. Sitting in Paine's office she had even experienced a sense of exhilaration as she presented her case, declining the opportunities he gave her to qualify or tone down her opinions, upping the stakes every minute. It was the thrill of the big gamble, exactly the kind of thing she would normally have avoided. But now, as the dark glass elevator climbed noiselessly towards the seventieth floor, she began to wonder if she had done the right thing. If all Krystal's words were only well-presented hype, if all the right things didn't happen, she wouldn't just be finished at Webber Atlantic, she would probably be finished on Wall Street. Perhaps that didn't sound so bad in principle, but what else could she do? She remembered what Paine had said to her one day as he'd walked by and seen her violin case leaning against her desk: *I hope you know how to play that thing.* She began to feel an uncomfortable trembling sensation in the pit of her stomach, and it had nothing to do with the slowing down of the elevator.

A moment later an electronic voice announced their arrival at level seventy, and the glass and steel doors slid open to reveal a large hallway with a domed roof and grey marble walls. A red carpet led Cathy and the others past rows of elaborate bouquets, standing in Grecian-style urns, towards a tall doorway, in front of which stood two lines of girls in knee-length crimson skirts, white blouses with bows at the neck and embroidered black waistcoats. They all smiled prettily. The girls on the left took care of the coats, while the girls on the right took each guest's invitation, and in return gave them a little metal badge with their name and company printed on it. Cathy saw that she had been sharing the elevator with the executive president of Bloomingdales and his wife, and a journalist from *Living* magazine. She pinned her badge to the lapel of the black jacket she had bought a few days earlier from a Spanish boutique in Greenwich Village. Under the circumstances it had been an extravagant buy – the jacket and the rest of the outfit that went with it – but it was all part of the same big gamble.

On the other side of the doorway Cathy was confronted with one of the most spectacular views over Manhattan she had ever seen. The reception was being held in a huge rectangular gallery at the south-east corner of the centre, somewhere up in the top section. Its two outer walls were made entirely of glass. To the south was an unimpeded view of the downtown area, dominated by the twin towers of the World Trade Centre, stark and lonely as she had never seen them before. Out beyond the mouth of the Hudson River, the Statue of Liberty was a floodlit speck in the distance. To the east was a complete panorama of midtown Manhattan, so close yet so silent that it looked like a gigantic model, something put together by the special effects team on a Spielberg movie.

In front of the windows about three hundred guests were already gathered, drinking champagne and talking excitedly. All around were tables laden with food, piled high with fresh fruit, elaborate hors d'oeuvres and tempting Swiss confectionery. In the middle of the room on a marble table stood an ice sculpture in the shape of an M. Around it, a bed of crushed ice cooled countless bottles of Dom Perignon champagne. In the far corner a group of musicians in tailcoats played Viennese waltzes. Cathy felt her confidence returning. If the product Mendelhaus were pushing was even half as good as their hospitality her worries were over.

Just inside the doorway stood a line of four Mendelhaus executives, shaking hands with the guests as they came in. This was unusually formal, but Cathy put that down to the company being European. One of the executives was the head of Mendelhaus Inc., the small US subsidiary which handled distribution in North America, and the other three all worked for the parent company in Switzerland. The most important was a handsome looking man of about forty, with a sun-tanned face and wavy blond hair. His name was Pierre Lambert, and his badge said 'MD – Cosmetics Division'. He took her hand with a warm smile, and held it in his for an instant longer than was necessary. His palm was unpleasantly moist. She wondered if he knew anything about her discussions with Ernst Krystal.

'Thank you so much for coming, Cathy,' he said. He spoke with a faint French accent. 'I do hope we have a chance to chat later.'

Cathy smiled back at him and walked towards the other guests. Her instincts told her that Lambert was attracted to her, and she couldn't help feeling a little pleased about it. She didn't like to flirt, especially not when she was on business, but there was something about these Mendelhaus people: they knew how to make you feel special. Whether it was business or pleasure, American men were always so preoccupied with showing you how tough they were. But if toughness was the most important thing, then a woman was always going to come off second best, wasn't she? There was no doubt about it: Europeans had more finesse.

Among the guests Cathy was able to recognise a lot of faces. It was much the same crowd as went to all these launches and presentations, only bigger than most. There were buyers and executives from all the big stores and retailing groups, journalists from a wide range of newspapers and magazines, and a good number of people like herself, from investment banks and broking firms. This was surprising in a way, because Mendelhaus was not a publicly quoted company: its stock was all in the hands of the founding family or the Union Bank of Geneva. On the other hand, it made all the sense in the world if a flotation of stock was intended in the near future. A good name on Wall Street could also be handy if acquisitions were planned. If she found Ernst Krystal, she thought, maybe he could tell her something about that.

She was standing on tip-toe, turning slowly round, when she found herself face-to-face with Ben Steiner. He had been right behind her.

'This is pretty good juice,' he said, holding up the fluted champagne glass. 'Here, let me get you some.'

Before she could say anything he had taken a glass of champagne from a passing waiter and handed it to her.

'I'm Ben Steiner,' he said. 'But of course you can read that for yourself. Dinky little badges, huh?'

'Cathy Ryder,' said Cathy, and held out her hand in a deliberately businesslike way. 'Webber Atlantic.'

Steiner shook it with a tight smile on his face, a smile which betrayed at once that business was not what he'd had on his mind. It was a smile that said: *Okay, I get the picture*.

'Good turn-out, wouldn't you say,' he said after an awkward pause. 'I wonder what we're in for.'

Cathy felt a moment of remorse for having been so defensive. It wasn't a good thing to go around denting people's egos, even if they did lay themselves open to it. She smiled and said: 'Some technological mumbo-jumbo, I expect, followed by a lot of beautiful models with grease on their faces.'

Steiner laughed. 'You've been to this kind of thing before, I can see that.'

'I have. In fact I was at the big Raeburn launch a month or so back.'

'Oh God, *Raeburn*,' said Steiner, rolling his eyes. 'I can't seem to get away from that name these days. How was it, by the way?'

'The Raeburn launch? Well, average I suppose. What did you mean you can't get away from *that name*?'

'Oh, you know, all these take-over rumours. The management down there are real scared someone's gonna buy up the company and restructure them all out of a job. They're making a major effort to talk up their stock price. I think they're about to spend a fortune on Madison Avenue.'

'Where are these take-over rumours coming from? Do you know?'

Steiner laughed again and took a sip of champagne. Cathy got the idea he *did* know.

'Well I couldn't say,' he said. 'You know how these things get started. Someone probably overheard something in a restaurant, that's all.'

'Overheard what though?'

Steiner looked into Cathy's eyes, her 'Egyptian eyes', and she realised suddenly, with a mixture of disappointment and anger, that the guru of the vanity sector would probably tell her anything she wanted to know, just to keep her engaged in conversation. His successful career, his big salary, none of that saved him from being the under-dog in this situation. That was where the anger came in, because all this made Cathy's own career seem unnecessary. Her looks were success enough.

'Well, the way I heard it,' Steiner went on, 'something was cooking down at Swift and Drew. But if they were working on a take-over of Raeburn I don't know who they would have been acting for.'

'Swift and Drew, you said?'

'Yeah, Swift and Drew, the old WASP nest. You know I was once dumb enough to put in for a job there – way back, mind you.'

'Why was that dumb?' Cathy asked. She'd heard that Swift and Drew were pretty good people to work for.

'You kidding?' said Steiner. 'With a name like mine? Easier to get elected as mayor of Damascus. If you don't mind me saying so, you don't look wishy-washy enough for a regular Anglo-Saxon yourself. Am I right?'

'I'm Jewish too,' said Cathy, 'mostly.'

78

'Mostly?'

'Three quarters. I had an English grandmother.'

'You don't say? So Ryder's a Jewish name?'

'Not exactly. My grandfather, I mean my paternal grandfather, was English too, only Jewish English.'

'I see. Well it sounds very classy. Maybe you would get into Swift and Drew after all.'

It was then that Cathy saw Ernst Krystal. He was walking towards her, accompanied by a blonde woman in a low-cut evening dress who seemed to be talking a lot between peals of high-pitched laughter.

'Good evening, Miss Ryder,' said Krystal. Standing next to Ben Steiner he looked taller and stronger than ever. 'I'm so happy you could come.'

Cathy looked at his badge. Beneath his name it just said 'Mendelhaus'. There was no mention of his position.

'And Mr Steiner of Salomon Brothers. Let me introduce you both to Mrs Beverly Stevens, of Harringtons.'

They all shook hands and the blonde woman immediately started talking again. Harringtons were a big chain of department stores in the mid-West, and Mrs Stevens, a Texan, was their cosmetics buyer. After ten minutes it seemed they knew just about everything about every purchase she had ever made. Finally, to Ben Steiner's dismay, but her own relief, Ernst Krystal managed to steer Cathy away, ostensibly to meet another guest.

'I must apologise for that,' he said as they made their getaway. 'One of the hazards of the job, I'm afraid.'

'Yes, I know,' said Cathy. 'But what exactly *is* your job? You never did tell me.'

Krystal smiled, as if the question amused him.

'Special projects,' he said. 'I go where I'm needed.'

'Like your competitors' product launches, for example?'

'Oh that. That was a very simple matter, Miss Ryder. And a perfectly ordinary one in such a competitive business. You can be quite sure that among our guests tonight someone will be taking notes for Raeburn Corporation.'

'But you're not just in public relations, are you?'

Krystal smiled again.

'Public relations? I would say personnel was more my line. Let's see, do you think everyone's here now?'

It was almost ten minutes to eight and the Mendelhaus executives were gone from the doorway.

'Yes,' said Krystal. 'I think we shall be ready to proceed quite soon. The presentation takes place in there.'

He pointed to another doorway on the west side of the room, above which a temporary sign said: AUDITORIUM.

'I just wanted to tell you to get a good seat, near the front. You'll be glad you did.'

'What are we going to see?' said Cathy. The champagne was beginning to have an effect.

'Something old and something new,' he said.

'Something borrowed, something blue?'

'Nothing has been borrowed, I assure you,' said Krystal quite sternly, missing the joke. 'It is all absolutely original.'

'Well I hope so,' said Cathy. 'That's what I've been telling all our clients for the past two weeks.'

Krystal handed her a fresh glass of champagne.

'So I hear,' he said. 'And I'm very pleased that you listened to my advice.'

For a few moments the trembling feeling returned to Cathy's stomach, in spite of the alcohol.

'The question is, will the clients be pleased?' she said. 'Will my boss be pleased?'

Krystal drained his glass in one. As he threw back his head Cathy took in the thick, heavy muscles in his neck, and the powerful torso.

'Don't worry about them,' he said. 'They're easily satisfied. In any case, you are destined for greater things altogether, I feel certain about that.' Someone touched Cathy's

80

shoulder. 'Ah, Monsieur Lambert, I believe you have already had the pleasure – '

'I certainly have,' replied Pierre Lambert, who had placed himself in front of Cathy, his back almost turned to Krystal. 'I had the opportunity of speaking to Mademoiselle Ryder at the door.'

He smiled at Cathy, but his eyes remained serious, observant. After the positive first impression she saw something predatory in him which was ugly. She looked at Krystal for help, but he had stepped back a pace and was looking at his watch.

'I hope Ernst has not been boring you with figures, Miss Ryder?'

Cathy flushed at the implied put down. His manner was patronising, and his eyes moved from her mouth to her breasts and back to her mouth as he spoke. A typical Frenchman.

'I don't find figures boring, Mr Lambert.'

Lambert looked up at her eyes, and seemed to notice she was a person for the first time. He laughed lightly and leaned forward so that she could smell his breath.

'Well I must say I am quite partial to figures myself.'

'Ah, the technical people are ready,' said Krystal pointedly from behind Lambert. Lambert glanced at his watch and after kissing Cathy's hand moved away. She let out a big sigh and then smiled at the expression of commiseration on Krystal's face.

'*Vive la France!*' he said raising his eyebrows. Then suddenly the musicians stopped playing and a calm female voice came on the public address system inviting everyone to go through to the auditorium.

Carrying their glasses, their mood barely subdued, the guests slowly filed their way into another large rectangular room, this time full of chairs arranged around a broad white catwalk, with a stage at the far end. Up on the stage, which was decorated with more flowers, was a lectern with

81

a microphone attached to it. Cathy, one of the first inside, took a seat behind the front row on the right hand side. As she waited, she wondered if this was to be the last product launch she would ever attend.

When everyone was inside, the doors closed and the lights went down except on the stage and the catwalk. Then the same detached female voice came over the public address system: 'Ladies and gentlemen, the managing director of the Mendelhaus cosmetics division, Mr Pierre Lambert.'

A little uncertainly at first the audience applauded as Lambert stood up from his seat near the door and walked briskly to the lectern. He smiled appreciatively to both sides of the room and began to speak. If there was anything written down in front of him, he never looked at it.

'Ladies and gentlemen, let me first say thank you for having taken the trouble to come along here this evening, and for welcoming us so warmly to the great city of New York.'

A group of guests at the far end of the room began clapping again, and the others all joined in. The Dom Perignon had been a smart move.

'Thank you, thank you again,' Lambert went on, the whiteness of his teeth set off by the depth and consistency of his sun-tan. 'I know that you are all very busy people, and so I will waste no time in coming to the facts about Erixil . . . besides which, I rather like the look of what the chefs have prepared for us out there, and I would like to get back to it.'

Appreciative laughter filled the room. Cathy caught sight of Ben Steiner on the other side of the catwalk, knocking back another mouthful of champagne. Beverly Stevens was sitting beside him.

'The facts are simply these: the development of Erixil is the fruit of a major breakthrough, not simply in skin care, but in our very understanding of how human cells function.

82

Where other products have sought to replace substances found missing in ageing skin, the Erixil three-stage skin treatment programme literally re-educates the epidermis to behave as it once did, creating *for itself* the structures and the biochemical environment necessary for a young, healthy-looking appearance. We at Mendelhaus believe Erixil represents nothing less than a complete revolution in skin care. Now I know what you might be thinking: how many times have we heard the words *breakthrough* and *revolution* on occasions like this? Too many times, I fear. So tonight, ladies and gentlemen, we shall not attempt to blind you with science. Instead we shall simply show you what those words really mean.'

In the background a fast electronic pulse had become faintly discernible. It was music and it got gradually louder. As Lambert finished speaking there came a series of dramatic chords and the lights on the catwalk became suddenly much brighter, so bright that Cathy had to shade her eyes for a few moments. Then she looked up and found herself staring at a procession of attractive young women, six facing her, six facing the left hand side of the room. They were all dressed in elegant black dresses of varying designs, and all of them had their hair swept back and tied with bows. They carried themselves with the assurance of professional models, their smiles cool and proud. They didn't blink, but rather their eyes unhurriedly opened and closed as if to punctuate the sinuous movements of their bodies. As she watched them, Cathy felt a terrible sinking feeling inside. Yes, the girls were beautiful, but they were just like the ones she had seen at the Raeburn launch. They didn't *need* skin care.

Then she heard Lambert's voice again: 'Ladies and gentlemen, I will not attempt to deceive you. The ladies you see before you have all been trained as professional models. In fact all of them have appeared at one time or another in the most prestigious fashion magazines. Perhaps you will even recognise some of them.'

Behind him the curtains parted to reveal a white screen. Simultaneously the models turned around and walked over to the opposite side of the catwalk, so that everyone in the audience got a good look at all twelve of them. The six who now faced Cathy were just as beautiful as the others. All the men in the room were spellbound. Ben Steiner sat staring with his mouth half open. It suddenly occurred to Cathy that this was the reason he had come to the launch in the first place.

'Here for example,' said Lambert, 'is Kelly Ramsey's first appearance in *Elle*.'

One of the twelve models turned around and walked back along the catwalk to the stage. At the same time a photograph of the magazine appeared on the screen: on the cover was a blonde, pouting outrageously, with her hand on the top of her head. It was clearly the same girl, although the pale lipstick and false eyelashes she wore looked very peculiar, very dated in fact.

'Kelly was modelling some of the year's boldest autumn collections,' said Lambert, 'and remained in great demand well into the 1980s.'

A look of puzzlement came across some of the faces in the audience: what did he mean, *well into the 1980s?* Somebody in the middle of the third row stood up.

'And here,' Lambert went on, 'we have Emilie Jobert, on the cover of one of *Vogue*'s Christmas editions. By 1973 she was already well established.'

Another picture flashed up on the screen, a second girl, a tall brunette this time, with very high cheekbones and a knowing smile on her face, strolled back onto the stage. From both sides of the room came a murmur of confusion. Cathy saw Ben Steiner sit forward, squinting through his horn-rimmed glasses.

'And this is Marie Chamant, photographed for the cover of *Harpers* by Norman Parkinson in 1967.'

This time an audible gasp went up from the audience. A lot of people suddenly stood up to get a better look, then more and more. Even Beverly Stevens, who hadn't stopped grinning throughout the entire show, looked astonished. The three models on the stage all spun round once, as if showing off their clothes, but everybody was staring into their faces, trying to find the wrinkles that just weren't there. The person in front of Cathy stood up and she had to lean to one side to see.

'Nor could I fail to mention Eva Sindermann,' Lambert continued, seemingly oblivious of the mounting commotion in the audience, 'for several years a favourite model of Sir Cecil Beaton. Here she is in *Vogue* in 1971.'

Another model spun around and walked back towards the stage. As she turned her back, her face reappeared on the screen behind her: she was wearing a pirate-style headband, the kind no one had worn for twenty years.

'Naturally, all these ladies have been in retirement for some time now,' said Lambert. 'But they have kindly agreed to make this brief comeback to demonstrate the effect of the Erixil skin treatment programme, which they have all carried out over the past eight weeks as we recommend.'

As he spoke the parade continued, each model walking back to the stage in turn. As they arrived, the others greeted them with embraces. Overhead, the magazine covers flashed by, one after the other.

'Ladies and gentlemen, when you look into the faces of these ladies,' said Lambert, 'what you are seeing is not a trick: what you are seeing is the result of scientific progress. We are not creating the *appearance* of youth, we are restoring youth itself. This is the Mendelhaus definition of a breakthrough. This is *our* revolution!'

The music was loud now, and the girls in the crimson

skirts who had been on the door appeared by the sides of the stage holding large mock-ups of the three different Erixil boxes, white cardboard with gold writing. At first Cathy could not believe what Lambert was saying. The models looked like they were in their late twenties at most, the same as her in fact. But then she began to detect here and there the signs of age: a lack of brightness in the eyes, a little too much breadth in the hips. But she had to look hard. These women were beautiful, and yet every one of them was old enough to be her mother. For the first time the full meaning of what she had been dealing with in her detailed reports came home to her. The applause had already begun.

'Ladies and gentlemen,' said Lambert, his voice at last loud with triumph, 'as the Erixil programme proves, there is nothing inevitable in decay, no corruption that cannot be redeemed. With the instruments of our own creation we can re-create ourselves!'

His words were all but lost in the din. Everyone in the room was on their feet now, clapping, cheering, three hundred and fifty fortunate people, witnessing a miracle. Finally, Cathy too had to stand. She applauded with the rest of the audience, but her eyes were not fixed on the faces of the rejuvenated beauties, but looking for Krystal, the man who had hitched her career to a rising star.

And then she saw him. He too was clapping and looking across the crowded room, looking directly at her. And as she returned his gaze, he smiled.

9

The flickering red numbers tumbled again and there was a
great whoop all around the room. Cathy lurched forward
losing her plastic cup, the warm champagne showering
Mike Paine's Hermès tie. Her apology was drowned in
the noise as the other analysts pushed to get a closer look
at the Reuters monitor.

'Nothing!' Paine shouted. 'Don't worry about it. A two
hundred dollar tie. What do I care?'

Cathy reached out to brush off the champagne, but
another foaming cup had been produced and was pressed
into her hand.

Paine slipped the tie over his head and looped it Red
Indian fashion over Cathy's thick black hair.

'It looks better on you anyway,' he shouted.

'Raeburn takes another hit!'

Cathy focused on the screen, glimpsed between the
shoulders of the jostling analysts. There it was, just like
Krystal had said. Less than two weeks after the Mendelhaus launch and the US cosmetics market was in turmoil.
And here she was taking the credit. The big sell had
started in Tokyo. Across the board the stock price of
pharmaceuticals with major cosmetics interests – Raeburn, Melos Pharm, Bio Factors, Pylos International –
had been tumbling. Wall Street had followed suit. No

sooner had the New York analysts switched on the screens than they were witnessing an avalanche. Cathy had gambled on Krystal's integrity, and it had paid off.

Overwhelmed now by the noise and the stark evidence streaming out of the Reuters screen, Cathy couldn't help thinking about all the help she had got from Ernst Krystal. He had been right behind her all along, answering her questions, even arranging a telephone conversation with some unnamed eminence in Switzerland. There had been so much information, so many powerful arguments. All she'd had to do was put it down in plain American so that the sales people could understand it. And now Michael Paine was ready to kiss her feet. It was a nice feeling.

'Hey, Cathy!'

Barney O'Toole, the red-headed financial analyst, was holding out the phone to her, his eyebrows dancing up and down like the thing was about to explode in his hand.

'It's *Fortune* again. Dave Woodrow. Says he wants to run a profile of you in their Heavy Hitters column.'

Cathy made her way across the room, taking a nervous sip of her champagne. At the mention of Dave Woodrow's name her mouth had gone suddenly dry. The guy was on the evening news all the time. He didn't do small-time profiles. But then, Cathy was slowly beginning to realise, she wasn't small-time any more. Nobody else on the street, in Europe, maybe nobody else in the world had called this sudden collapse with the accuracy that she had. It was pure luck – she realised that – but then being lucky, being in the right place at the right time, wasn't that always a part of success? What was it that Howard Hughes used to say about getting rich? *Rise early. Work hard. Strike oil.* Wasn't that part of the same thing?

Cathy gripped the phone with both hands. The room was suddenly quieter. Smiling faces were turned on her from all over the room.

'Cathy Ryder?'

It was true. She'd recognise the voice anywhere. The voice wanted to know if she could find time to meet.

Congratulatory notes came in from different departments. People she had never met, people high up in the firm, wrote to her saying thank you. One of the analysts estimated she had saved Webber clients over thirty-five million dollars. Mike Paine confided that he had even gone out on a limb shorting Raeburn Corp. on Webber's own book. He didn't say how much had been made, but Cathy got the feeling it was a lot.

After a noisy, alcoholic lunch in a favourite Chinese restaurant, the research team had returned to the office, and a degree of normality had returned. But every five minutes the phone would ring with a different journalist asking for the analyst that had called the crash. Then at four o'clock a call came through from Goodney Walker, a flunkey working for J. W. Webber, the old man himself.

Webber wanted to see Cathy in his office. Immediately. Cathy tried to push her hair into place, the guys giving playful wolf whistles. She had just reached the door when her phone rang again. Barney took it. Cathy paused in the door.

'Cathy, it's some UK magazine, *Euromarket*; something like that.'

Cathy felt herself colour, poised to leave the room, but flattered too that her reputation had flashed across the Atlantic already.

'Tell them I'm busy,' she said.

In the elevator she touched the button and turned to the smoked mirror set in the back of the car. In spite of the excitement she looked composed. She smiled at herself. The elevator carried her up to the forty-second floor.

J. W. Webber was standing in the middle of the room.

Next to him was Paine, sporting a new tie. Both men were smiling.

'Cathy.' Webber held out his hand revealing a battered Rolex under his crisply starched cuff. 'Cathy I can't tell you how much we appreciate your work on this. You've done a great deal for the company's position in the market.'

Cathy blushed, and offered a stammered disclaimer.

'Luck! Come, come.'

Webber guided her across to a suite of furniture set around a low marble table on which there was a small Henry Moore.

'You shouldn't be so modest. You know what Arnold Palmer said about luck?'

Webber turned to Paine for the answer, but Paine was shaking his head and smiling. No he didn't know, but he wanted to hear it from Webber's own lips. Cathy almost burst out laughing at the sycophantic expression on Paine's face.

'He said *the more I practise the luckier I get*. Hard work gets you in the right places at the right moment. Mike was telling just now how you went along to the launch and made contact with an insider there.'

'Well yes I – '

'So let's have no more talk about luck! And the way you presented the material. Lucidity itself. You had the courage of your convictions, a rare thing.'

Cathy sat back in the leather chair and stared at the Henry Moore. Paine placed a flute of champagne in front of Webber and then herself. Webber raised his glass to Cathy and smiled.

'Here's to you, Miss Ryder, and to your promotion in the firm.'

For a moment Cathy looked confused. Webber looked to Paine who was sipping at his champagne.

'Don't tell me you forgot to tell her, Mike?'

Paine looked stricken. He lowered his glass as though he had discovered a dead fly in the bubbles. Webber turned to Cathy, talking to her over his glass.

Back in the elevator Cathy checked her face again. This time to see if she had changed. Everything had happened so suddenly; such dramatic changes! She couldn't help feeling she must have changed too. But it was her face smiling back, the face of Cathy Ryder, head of European Research at Webber Atlantic. A woman earning $175,000 a year.

10

Manhattan. November 15th, 1995.

'Be reasonable, Mr Conner. We – '

Ben Steiner gripped his forehead and leaned forward into the telephone as though trying to withstand a hurricane. Nobody else on the desk appeared to be listening, but they could all hear that the client on the other end was furious.

'Of course I'm sorry. Jesus, we all made a loss Mr – '

Again the storm at the other end of the phone ripped loose. All Steiner could do was wait. After another minute there was what sounded like a scream and the line went dead. Steiner took the phone away from his ear and put it back in its cradle.

'Not too happy, right?'

It was Melvyn Tambow who put the question. Steiner looked him in the face for a moment, running his tongue over his dry lips. Then he told Tambow to fuck himself and walked out of the office.

In two days his clients' portfolios had shrunk an average eighteen per cent in value. All because of overexposure to the 'sure-fire' vanity sector. It was a disaster. What made matters worse, Steiner was just beginning to hear rumours of what was going on over at Webber, a house which normally ran along behind Salomon picking up the scraps. They were saying Cathy Ryder had called the market slide. It gave him a very bad feeling. Standing in the men's room, he looked in the mirror at his pouchy, bloodshot eyes.

'Well, Cathy. It looks like we're gonna have to get to know each other a little better,' he said to the scowling reflection.

11

Manhattan. November 29th, 1995.

Mike Varela sat on a packing case in the empty sitting room, staring at her photograph on the cover of *Fortune* magazine. She looked like the perfect Wall Street woman: neat black suit, crisp white shirt with the high starched collar and the golden bar-pin, flowing black hair tied back sensibly but not starkly with a bow. She was standing on the threshold of a busy-looking dealing room with a bundle full of papers and documents under her arm. Beneath her the coverline read 'Kings and Queens of the Crystal Ball.' She was the dream of a million career women: success *and* femininity, brains *and* beauty. And she was beautiful, this Cathy Ryder of Webber Atlantic. Varela had to admit that. She had dark, exotic-looking eyes, a fine straight nose and a generous mouth. And he liked the way she was smiling: it was humorous, self-conscious, as if the title 'Queen of the Crystal Ball' was not one she took too seriously. Mike could just imagine how it had been at the photography session: all the dealers wolf-whistling and cracking dirty jokes as the photographer danced about in front of his subject, giving instructions. A woman had to get used to that kind of thing on Wall Street, because the best she could do career-wise was get herself treated as an honorary man. As soon as her male colleagues started being polite and courteous with her, it meant she was no longer part of the competition, that she was out on the sidelines. On Wall Street men were only polite and courteous to their secretaries or their bosses.

As a photostat letter inside the front cover reminded him, this was the last copy of *Fortune* that Mike was due to receive. He had already decided not to renew his subscription. Even when he'd been in work he'd never had much time to do more than flick through it at weekends, and now the very sight of all those grinning multimillionaires made him feel ill. Besides, he had to make economies now. Selling the flat and giving back the BMW got him out of debt, but his remaining capital seemed pitifully small next to the big numbers he'd expected to earn in just a few months at Swift and Drew. He certainly couldn't afford to get another place until somebody gave him a job. In the meantime he was moving back to his dad's house in Queens, back to the little bedroom where he'd slept as a teenager, with the enamelled picture of the Virgin and Child over the bed, and the faded space shuttle poster inside the door of the wardrobe. There wasn't room in the house for very much of his stuff, but they had arranged to have it stored for free at an old warehouse in Brooklyn. The owners were Hispanics and knew old Joaquin Diaz from his days in the champagne business. It came as a complete revelation to Mike that being Hispanic could actually be useful. On the sides of the packing cases he had written his name in full for the first time in years: Miguel Diaz Varela.

Taking a sip from the mug of instant coffee at his feet, he flicked through his copy of *Fortune* as if it were some memento of an exchanged past. It was a Wednesday morning, and here he was in jeans and a thick sweater, doing nothing – *earning* nothing – while Wall Street, once his whole world, carried on as usual just the other side of the East River. Right now there was someone in *his* office at Swift and Drew, working at *his* desk, doing *his* deals, and there wasn't a damned thing he could do about it. He wondered who the usurper was. When he'd called up Walt Simmonds a few weeks back some woman he didn't know had answered the phone. Perhaps it was her: some cold-hearted bitch with a second-rate MBA but the ability to turn all charming whenever one of the bosses walked into the room. Doubtless a woman just like Cathy Ryder.

He found the cover story and began reading. It was just one of those dumb things all the financial magazines did: a poll, conducted among institutional investors, to determine the year's top securities analysts. There was a first, second and third place for each sector: communications, electricals, petroleum, pharmaceuticals and many others. The winners in each category were photographed and had a story written about them. Sometimes the stories were small and sometimes they were big. The biggest of them all, which had Dave Woodrow's by-line beneath it, was about Cathy Ryder. It started with a few anecdotes about her career at Webber Atlantic and then went into a story about a big shake-out in the cosmetics industry.

Then Mike saw the name that had been haunting him ever since that final interview with Harvey Swift: *Mendelhaus.*

The mug of instant coffee went flying as he jumped to his feet, but he didn't even notice. He hurried over to the window to get more light and read on: Mendelhaus, it said, were about to make a big splash in the market with some new skin treatment products and the rest of the industry was worried. Cathy Ryder alone had foretold what would happen, and as a result, Webber Atlantic's clients had saved themselves a fortune. Her boss, a guy called Michael Paine, put her success down to 'persistence, a thoroughgoing knowledge of her field, and a determination to see that the Webber clients get the best.'

Mike read the article again, open-mouthed. Only a few

months back he'd been working with the Mendelhaus people, preparing the Raeburn take-over deal. With their co-operation he'd gone into every aspect of Mendelhaus's business – not just their financial position, but their prospects, future earnings, everything. He'd been on the inside, far closer than any stock analyst ever got, and yet he'd heard nothing, *nothing* about this. In fact, the figures the Mendelhaus board had given him suggested that research spending in the company was relatively modest. It would only have made sense to conceal a thing like that if they hadn't expected to get anything worthwhile out of the money they'd spent.

He told himself to calm down and tried to piece it all together. There was one thing at least that did add up: if Mendelhaus had discovered they had a world-beater on their hands then they wouldn't have needed the expensive take-over that Mike Varela had planned for them. The main point of acquiring Raeburn Corporation had been to get hold of their big distribution network in North America, and some of their production facilities in New England and the Carolinas. Reduced costs and higher margins were supposed to compensate for the huge chunk of debt that Mendelhaus would have to take on. But if the company were just about to strike gold, the whole situation was different: they could afford to set up networks and facilities of their own. And even if growth through acquisition was still desirable, Raeburn's stock price was bound to fall once the new Mendelhaus product had been launched. The operation would simply become much cheaper. And yet how come they hadn't said anything about it? How come a kid called Cathy Ryder, at a second-rate outfit like Webber Atlantic, had found out, when he'd known nothing? It was crazy.

He picked the telephone off the floor and dialled up a number in the sales department at Webber. He had a friend there from his old days at First Chicago called Brad

97

Matthews, at least he'd been a friend once. Mike didn't take that kind of thing for granted any more.

'Hey, Mike, good to hear from ya!'

'It was Brad's voice all right. He always talked like he was standing on the touchline at a football game.

'Hi, Brad.'

'Hey, I been trying to call you at S and D, but they told me you don't work there no more.'

Mike inwardly groaned.

'Well hell, Brad, I got fired three months ago. I thought you knew.'

'Fired? Jeez, Mike, they never told me. That's tough. So how you doing?'

'Oh fine, fine. I got it all under control. How about you?'

'Oh great, man. Things is really cooking, let me tell you. Too bad about your being fired though. Still, you coming to my party?'

'A party? Well sure, Brad, I'd love to. When is it?'

'A week on Friday. Get you in the mood for Christmas.'

Christmas. He hadn't given it a single thought. Unemployed at Christmas . . .

'Listen, Brad,' he said, his voice sounding hard, flat. 'I need some information.'

Matthews laughed, his hearty footballer's laugh.

'Hell, Mike, that's what I always used to ask you! Just gimme inside information, right?'

'I'm serious, Brad. What do you know about Cathy Ryder?'

For a moment there was silence on the line.

'Well, what do *you* know? I mean I didn't even know you'd met her.'

'I haven't met her. I just read about her in *Fortune*. She just got herself onto the cover because of some work she did.'

'Yeah, yeah, we all seen it. She's flavour of the month

upstairs for sure. But hell, trying to make a buck telling everybody to sell things ain't easy. I just hope she tells 'em what to *buy* next time. I mean, head of European Research, Jesus!'

'Do you know her, Brad? Do you see her much?'

'Well, as much as anyone does, I guess.' Mike detected a touch of discomfort in his voice. 'I mean, you know what we used to call a piece like her in college: a real Virgin Mary. You know what I mean? She works hard, she keeps her shoes shiny, and she prays before bedtime. That kind of stuff. A real fucking Virgin Mary.'

From the way Matthews was talking about her, Mike got the feeling that he'd tried hitting on her some time and been told to back off.

'Listen, Brad, I can tell you why later, but I have to speak to her – and not on the phone. Can you arrange it?'

Matthews hesitated again. 'Well I guess so. Hey! I got it. You remember Pete Sweeney? He's giving a party the day after mine. I'm almost certain she'll show. No guarantees though. She's pretty picky. But hell, a lot of the guys in Equity Research'll be there.'

'But how does that help me?'

'Well you can tag along with me. Pete won't mind.'

Mike gave a twist to the telephone flex.

'I'm not sure how I feel about crashing this guy's party, Brad.'

'Come on, Michael. There'll be plenty of people there without an invite. It's kinda open house when Sweeney throws a party anyway.'

'Well if you say so Brad.'

'Hey, do you wanna meet this broad or not?'

Mike gave another twist to the flex.

'Yea. Yes I do.'

12

La Jolla beach, San Diego. December 1st, 1995.

Waterman stood on the terrace of Delano's Workout Shop watching a pair of surfers as they wheeled and dodged on the foamy green waves. There was a stiff wind blowing from the north and a film of high cloud covered the sun, making the shadows pale. The surfers were wearing wetsuits, and the beach was deserted except for an old man with a dog and a young couple walking along holding hands. They were both in burgundy-coloured tracksuits and bright white trainers. For San Diego it was cold.

Waterman put a cigarette in his mouth and cupped his hands around his lighter to keep the flame from blowing out. You couldn't smoke anywhere in Delano's except out on the terrace. There wasn't an ashtray inside, and as soon as you reached for a packet everyone *looked* at you, like you were just about to set fire to the place or something. So he had decided to wait for Marty Kingman out on the terrace where the parasols and the wickerwork furniture would shield him from the hostile looks.

On the other side of the perspex doors seven or eight men, most of them in their forties or fifties, were exercising on an array of gleaming machinery. Nearest to him a man with silver hair was lying on his back lifting a bar up and down at chest level. A few inches from his head a pile of weights slid up and down to the same rhythm, clanking noisily each time they came to rest. The man didn't look very dignified as he strained at the bar, his face red, and the veins on his neck bulging ominously. But then he stopped and stood up. His whole body was neat and firm, and there wasn't an ounce of fat on it. Waterman felt a stab of shame. He hadn't looked like that in twenty years, if ever. And it would have been nice. He finally got his cigarette lit and took a drag. For some reason it didn't taste good at all.

Marty Kingman had been Ray Bladon's favourite stunt-man. In the early days Bladon had done a lot of the dangerous stuff himself, one of the things that had contributed to his tough-guy reputation. But once he became a big star, the producers and insurance stiffs began insisting that stand-ins be used. Bladon was simply too valuable. Kingman had been used a lot because he had the same colouring as Bladon and exactly the same height and build. There was even a passing similarity in the face. Furthermore, after a couple of pictures together, Kingman was able to imitate Bladon's way of moving and gesturing, so that he could be used in quite extensive sequences. According to Bryan Oplinger the two of them had become friends, and Bladon had got Kingman onto the sets of most of his later pictures.

In any case, it was the last lead Waterman had. He had received a call from Bill Miller two days before, telling him to drop the case – couldn't justify the expense, he said – but Harry didn't want to quit just yet. Maybe it was just the way all Bladon's old friends and colleagues had been slamming the door in his face for the past few weeks that made him want to carry on. Or maybe it was the idea of going back to Bill Miller empty-handed. There was no telling what Miller would come up with for him to do next. In any event, it was just a case of rounding things off. After talking to Kingman there wasn't really any more he could do. No one seemed to know anything about any cosmetic surgery, or if they did they weren't telling. Kingman was the only one he hadn't tried.

Waterman watched the young couple in the burgundy tracksuits walking away into the distance and realised that there was another reason why he was still working on this case: he'd *liked* being in Bladon's world, even if he'd only been on the fringes of it for a few moments at a time. Everything was so *right* there, so successful, so smart, above all, so exclusive. It was a world where everybody knew who you were, and most would give anything to be in your place, a world inhabited by every movie star since movies began, by every movie star on the walls of the Sierra Madre on Sunset Boulevard, for instance. He hadn't been able to admit it until that moment, but he'd got the same buzz picking through the traces of Ray Bladon's life that autograph hunters got when one of their heroes signed his name on the back of a programme or a menu or something: an instant of association, of belonging to that exclusive world of fame which they would otherwise never experience. Never. Waterman threw the cigarette away and swore to himself. The CDC were right to close this case. There was nothing so damned significant about Bladon and McArthur. They were only a pair of fucking actors, after all.

Kingman appeared in the exercise room in a pair of red running shorts and a faded Batman III T-shirt. His hair was wet and there was a towel around his shoulders. He wasn't a Mister Universe, but he was tall, and his whole body had a solidity, a compactness that made Waterman feel puny. His hair had gone mostly grey, but he still had plenty of it. Waterman tried to guess Kingman's age, and realised with another moment of discomfort that it was probably about the same as his.

Kingman went straight to one of the machines and began doing sit-ups on a board that was all of forty degrees from the horizontal. After watching for a minute, Waterman walked over and stood by his feet.

'I thought you'd done this part already,' he said. 'Haven't you done this already?'

Kingman did another couple of sit-ups before answering.

'I have. I do it twice.'

'No kidding.'

'It's better this way.'

Two more sit-ups.

'Less strain, more exercise.'

'No kidding,' said Waterman again. 'So two lots of thirty . . .'

'Fifty.'

'Two lots of fifty is better than one lot of a hundred?'

Two more sit-ups.

'Yeah.'

'Do you have two massages as well?' Waterman couldn't think of anything else to say.

Two more sit-ups, and now you could hear Kingman counting them under his breath.

'Thirty-six. No. Just a shower.'

This was no way to conduct a conversation. Waterman decided to wait until Kingman got to fifty. Then he said: 'I hope you don't mind me bothering you like this, Mr Kingman. But I know Jim Bladon was a friend of yours.'

Kingman lay on the board, breathing deeply. He looked at Waterman, sniffed and got up.

'No bother,' he said. 'I'm gonna do some cycling now.'

He went over to a white exercise bike and began pedalling hard. Waterman followed him over. He felt self-conscious just standing there, waiting for Kingman to pay attention, but there wasn't much he could do about it. It had been the same story with almost all of Bladon's old pals. Micky Harborne's article in *Exclusive!* magazine had touched a raw nerve, and everybody assumed that he,

103

Waterman, was digging over the same old dirt. The fact that the Centre for Disease Control were interested in the case didn't impress them very much at all. Waterman decided to get straight to the point.

'You see, Mr Kingman, there is a possibility that the cancer which killed Ray Bladon may have been caused by a virus. I'm trying to establish where such a virus may have been picked up.'

Kingman adjusted a dial on the handlebars of the bike and started pedalling faster. He kept his gaze on the opposite wall.

'And you think you might find it in here?' he said.

'Hell, no. But if I had to put money on it, I'd say wherever he had that chin tuck done was the likeliest candidate. You'd be amazed the number of new bugs that turn up in hospitals.'

Kingman stopped pedalling and looked at Waterman for the first time.

'You know about that? How do you know about that?'

Waterman was suddenly glad he'd come.

'About the tuck? It doesn't matter, does it? The point is we have to check the place out.'

Kingman went back to pedalling.

'The trouble is, we don't know where he had his surgery done. No one seems to know anything about it.'

Kingman smiled knowingly. It was the smile of the world of fame, confident in the knowledge that the likes of Harry Waterman would never get in and spoil things.

'Well, that makes two of us, my friend.'

The hell it does.

'The trouble is all these private clinics out here, they're kind of committed to secrecy,' Waterman went on, ignoring Kingman's answer. 'It's part of the deal, I guess. And this is really just a low level enquiry. On top of which, the very idea that there might be a virus on their premises could be very bad for business. I mean nobody would go near a place if that idea got around, right?'

Kingman smiled again.

'I suppose so, but you're wrong about the secrecy. A lot of these places out here are only too happy to let on about their big name clientele – in a discreet kind of way. It's worth a lot of bucks to them. You got Jack Nicholson on your books, then a lot of other people are gonna want to sign up too. Just to be able to talk about it at dinner parties.'

In other words, Waterman thought, even the rich wanted to rub shoulders with the famous. He could understand that. It must have been frustrating to have millions in the bank, and still find that nobody was interested in you. He guessed that was why so many rich people became patrons of the arts. They didn't want to have to tell people that they'd made their fortunes in the dog food business, or insurance. They wanted to be spoken of in the same breath as the famous names, like Nijinsky and Diaghilev.

'Are you saying that if you really didn't want people to know where you were going, you couldn't go to *any* place on the West Coast?'

Kingman was pedalling now at top speed, and there was a patch of sweat showing through on his chest.

'There are quieter places,' he said.

'Like where?'

'Like abroad. You gotta get out of the US altogether. Some place where people really don't know who you are, or don't care.'

'And that was where Ray Bladon went?'

Kingman stopped pedalling and let out a deep breath. The pedals flew round and round on their own.

'I told you. I don't know where he went.'

'But you must have some idea. Where outside the US?'

Kingman shook his head.

'Look, what's this all about? Hasn't the guy had enough people poking about in his life already? What the hell difference does it make if he had a chin tuck or not?'

He got off the bike and wiped his face with the towel.

'Mr Kingman,' said Waterman. 'I can understand your being anxious to preserve Ray Bladon's reputation, and I sympathise with that. But I don't see that concealing information like this, information that may shed light on his real cause of death, is any help on that score. I mean, they're saying that the guy was really a fairy already, aren't they? And that the big A was what got him. If it does turn out to be a new virus, which I very much doubt, then at least we can nail that idea, can't we?'

This was Waterman's last throw, appealing to a sense of wounded honour, making Micky Harborne and his kind the common enemy. Kingman sighed.

'You said all this would be in confidence, right?'

'It is.'

'All right. All I know is he was a big fan of this place in Europe, in Switzerland I think, or maybe Austria. I don't remember the name of it, but he said it was great. Came back from there last spring saying he felt twenty years younger.'

'And you really can't remember the name?'

Waterman was already flicking back through his notebook, searching, searching.

'No, I didn't really take it in. It's not something I'd go for. Anyway I don't have that kind of dough. I think this place wanted pretty major bucks.'

'To your knowledge did he tell anyone else about it?'

'Yeah, I think he recommended it to a few people. People he knew real well.'

'Like who, for example?' said Waterman. He had found what he was looking for in his notebook: it was right at the front, part of the information he'd taken from Micky Harborne's article. A name.

106

'Let me think . . . well I'm pretty sure Matt McArthur was one.' Waterman drew a heavy line under the name.

'And was the clinic owned by a Swiss company called Mendelhaus?'

'Mendelhaus. Yeah,' said Kingman. 'Yeah, that was it. But you never heard it from me, okay?'

13

Manhattan. December 9th, 1995.

It was a great place to throw a party, but Mike wasn't in the party mood. Pete Sweeney's apartment covered two floors of a converted warehouse on the lower east side. The 1930s features had been retained: riveted beams, carved stone lintels over the big arched windows. On the first floor Pete had installed a huge fireplace. Standing near the bar, next to the smart-looking Latino guy who was shaking cocktails for Sweeney's noisy friends, Mike considered the burning logs which from time to time sent showers of sparks up the brick flue.

For over an hour he had been nursing a warm martini and watching the group of sharply dressed men standing around the tall dark girl in the black cocktail dress. She looked different from the picture in the magazine. He'd expected something more conventional, more poised. The way this girl's big dark eyes fixed on the person she was talking to! There was something odd about her, un-developed.

'Mikey!'

For a second Mike's view was blocked by an expanse of pristine shirt front and a painted silk tie. Bob Gibbon, a Swift and Drew corporate relations air-head, pressed his long index finger into Mike's midriff.

'Jesus Christ, Mikey! Too bad about you getting the push. Jesus Christ!'

Gibbon's contracted pupils were tiny dots in his blood-shot eyes. His breath smelt rank. He watched Mike for a response, sucking hungrily on his blue cocktail.

'Looks like you're flying high as ever, Bob.'

Mike tried to look past Gibbon. The girl in the black cocktail dress had accepted a cigarette and was smoking with little nervous pulls, blowing smoke up into the air in urgent exhalations. She jerked back her thick black hair revealing her pale throat. A toothy grin spread over Gibbon's flushed face.

'You know me, Mikey – never a party without a little something on board.'

The girl looked across to him and for a moment their eyes met. She frowned and Mike looked down at his drink.

'Hey Mikey! You look as though you could do with a little lift yourself.'

Mike refocused on Gibbon's grin.

'Yeah, well don't worry about me, Bob. I'll be all right.'

Gibbon straightened up a little at the tone in Mike's voice, and tried to gather himself by pulling up his trousers by the belt.

'Listen Mikey, if there's anything I can do. Anyone I can talk to.'

Mike swallowed the last of his martini and moved away. Pushing between the laughing people he moved towards the fireplace where Brad Matthews was telling a joke. He felt hot in the face – angry. Gibbon meant well. But to have him sympathise, a guy that Mike would normally avoid like anal surgery, it brought it home to him how far he had fallen. Other people, people that could help him if they wanted to, now avoided him. A number of them were at the party. Sure, he could go up to them and explain his situation. They would listen and sympathise

109

like Art Prentice who he'd met in the lift coming up – *breaks my fucking heart Michael, seeing a good man go down* – they would sympathise, but they wouldn't really want to know. Why should they? The guys here, Bob Gibbon included, were still pulling down their big salaries. They had driven to the party in their streamlined European cars. Mike had seen Prentice climbing out of his Lotus Sprint, as he entered the building. These guys could help if he asked, but he didn't think they would. Losing your job was embarrassing. It embarrassed them. It embarrassed him, and somehow or other, deep down, he felt guilty, as if he had deserved what he got. The thought confused him. He felt that if he could find out what had happened on the Mendelhaus deal he could start to dig his way back out of his hole.

Mike reached the fireplace, within earshot of the girl from the magazine, and tapped Brad Matthews on the shoulder.

'Yo, Michael.'

Matthews turned from the group which had gathered around the girl and stood square on to Mike like a doorman.

'Nice party last night, Brad. Really enjoyed it.'

Brad nodded and took a sip at his drink. Mike looked across to the girl and, lowering his voice, said: 'This is the lady, right?'

Brad nodded conspiratorially. He put an arm around Mike's shoulder and drew him away from the animated group.

'This is indeed the lady: Miss Cathy Ryder in person.'

Both men turned to look at the girl. She was smiling up at a tall guy in a Lacoste sports jacket. Standing this close Mike could see how special she really was. Her fine skin glowed in the light of the fire and her dark eyes glittered. In the subdued light they looked oddly deep, the iris drowned in the dilated pupil. Mister Lacoste was asking her about her research at Webber Atlantic. His droning voice and the serious dips of his long head in affirmation made it look like a job interview. Again Mike was struck by the girl's manner. As she answered the dull questions she sounded brittle, almost annoyed. He began to think he might be able to smooth-talk her away from the other guys.

'So Mike, what's new on the Street?'

Mike turned back to Matthews and gave an account of the week he'd spent, putting everything in a favourable light.

'I heard about Karen. That must have been hard.'

Mike took the cigarette Matthews offered. He smiled, shaking his head.

'I've forgotten about it already.'

'But you had been together for a while – how long was it?'

'A year, maybe a little more. I don't remember.'

Mike watched the girl detach herself from the group. She made her way across the room to the bar and said something to the Latino. She was in *very* good shape.

'She's quite something isn't she?'

Matthews followed Mike's gaze.

'Friendly too.'

Mike looked at Matthews through his rising smoke.

'That's not what I heard,' he said, drawing at his cigarette. 'That's not what you said.'

'No, *friendly*, Michael. You know – friendly, like your friends from school, like me, friendly.'

Matthews looked across at Cathy who was holding a tall drink.

'I don't know about the other thing. She's a dark horse, as they say.'

'She's dark. That I will say.'

Suddenly Mike felt hungry.

'What about an introduction, Brad?'

Matthews shrugged.

'Come on Mike, I hardly know the girl. Maybe Pete can . . .'

He was turning away looking for Sweeney who had come into the room carrying a basket of logs. Mike put a hand on Matthews' arm. He didn't want to be introduced to Sweeney. Here he was at the guy's party and he had to be introduced. It made him feel like a freeloader.

'No, don't bother Brad. I think what I really need is a drink.'

He made his way across the room, but when he got to the bar the girl had refilled her glass and was talking to another guy. She looked at him as he approached the bar and went on with her conversation. When Mike heard the word Mendelhaus he stiffened so that the barman had to ask him twice what he was drinking.

He took his fresh martini and turned to face the room. He could hear little of what the girl was saying. She stood with her back to him, but he knew she was talking about the company. He tried to think of a way of introducing himself, of getting her to talk about the deal.

'I'm starving,' he heard her say. The Yale stiff mumbled something about a buffet in the dining room. Then he asked her another question. *Playing for time*, Mike thought.

Then she moved off and Mike found himself following her across the room to what he assumed would be the dining room. He followed her close, hoping she wouldn't turn. The group seated by the fire looked up as she went past and Pete Sweeney said something to her. For a moment Mike thought she'd pause and he'd have to go on past her, but she said: 'Back in a minute,' and went out of the room, Mike walking beside her as though they were a couple. He felt the blood beating in his ears. They came to the dining room, but instead of going in she went on down the corridor.

Mike stopped at the door of the dining room which was crowded with men, and watched her go on. She went on down to the end of the corridor and into what looked like the kitchen. Mike was thinking fast, unsure what to do next. If he followed her into the kitchen she'd think it was a come on, and it was important to him to get the information about the deal. She might not know about the take-over, but maybe she had seen the problem from another angle. She had to know something.

He started along the corridor and burst in on her in the kitchen so that she gave a little yelp. She was looking in at the refrigerator.

'Hi!' Mike stepped past her to the sink and turned on the cold tap, letting the water flush over his hand. He suppressed a cry of pain.

'What did you do?'

She came away from the icebox and stood next to him at the sink so he could smell the warm perfume smell of her body.

'One of Pete's tongs. I guess it was in the cinders. It didn't look hot.'

'Ouch!'

It was the girl who yelped. She looked at the hand he worked under the tap.

He turned off the water and took the tea towel she offered.

'Mike Varela,' he said and offered her his reversed left hand.

'Cathy Ryder.'

'Oh right.' Mike stepped back and leaned against the dishwasher. 'I thought I recognised you. You're the girl who called the cosmetics slide.'

Cathy made a wry mouth.

'I'm beginning to wish I hadn't,' she said.

Mike raised his eyebrows inquisitively.

'It's just that everyone I've met here tonight has said

113

exactly the same thing,' she explained. 'It's weird. I get the feeling they're all talking about someone else.' She looked vacant for a moment. Her eyes were so dark. Mike felt his scalp draw tight. 'How's your hand?'

The question surprised him. Mike looked down at his hand, flexing it.

'Fine. I guess I let go of the tongs in time.'

She held her eyes on him for a moment. He thought she was smiling. He had the feeling she could see inside him. It made him blush. Then she turned away.

'I'm starving. I didn't want to fight my way to the buffet. All those questions.'

She opened the door of the refrigerator and was bathed in the eerie blue light. Mike came across and looked into the cold blue box. It looked like a woodman's freezer: thick steaks, cans of Budweiser, a block of butter, ham on the bone, cheese.

'God,' she said. 'Underneath the Armani suits Sweeney's a real Davy Crockett.'

She took a knife and hacked a piece of meat from the ham bone and then some cheese. She was kneeling down, concentrating on her slender hands and the knife. Mike looked at her brilliant hair and the nape of her neck as she leaned forward to cut.

'Want some?' she asked, her voice sounding odd in the confined space.

She cut more for Mike and handed the strips of cold meat from her hand to his. He laughed.

Music started throbbing in the other rooms. Cathy popped the last of the ham into her mouth and wiped her hands on the tea towel.

'I'm going to dance,' she said and was gone.

Mike stood for a long time, looking at the strip of ham in his hand. There was a mark where she had pinched it. He raised it to his lips and then put it back on the plate in the refrigerator. A moment ago he had been hungry

114

and now his appetite had gone. He thought about the way she had looked at him when she asked him how his hand was. Those eyes. He looked down at his unmarked palm and closed his hand. Had she realised he was faking? The music in the other room was unbelievably loud. Sweeney was showing off his new Danish sound system. Mike was pleased with the way things had gone, but he had let her get away. He felt if he could get her on her own again he could work her round to the question of Mendelhaus.

As he thought it over, he was surprised to find that Mendelhaus didn't really matter. She was the one. He just wanted to talk to her. Mike made a face, annoyed by his lack of purpose. *I get close up to a good-looking woman and my knees start to knock. Fucking dumb-ass wetback!*

He turned and looked at the window. Outside it was pitch dark, his face clearly reflected. He pushed his hair back from his forehead, thinking hard. The sight of the cold food gave him an idea. He took an egg and put it into his jacket pocket. As he went along the corridor he had the feeling he was just behind himself, following himself somehow, waiting to see what he would do next.

When he returned to the room it looked like more people had arrived. Everybody was up on their feet dancing. It was a while before Mike could make out Cathy dancing in the firelight. When she saw him she pointed at his hand and said something he couldn't hear. He moved across to her and started dancing, one of a group of three men all with their eyes on Cathy's athletic body. Mike felt ridiculous, but was encouraged by Cathy's smile. From time to time he checked the raw egg in his pocket.

He was waiting for a pause in the music, but Sweeney's CD was in some kind of disco programme and just skipped any gaps so the music was seamless. After what felt like

115

ages, Cathy made her way across to the bar, Mike following.

The Latino was showing Cathy his best smile when Mike tapped her on the shoulder.

'Excuse me,' he said. 'I think you dropped this.' And he handed her the egg.

Cathy held the cold egg for a moment, confused. Mike thought she was going to take it badly, though he couldn't see how she would do that. It crossed his mind that she might take it as some kind of strange fertility display, but the thought evaporated as she began to smile.

'You're a very sick person, Mister Varela,' she said, still smiling and nodding her head in approval. Something strange had happened between them.

People started to move off at about four o'clock. Some soft jazz was exchanged for the disco thump, and the Latino started to serve coffee. One or two couples were dancing slowly on the wooden floor in the light of the fire which burned lower now.

Mike watched Cathy as she talked. She was explaining something about the violin to him, something about the way Bach had put together a specific partita, the exact number of which he had already forgotten. They had been talking now for maybe two hours and had covered so much ground, it made him tired to think about it. There was something confessional in the way she spoke – facts, information tumbling out, her childhood in Maine, her relationship with her mother, the life she led now, her music. Mike had talked too, but less used to being so frank and wanting to avoid too many references to Pop Varela and his Mexican champagne, he found it hard to be truly open. And all the time he was trying to get onto the question of Mendelhaus. But after her complaint in the kitchen he thought it might spoil things if he talked business with her. And she was beautiful, and witty, and

116

vulnerable somewhere, and as they talked he thought maybe it was the beginning of change for him. The beginning of better luck maybe.

At half past five Cathy looked at her watch and gave a little start. Only now did she realise how long they had been talking; how long *she* had been talking. And that was the oddest thing. She *never* talked so openly. Men asked her questions all the time, but it was so that they could give their answers. Or their questions were directed somehow; strategic, and she felt like they were trying to winkle her out of her shell. But with Mike, this complete stranger she had only just met, who had handed her a cold raw egg as a joke which she didn't understand at all, but which had amused her somewhere deep inside, with him she felt safe, good, happy.

'What's up?'

His voice surprised her. It was like a soft brush going across her. She liked his voice. She liked his smile.

'I have to go,' she said.

He looked down at his feet. They had removed their shoes to dance. He had the beginnings of a hole in the heel of his left sock. Cathy laughed. That was the thing about Mike – spontaneity. He seemed so natural compared to all the other people. He hadn't even mentioned his job or hinted at his salary as nearly everyone she knew on Wall Street always did.

Mike looked up from his feet and felt his face flush for the second time that evening. Her beautiful black eyes seemed to go right into him. He would have liked to offer her a ride, but the thought of the second-hand Toyota made him pause.

Then she said: 'Can I drop you anywhere? My car's outside.'

14

Boston, Massachusetts. December 11th, 1995.

Dr Geoffrey Andersen was horrified to discover just three
people in the conference room. From the memo he had
received two days earlier – just before the weekend – he
had formed the impression that he was to deliver his
report to almost the entire board of Raeburn Corporation. It would be like giving a lecture: no one would
interrupt and there wouldn't be too many tricky questions. But now he saw that it wasn't going to be so easy.
He was face to face with the chief executive, Peter Woodridge, his deputy Richard Newell, and another man he
didn't recognise. That was all. A tremor of panic went
right through his wiry frame: they were going to grill him.
They wanted to know where Raeburn had gone wrong.
They wanted to know where *he'd* gone wrong.

'Come in, Dr Andersen,' said Woodridge. There wasn't
a trace of humour in his voice or his countenance. He
seemed very different from the smiling, respectful man
that had hired him four years earlier. But then, Raeburn
had been number one in those days.

Andersen smiled fleetingly and walked over to the near
end of the conference table. Woodridge sat at the other
end with Newell on his right and the other man a few
seats away on his left.

'Mr Chaney, Dr Andersen is our head of Research and

Development,' said Woodridge. 'This is Sam Chaney. He'll be advising us over the coming months.'

Chaney got up and held out his hand. He was a big man with neat grey hair, a thick moustache, and several small, deep scars on his face. He looked like a cop. He sure as hell wasn't a scientist.

'Good to meet you, Dr Andersen,' he said. His grip was uncomfortably strong.

Andersen nodded back and sat down. Woodridge and Newell were both looking at him with their hands resting on the table in front of them: Woodridge, fifty-seven years old with narrow gold-rimmed glasses and a suntan from his last trip to the Virgin Islands, Newell, barely forty, with an immaculate head of black hair and a face that was almost too well-proportioned to be handsome. Andersen could feel his own pulse beating in his ears.

'Well, Dr Andersen, what are we looking at here?' said Woodridge. 'What the hell are we up against?'

Andersen's fastidious scientific mind sought a clarification of the question, but he could see that no one here was in any mood for that. He took a deep breath.

'In a word, sir,' he said, trying to sound as steely as he could, 'a regulatory protein, or rather a series of regulatory proteins. That's what it has to be.'

Woodridge and Newell exchanged glances. Then Woodridge said: 'And what's so fucking special about them? What *are* they?'

Andersen cleared his throat. He had never, *never* heard Woodridge swear – not so much as a 'god damn'. Newell and Chaney were still looking at him impassively. They registered no surprise at the old man's language.

'I must point out first that we haven't established just how effective the Mendelhaus product really is. Our own tests are still a long way from completion. However . . .'

'Are you saying that Erixil is just a load of hype?' said Woodridge. 'Is that what you're saying?'

Newell folded his arms. There was a look of hard impatience on his face.

'I'm afraid not, sir,' said Andersen. 'I'm simply saying that it will be easier to assess what the product is when we get a better idea of how it performs. That's not to say we don't have some ideas, but . . .'

'Well let's hear them, if you don't mind,' said Woodridge. 'Because while you're waiting for your tests to come through we're being wiped off the face of the market. That puts us *all* in a very dangerous position, Dr Andersen. I'm sure I don't have to tell you that.'

Andersen wanted to swallow, but he didn't want the others to see him do it. His cheeks were already burning.

'If Mendelhaus's claims are justified,' he said, 'then it is my belief that we are looking at a breakthrough in the identification of certain regulatory genes and of the proteins that induce them to function.'

It struck him how breathless he sounded, but he couldn't stop to get a deep breath.

'It's an approach that hasn't been attempted before in this field,' he went on, 'at least not to my knowledge – because no one has yet come up with a satisfactory method of isolating the regulatory proteins. The body of scientific knowledge available on the regulatory system of human cells simply isn't available.'

Chaney reached into his jacket pocket for a ball-point. Then he said: 'Just for my benefit, Dr Andersen, could you describe the approach that you have been following in this field? It may help.'

Andersen wondered what Chaney's role in all this was. He looked at Woodridge and Woodridge nodded back to him.

'We have simply been trying to identify missing elements in skin that has begun to age, and to replace as many of them as possible. Our approach has been essentially empirical. We look at a young, healthy epidermis, and track the process of degeneration as closely as we can. When certain substances or structures are found to be lacking or inactive, we try to discover if that has something to do with the problem and, if so, to replace them artificially. And we've had our successes. However, our solutions are bound to be only partial because the ageing process is so complex and so all-pervasive. The epidermis is a lot more complex a system than most people realise, and simply understanding the interaction between the various structures is a challenge. We know that with the passage of time there is a slow-down in the rate of cell replacement and diminishing efficiency in the micro-circulation, and we have a pretty good idea why, but until we can find some way to reverse these tendencies, we are always going to be dealing with the symptoms of degeneration, never tackling the actual causes.'

Chaney was writing on the notepad in front of him. The ball-point looked like it might snap under the weight of his big prize-fighter's hand. Andersen wondered if all this was over his head, but he didn't seem to be having any difficulty with it. Chaney looked up a few moments later.

'And you believe Mendelhaus may have found another way?' he said. 'Why do you think that?'

'Firstly because Erixil is so effective, and secondly because Mendelhaus has no record in this field.'

'What?' said Chaney. He was looking at Woodridge.

'It's true,' he said. 'They came out of the blue at us with this one. They always used to trade on image in this field. Their products were low-tech – just moisturisers mostly.'

'So if they'd been following the same path as us,' said Andersen, 'we'd have seen some intermediate products by now.'

Chaney turned to a fresh page on his notepad.

'Okay, Dr Andersen,' he said. 'Suppose you give me

some details on what you think they've got. And how they got it.'

Andersen realised that he was sweating. He could feel the moisture on his brow. He wanted to dab it dry with a handkerchief, but he didn't want to show them how vulnerable he felt. It would look too much like guilt.

'The preliminary results of our tests show an improved performance of collagen in the epidermis,' he said, 'and, latterly, a similar improvement in elastin and reticulin, although we can't be sure about that yet.'

'And just what are these substances?'

'They are what we call connective proteins. They make up the basic materials in connective tissue. The proteins themselves are made up of twisted strands of amino acids, and collagen is the most important. In fact collagen makes up more than forty per cent of the body's protein. The connective tissue acts like the mortar of the cells – it lends them structural support. Furthermore, all the things that a cell needs to function properly – oxygen, nutrients, water, and the removal of waste products – have to pass through the collagen network. One of the key factors in the ageing process, at least as far as the epidermis is concerned, is the loss of efficiency in the collagen network. Cells do not get properly nourished, waste products build up, and from a cosmetic point-of-view the whole structure of the epidermis loses in firmness and elasticity.'

'Do we know what causes this loss of efficiency?' said Woodridge. 'Do *they* know?'

'Actually we've had a pretty good idea for some time now,' Andersen replied. 'And the most important factor seems to be attack from electrically charged particles called free radicals. As I explained, collagen is made up of twisted strands of amino acids – a triple helix in fact. To service the cells they surround most efficiently, and for connective tissue to remain supple, these strands must be able to move back and forward against each other unimpeded. Free radicals, which are mostly unwanted by-products of other reactions taking place in the body, form chemical bonds with parts of neighbouring strands of collagen, thereby tying them together. This process is called cross-linkage, and though it occurs naturally in the formation of muscles, the free radical variety slowly adds up to major impediment to the efficient functioning of the body.'

Chaney was writing, but Woodridge and Newell were still staring back at him. All they wanted were answers.

'The point is, sir,' he went on, 'that some cells do produce enzymes which break up unwanted cross-linkages, restoring the flexibility and efficiency of the connective tissue, but these enzymes seem to be produced at a much lower rate after adolescence. I believe that Mendelhaus have found a way to stimulate the production of those enzymes – or failing that of the connective proteins themselves.'

'And exactly what kind of research would that involve, Dr Andersen?' Chaney asked. 'What kind of expertise would you need?'

'Well, I suppose you could divide your research into three stages. The first would be to identify that part of the human genetic code that produces the enzymes and the connective proteins. I'm sure I don't have to tell you that the genetic material in the nucleus of every cell – the DNA – contains a complete blueprint for the entire body: the information and the means to produce every substance, every component, every type of cell. Which parts of this blueprint are put to use in an individual cell is determined by the regulatory genes which effectively activate the other genes as and when they are needed.'

'So you would need a strong genetics team,' said Chaney. 'Would that be a lot of people?'

The question puzzled him, but Andersen answered it anyway.

123

'Well, yes, assuming this research was yours. But mapping out the human genetic code has been going on in a number of institutes all over the world for some years now. Admittedly things have been badly slowed up by restrictions on this field of research, but if you had a good idea what you were looking for, you might be able to pick up that kind of information without having to do all the grunt work yourself. The Europeans, for example, have taken great strides in pooling their research findings in computer data bases.'

Chaney looked disappointed.

'OK,' he said, 'what about the second stage?'

'Well this would be a lot harder. In order to activate the right regulatory genes you would have to identify the correct regulatory proteins. These proteins act as messengers, if you like. They tell the genes in the nucleus what the cell should do, and are presumably produced by other cells according to their circumstances. The regulatory genes in each type of cell probably only react to certain types and concentrations of regulatory protein according to the type of cell they are in. As cells specialise, so the range of their functions must narrow. But I have to tell you that this part of the picture has yet to be established beyond the realms of theory. Apart from anything else, without embryo experimentation we have virtually no hope of tracking the process of interaction between the nucleus and its environment. And with the laws as they are at the moment you can't . . .'

Chaney interrupted him: 'You're saying this whole approach has been held back by restrictions on embryo experimentation?'

'I'm afraid so.'

'And when were those restrictions imposed?'

'Over here about four years ago. In Europe and the Far East more recently. But don't misunderstand me. This kind of research has not been, normally associated with the cosmetics industry. Even a partial knowledge of regulatory genes and how they are manipulated holds out vast possibilities for the treatment of disease and the prolongation of life. Already our knowledge of the genetic code – limited as it is – is helping us combat hereditary diseases and . . .'

'Do you know if any research of this type, research into the regulatory system of cells, was undertaken here in the US or in Europe prior to the imposition of the restrictions you've mentioned?'

Andersen pulled the handkerchief from his pocket and caught a pearl of sweat as it ran down his cheek. Just when he thought he'd stumbled on a scapegoat for his failure, Chaney had started grilling him like he was a common criminal. And still Woodridge and Newell stared.

'Well I think there were a lot of them. Most of the biotech companies went into human genetics at one time or another, although most of them concentrated on specific disease-related problems. And of course it wasn't just the legislation that killed the research. I mean a lot of the most impressive projects, the ones funded by corporations, were abandoned because of worries about public opinion. I remember that happened at Westway Pharmaceuticals in the early 1980s.'

'I remember that,' said Woodridge. 'They had protesters outside the gates and all that. Went on for weeks.'

'Was there anything special about the research there?' asked Chaney.

'The most special thing was Edward Geiger,' said Andersen. 'He was Stanford's number one, a real thinker and a mathematics prodigy. Back then it was thought of as a real coup for biology – and genetics in particular – that he chose to specialise in that field. Everyone had assumed he'd go for physics.'

'And what was this man Geiger looking at?'

125

Andersen shook his head.

'I don't remember. He was working on the cell differentiation I think. Anyway after five or six years at Westway he had half his projects cancelled and he left. I don't know what happened to him.'

Newell, who had been silent throughout the meeting, suddenly cleared his throat and said: 'Perhaps we could leave the history lesson aside for a moment and turn to the practicalities. What do you think, Peter?'

Woodridge nodded.

'Right,' said Newell. 'This Erixil stuff. One: how long before we get a complete analysis of it? And two: how long before we can make it ourselves?'

Andersen shifted in his chair. These were the questions he had been dreading, but he wasn't going to make excuses. If they wanted to fire him, they could fire him.

'I'm afraid this is no simple matter,' he said. 'Complex proteins can only be identified using X-ray crystallography, and even this method is unreliable unless undertaken in zero gravity.'

'Great!' exclaimed Newell. 'The guy wants a trip on the space shuttle!'

'With molecules of this complexity there is no other dependable way!' Andersen shouted back. Newell always had been an ignorant sonofabitch. 'And in any case, there is a second problem.'

'Which is?'

'That unless Mendelhaus are pretty stupid, they will be sure to put a considerable number of irrelevant proteins in with the active ones – dozens, perhaps hundreds. That way it will take a great deal longer to isolate the ones that matter. All in all, it would be a lot easier and probably cheaper to steal the information you require. No organisation can be completely watertight, and even scientists have their price.'

There was silence in the room. Chaney was looking

126

down at the table as if determined to show no reaction to what he had just heard. It was then that Andersen understood.

'Thank you, Dr Andersen,' said Woodridge. 'We will call you if we need you.'

Andersen pushed back his chair and stood up. The others remained seated. He left the room without another word, conscious of three pairs of eyes on the back of his neck.

Once the door was closed Woodridge turned to Chaney.

'Well?'

'It's what I expected him to say. Given the time parameters it seems there's no alternative.'

'And you believe the girl, what's her name again?'

'Ryder.'

'You believe she is our best way in?'

Chaney shrugged and put down his pen.

'No doubt about it. She's been making all the right calls since the beginning. She didn't pick up on this in the normal way is my feeling. The research Webber put out was too detailed and too punctual. She knows someone inside Mendelhaus. And the person she knows, if he was important enough to be responsible for the leak, probably knows enough himself to help us, or at least has access to the information we need. It has to be the best line we've got.'

'And, I hope, the quickest,' added Newell, looking at his watch. 'Apart from our own internal situation, which is in danger of becoming grave, there must be other people drawing the same conclusions we are. It might get a little hairy out there if they all start playing hardball at once.'

'That's right,' said Woodridge with a single nod. He turned to Chaney and looked him straight in the face. 'Time is what we don't have. Another few months of this and we're history. If you have to cut corners, do it. Just get us the information we need.'

Chaney looked down at his notebook.

'And, Mr Chaney. I want you to understand you have my personal support on this. Come up with the goods and you will be generously compensated for your . . . trouble.'

15

Manhattan. December 22nd, 1995.

It started to snow just after Cathy left the office so that by the time she reached Bloomingdales her shoes were soaked through. Christmas had never been a big thing at home, but since she was a child she had always enjoyed the window displays, the warmth of the shops, even the talk of peace and goodwill – when it wasn't soaked in too much Christmas spirit.

A lot of spirit had been in evidence at Webber that afternoon and Cathy had found it difficult, particularly given her unfamiliar position of authority, to cheer the opening of yet another bottle of champagne. But as soon as she had left the office and seen the snow spinning down between the towers crowding Fifth Avenue, her mood had changed. She realised with an excitement bordering on vertigo that this Christmas was special.

It was crowded in Bloomingdales and Cathy had to push to get through to the books department. She was tired, but now at last she was on the home straight. In the stylish bag under her arm she carried a blue cashmere sweater for Mike. It had been a difficult choice, and she had stood there for almost an hour before finally picking it out of the row of sweet-smelling knitwear in Saks. Even then she'd had her doubts. It was an expensive present and it occurred to her more than once that Mike might

129

feel she was putting pressure on him by buying it. But she wanted to show him how she felt.

Since she had met him at Pete Sweeney's party they had seen each other almost every day. It was unlike anything she had known before. Instead of being 'taken out' to grand restaurants by someone who was obviously going to great pains to impress her, she had found herself walking alongside Michael under an umbrella with no particular sense of urgency or purpose; found herself eating simple food in modest restaurants; found herself curled up on the couch in her apartment with a glass of wine, and Michael's head in her lap, and found in all these simple things that she was deeply affected by him, by *them*, the way they were together. The spontaneity, the simplicity of the whole thing was all the more striking in the context of what her daily life had become since she had been promoted.

Had she known what it would mean, she would probably have hesitated to write her report on Mendelhaus and Erixil. It wasn't just a question of the increased pressure which came with promotion. There was something vaguely scary about having been at the heart of something which had caused people, powerful people, to lose millions. In the midst of what seemed sometimes like the ocean of ulterior motive and hidden intention in which she now had to swim, Michael had bobbed up like a life belt. Strangely enough she got the feeling that their relationship seemed to afford him the same kind of relief. He seemed to come to her as if her apartment were a sanctuary. She only had to touch him and he would relax immediately. And when he touched her it seemed to be a natural extension of their discourse, their communication. True, he sometimes wanted to go further than she was ready for, but she believed that in time even *that* would no longer be a problem.

As she handed over her credit card in Saks, she had

realised that by buying the sweater she was in a sense putting an end to the simplicity which had characterised their first contact. So now she had come to Blooming-dale's to pick up something amusing; any embarrassing silence caused by the sweater could be broken with a good laugh. She knew what it was she wanted, but pushing through the crowd and looking between the heads at the shelves of books she was making little progress. Then she saw it: *A Hundred Ways to Cook an Egg* by Norma Phillips.

Mike had never been able to explain to her why he had offered her an egg at Pete's party and had always denied having meant anything by it. After a couple of lengthy discussions he had said 'Cathy, let's drop the egg.' Since then it had been a standing joke between them. In-jokes already! Suddenly she felt the hair creep on the back of her neck. Two rows down, a tall man in a Burberry raincoat was looking straight at her. The instant she raised her eyes he looked down at his book. Now he was brows-ing just like the guy next to him. But in that moment of recognition Cathy had got a clear picture of his face. She felt sure she was not mistaken. He was too big to confuse with someone else. He looked like an out of work heavy-weight boxer. He had a grey moustache and several deep scars in his face. She had seen the same guy in Saks and again in the street when she had stopped to look in the window. He had been walking close behind her. Then, when she had stopped, he had slowed down a few paces on and looked in at the display.

Her hands were suddenly moist. She put the book back on the shelf and slowly, just as if she too were just another customer browsing, she made her way towards the stairs which led down to the door. Once on the stairs she started to run. She ran two blocks holding her package tight.

Mike looked out of the window, his eyes drawn down to

the street by the falling snow. It was a quarter past seven. For no reason a shiver went through him. *What if something's happened to her?*

He shook his head and turned away. Expecting the worst had become a reflex in the last few weeks. After so much bad luck, Mike had trouble believing anything could go his way. He was starting to behave like a victim, a loser. He walked across to the hi-fi and switched on the CD player. The sound of a Bach violin partita filled the room. He picked up the cover and smiled. Two weeks ago and he would have said a partita was some kind of curry dish. In a childhood spent listening to Bruce Springsteen, Steely Dan, Leonard Cohen, the Partita just hadn't come up. The evenings spent with Cathy at her three-room flat on 87th Street were full of partitas; partitas, sonatas, preludes. Then, after dinner when they curled up on the old leather couch, nocturnes – or the odd choice adagio maybe, picked out by Cathy from the pile of CDs which threatened to topple off the shelves at any moment. The whole flat was like that. Dishes stacked anyhow in the cupboard. Three damp towels jammed on the towel rack. Cathy's shirts hanging from the skylight over the bathtub. But everything clean; a smell of clean everywhere.

Mike went through to the kitchen and switched on the kettle. He took off his raincoat and tossed the door key onto the table. Cathy had given him a key the third time they had met. At first Mike had been taken aback. It went through his mind that she was going to be another easy lay like Karen. Not that he minded easy lays, but he had come to expect something different. If anything, Cathy seemed nervous when he touched her. In their lengthy bouts on the couch, for all her obvious excitement, she had kept her clothes on. Then she gave him the key. *If I ever get back late, you can just let yourself in*. He had taken it, of course, but at the same time it had thrown him. She was always surprising him.

Since then, he had come every single night and let himself into the warm, clean-smelling flat with a feeling of almost childish happiness. Perhaps it was just that his days were not so hot. Walking for hours from interview to interview or sitting in his dad's front room making phone calls got him so low he thought he would sometimes give up, throw in the braces and Ivy League tie. There was nothing for him, anywhere. Then, at about six o'clock, he'd button up his filofax and make his way across Queensboro Bridge, turning north on Second Avenue. After a day like that he was bound to feel good about letting himself into a beautiful girl's apartment, but then again there was more to it than that. He had spent all afternoon trying to find her a Christmas present. Wasn't that proof of the way he felt? He had finally chosen a gold chain with a little medallion upon which a treble clef was engraved. It was Cathy who had told him that the little symbol marked G on the musical stave. He was pleased with the find. It seemed to him to show that they already shared secrets.

'This is very serious, Mikey,' he said to the empty kitchen. It was all the more serious in as much as he had yet to broach the subject of Mendelhaus. Cathy was touchy about her sudden rise to fame. For some reason it had made her feel insecure. She said she had seen a different side to people since her promotion, a side she didn't like. *Everyone wants something from me all of a sudden*, she had said. Mike didn't dare talk about it, even though it was often on his mind. Every time she opened her attaché case he had to restrain himself from taking a peep at the papers.

He was taking his first sip of coffee, when the front door opened, and Cathy, her skin flushed with the cold, her black hair tumbling over her face, rushed into the

133

kitchen. For a moment she could say nothing, breathing hard. Mike kissed her fragrant face and helped her out of her coat, freezing air escaping from the stiff folds and vents.

'There was a man in Bloomingdales,' she said after a moment. She looked up at Mike, her deep eyes serious, drinking in the light. 'I'm sure it was the same guy. He's been following me since I left the office.'

Mike sat down and offered her his coffee.

'And that's not the only thing.' Mike was sitting on the sofa looking up at Cathy as she paced back and forth across the room. 'I've had some weird calls at the office over the past few days. In the end I had to tell the switchboard to screen the calls as they came through.' She looked down at her violin, her reference point, he had noticed, in moments of anxiety.

'It's that article in *Fortune*, I'm sure of it. Anyone can pick it up and there I am, smiling Cathy Ryder, just waiting for your call.'

'Come on Cathy, there's no reason for anyone to want to hurt you.'

She looked at him, her expression severe for a moment.

'I worry that people think I know more than I really do about this Erixil thing.' She sat down and pressed herself against him. 'I'd like to explain to everyone, especially Ben Steiner – you know that creepy guy from Salomon? – I'd like to tell them that I've no inside information. Everything I knew I reported.'

Mike felt the truth of what she was saying, but he didn't want to alarm her by seeming to take it too seriously.

'You're not saying Steiner is paying people to follow you around?' he said, smiling.

'No, but – '

'Maybe it's some journalist hoping to see you meet someone or something like that. Maybe it's just a guy

134

who likes the way you look. Christ knows there's enough weirdos in this city.'

Cathy's head snapped round.

'Oh, I see: you think a person would have to be weird to think I was good looking?'

Mike laughed at her mock severity.

'Come here and I'll show you how weird a guy can get.'

She looked at him for a moment, standing over him. Then she smiled, and shook her hair away from her face. She sat next to him and pushed her head against his shoulder.

'And how was your day, Michael Varela?'

Mike smiled blankly. This was always a difficult moment. He never knew what to say. He was afraid if he told her the truth about losing his job, it would lead to questions which would eventually bring them round to Mendelhaus. Even so, he knew it was only a matter of time before she found out anyway. Sooner or later someone at Webber would tell her about Miguel Varela and once again the deal would be off. Mike didn't know if he could take another fall. She would ask him if that was the reason for his picking her up in the first place and he would have to admit the truth, or lie – which Cathy with her all-seeing eyes would perceive immediately.

'Oh, fine. You know the kind of thing, revolving credit facility, tender panels for the insurance of CP – let's forget about it.'

Luckily Cathy was always ready to talk about anything other than finance. It had surprised Mike to see how little interest she took in Webber, her position, her success. If anything she talked like someone who was slowly detaching herself from the industry. Another of her mysteries.

So they talked about other things. And then when they had talked Bach was replaced by Chopin and they sat staring into each other's faces and kissing, the kisses seeming to go on for hours. Sometimes, coming up for air,

Mike almost laughed. He hadn't been through such sessions since adolescence. But their passion *had* to be taken orally. It could never go to the next phase. If Mike touched her breasts, Cathy stiffened and withdrew her face to look at him with her mesmeric eyes. Unable to bear any more of Cathy's deep probing kisses, Mike stood up. He wavered for a moment, and then began to undo the belt of his slacks. She shook her head, smiling. He paused. And then sat down next to her, where she immediately drew him into another long kiss. He detached himself after a moment and asked her why.

She flushed, and said simply, 'Because you frighten me.'

Mike kissed her hair.

'Are you still – '

She nodded once and looked down at her clenched hands. She was so vulnerable and perfect. Again Mike kissed her fragrant hair. He didn't know what to say to reassure her. Then she drew away from him and stood up.

'It's ridiculous, I know.'

'No, I – '

'No it is. It *feels* ridiculous. I don't know why I am, but I am. Being with you like this feels like the most natural thing in the world, but to actually . . . to make love – you in me. It's a difficult thing. It's become a difficult step. I don't know. If I'd had sex like all my friends did when I was a girl it would have been simple enough.' She walked over to the window and was talking more quietly now, almost as if Mike were no longer there. 'But I didn't like the boys. They were so stupid, so selfish. Then later, when it meant more, it became more difficult.' She looked across to him, smiling. 'You develop defences. You try to intimidate people so that the situation doesn't arise, and then you get so good at it, that nobody comes near you. Life's too short. That's what everybody thinks. And

136

then – and this is the really weird thing – then it becomes so important, it feels like such a . . . such a momentous thing. It becomes as if you were saving yourself. As if you knew something was coming, and that you were saving yourself for that.'

'I see . . . I think.'

Cathy came and kneeled before Mike. She took his hands in hers.

'I don't mean that you're not the one. I think you are. I have never . . . no one has ever made me feel like this, Michael. You must see how important all this is.'

'For me it is, Cathy. You're the girl. You're the one for me. You – '

She put her hand softly against his mouth.

'Then wait a little. That's all I'm asking. I just want a little time. That's all.'

16

Los Angeles. December 24th, 1995.

A two-foot-high plastic Santa sat on the edge of the bar with a bell in one hand and a sign in the other. The sign said: 'The Golden State Charitable Foundation. Please give generously. Yo! Ho! Ho!' Inside the Santa an electric light flashed on and off and there was a slot in the top of its head for the money. For a moment Harry Waterman fingered the change from his Johnny Walker, but then he thrust it back in his pocket. That kind of stuff wouldn't work on him: even as a kid he'd never believed in Santa Claus and these days he didn't even believe in Christmas. It was just a whole week or more without work and a lot of time wasted in front of the TV. He hadn't been to a midnight mass – or any mass for that matter – for more than a decade. From a loudspeaker above his head he could hear a choir of syrupy female voices singing 'Jingle Bells'. He wished to God they'd turn it off.

Just in time he stopped himself from gulping back the scotch. He had to make it last a little, else he would be drunk by nine o'clock or even earlier, and he didn't want to get drunk. Ever since his trip to Delano's Workout Shop he'd been painfully conscious of how bad a shape he was in. He'd even made a couple of resolutions to go running, although as yet he hadn't found the time. In the New Year he would start: twice a week down on the beach, early so there weren't too many people. He would get trim in a few weeks. Maybe even do some of that weights stuff once he'd got his gut under control. His resolution pleased him and he slugged back the rest of the glass to celebrate. 1996 would be a healthier year.

He sat looking at his empty glass for a minute and then his flush of optimism vanished. Who was he kidding? The way he was drinking these days he would be doing well just to *see* a morning. He didn't even own a decent pair of running shoes. Besides, he had more important things to worry about: like what the hell he was going to do with his life.

He looked at the pair of Christmas cards he had picked up from his mailbox on the way out. One was from Eddy Shorten, an old pal in San Francisco who he hadn't seen in three years, and the other was from 'the guys at the CDC.' Eddy's card was the same one he had sent the year before: a sentimental watercolour of Bethlehem under a foot of snow. The CDC's was classier: a reproduction of a renaissance painting. 'Detail from the "Madonna di San Sisto" by Raphael (1483–1520)', it said on the inside. Altogether that made four cards this year, four lousy cards – three really, because the CDC one didn't count. It was business, and not much business at that.

After his visit to Delano's he had called Miller again. He had explained the Mendelhaus connection between Bladon and McArthur but Miller hadn't been too impressed. At least not impressed enough to put him back on his $275 a day. After all his hard work it had been a real let-down. He'd tried to find out more about the company by doing a search on the NEXIS data base, which they let him access, for a fee, down at the *Herald*, but the machine hadn't turned up much. Mendelhaus was a private Swiss concern with interests in cosmetics, over-the-counter drugs and private health care, but Waterman knew that already. A couple of stories on Matt

McArthur's death mentioned the company, but gave no details.

The only bit of information he didn't have came from an article on the Union Bank of Geneva in some finance magazine. The article, which was dated July 1994, said that UBG had 'under-estimated the impact of greater financial integration within the European Community,' and was 'seeing a serious decline in its foreign business as a result.' The journalist speculated that the bank would be demanding bigger returns from the companies in which it had major holdings, so as to buoy up group profits. Among the companies listed was Mendelhaus. The only other mentions of the company came from retail industry trade magazines, in which prices and market shares for various cosmetics products were listed. There was certainly no word about viral cancers.

And that was that. Waterman had felt proud of the work he'd done, but without the CDC picking up the bills he couldn't afford to take the case any further. Unless some guru turned up out of the blue there was no way he could find out more without going to Switzerland, and that was beyond his budget. It was a pity though. For a while there he'd begun to think he was really on to something big, something that might pull him out of the rut he was in. With the booze the disappointment came back to him. Thanks a lot, Atlanta! And a Happy Christmas to you too! He took the card with the Raphael Madonna on it and tossed it into the waste bin on the other side of the bar. Then he summoned the barman and ordered another Johnny Walker.

A couple of stools down, a tired-looking businessman in a creased steel-grey suit was drinking a beer and staring at a magazine which he had spread out in front of him. Every few seconds he would turn over another page, but nothing seemed to grab his interest. In fact the guy looked washed up. Eventually he looked at his watch, climbed off his stool and left, leaving the magazine behind. Waterman leaned over and picked it up. It was an out-of-date issue of *Fortune*, which explained the dejection: any businessman working late on Christmas Eve had to be either extremely enthusiastic about his work or seriously worried about it – and this guy hadn't looked enthusiastic at all. Yet when you looked through this edition of *Fortune*, all you saw were the smiling faces of success: an ice cream entrepreneur in Wisconsin, a mail-order millionaire in Baltimore, a bunch of smart-ass stock analysts in New York City. It was enough to make any normal person feel dejected.

One of the smart-ass stock analysts wasn't bad looking, though: a classy looking brunette with sexy eyes and a shy kind of smile. Waterman speculated whether she hadn't got where she had through being a cute-ass rather than a smart-ass. She sure as hell wouldn't have been the first. But as he started reading the story about her he began to change his mind. It said she had anticipated a huge shake-out in the cosmetics industry caused by a technological breakthrough at a Swiss company called . . . *Mendelhaus*. Waterman put down his glass. It seemed that this girl had found out about it ahead of everybody else. The way the story told it, you'd think she just read the science journals a bit more thoroughly than everyone else, or was better at handling a pocket calculator. But Waterman knew better: you didn't get that kind of information unless you had friends on the inside, because information like that was big money.

He slung the magazine under his arm and finished off the Johnny Walker in one go. Then he pulled out the change from his pocket and stuffed it all in the top of the plastic Santa. It lit up gratefully and an electronic voice said: Yo! Ho! Ho!

17

Geneva. January 10th, 1996.

The door was opened by a uniformed footman with a long wrinkled face.

'Herr Doctor Kessler?' he enquired.

Kessler nodded and the door was opened wider to reveal a small cobbled courtyard, with neatly cut bay trees growing in each corner. From the overcast sky snowflakes were falling. The footman led him to the opposite side of the courtyard and up a stone staircase to the first floor. Behind another large door was a kind of reception area with a polished wooden floor and modern paintings on the walls. There was also a sofa, some armchairs and an antique desk on one side. The footman took Kessler's overcoat and scarf and disappeared. From somewhere inside the building there came the faint ringing of a bell.

An instant later a neatly-dressed lady, in what he accurately guessed to be her mid-forties, came to greet him. She was all in grey, with an elegant gold bracelet on her wrist, gold earrings, and a small gold watch pinned to the front of her jacket. She held out her hand.

'Good afternoon, Herr Doctor,' she said. 'I'm honoured that you should take the time to visit us.'

Kessler bowed slightly as he shook her hand. 'Good afternoon, Madame Beauvais.'

'I do hope we can be of some assistance,' she went on. 'Would you care for some tea or coffee?'

'Thank you, no, madame,' he said.

'Something stronger perhaps?'

Kessler shook his head. 'No again, madame. I'm afraid my time is short.'

'Of course. Forgive me. If you will follow me, all is ready.'

She led him down a white panelled passage to another room, this one with a Persian rug on the floor and two Empire couches at right angles to each other. There were white shutters on the windows.

'Please take a seat, Herr Doctor,' said Madame Beauvais. 'I shall not keep you a moment.'

She left the room through a door in the opposite wall. Through the doorway Kessler caught a glimpse of three girls sitting in a row on a couch just like the one he was sitting on. They were laughing. When Madame Beauvais opened the door again a few moments later, however, they had all disappeared and the laughter had stopped.

'Your requirements were unusually exacting, Herr Doctor,' she said with a smile, 'but in order to meet them I have left no stone unturned.'

'Just as long as you have been able to proceed with discretion, madame,' said Kessler. 'I cannot stress how important we regard this aspect . . .'

Madame Beauvais interrupted him with a wave of her hand.

'Discretion is something we understand *very* well here, Herr Doctor. Please have no doubts on that score. Indeed is it not the greatest virtue of the Swiss nation itself?'

Kessler nodded in agreement.

'Then let's proceed.'

She opened the door again and one of the girls Kessler had seen a few moments earlier stepped into the room. She was slim and very pretty with big brown eyes, high cheek-bones and short auburn hair. She wore a simple white blouse with embroidery on the collar, a flowing black skirt with a leather belt and black leather boots to match. She went to within a couple of yards of where Kessler was sitting and smiled, her hands linked together in front of her. Through the material of her blouse Kessler could easily make out the dark circles of her nipples.

'This is Claudia,' said Madame Beauvais, walking over to the mantelpiece and lighting a cigarette. 'You saw a photograph of her before. She has some very distinguished followers, don't you my dear?'

The girl smiled again and looked into Kessler's face with an expression of complete confidence.

'Charming,' said Kessler. 'But I'm afraid I failed to appreciate . . . how tall is she exactly?'

'One metre fifty-seven centimetres. Somewhat less than you specified, I know, but I thought in case . . . No matter. It was only an idea. Thank you, Claudia.'

The girl smiled again and walked out of the room.

'I'm sorry,' said Madame Beauvais. 'Would you care for a cigarette?'

'No thank you,' said Kessler. 'Do you have any other candidates?'

Madame Beauvais smiled gracefully as the door opened again. This time another girl, younger but markedly taller, came into the room. She had long brown hair which she held back with a white head-band, a fine straight nose and green eyes. She wore a sleeveless dress of pale pink cotton, which buttoned up the front. She smiled a little nervously as she crossed the room, and then curtsied quickly. From where Kessler sat the scent of perfume was powerful.

'This is Brigitte,' said Madame Beauvais, coming up behind her and putting her hands on the back of the girl's shoulders. 'I'm sorry I wasn't able to give you a photograph of her before, but she only arrived in Geneva a week or two ago. She is young, but I thought I would show her to you anyway. She is quite a find. She speaks English very well, and is quite accomplished at the piano.'

As soon as Madame Beauvais's hands had touched her shoulders the girl had begun to undo the buttons on her dress. Now she cautiously drew out her arms so that Kessler's view of her breasts was unimpeded. As the material fell away she smiled again fleetingly and momentarily folded her arms.

'Madame,' said Kessler. 'Have you told these ladies of the nature of the work we have for them?' – A look of uncertainty crossed the girl's face. She was blushing in spite of her smiles – 'Because really this is not strictly necessary.'

'Herr Doctor,' said Madame Beauvais. 'I have treated the whole matter with the discretion you requested. I have spoken only of the generous fee we discussed.'

The moment of disagreement made the girl hesitate. But then she continued to divest herself of the dress. Kessler watched for a moment as she stepped out of it. Her legs were long and perfect. Then he asked: 'How old are you, please?'

A look of confusion crossed the girl's face. Then she answered: 'Nineteen, sir.'

'As I thought, madame,' he said. 'The height is good but the age is not. The colouring is far from perfect also.'

Madame Beauvais smiled through her cigarette smoke.

'At least we are getting closer, Herr Doctor,' she said. 'Thank you Brigitte.'

The girl, naked by now but for her shoes, gratefully gathered up her clothes and left the room. Kessler sighed and sat back on the couch. For the first time Madame Beauvais sat down too.

'The age is something of a problem, I must confess,' she said. 'Ladies of this calibre do not generally stay in this field for more than two or three years. By twenty-five, most have found themselves husbands – bankers as often as not. But, as I said, I have left no stone unturned to help you.'

As she was speaking a third girl came into the room. She had curly dark hair and brown eyes. In fact there was a proud gypsy quality about her whole demeanour which her business-like clothes did nothing to conceal. She was older than the other two and more casual than either. She stood at a greater distance from Kessler than they had done, with her hands planted a little theatrically on her hips.

'This is Katrine,' said Madame Beauvais. 'You said you preferred a Swiss national, but for looks like hers you have to cast your net wider.'

The girl seemed to take these words as a compliment and smiled proudly. Then she began to undress, throwing down each article of clothing as if it were a challenge. Kessler got the impression that maybe she had worked on a stage somewhere. He had seen girls carry themselves like that in the private clubs the directors sometimes frequented. Those kind of places didn't much appeal to him, but sometimes he felt obliged to go along in case his superiors should detect his disapproval. Their support was still not something he could take for granted.

A few moments later the girl called Katrine stood in her silk camisole. Her skin was a little dark, but she was above average height even without high heels.

'How old is she?' he asked Madame Beauvais.

'Twenty-six,' the girl said before the older woman could reply. Then she walked over towards him, and added: 'last July.'

She took off the camisole and, last of all, untied her hair which she shook until it flowed over her shoulders. Her breasts were large but firm and the rest of her body was almost muscular. There was no sign of a bikini line anywhere on her hips or thighs, as if she had spent most

146

of her life naked under the sun. Unprompted she turned around, looking at him over her shoulder, anxious, it seemed, to gauge his reaction.

'She's as close as you're likely to get, Herr Doctor,' Madame Beauvais observed, her gaze resting on the girl's thighs. 'And I think she meets most of your criteria.'

'Yes,' said Kessler after a moment's consideration. 'I believe she does.

18

Manhattan. January 12th, 1996.

Instead of driving down into the basement carpark Mike
eased the used Toyota hatchback into the tight space
behind a rusty Ford van. It was the closest space available
to the street door of Cathy's building. As he climbed out
of the cab he failed to notice the guy leaning out of the
phone bubble on the opposite sidewalk. The guy was lean
and unshaven with dried soup in the corners of his wide
mouth from a breakfast eaten standing in the warm stream
of peanut-smelling air rushing up out of the subway at
West 86th Street. He had lank brown hair that was too
long for him.

Keeping an eye on Mike, he leaned into the plastic
bubble and shot a dime into the slot. Whoever it was on
the other end was a long time picking up the phone. The
man cursed, a fleck of spittle flying from his mouth.

Mike slowly emerged from the car mostly hidden by a
large weeping fig in a terracotta pot.

'Yeah!' said the man, 'who else? And I'm fucking freezing down here.'

Someone shouted at the other end of the line and the
man smiled. He felt in his pocket for his cigarettes. He'd
had nothing to report for three days of standing around
in the cold and now that he did, he felt like stirring things
up a little.

There was another long pause. Mike was taking a suit-case from the trunk.

The small man stood upright suddenly and changed his tone.

'Yes, sir, Mr Chaney. Like you said. Anything happens I tell you about it.'

He nodded, listening to the careful, authoritative voice of a man he had never seen.

'It's the guy. The boyfriend, yeah. Normally comes on over at about six o'clock, but he's here early today and he's brought a load of junk with him.'

He listened for a moment and then looked across the street. Mike was just disappearing into the building.

'Yeah. I think maybe he's movin' in or something. Like I said before, he must have his own key. Must be fuckin' this piece on a regular basis, lucky son of a bitch.'

On the fourth floor Mike put the plant down and rested against the wall. Even now he wasn't convinced of what he was doing. He had only known Cathy for a month and while he felt stronger than he had ever done, felt certain that what was happening in him was different, special, at the same time it was impossible to untangle that pure golden thread of truth from the web of circumstances. If he was moving into Cathy's guest room it was because he loved her . . . hell, and she loved him back, but it was also because he had lost his own flat at the Continental Guardian building and was tired of the conversation at Pop Varela's in Queens, tired of the poky room at the back of the building – tired of seeing his suits hanging on the back of the door. Mike suppressed a shudder of dis-taste. When he got back from Cathy's at night, lying on the narrow bed and looking up at the low ceiling, he had the impression he was drowning in his low rent past.

And the state of his finances made it impossible for him to get a flat in the right kind of area. He still had his old

149

business cards and couldn't face having new ones printed with the Queens address on them. But on his résumé there it was, plain as daylight. He had seen the faces of potential employers become distant, less interested. *Oh, Queens, that's a colourful place to live.* There he was in his $1000 suits and expensive haircuts with an address in Queens. *Isn't that street where the old fruit and vegetable market was?* It just didn't fit. They wanted to know what he was doing living in Queens if he was the hot shot he made himself out to be.

But Cathy's address, that was a different matter. He *could* print cards with an address on West 87th Street. It wasn't Ritzy exactly, but it was respectable. Mike frowned. Was that why he had come? He looked at the plant as if expecting an answer. Then he took a cigarette from his case and stood with it unlit in his hand, his thoughts going round and round.

It was the same tangle with Cathy. He persuaded himself that he had never met anyone like her. That she was, for him, *the* woman. Everything about her drove him crazy. Her beauty, her intelligence, her music, even her hang-up about the sack. He loved that hesitation in her. It made everything so much more intense. But at the same time, he could not forget his original intention. He could not forget Mendelhaus. He could not put it out of his head that she knew about the company from the inside. She had hinted as much when they had touched on the matter obliquely (he didn't dare go at it head on). He kept telling himself that the time would come when he could be open with her about everything. But that time didn't come, and he got deeper and deeper into lies about what he did with his days, what it was that had drawn him to her that night at Pete Sweeney's party.

Mike lit his cigarette and blew smoke at the leaves of the weeping fig. He thought about leaving her the plant with a note telling her the truth, and then driving back across town. *I love you, Cathy. Can you still love me?* But what if she didn't understand? Stranded on the narrow bed in Queens with the yellow ceiling pressing down on him he knew he would suffocate in a week. And if he moved out, found a place in a cheaper part of town, how long would it take him to get back on track? He might never get back. And she wanted him there. She had asked him if he wanted to live with her, even if she had set some pretty weird terms. Why fight it? Tossing his finished cigarette into the stairwell, Mike picked up the plant and went on up to the sixth floor.

Cathy saw the guy immediately. She was coming along the street from where she had parked the car, and had known at once, instinctively that he was watching her. He was leaning against the wall, reading a newspaper, a cigarette in his mouth. But she knew that if she had turned, gone back to the car for something, or simply crossed the street, he would have known it even without looking up.

Things had changed in the last few days. Things had taken a turn for the worse. Calls still came through to the office, and she had the feeling she was being watched. The previous night soaking in the tub, looking up at the blue square of the skylight, she'd had a sudden expansion of fear. She had been sure that someone was watching right through the frosted glass. She'd sat up and covered her breasts, water surging over the sides of the bath and onto the floor. It was a while before she could convince herself that this was impossible.

And then there was the man she had seen in Bloomingdales. He kept his distance now, and she could go for a long time without thinking about him. But then, just as she was buying a hot dog or maybe a copy of *The Post*, she'd look up, and he'd be there, parked by the side of the road, or talking to someone in the street. He made no sign of having noticed her, but again she felt instinctively that he was watching.

Approaching the street door she gripped her key hard, not frightened but angry at the continual intrusion. How could they think she was so stupid as not to notice them? She was almost tempted to cross the road, walk straight towards him, just to see what he would do. But something stopped her. Underneath her anger she knew she was afraid.

Inside the building she tried to reason with herself. Maybe it was just the pressure she was under at the office. People called her all the time, asking her for information about Mendelhaus. She was tired of having to disappoint them. Given her status, she really ought to know something about the company's future projects, but the truth was she knew nothing. It had been weeks since Krystal had called, and she was now as much in the dark as everyone else.

When Ben Steiner called from Salomon, she felt herself flush to the roots of her hair. He flattered and wheedled, asking her if she wanted to have lunch, and she knew that the only thing he really wanted was to get information about Mendelhaus.

Thank God there was Mike. At least with him it was simple. She thought about him all the time. She thought about their conversations. It was an enormous relief to her that he seemed to positively avoid talking about finance. She didn't know much about what he did, and she didn't particularly want to know. By leaving out their professions they were able to talk about all the things that really mattered. Mike knew little about music, but he seemed so ready to listen. Talking to him she felt her inhibitions dissolving bit by bit. She had even played the violin for him, something she normally reserved for the little music academy in the Village. And she knew that given time other inhibitions would leave her. If he only gave her a little time . . .

He was standing with the door open when she arrived on the landing.

'I heard you coming up,' he said with a smile. She pressed herself against him, breathing deep his familiar smell. After a moment she leaned away from him slightly and looked into his warm Mediterranean eyes. When he held her she felt light, energised somehow. She no longer thought about the man in the street.

'Cathy?'

His voice was soft. It came to Cathy that he would make a good tenor. She realised she had never heard him sing.

'Cathy. What've you got there in your hand?'

They separated and Mike took her by the wrist of her clenched left hand. Cathy was as surprised as Mike to see her doubled fist, the knuckles white with the strain. Slowly she opened her hand to reveal her door key. The palm was marked red where she had held it tight.

Mike looked into her dark eyes, holding his breath as they filled with tears.

'What is it, Cathy?'

She pressed her eyes shut so that the tears spilt like the beads of a broken necklace. He held her as she cried, shaking her head. Then, after a moment, she looked at him through her long wet lashes.

'I'm scared, Michael.'

And she told him about her day, the calls, the men following in the street.

'You don't believe me, do you?'

Mike looked confused. It all seemed so unlikely. Why would anyone be following her? She came across the room and put her arm through his.

'Let me show you something.'

She took him to the window. They both looked down.

Mike saw the street still striped with slush left from the previous night's fall of snow. There were a couple of people walking along with a dog. It was just a street.

'Do you notice anything?'

Mike looked Cathy in the eyes.

'Take another look. Can you see that little guy standing near the telephone?'

Mike looked, and for the first time he did see the guy. He looked cold, flapping his arms for warmth.

'What's so special about him?' he asked, keeping his eyes on this man who had suddenly become sinister.

'He was waiting this evening. Waiting for me to come home. I saw him when I left this morning. I think he's been hanging around for a while, but I don't know why. It's just an impression I have.'

'What makes you think he's waiting for you especially?'

Cathy turned abruptly, her eyes hard under her emphatically marked eyebrows.

'There's no evidence, Mike. It's just a feeling I have. It goes with all the other business. The guy in Bloomingdales, the people I see in the street.'

She was losing control, her eyes glittering, full. Mike held her to him, trying to think what to do. After a moment he said, 'It's okay. I'm gonna go down.'

She looked back at him, looking deep into his eyes. She drew in her bottom lip, thinking.

'What are you going to do?'

'I don't know. I'll just go and talk to him. Tell him to clear off if I have to.'

Suddenly the expression on his face, so serious and brave, made Cathy laugh. And this seemed to push everything into a different perspective. He came towards her. He wanted to do something, let her know he was there and that she was safe whatever happened.

'Don't do that. Maybe I'm just – '

'Cathy, I'll do whatever you say. We should call the

police, maybe. But they won't come out just because there's a man standing by the telephone down in the street. And they might want you to go down to the station to file a complaint. Are you sure you want to go through that?'

Cathy shook her head.

'Listen, if that guy is there tomorrow morning I'll kick his ass, okay?'

He showed her his biceps and smiled. Then he took her in his arms and kissed her moist face until she was smiling again.

'Now let me show you something,' he said.

He took her through to the box room where he had installed himself.

'As per the agreement. A totally independent room. We can meet in the lounge and other common areas of the flat, but this is my room and your room is – '

'Don't laugh at me, Michael.'

He looked at her where she stood leaning against the door. She had a look he hadn't seen before. She seemed more vulnerable than ever. He went across to her and pushed his face into the rich hair tumbled on her shoulder.

'Cathy, Cathy, Cathy.'

He breathed her scent and touched her fine skin with his lips. Being close, he felt a heaviness in his throat. He wanted her so much, it was difficult to keep control, to keep the thickness out of his voice. And then suddenly she held him too. She pressed against his groin, straining against him as though he were in fact trying to push her away. He tried to look at her face, but she kept her head pressed against his shoulder. She stayed like that for a long time, just pressed against him, breathing through her mouth. He couldn't move. He wanted to step back, kiss her full mouth, undress her, but she wouldn't let go. Then, just as suddenly as she had held him, she let him

155

go, almost pushing him away. She was leaning back against the door, her face flushed.

He was about to say something, but she put her finger to his lips. Then, without saying another word, she began to undo the buttons of her blouse. Mike wanted to look as her fine hands worked down the row of buttons, but he was afraid she would feel watched. So he kept his eyes on hers. As she dropped the blouse from her shoulders he caught the warm intoxicating scent of her skin and looked at her body for the first time. She was perfect, fuller than he had expected, more womanly.

She stepped towards him so they were standing up close. She put her burning hand on the back of his neck.

'Kiss me.'

Her voice came soft but charged with an edge of urgency. Hardly breathing, his heart beating in his throat, Mike bent forward and touched her breast, feeling its weight and the smooth pliancy of the pale skin. Cathy shuddered at the first contact of his fingers and then leant against him slightly. Then he kissed her, slowly rising with each kiss to the base of her throat.

He drew his shirt over his head, and stood lightly against her. Keeping his eyes on hers he began to undo the zipper of her skirt, Cathy smiling at the small tearing sound of the zip. The skirt fell and she stepped out of it. She was all but naked now and beginning to feel self-conscious. She went across to the bed and climbed in. Mike stepped carefully out of his pants and sat down on the bed. Then he slid in against her and they lay for a long time, looking into the warm shadows of each other's face. Then, deliberately, raising himself up on one elbow, Mike began to kiss her throat and breasts. Her breath came faster, and as he kissed her nipples or the soft arches of her ribs she gasped with pleasure. But when Mike slipped off his shorts and lay naked against her, she froze.

He looked into her eyes, sure that he would see the

fear which was becoming familiar to him. She looked at him, her brows compressed in a line over her great dark eyes.

'I'm sorry, Michael. I'm not very good at this.'

And her expression, and the way she spoke, her beautiful disarming frankness, filled him with love.

'You are perfect, Cathy,' he said, the words seeming to come from him of themselves. He kissed her eyes and her fragrant hair.

'Immaculate, perfect.'

19

Manhattan. January 25th, 1996.

Mike turned on to Beaver Street and had to drop the visor, the sun was so strong. Trying to hold himself down, trying to contain himself, he couldn't stop the smile which spread slowly over his lips. First a phone call from Rudd and Martens asking him to come down town for a second talk and then the sun comes out. It had to be his day. There was no other way of looking at it.

Rudd and Martens were new on the Street and he'd had to do some research to find out about how they made their money. Peter Rudd had left Morgan Stanley in the spring of '95 to set up a consultancy boutique specialising in European corporate finance with an East European slant. There had been a lot in the press at the time of his departure, Rudd having creamed off some of Morgan's best clients on his way out the door.

From the first meeting Mike had Rudd down as a feisty numbers genius with a lot of ideas and little in the way of manners. They had gone through a couple of Napier Drew deals in which Mike had played a leading role with Rudd laughing his adolescent laugh, turning round equations, re-routeing money through tax loopholes, smiling triumphantly with his proof of savings for the buyer. He let Drew have it with both barrels: *nice deal, Mike, but the math stinks*. Mike thought Rudd must have gone down like a lead balloon in the panelled boardroom at a blue-blood outfit like Morgan. Naturally enough, they had hit it off immediately.

When the call came through that morning Mike had been surprised because it was the first time his luck had showed any sign of turning, but driving to the office he had hit the wheel with his fist and shouted above the deafening traffic noise: *it makes sense, damn it!* Rudd liked him. They came at the target from the same direction: wrong side of the tracks, pushy, smart. Mike parked the car, checked the papers in his attaché case once more, straightened his tie in the mirror and climbed out into the January sun. If everything went well he would call Cathy at Webber and invite her to lunch.

Cathy leaned back from her desk and pushed her fingers against her eyes. It was only twelve and already she felt exhausted. The whole morning had been burnt up under the strip lighting in Michael Paine's office. The pressure was on to come up with more hot tips on vanity stocks. Paine, more careful since her promotion, had nevertheless taken obvious pleasure in explaining the situation. *It was the quality of the material we put out on Mendelhaus, Cathy. It raised expectations to the ceiling. Now they're starting to think we're holding something back . . .*

For the hundredth time Cathy had cursed Mendelhaus under her breath; Mendelhaus, Krystal, the whole business. She had been taken up by the press as one of the Street's hottest analysts, but underneath she was just Cathy Ryder, average corporate analyst, and part-time violin player. In spite of her doubts she had been astonished to hear herself say: *I'm expecting something interesting to come through in the next few days.* So what was she expecting? She tugged at her lip. All she had were the original reports from Krystal which she no longer even carried around in her bag, they irritated her so much.

159

Krystal hadn't been in touch for a couple of weeks now and whenever she called his New York number she just got the engaged tone.

A call came through on her direct line. She pressed a button and leaned forward to her microphone. Ben Steiner's schoolboy tenor burst out of the speaker like Pavarotti on coke. Cathy made a face, flipped the switch and picked up the phone.

'Ben, how are you?'

Of course she knew how Ben was. Ben was fine. She could picture him perfectly sitting in his glass tower over at Salomon's smiling into the receiver and drawing a hairy hand along his polka-dot tie. And the way he talked, you could hear he thought she was fine too. If she had said she wanted to go back home and play her violin he would have thought she was joking. But the joke was her sitting in the high-tech chair in her blue suit, Miss Corporate America.

'I just wanted to confirm lunch today. Half past one, right?' She could hear him breathing eagerly into the phone.

Cathy's dark eyes rolled up and she stuck out her tongue, gagging. She had a flashback of Ben wheedling this lunch out of her last week. She had already refused him three times and now she had no more excuses. Ben was already explaining how to get to The Factory, an expensive new restaurant in the village.

Standing at the bar, Mike re-ran the moment in the interview when Rudd had turned to Benny Martens and Martens, without moving a muscle in his long Pennsylvania Dutch face, had shrugged. Mike sipped at his tepid coffee and shook his head. Up to that point it had been pretty much a repeat of the previous interview, in fact it had if anything gone even better. They had gone back over the same Drew deal and Mike had the distinct impression that Rudd was feeding him all the best lines. He found himself repeating part of what Rudd had said in the first interview, but Rudd acted like he had never heard it before. He continued to talk to Rudd who was putting the questions, but he knew it was Martens he had to impress. Finally it was Martens who had broken the silence. *I'm sorry, Mike. I know Pete is keen to have you on board, but it's not another deal-maker we need.*

He had then gone on for what had seemed to Mike like an hour, explaining about the client base, about the need they had for someone with just a touch of WASP. Having been at Swift and Drew he, Mike Varela, had been a strong candidate in that respect – *a strong candidate, Michael* – but it came down to a question of style. As Martens spoke, Mike's eyes had drifted across to Rudd, who was looking down at his shoes, a little vertical crease dividing his puckered forehead. At the door Rudd had been apologetic, encouraging.

So Mike was out of gas. Grounded. All used up. And once again, staring into his coffee cup, he tried to understand how it had all happened, starting with Mendelhaus.

'Don't worry about it, fella. It may never happen.'

Mike looked at the guy who had pulled up on to a bar stool next to him. He was a fat guy with thick spectacles and grey stubble on two of his three chins. He looked as if he spent at least one out of every two weekends wrestling grizzlies; slept with them too, by the smell of him. Not yet needing conversation with drunks, Mike pushed away from the bar and found the door to the street. It was raining. Of course.

'Yeah, all kinds of things trickle down to me at Salomon's. Things you would not *believe*.'

Cathy watched Steiner push another spoonful of ice cream into his mouth. It wasn't that he was a greedy eater, but everything he did, he did with the same intensity. His

161

eyes followed the spoon to his mouth even as he was talking to her about the Street grapevine and the ins and outs of being the Greatest Analyst in the World. It made her shiver.

'Cold? Too much Perrier, Cathy. Have another hit of this Bourgogne.'

Steiner poured, his eyes fastened on hers.

'Mendelhaus for example. I heard some interesting stuff about that little-known Swiss operation only yesterday.'

Cathy straightened slightly in her chair. Steiner had managed to get through the whole meal without mentioning Mendelhaus, and now that he did she was on her guard immediately. Not that she had any secrets to tell, but she didn't want him to see how little she really knew. It had been clear from the moment they sat down that Steiner had got her there in order to find out where she got her information. He had even hinted that he knew. Cathy felt herself flush, wondering if Krystal's absence was to be explained by the fact that he was on the phone all hours of the day to Steiner.

Steiner was eyeing her across the table.

'I bet you didn't know, for example, that our little-known Swiss company pulled out of a very big take-over in September last year – at the very last minute?'

Cathy blinked. What Steiner was saying seemed unlikely, and if it were true it seemed unlikely that Krystal shouldn't have mentioned it. It was about that time, after all, that she had first met him. But there was no time to think it through. Steiner, his eyes on hers, was waiting for his answer. Cathy shook her head.

This seemed to amuse Steiner immensely. A wide grin pushed deep folds into his cheeks, and he leaned back from the table.

'Come on, Cathy. Hey, we all have sources we want to protect, but you can't have secrets from me.'

Then, when she said nothing, he was suddenly very

162

serious, angry even. Slowly he came forward, and put both his elbows on the table.

'You see, Cathy. My name is Ben Steiner and I know.'

Cathy brought her glass to her mouth. She felt the weight sliding away from her. Suddenly she saw Steiner as if from a long way off, his hairy knuckles joined on the immaculate white cloth. She almost wanted to smile. It had all been so brief. Raised up by powerful friends – people who could move a whole market – she had made powerful enemies. Here she was sitting opposite one. A man who could not bear to be challenged in his field of expertise. A man who had used all his power to find out what was behind the upstart. In a couple of days the whole story would be out. Ryder was a featherweight, a cupcake. She knew nothing about the cosmetics industry and her information, her analysis was worthless. She would lose her job. Cathy sipped at her wine. The real question now was how to play it. Steiner still watched her over his empty bowl so thoroughly delved and scraped as to appear clean.

'What do you know, Ben?'

She was surprised at the cool authority of her voice. She had almost forgotten what it was like to feel sure of herself. Steiner sat back again, composing himself a little before speaking.

'I happen to know that Michael Varela, someone who I believe you are not unacquainted with, was in on that deal, and lost his job at Swift and Drew when Mendelhaus pulled out, and that one of the reasons he *lost* his job was a certain lack of discretion, a certain inability to keep a secret from those near to – '

Steiner stopped, shocked by the change on Cathy's face. She had stood up, steadying herself against the table as she rose, her eyes full. She stood like that for a moment, swaying slightly, and then abruptly brought her napkin to her mouth.

163

'I've bitten my tongue,' she said in a quiet voice, and she showed him the smudge of blood on the white cloth.

Leaving the lights off, Mike went through the silent apartment to the lounge where he sat heavily on the sofa, pushing his legs out straight. He had been drinking since lunch-time, and it had left him low, exhausted. In one of the bars he had come to the decision that he should tell Cathy the truth about Swift and Drew and the reason he lost his job. But now that he was back in the flat, breathing its smell, feeling the warmth of what he shared with Cathy, he felt his resolve draining away. He wanted things to stay the same. But he also wanted the pretence that he went out to work every day to end. Maybe there was some ground in between, not the whole truth and yet not outright lies either. He tried to think, but he was tired. Events would take their course. Cathy would come in and find him sitting in the dark. She would see that something was wrong and she would want to know what it was.

Mike pushed back against the sofa. Then he stood up and went to the door. He turned on the lights, removed his coat and went into the kitchen to make coffee, his mind racing. There were a hundred things he could say. He could tell her he had just lost his job. He could tell her he had been working for Swift and that he had just lost his job, that would at least be half of the truth and it would explain why he was in such a state. Mike looked at the sleeve of his suit and registered that he had removed his coat and was now standing in the kitchen making coffee.

He realised he had already taken a decision without knowing it. Here he was in the kitchen making coffee. Cathy would come in and she would suspect nothing. Maybe that was for the best. Maybe tomorrow something would turn up. He could call Rudd and ask him for a favour. The guy sympathised, anyone could see that.

Mike leaned forward and covered his face with his hands. His face flushed with anger and he brought his fist down on the counter making the kettle jump.

'Fuck it! You just have to tell her, Michael. That's all there is to it. If she wants to kick you out that's her business.'

There was a noise on the stairs and something brushed against the front door. Mike froze. Then he heard steps going on up to the floor above. In his panic he had forgotten his anger. His head was clear now. He felt as though he had entered a new space. He wanted the truth to come into their life. He loved Cathy. She loved him. She would listen and understand. He stood leaning against the sink sipping at his coffee, his eyes resting on one object and then another. And then he saw it.

It was on the crowded bookshelves which stood to the left of the kitchen door. It was buried under a pile of papers and half hidden by one of Cathy's numerous trailing plants. But Mike had so often looked at it with disguised curiosity he knew what it was immediately. Looking through the kitchen door to the front door of the flat, he went across the kitchen and removed the dossier from the shelf and put it on the kitchen table.

It was in a stiff cardboard document wallet. There was nothing marked on the outside except what looked like a telephone number written in ball-point diagonally across the front. Mike walked around the table sipping at his coffee. It was five to seven. Cathy wouldn't be home for at least another five minutes and more likely fifteen. He opened the wallet, withdrew the thick sheaf of documents and sat down.

It was difficult. There were some notes and a lot of statistical tables and then a sheaf of twenty pages held together by a paperclip, pages full of information about Erixil. A lot of it was over Mike's head but certain facts did mean something to him. It said, for example, that

165

Mendelhaus had only recently branched into advanced cosmetics as an application of technologies the company was developing with other ends in mind, and that this explained the lack of pedigree in the Mendelhaus product line. Mike read, a hand pushed into his thick brown hair, unaware of the time. *While the company has moderate penetration in several European markets with low technology products such as AubeBleue (France) and Giovanni (Italy), Erixil represents its first push into the high value added segments – for so long the sovereign territory of L'Oreal, Clarins and of course in the US of Raeburn Corporation.*

Mike sat back in his chair, his hand still pushing back the hair from his forehead, now drawn in thought. It had always been a mystery to him that Mendelhaus should be planning to buy out Raeburn when it was about to launch its own product. Could they be that uncoordinated in the company? You didn't spend millions developing a product based on market research that would be invalidated once the finance department made its move. Whoever wrote it seemed to have no doubt about the potential of the product: *Erixil breaks new ground in the application of genetic science to cosmetic treatments. In fact to say that it breaks new ground is to a certain degree misleading, for Erixil has been conceived on a different plane and is in no way a continuation of the 'research' carried out in other laboratories since the early 1970s.*

Then Mike saw the answer he was looking for: *Erixil is in fact an unanticipated spin-off from an entirely separate field of medical research being supported by the company's Medical Services Division. The real commercial potential of this spin-off was only understood very recently. The remarkable speed with which commercially available products have been manufactured and tested is a tribute to the drive and organisational abilities of Mendelhaus's management team.*

Now he understood at last: *The real commercial potential was only understood very recently.* In other words, after work had begun on the Raeburn takeover.

Mike read on. There was a list of figures relating to the technical performance of Erixil, projected out to two years. In spite of his lack of science even he could see the claims were outrageous. One comparison in particular took his notice. It was two templates of an idealised epidermis, one belonging to a nineteen-year-old girl and one to a thirty-five-year-old woman who had had the treatment. At the bottom of the page there was a note claiming a ninety per cent correlation in levels of cross-linkage. Mike frowned at the unfamiliar word, but was impressed nonetheless by all the numbers that seemed to match up. Almost unconsciously he voiced his thoughts.

'So if it was such a hot product why waste millions buying out a company you've already left behind?'

'We may never know, Michael.'

Mike's head snapped round. Cathy was in the doorway, a twisted smile on her lips. Her eyes were red, feverish, their colour all the more startling against the terrible whiteness of her skin.

'Cathy.'

'NO!'

The sudden explosion of her voice in the quiet kitchen startled them both. She started forward and snatched the documents from the table, but she was so distraught several sheets fell to the floor as she clutched them to her. Mike stared, unable to move or speak.

Cathy tried to control herself, though the tears were streaming down her face now. She closed her eyes and shook her head to clear her vision. When she spoke her voice was trembling with rage.

'I spoke to Ben Steiner this afternoon, Michael, and he told me everything about you. He told me how you had been involved in Mendelhaus on some kind of buy-out.'

167

She looked at him, her great black eyes glittering.

'Why didn't you tell me, Michael? Why did you have to lie to me?'

'Cathy.'

'LISTEN, Michael. Listen to me. I want you to leave. I want you out. Now.'

And then her head dropped and the papers began to slip from her grasp to the floor.

Michael stood up and walked towards her, his hands held loose at his sides. He didn't know what he was doing. He had never seen her in such a state, and she frightened him. He thought she would tear in two. He put his hand on her shoulder.

What happened next was unclear. She had struck him in the face, he knew that. Not a glancing blow, but directly, striking him full in the face. And a ring she was wearing or something, there must have been *something*, struck his gum so that his mouth was suddenly full of blood. And then she was screaming, tearing at him and pushing him out on to the stairs, pushing his heavy body with all the strength of her long legs. The door had closed. He had hesitated for a moment, the blood welling from the cut opened in his lip and gum, and then, shakily, his foot had found the first step down, and unable to resist the pull of the earth, the ground, the street, he had stumbled into the stairwell, down and around and then out into the rain.

20

Manhattan. January 29th, 1996.

A week in New York and Waterman still hadn't got used
to it. As he walked back to his hotel that night, with a
half-pint bottle of scotch in his pocket, he cursed the icy
wind, the slushy sidewalks, already brown with filth, the
sheer bare-faced ugliness of all that modernity gone to
seed. His raincoat didn't do anything to keep out the
cold, and even the scotch wasn't much help. He'd tried
to buy a real overcoat that morning, but the prices midtown were unreal. The only bargains to be had were made
of imitation fur, and somehow he couldn't see himself in
that kind of stuff. As he dodged the spray of slush from
a passing Cadillac he promised himself that, however bad
things got, he would never come and work in New York.

'Here's another fine mess . . .' but he was too tired to
finish the phrase. He unscrewed the cap on the bottle and
took a good long pull. It was a Korean scotch he had
never bought before and it seemed to light up two cold
little flames behind his bloodshot eyes. He stared at the
bottle astounded as it burned into his guts, and then
leaned back against a graffiti-covered wall. Coming to
New York had been a mistake. There was no way the
CDC would have put up the money for the trip, so he
had told Miller he was taking a week to see his sister. He
had been so sure that something would turn up. Two days

after he'd read the *Fortune* article he'd gone out to buy some of the Mendelhaus product, Erixil, which was supposed to be at the bottom of the upheavals in the cosmetics industry in the hope that it would suggest something. He carried a jar of the stuff in his pocket like a lucky rabbit's foot all the time. But since then nothing new had come up. Now it was impossible to see why he had been so optimistic. He had always followed his instincts, and they had proved, generally speaking, and with the notable exception of his marriage, reliable. The trouble was he was running out of room in which to make his mistakes. He took another pull at the bottle and was surprised to find it almost empty. Then he lurched away from the wall and started to shuffle off in the direction of his hotel.

He was still a block away from his front door when he saw the little Catholic church tucked away between two 1950s tower blocks. He had walked past it at least a dozen times before, but this was the first time he'd really noticed it. The door was ajar and from inside came a friendly yellow light. Waterman didn't normally feel too good about churches. He hadn't taken communion since well before the divorce, and that was more than ten years ago now. Ten years, eight months, to be precise. But tonight the street was so cold and the light so welcoming that he felt an odd kind of curiosity. Besides, he was in no hurry to get back to his room. He'd had enough of the spongy bed with its blue polyester cover, the swirly brown pattern of the carpets, and the ceaselessly flickering TV.

It certainly wasn't a church like the ones he'd been used to. Out West they were big, airy and modern, all fitted out with PA systems and modern sculpture. This church was old, a place of candle-light and shadows, almost clandestine in comparison. The stone angels who stood on either side of the narrow windows were like sentinels, and one of them carried a sword. There was a link here, Waterman sensed, with the early days of Christianity, when the faithful worshipped in secret, fearful of persecution, their chapels sometimes hidden away below ground, where no one would think of looking for them. He stood for a few moments by the door, afraid that his presence might not be welcome, that they might take him for a drunk and throw him out. But who were *they*? The place was completely empty.

He sat down on the end of a pew, half way down the aisle, and looked up towards the altar. There were two banks of candles just in front of the wooden altar-rail, supported by iron frames. Most of the candles were burning low, and long fingers of wax hung down underneath. It was cold, but the sweet, morbid smell of incense was still heavy in the air.

High above the altar was a plaster representation of Christ crucified. In the newer churches the image of the crucifixion was usually restrained, artistic: a bronze sculpture or a wooden carving, the body of Christ one or two feet high. This model had nothing to do with art: nearly life-sized, its only aim was to show the meaning of agony. Crimson blood poured from Christ's hands and feet, from around the crown of thorns, from the wound in his side. Waterman had seen pieces like this before, in some of the old Mexican churches over the border. To him they spoke of the cruelty of man, of his guilt: *this is what you did*, they always seemed to say. And with the guilt came the fear. Waterman sometimes wondered if he would ever really be rid of it. He looked at the figure again: the thick black nails, the crown of thorns, the wound in his side . . .

When he woke up he saw that an old woman was standing in front of the altar. She seemed to be crying. Every now and then her shoulders shook, but then, as she turned her face to the side for a moment he could see that she was in fact laughing. Harry frowned, and leaned forward. New York was full of crazy people. *And*

171

I'm one of them, he thought. But there was something else. Something had come to him while he was asleep, or maybe it was before he nodded off. He looked at the laughing woman, trying to think what it was. Then he looked up at the crucified man. The sight of the wound jogged something in his memory, something he had almost forgotten: on Ray Bladon's body his regular GP, Dr Fanshawe, had found a small scar that he couldn't account for. It had been a few inches below his heart, the aftermath of some minor operation, so Fanshawe had guessed. Presumably the operation had taken place at Mendelhaus around the same time as the cosmetic surgery.

And that was why the memory came to him now: the water that sprang from Christ's side had been a symbol of regeneration, like the water which sprang from the rock when Moses struck it with his staff. Waterman remembered that from Sunday school, although he didn't know where it came from. Bladon had been seeking his own kind of regeneration, McArthur too. They wanted their own private miracles, courtesy of the cheque-book and the gold card, miracles reserved for the few. And yet what had they come away with? Death had claimed them within a matter of months, a matter of days in McArthur's case, as if they were being punished for their presumption.

It wasn't so different from Mendelhaus's other customers: the ladies who queued up for the latest miracle products. He reached into his coat pocket and pulled out the neat white cardboard box with the jar of Erixil inside it. There was writing on the side, elegant palace script, but too small for Waterman to make out easily. He got up and moved closer to the altar. By the flickering light of the candles he read: *There is nothing inevitable in decay, no corruption that cannot be redeemed. With the instruments of our own creation we can re-create ourselves.*

The words struck him as somehow blasphemous: Man

172

usurping God. Except that it wasn't *Man*, it was *men*, a few men, working away behind closed doors for a Swiss company that was about as accessible as the Pentagon. For weeks now he'd been trying to establish if Ray Bladon really had gone there for treatment before his death, and he hadn't gotten anywhere. The furthest he had gotten on the telephone was the public relations department. As for the girl he had seen on the cover of *Fortune*, the one who was supposed to know all about them, she hadn't returned his calls to her office. And now that he finally had her home number there was no answer at all, just the same dumb answering machine: *This is Cathy Ryder. I'm afraid there's no one here at the moment, but if you'd like to leave a message . . .*

He read the writing on the Erixil box again. It was just a load of marketing nonsense, he told himself, and it wasn't even original. He was sure he had heard those very words before, although he didn't know where. The problem irritated him. He reached into his paper bag for the scotch but then remembered where he was. It had been years ago, he was sure of that, probably when he was still at Stanford. And yet that meant it had to have made a big impression on him, whatever it was, otherwise why would he remember it? He stopped looking at the words as printed on the Erixil box and tried to visualise them differently: in conventional print, on a TV screen, in his own handwriting.

It was then that it came to him. The very same words had been written in capital letters in his lecture notes, notes he had studied over and over again in preparing for his final exams. The lectures had been given by a young professor. What was his name? Gerard? Gaynor? Harry squeezed his eyes shut and sat back against the pew. Geiger. That was it. Edward Geiger. He remembered it now. Geiger's main themes hadn't been that close to Waterman's specialities, but he'd gone along to the lectures because of the man's reputation. Everyone raved about his ideas on genetics, which were bold although often, Waterman had found, quite impossible to follow. It was all the math that made it tough. Still, at the time he'd been impressed enough to write Geiger's words in red ball-point along the top of two pages. And presumably someone who had ended up working for Mendelhaus had been equally impressed. Unless, of course, it was Geiger himself . . .

But that was absurd. Geiger was a man of science. He had always been cut out for the very forefront of pure research, whether it was biology, math or physics. His work would go on at universities and institutes, free from commercial pressures. He would never have wasted his time producing face creams, even if the face creams were good. He'd always given the impression of thinking much bigger than that. Waterman resolved to check it out. Geiger would probably turn out to be at M.I.T. or something, but you could never be sure, maybe he would be able to tell him something about viral cancers.

He shook his head. For a moment he had been carried away by his own ideas. Where was the money to come from for further research? Suddenly overwhelmed with a feeling of anger and frustration, he finished the bottle in one go. Then he lurched up out of his seat and made his way along the aisle.

As he reached the door he noticed a little shrine in the wall to his right. Inside the shrine was a cross and a painting lit by three candles of the Archangel Gabriel appearing to the Virgin Mary. The angel was resplendent in gold and silver, the Virgin a small figure, dressed in a dowdy grey.

'Just a poor Jewish girl,' Waterman thought to himself, 'after all.'

21

Manhattan. February 3rd, 1996.

The milk in the carton was sour. Mike went through to
the lounge and put his coffee on the television set. It was
after eleven and his father had just left for his Saturday
walk down to the pool hall. Mike sat for a long time
listening to the rain on the window, sipping his drink and
staring into space. He had been awake since six, but
hadn't wanted to get out of bed until his father had slammed the door.

He was alone now, struggling, trying to work out his
next move. After he had left Cathy's apartment he had
waited for a time in the road, a Kleenex against his bleeding lip. He had wanted to go back up, to explain everything, but the driving rain and the pain in his lip and
mouth made him so angry all he could do was walk away,
almost knocking over the man standing on the sidewalk
drinking tomato soup from a styrofoam cup. That was
just over a week ago. To Mike it seemed like it had only
just happened.

Nine days. They were stacked against him like the dirty
dishes in Pop Varela's chipped enamel sink. On Thursday,
exactly one week after everything had fallen apart, he had
called Cathy's apartment, getting the answering machine.
The sound of her voice, even recorded, made him feel
like he had been turned inside out. He had put down the

175

phone without a word, and regretted it instantly. Maybe she was waiting for his call. Maybe she was sitting by the answer machine waiting. He only had to speak for her to pick up the phone.

He had redialled, his hand shaking.

'Cathy, this is Mike.'

There was nothing. He had so expected her to pick up the phone that the silence threw him completely. As always, when unsure of himself he tried to be funny.

'So. You don't want to answer. There are only three possible explanations for this: either, one, you are not there; two, you are there but don't want to speak to me; or three, you are there, desperately want to speak to me, but are trapped under something heavy and can't reach the phone.'

Then it seemed to him that his tone was all wrong. She knew he could be funny. He had to prove to her that he could be serious; honest. He had slammed down the phone, cursing his own stupidity.

Since then he hadn't been near the phone. It made him angry to think that even though he had left a message she still wouldn't call him. It seemed to show how little she felt for him. How little she trusted him. Staring out at the driving rain, he brought the cup to his lips, his mind drifting back over the time they had spent together. How could she believe, after the times they'd had, that all he wanted was to find out about Mendelhaus! Mike sipped at his coffee. He was ready to forget the whole thing.

He stood up and walked around the tiny lounge. He switched on the ABC news and watched. There was a shot of the Big Room at Salomon with a trader screaming into the phone. He switched it off.

He put on his old green combat jacket, pulled up the hood and went out into the rain. He didn't know where he was going and he didn't care as long as it got him away from the house and his thoughts.

At four o'clock he was back in front of the window, looking out at the dead light, a cold cup of coffee in his hands.

He stood up and walked around the room anti-clockwise. Then he switched on the TV without turning up the sound. He watched the images for a while. Then he walked over to the oval mirror hanging over the gas fire by a chrome chain. He looked at himself. He hadn't shaved for three days. He closed his eyes. Then he opened them again.

'You look about ready to jump,' he said, smiling nervously. Then, exhaling noisily he went to the phone and dialled the number. Her recorded voice. She sounded vulnerable, far away.

'Cathy, this is Mike.'

He took a deep breath, and tried to control his voice.

'Like they say in the films – I'm losing altitude. No, don't worry, I'm not gonna crack another joke. I just wanted . . . I have to see you, Cathy. It may seem impossible from where you are, but that night, the way things looked, it was all wrong. I just wanted to find out . . . oh, hell.'

He held the receiver away from his face, as though he might see Cathy there, reduced, looking back at him.

'Cathy it's too complicated to explain on the phone. We have to – I have to see you.'

He looked around the room, his mind racing.

'That bar. You remember that bar we used to meet in near Webber. What's the name, Malone's, Molloy's – you know the one. It has a grandfather clock in the bar. I'll be there at seven o'clock Monday evening. Please – be there.'

He put the phone back and looked across at the TV screen. A young woman was talking into the camera, looking out at him and smiling, but he couldn't hear her voice.

177

22

Manhattan. February 5th, 1996.

The door gave way with the second kick and they were inside. The apartment was dark: the blinds were closed and just a few shafts of daylight reached up to the ceiling above the window. There was a faint smell of perfume in the air, and a trace of stale liquor. In the corner of the big room, the small red light on the answering machine winked silently on and off.

They were two men: one in his forties, big, with a grey moustache, the other man leaner, with greasy brown hair and a mass of uneven stubble on his chin. The big man pulled on a pair of white cotton gloves and went to the desk. He switched on the angle-poise lamp and began looking rapidly through each drawer in turn. On one side of the knee-hole he found heaps of old bills, bank statements and tax demands, on the other side sheet music, letters and several plastic wallets full of photographs. He put the letters into the pocket of his Burberry raincoat without attempting to read them and flicked through the pictures. Most of them had been taken at a graduation ceremony somewhere, others at Christmas or Thanksgiving: groups of young people mainly, smiling, drinking, pulling faces at the camera. Cathy Ryder herself was only in a few of them. He noticed that her hair was longer. He put one picture in his pocket and dropped all the rest on the floor. The bookshelves beside the kitchen door were next.

A minute later the other man came out of the bedroom.

'This is all I got, Mr Chaney,' he said, holding up a large volume with a Japanese-style watercolour on the front.

Chaney leafed through a couple of pages.

'It's just a goddamn scrapbook, right?' he said. 'History.'

'Yeah, but this?'

He pointed to a group of yellowed cuttings covering two pages near the front of the book. They were nearly twenty years old.

'History,' said Chaney. 'Check out that shit over there, okay?'

He dropped the scrapbook and carried on searching through the shelves, pulling out the books and any scraps of paper in between them. O'Brien left the scrapbook open on the sofa and began going through the cupboards beside the fireplace. He found a ten-dollar bill lying behind a pile of CDs and stuffed it into his top pocket. Outside, a car went by sounding its horn. Someone in the street shouted *fuck you*.

'Oh boy, oh boy,' said O'Brien sarcastically as a wine glass rolled off the top of the amplifier and smashed on the floor. 'This place is a real mess.'

'We want a mess,' said Chaney. 'Make it look like a crack addict. And take some jewellery or something. Take the fucking CDs.'

O'Brien left the cupboards and went back into the bedroom. He came out a minute later holding a silk kimono up against him showing his yellow smile. Chaney was too absorbed to notice. He had just found the document wallet with the Erixil notes inside it. He pulled out the contents and looked at them closely.

'Something here,' he said. He slipped the notes into his bag. 'You check around the phone.'

The phone and the answering machine stood on a little mahogany card table, covered in green baize cloth. O'Brien swept all the papers off the surface into a big leather briefcase; the two notepads, the handful of business cards lying on a porcelain plate, even the junk mail with the postage-paid envelopes. As he did so a book of matches with a restaurant logo on the cover fell to the floor. He didn't bother to pick it up.

'Okay, that's it, right? Now the crazy stuff, right?'

'Wait,' said the big man. 'I want the messages. Then you can do your thing.'

He walked over to the answering machine and carefully picked it up. On the bottom was a small card held by two little plastic brackets. On the card was printed: REMINDER, with the number 717 written in ball-point underneath.

'Seven one seven,' he repeated, putting the machine down again and pressing the play button. 'Got that, O'Brien?'

An electronic female voice said: '*Number of messages received: six.*'

The incoming cassette rewound for a few seconds; then there came a high-pitched bleep and it began to play. They stood in the half darkness listening.

'Cathy, this is Danielle here.' It was a young woman's voice. 'So what happened about our lunch date? I hope nothing's up, or did you just forget? Anyway give me a call, okay? Maybe we can do something else. Well, *ciao bella.*'

The electronic voice followed: '*Monday, eight twenty-two pm.*'

'She's been gone more than a week,' said O'Brien. 'Just like I said.'

180

There came another bleep, a moment's silence, then the sound of someone hanging up.

'*Tuesday, seven forty-five pm.*'

Another bleep. Then the same thing again.

'*Wednesday, ten o'clock pm.*'

The two men exchanged glances.

'Hello, Cathy, this is Michael Paine. I'm just calling to ask if you could ring the office soon. We tried calling you at Mendelhaus but they say you left already. Your secretary doesn't seem to know where we can reach you, so if you call to get your messages perhaps you could get in touch. Thanks. Bye . . . *Thursday, nine fifty-one am.*'

'Why don't we just take the tape?' said O'Brien. He was getting nervous.

'Don't be stupid,' said the other man.

Now there was another voice, another male caller, only this one was different, anxious. There was a tremor in his voice.

'Cathy, this is Mike . . . So you don't want to answer.' – A shaky laugh, then a kind of TV commentator's voice. 'There are only three possible explanations for this . . .'

'I think this is lover boy,' said O'Brien.

The big man was writing in a pocket-book.

'Sounds like they had words or something, don't it?'

'. . . you are there, desperately want to speak to me, but are trapped under something heavy . . .'

There was a click and then: '*Thursday, nine thirteen pm.*'

The big man kept on writing. Then the last message began: 'Cathy this is Mike . . . Like they say in the films – I'm losing altitude. No don't worry. I'm not going to crack another joke. I just wanted . . . I have to see you, Cathy. It may seem impossible from where you are . . .'

'The guy's got it bad,' said O'Brien. 'I think he wants her even more than you do.'

'. . . I have to see you. That bar. You remember that

bar we used to meet in near Webber. What's the name, Malone's, Molloy's . . .'

'I think he means O'Malleys.'

'. . . I'll be there at seven o'clock Monday evening. Please be there.'

Chaney looked at his watch. It was almost half past three in the morning.

'Time to go,' he said and switched off the light. 'I'll see you later.'

Leaving O'Brien by the telephone he picked his way back to the door.

As it closed behind him the electronic voice said: '*End of final message.*'

23

Manhattan. February 5th, 1996.

The Data Centre was housed in a long gallery at the top
of the library building. It was half past eight and sunlight
streamed in through the windows in the far wall, blanking
out the computer screens on the other side. In the corridor
outside a team of women cleaners were wheeling a trolley
around, breaking the silence with the occasional burst of
Spanish that carried into the furthest corners of the building. It was still too early for most of the students, although
on his way in Waterman had seen a handful of them in
the big Reading Room, each one seated at least ten places
from the next.

There were two sources of information in the Data
Centre: a computerised index of all the books and articles
in the library, and, on microfiche, copies of major newspapers going back to the 1950s. It was old technology,
but it was good enough. Waterman began with the index.

The program was easy to use. You could search through
the library according to author, title, subject, date of
publication, or any combination of the four. You could
further narrow the search by choosing articles or books
only. Waterman asked for articles only, defined the search
period as 1975 onwards and opposite AUTHOR, typed
in the letters G-E-I-G-E-R.

SEARCHING SEARCHING SEARCHING

183

The word flashed on and off in the middle of the screen. Waterman folded his arms and waited. A student, a freshman judging from the tweed jacket and the short cropped hair, came in and sat at one of the other terminals. Neither of them said anything. Waterman wanted a cigarette but there were big NO SMOKING signs everywhere. He could feel his pulse quickening, like a finger tapping against the wall of his stomach.

SEARCHING SEARCHING SEARCHING

The system worked at stone-age speed. If he had been back home he would have called in to the *Herald* and used the Nexis database. It worked a lot faster, and for anything since the early '80s was a far bigger source of information than a campus library. You could use more sophisticated search terms too. But Geiger was a scientist, and scientists published papers. A look at his titles should be all that was needed to get a good idea what he was working on – and where. *If we use the instruments of our own creation we can re-create ourselves . . .*

Suddenly the screen went blank. Then a panel appeared announcing that there were fifty-three items conforming to the search criteria. *Fifty-three*. The man had been busy. Waterman stabbed a button and the screen instantly lit up with text.

The articles on the library system were listed chronologically. The first two were by a Dr Rudolf Geiger, one published in *Antiquity* and the other in *History Today*. They were both about military technology in ancient China. Then came an article by Marie Herbert-Geiger on adult education in Germany. On the bottom of the first page was listed an article in *Nature*, published in 1978 entitled 'Towards mathematical prediction of protein folding'. Waterman had to go to the next page to see the author, but he already knew he had found his man. The behaviour of proteins had been the subject of Geiger's lectures at Stanford. The screen went blank again for an

184

instant and then the name appeared, right on the top left-hand side: Dr Edward Geiger.

Waterman looked down the rest of the page, and then on to the next. The articles listed were all by Edward Geiger, only some time in 1980 he had become a Professor. Waterman took out his notebook and scribbled down the details. Geiger had specialised in cell biology and biochemistry, but the range of problems he had covered was extraordinary. A year after work on protein folding – an area of vital importance in the manufacture of man-made proteins – he had moved on to problems of how the cell cycle was controlled. He published a paper in *Annual Review of Biochemistry* entitled 'The action of cyclin and cdc2 in the regulation of mitosis'. A year later he was looking inside the cell nucleus at how genes were activated and de-activated. There were several papers in that field including two in *Science*: 'Protein control of regulatory genes – theoretical models', and 'Studies on the regulation of protein encodement'. Waterman sat back from the screen and blinked. He had read articles covering the same subject, but it looked like Geiger had studied the issues years before the rest even if much of what he published at the time was described as 'theoretical'.

By 1982 the rate of new papers was accelerating. It looked like Geiger had begun to concentrate on the key control functions of the living cells and the genes within them. He seemed to approach each subject from a number of different angles, exhausting one avenue of research before hurrying on to the next – then going back again to apply his newly-acquired knowledge to older problems. In *Cell* he published 'RNA fragments used in the inter-regulation of gene blocks', in *Nature* there followed 'The action of extra cellular substances on the Ribosomal gene block'; in *Science* he wrote 'Recurring patterns in box genes: accelerating the analysis of regulatory functions', and two other papers in the same field. Even staring at the humming grey and white screen, Waterman could sense Geiger's restlessness, his impatience. It was as if the pursuit of knowledge was not enough in itself, as if Geiger had been seeking an answer, a key, some great advancement that would not wait. The pace of his work was frenetic. He was one child prodigy who hadn't burnt out at nineteen.

Then, in 1986, the papers stopped. In *Scientific American* Geiger published an article entitled 'Homeobox genes and positioning of vital organs in insects and vertebrates'. It was the last item against his name. Waterman ran another check on the computer, asking for books as well as articles this time, but the result was the same; for ten years Geiger had published nothing.

Waterman took down the reference number of the last article and followed directions to the periodicals section. The *Scientific American*s were stored in dark red binders, twelve at a time. Geiger's piece was in the May issue, illustrated by colourful diagrams of DNA strands, with systematic breakdowns of functional groups of molecules. It was clear that Geiger had been making comparisons between genetic codes of insects and human beings – not simply vertebrates as the title of the article suggested.

As usual, at the bottom of the opening page there was a box containing a short biography of the author. It was the richest catalogue of academic excellence Waterman had ever seen:

> Edward Geiger is Sterling Professor
> of Molecular Biophysics and Bio-
> chemistry at Yale University. He is
> a fellow of the University of Cali-
> fornia, Berkeley, Honorary Pro-
> fessor of the Institute of Chemical
> Physics of the USSR Academy of
> Sciences, and a fellow of All Souls

College, Oxford. He is currently employed as a senior research director at Westway Pharmaceuticals Inc. He graduated from Princeton in 1970, aged 17, and obtained his PhD from Harvard. Shortly afterwards he received a MacArthur Fellowship and two years later the Sakurai Prize for Mathematics thanks to his pioneering work on the quantum mechanics of complex molecules. He is currently spending a one-year sabbatical at the Lawrence Livermore Laboratory.

Waterman read through it again. The biography confirmed his impression of Geiger as polymath, yet he could not believe that the course of studies had been random. It was all moving in the same direction, one that the man himself might only have perceived dimly. The one part of the biography Waterman could not make fit was the last: the Lawrence Livermore was best known for its work in high energy physics – lasers and that kind of thing. What help could all that be to a biochemist?

24

Manhattan. February 5th, 1996.

At a quarter to eight Mike went through to the phone and dialled the number. There was no Cathy, just the machine: *There's no one here at the moment, but if you'd like to leave a message* . . . Mike rested his head against the dirty perspex of the cabin. From where he stood he could see a stretch of the dark wooden bar, and a swing door going through to the kitchens. He let the message run and then hung up. There didn't seem to be any point in saying anything.

He sat for another quarter of an hour watching people come in and out. There was a young couple sitting in the opposite corner of the room, whispering to each other, and a big guy sitting with his back to him, hunched over a beer. The place was done up like a Dublin bar around the turn of the century. There were ceramic pumps for the beer, and old photographs of people in high collars with constipated expressions. On the opposite wall a long mirror proclaimed that Guinness was good for you. The bar was quiet except for the whispering of the couple which was beginning to get on Mike's nerves.

He didn't want to move. He couldn't bring himself to believe that Cathy wasn't going to show. He imagined her rushing along the street, her heavy hair blowing like a black flag in the wind. Every time someone walked into the bar he looked up expecting to meet her eyes.

Nine o'clock came and still there was no sign.

Then the young couple got up to leave and the guy said something which made his friend, a greasy brunette with a big whore's mouth, laugh out loud. Mike shot an irritated glance across the room and felt his blood run to ice. Reflected in the mirror on the other side of the bar he saw the face of the big guy who was hunched over his empty glass. In the moment he looked up he had caught this man's eyes fixed on him. Now he was looking down at his glass and all Mike could see was his grey hair combed back over his big brute head.

The couple left the bar and Mike was alone with the man. The stranger lifted his head slightly and Mike lowered his eyes which were on the table either side his empty glass. He didn't want the guy to think he was watching him. Maybe he was just a fag. Maybe this was a gay bar. Mike looked across at the bar where the barman was talking to a customer in jogging clothes and cleaning a glass. Then his eyes drifted back to the stranger.

This time there was no room for doubt. The man looked him straight in the face and smiled. Mike looked at him for a moment and then lowered his eyes. He had a big head and was marked with deep scars like shrapnel wounds. His mouth was overshadowed by the bar of a thickly growing grey moustache. Then he remembered Cathy's stories about being followed and his heart started going like someone was elbowing him in the ribs. He felt the sweat break out on his brow.

Where was Cathy? What was happening? He had the clearest feeling that she was in danger and that the man on the other side of the bar knew something about it. His mind was racing, but he couldn't make any sense of what he knew. How did the guy know he was going to come here to meet Cathy? Was he tapping her phone? Mike

189

looked up, his fists clenched. He was ready to wipe the smile from the other guy's face, but he was no longer looking at him. And as Mike watched him the certainty of recognition began to evaporate.

Without knowing what he was doing, he got to his feet and started to move across the room. The other man kept his head down, but Mike felt he was tensed, ready. A tremor of fear shook him. He was afraid. For himself. For Cathy. In the next moment he was out in the street running for his parked car.

He drove hunched over the wheel, white-knuckled. At West 88th Street he threw the wheel over, and smacked the tyres of the Toyota up onto the sidewalk. Not even bothering to close the door, he sprinted across the street and up to the door of Cathy's building. He pressed her bell for a couple of seconds and then let himself in. As he ran through the lobby he noticed a fat mail order catalogue sticking out of her letter box. He ran up the stairs, taking the steps three at a time. It seemed to take for ever. He felt the heavy Irish beer at the back of his throat. He was ready to vomit.

At her door he stopped and tried to control his breathing. In a sudden lucid instant he had a picture of the apartment on the other side of the door. Cathy was there, looking up at the ceiling, already stiff and cold. Her legs were spread apart, the bare feet twisted outwards. There was blood on the floor. Hardly able to control his hand Mike pushed his key into the door and watched with horror as it rode back on the hinges. The wood around the mortise lock was splintered. Squeezing his eyes shut, he stepped through into the darkness and switched on the light.

The air rushed out of him as he took in the scene. There were papers scattered everywhere. One of the drawers from the desk in the study was on the kitchen table. Cathy's clothes were strewn along the hall where several of the pictures had been smashed. A draught blowing along the hall told Mike a window was open in Cathy's bedroom. Papers stirred on the floor.

'Cathy?'

His voice sounded weak, scared. He cleared his throat, and started to make his way along the hall towards the bedroom.

'Cathy?'

Her door was pushed to but not closed. The current of cold air opened and closed it. For a moment Mike couldn't bring himself to push the door back. There was a smell, a bad smell coming from the room. He brought his hand to his mouth. He thought he would be sick. Suddenly the thought of the car in the street, left open to anyone who wanted to take it, brought him up sharply. He turned and started to make his way along the passage to the door. But then he stopped and as if being pulled by wires, walked back to the bedroom and pushed open the door.

The smell in the bedroom was so powerful he gagged for a moment, bringing his sleeve across his mouth. He fumbled for the light switch, but when he found it nothing happened. From the light of the hallway all he could see was the opposite wall. The area of the bed was in darkness. He froze. There was writing on the wall; daubed clumsily, two words: *PORCA MADONNA*. By now his eyes were nearly accustomed to the half light and he could make out a bedside lamp. He went across the room unsteadily.

What he saw in the sudden brilliance was Cathy's bed, the sheets twisted and smeared with something dark. He looked closer and then brought his hand to his mouth. He stumbled out of the room and into the bathroom.

Even when he had finished vomiting his stomach still convulsed. But there was nothing left to spew. He wiped the perspiration from his face and then, taking some more paper, wiped his mouth and chin. His legs were trembling and the shit smell which seemed to fill the air frightened him. Her room had been empty, but that didn't mean a thing. He had read about bloody torsos in cupboards, pieces of flesh jamming the waste disposal. He had to look.

25

Manhattan. February 6th, 1996.

'So you don't know if anything's missing, is that right?'

The cop stood in the middle of the room with his fists on his hips, as if he thought the whole thing was a waste of his time. He was a shortish, stocky guy with a pock-marked face and lot of angry-looking spots on his neck. His name was Officer Bales.

'I don't want to touch anything,' said Mike defensively. 'And I wouldn't know if something was really missing anyhow. It's not my stuff.'

'But you *are* living here, right?'

'No. I kind of did for a while, but not any more.'

'I see. And you moved out when?'

Officer Bales reached into his top pocket and pulled out a notebook. Mike felt the blood rising slowly to his face. He hadn't wanted to talk about all this.

'About ten days ago.'

'But you still got keys. A set of keys.'

'Yes.'

'And you let yourself in, you said. Yesterday night.'

'Yes, but I could see the door was damaged.'

Officer Bales was writing it all down. Mike hoped that was that, and that they could turn to more important things, but he was disappointed.

'And why was it that you moved out, sir?'

Mike sighed.

'I . . . I didn't feel comfortable . . . I mean we decided . . .'

'You had a bust-up or something?'

Mike sat down on the arm of the sofa. The scrapbook was still open where he had found it.

'Yes, kind of.'

Officer Bales nodded and wrote down some more.

'And you came back for what reason?'

'I arranged to meet her. She didn't show up, so I got worried. She'd said she'd seen some men following her a week or two back. I didn't think anything of it at the time, but . . .'

'Why didn't you just call up, Mr Varela?' said Officer Bales. 'I mean, what made you think she'd be in?'

'I told you, I was worried. I'd called up a couple of times before and left messages, but I didn't hear anything back. I thought maybe someone in the building might know something.'

Officer Bales looked puzzled.

'I thought you said you'd arranged to meet her. How was that?'

'Well it wasn't a firm arrangement,' said Mike. What would it take to get this guy off his back? 'I mean I asked her to meet me. I left a message on the answering machine – right over there.'

For the moment Officer Bales seemed to have run out of difficult questions. But he didn't look very convinced. He sucked his teeth as he wrote down what Mike said, as if resisting the urge to put the cuffs on him right away. Then he put the notebook back inside his pocket and began walking about.

'They did over the whole place like this, huh?'

'The bedroom's even worse,' Mike said, and immediately wished he hadn't.

'Yeah? Let's take a look.'

Mike got up and pushed open the door into the bedroom. He'd had the windows open since the night before, but the stink was still there. So was the graffiti, written in shit, on the wall.

'Finger painting,' said Mike. 'Nice isn't it?'

Bales looked at it.

'*Porca Madonna*?' he said. 'Is that Italian?'

'Yes,' said Mike. 'I guess so.'

Bales wrote down some more in his book. Then he asked: 'Ain't *you* Italian, Mr Varela?'

'No, I am not,' said Mike. 'I'm an American. And if you want to know, my father was born in Mexico.'

'A Mex, no kidding?' said Bales. And Mike could sense his pleasure: all along he'd been struggling with a sense of social inferiority and now it was gone. *He was just another spic after all . . .*

'Well we see this kinda stuff a lot I gotta tell you,' he said, relaxing a little. 'Usually they're lookin' for a fix – hell, they don't know what the fuck they're doin' half the time. Outa their heads, you know?'

They walked back out into the main room. Mike didn't say anything.

'And you say you still have no idea where Miss Ryder is?' Bales asked.

'None. She didn't say anything to me about going anywhere, and when I rang up Webber Atlantic they wouldn't tell me. Said they had to be specially careful these days, whatever that means.'

Officer Bales nodded slowly.

'Well, we called them up this morning too. And they told us she'd made a trip to Europe more than a week ago. In fact just about the time you say you moved out.'

'To Europe?' said Mike. 'Where in Europe?'

'I'm not sure if we established that, but it does seem like your concern was a little premature, don't it.'

Mike sat down again on the arm of the sofa. He felt a

wave of relief break over him. So she'd gone to Europe.
It meant she hadn't ignored his messages, she just hadn't
received them. Maybe when she returned things would
be calmer, and he'd have a better chance to sort things
out, unless . . . unless she hadn't gone alone.

'Did they say if she was on business?' he asked anxi-
ously.

Officer Bales shrugged and shook his head.

'We've asked her employers to tell her about all this as
soon as they can. In the meantime we'll want to dust for
prints some time, okay?' He looked around at the papers
and books strewn all over the floor. 'You can clear this
up if you want to, only try not to touch any smooth
surfaces, okay? Especially not around the handles of
drawers and cupboards and stuff. You'd better give me
your address and number so we can fix up a time. That's
if you don't mind coming back, of course,' he added.

Mike said he didn't mind and gave Officer Bales the
information. Bales stood for a few moments, surveying
the mess as if trying to commit the scene to memory.
Then he headed back to the door.

'We're assuming of course that since you got a key from
the owner, she still don't mind you coming and going,
OK?' he said, looking back from the passage. 'If we hear
different, we'll be sure and let you know.'

Mike closed the door and stood for a moment in silence.
He burned to know more about where Cathy had gone,
and why, and – he couldn't shut out this new anxiety –
with whom? But he was being stupid, he told himself. It
sounded like she'd left town just a day or two after their
bust-up. She couldn't have found someone else that fast.
On the other hand, who could say what standing offers
she might have had? Or what old flames to go back to in
times of crisis. More than likely there were scores of guys
in her circle who would have been only too glad to let
her cry on their shoulders. He could just imagine their

friendly advice: *Cathy, you need a break, a change of scene. Why not come to Europe? I've been looking for an excuse to go myself* . . . No, by the time she got back it would be harder than ever to explain that she had been wrong about him. She would have made up her mind. A dreadful certainty began to grip him: he had lost her, he was too late.

He looked at the room with anger now. A minute ago he was getting ready to do everything he could to put things right. He would clear up the mess, repair the door, deal with the cops – all so she would see that he was still looking out for her, that he really cared. But now he feared she would only resent his interference. Maybe she would even think he'd ransacked the place himself, like Officer Bales had done. Well, she could clear up the place for herself.

He picked up his jacket from the arm of the sofa and pulled it on. As he was walking back to the door he noticed the little book of matches lying on the floor beside the desk. It came from a restaurant in the South Street Seaport called La Villa where they'd gone together on their first date. They had been back there twice, the last time just a few days before it had all gone so wrong. He stooped down and picked it up. At least she could let him have one small souvenir.

26

Manhattan. February 9th, 1996.

'I'm sorry, but I'm afraid we're not allowed to give out information on the movements or whereabouts of staff.'

The female voice on the end of the line was unemotional, mechanical. It could have belonged to a robot.

'But we'll be sure to pass on your message at the earliest opportunity.'

'Look,' Mike implored, 'I just want to know when . . .'

'Thank you for calling, Mr Valera.'

'*Varela!* My name's – '

He heard a click and then the line went dead. He took the receiver from his ear and closed his eyes for a minute. It was his sixth call to Webber Atlantic in three days, and always he got the same answer: *We'll be sure to pass on your message.* He had tried everything to get more information, but they had every angle covered. He'd tried asking for Cathy in person, for the European research desk, for the personnel department, hoping to find someone, anyone, who would tell him where she was. But no matter how he went about it, he always ended up talking to the same woman, the same robotic voice. It was as if they had some special procedure for protecting Cathy Ryder from unwanted calls, a procedure that had been perfected with constant use. He remembered Cathy telling him about a lot of weird calls at the office. Maybe

198

that was why they wouldn't tell him anything. His best hope had been Brad Matthews in Institutional Sales, but it turned out he was on a training course in Chicago and wouldn't be back for a week.

Of course, they could have been keeping him in the dark for quite a different reason: she was in the office all the time and didn't want to speak to him. It was a crazy notion, but maybe she was really right here in New York. She could have come back to the apartment already knowing about the break-in, seen how he had cleared everything up for her, and decided simply to avoid him. She could have been staying all the time with her new boyfriend, the one who had taken her to Europe. *You need a complete change of scene, Cathy. Why don't you take the spare room for a while?* She could be waiting for Michael Varela to give up and disappear. Maybe she hated him that much. For the hundredth time he berated himself for not telling her about his connection with Mendelhaus. If he had been honest from the beginning, honest instead of trying to be clever, maybe she would still be there for him.

He slammed the receiver down and got to his feet. He was thinking like a madman! She had been in Europe and she was still in Europe. The same six messages waited for her on the answering machine, two of them his. If she had been back she would have heard them. She would have heard how he wanted to speak to her, how he needed to talk to her more than anything. She would have been in touch. She couldn't have buried all her old feelings for him so quickly. And she wouldn't have steered clear of her own apartment just because he had a key. Cathy wasn't like that: she was strong. And yet he still came to her apartment every night, just to see whether she was there, or if the answering machine had been re-set, or if the mail-order catalogue sticking out the top of her mail box was gone. He didn't care any more if she thought he was trespassing. She couldn't just vanish from his life like this, without even giving him a chance to explain. It wasn't adult. It wasn't fair.

He threw himself down on the sofa and stuck a cigarette between his lips. Then he looked around for his disposable lighter. He searched his pockets but all he could find was the book of matches from La Villa in the South Street Seaport, the one he had found on the floor. He stared at it for a moment, remembering the last time he and Cathy had dined there, the silly jokes he'd told her and the way, over coffee, she had looked at him with a big smile on her face for no reason at all. He had asked her what she was smiling at, and she'd said because she was happy. And he remembered the giddy, almost overwhelming joy that he had felt: *She wants me, she wants ME.* He shook his head in disbelief now. How could he have imagined that it would be so easy?

He opened up the book of matches and was about to tear one out when he noticed something written on the inside of the flap. He went over to the desk light so that he could read it more clearly. It said: *Ernst Krystal (212) 623–9111.* It was Cathy's handwriting.

Mike's mind began to race. He and Cathy had been at La Villa just a few days before she had disappeared. Unless she had been there earlier without his knowing it, she must have written this name and number down after that. And the name, Krystal, was European. Maybe it was *he* who had gone with Cathy to Europe, maybe it was with *him* that she was staying now! He told himself to calm down. He was letting his fears run away with him. The likelihood was that she had gone to Europe on business. She was head of European Research, for Christ's sake! But the trip had been so sudden, and the way she had this number scrawled on the inside of a book of matches, a Manhattan number – it looked so impulsive.

It was nearly seven o'clock. He stared at the number

for a while and then picked up the phone. First, find out who this guy is.

The phone at the other end rang a couple of times and then Mike heard another female voice, only this one deeper and smoother.

'Union Bank of Geneva.'

A Swiss Bank. *Jesus! Mendelhaus's bank!*

Mike disguised his voice with a Southern accent.

'Good evening there, Miss. My name's Jack Fairweather from Transpacific. I'm calling to ask if you'all could tell me what Mr Krystal's exact position is within your organisation. We've received some correspondence here from the gentleman, and we weren't sure of his department.'

The woman hesitated. Mike heard her say something to someone near her. *Come on, come on*, Mike thought, *buy it!*

'Mr Krystal is a vice-president and advisor to the general manager.'

'Thank you kindly, miss.'

'Could I enquire . . .'

'Take care now.'

It was Mike's turn to hang up. He waited three minutes, then dialled again. The same woman picked up the phone. This time Mike used his own voice.

'Hello,' he said, sounding a little preoccupied. 'Er, yuh, the GM's advisor, please, Ernst Krystal.'

His heart was beating so hard he could feel it. The line buzzed for a moment.

'Krystal.'

He was through! He crouched forward, gripping the phone hard.

'Good evening, Mr Krystal, my name is Michael Varela, I'm a friend of Cathy Ryder's.'

There was no reaction. Just silence.

'Hello?'

201

'Yes.'

'I'm calling because some things have come up and I need to get hold of her. It's kind of urgent.'

Mike waited. He wanted a reaction, something to go on. He didn't want to bluff more than he had to.

'I'm sorry. What did you say your name was?'

'Michael Varela.'

Another pause.

'And what makes you think I can help you, Mr Varela?'

Still nothing to go on . . .

'Well, er, Cathy said you'd know where to reach her. I mean she talked to you just before she left, isn't that right? And you talked about, about the whole thing. That's what she said.'

'I'm afraid I'm very busy at the moment, Mr Varela, and I'm not in a position to discuss the bank's business with unauthorised people.'

You do know where she is, you sonofabitch! And you want her all to yourself! Mike wasn't nervous any more. He was angry.

'Well, Ernst, I don't think we're talking about the *bank's* business, are we? I think we're talking about a different kind of business altogether. You know, Cathy's told me an awful lot about you. Enough so I could figure this whole thing out. I mean, Cathy isn't the kind of lady you meet every day, is she? She's kind of special.'

He stopped. He could hear Krystal's breathing on the other end of the line.

'I believed that she mentioned you also, Mr Varela,' he said. He sounded just as calm as before. 'She mentioned how persistent you had been in your enquiries. In fact, as I recall, she was somewhat perturbed about it. But I'm afraid you are wasting your time. I do not have the information you want.'

His voice was growing harsher, the impatience beginning to show through. Mike felt a moment of doubt.

Maybe it was all just business, maybe this guy Krystal *didn't* know.

'Well if you hear from her, would you tell her people are looking for her, especially me. There are some things she ought to know. You can get me at her number – you got that number, Mr Krystal?'

Krystal hesitated.

'Yes, I think I have it somewhere,' he said. 'Goodbye.'

Mike closed his eyes. He was making a fool of himself over this whole thing. She had thrown him out, and yet here he was worrying about her whereabouts like he was her big brother. All the same, he couldn't shake the uneasy feeling that she had been gone too long.

He turned off the light and went over to the window. On the other side of the street the phone booth stood empty and he couldn't see anyone standing around. He always checked that before he went out now, just in case the skinny guy with the greasy brown hair was there again, the one Cathy had pointed out to him. He watched for a minute and then slowly pulled on his jacket. He would grab a chicken dinner or something from Larry's on West 90th and then check back one more time before heading back to Queens. Maybe Cathy would call him there. There was always a chance.

He was just reaching for the latch when there was a loud knocking on the door. It made him jump. *Cathy!* He reached for the latch again, but them something inside him made him hesitate. Why would Cathy knock? She had keys. He leaned forward slowly and looked out of the spy-hole. A man was standing there in a raincoat without a belt, one hand buried in the pocket. The light was behind him and the lens made it impossible to judge his size, but Mike could see a square kind of face, with watery eyes and thinning grey hair. The man leaned forward towards the spy-hole, his head distorting, and then knocked again, harder this time.

Mike froze. He wanted to back away from the door, but he was afraid in case he made too much noise. Slowly he put one foot behind the other, shifting his weight back carefully, so that the only sound was the faint, almost inaudible creak of his shoe-leather. Then, underneath the gap in the door he saw the man's shadow suddenly widen, blocking out the dim light of the landing. *He was trying to look under the door*. Mike stopped moving. The sodium glare of the streetlights cast his own shadow in front of him. A twitch and the stranger might see him. The lock was still damaged from the break-in. It would only take a good kick to get in. What could he reach for to defend himself? He would only have a second.

From the landing came a click and the light went out. There came a faint rustle as the man stood up. Then Mike heard footsteps going away down the hall. He stayed where he was for a minute or more, listening, still not daring to make a sound. Then he went back to the window and looked out onto the street. For an instant he thought he caught sight of a man standing on the corner of the block, looking up at the building, but then he was gone. Mike couldn't tell if it was the same man or not.

Downstairs he found that the front door had been left off the latch. Anyone could just walk in. He flipped the lock closed and walked quickly out on to the sidewalk. It was quiet: on the other side of the street there was a woman in a smart-looking coat unloading groceries from the back of a BMW, but that was about all. He walked quickly towards the corner and then up towards 90th Street. It was just beginning to rain, and there was a wind blowing in from the west. He wondered where Cathy was, and why she didn't call. He told himself he would pay anything, do anything, just to see her one more time.

Larry's wasn't somewhere Mike would ever have gone to in the old days. It was too earthy for the Wall Street

204

crowd: no Japanese Kirin beer on the menu or macadamia nut salad. But times had changed. Now he couldn't help appreciating the sheer volume of calories you could get in a place like this for just a few bucks. He didn't care any more about the bright neon lighting or the plastic table-cloths, or even about the fact that everyone going by outside could look in and see you there, as plain as daylight, eating on the cheap. If it was good enough for Cathy – and Cathy often had breakfast there – it was good enough for anyone. The Wall Street crowd could go hang by their scarlet suspenders. Their whole world seemed a thousand miles away.

In Larry's that night there was the usual mix of people: cab drivers with tattoos on their arms, stuffing their mouths with hamburgers, students from Columbia, wearing tweedy coats and coloured scarves, drinking beer or diet coke, and a couple of salesman-types in chequered suits and beige raincoats, knocking back the shorts. Mike took a table in the corner, and sat with his hands in his pockets, watching the street through the plate-glass windows. He could not get out of his head the idea that Cathy might be out there, that she might walk past any moment and see him. And he wanted to be sure that he saw her first.

As he waited for his order he ran through the memories of their weeks together for the hundredth time, looking for reassurance that she would return to him in the end, that her love was strong enough not to be swept away by the events of a few hours. She had to give him another chance, she had to! And yet he knew that every day they spent apart would make it harder to go back. *If only I'd told her the truth, I'd be with her now.* He pressed his eyes shut. One stupid mistake and his chance of happiness was gone. It couldn't be right! Somebody somewhere was cheating him.

He had no appetite for the chicken dinner. He picked

at it with a fork, propping his head up with his other hand. What he wanted, really wanted, was to get drunk, so drunk he couldn't think, couldn't feel anything. But for more than a week now he hadn't touched a drop, in case Cathy showed up or called him. It might be his only chance to put things right and he didn't want to blow it because he couldn't think straight. In his mind he began to rehearse what he would say. He had done this a hundred times too, but every time he began it seemed that the words he had prepared before were all wrong. What could he say? Every day it got harder and harder to work out.

As he pushed the plate away from him, Mike noticed that he was not the only one sitting on his own that night. In the far corner, mostly hidden by the two salesmen, was another guy. He had a glass of beer in front of him and was reading the *New York Times*. There was something about him that was familiar: the grey hair, the plain kind of raincoat. Then he put down his newspaper. It was him! The same man Mike had seen through the spy-hole less than an hour beforehand. The man looked up and for a moment they were staring at each other. Then the other guy went on reading.

Mike left some money on the table and walked out. If the stranger had called to see Cathy then he couldn't know where she was either. And if it was him he had wanted to see, then how come he knew where to come? He walked fast along 90th Street, pulling up the collar of his coat. It was still raining a little and the traffic on Broadway was all snarled up. Farther down a lot of cars were impatiently sounding their horns.

As he turned the corner of 87th Street he slowed down. The guy in the restaurant was probably an insurance sales-man, he thought, or something like that. Maybe Cathy had made an appointment to see him and forgotten to cancel it. Or maybe it was just a neighbour who knew she was supposed to be away and had become suspicious when he heard someone moving around. Besides, it might not even have been the same guy in Larry's. It had been pretty dark out there on the landing.

He was just crossing the street when he saw the man again. He was standing on the other side of 9th Avenue, lit up in red by the DON'T WALK sign. He was a hundred yards away at least, but Mike knew it was him. There was even a newspaper folded up under his arm.

Mike didn't try to get away. He walked slowly without looking around until he reckoned the other man was no more than forty or fifty yards behind him. He walked right past the front entrance to Cathy's building and all the way to the corner of 8th Avenue. Then, knowing he was out of sight, he ran, one block north and then back along 88th Street. There was a back way into Cathy's building via an underground parking lot. At the corner he almost collided with an old woman pushing a shopping trolley. He wasn't exactly sure what he was doing, but if he got back to Cathy's apartment with enough time, then he could call the police.

The parking lot was small, with enough bays marked out for about twenty cars, most of them taken. It was lit by two small neon striplights in the ceiling, one of which flickered on and off. As Mike walked down the steps from the alley at the back of the building he saw the tail-lights of a car driving up the ramp on the opposite side, the electronic door closing automatically after it. He walked over to the elevator but the red light above the call button told him that it was occupied. He took the stairs. In one of the apartments on the second floor a TV was on loud.

As he approached the third floor he heard the elevator doors closing somewhere above him. Then the stairway lights went out again – far too soon, as they always did. He climbed the last flight carefully and reached out towards the switch which was visible thanks to a tiny yellow light which was always on just above it. As he got there he found someone else's hand on the button. He let out a gasp and almost lost his footing on the stairs.

'Mr Varela. You're a hard one to find.'

It was the man he had seen in Larry's. He wasn't so young or so big, but he was on the landing and Mike was still a couple of steps down. The stranger's eyes were bloodshot and his skin was shiny. A faint smell of booze came off him.

'Who are you?' Mike said. 'How did you get in here?'

The man smiled. He kept his left hand buried inside his raincoat.

'I'm afraid access is not a big problem in an old place like this. I'd have thought that was pretty obvious by now.'

He motioned towards the door of Cathy's apartment. The damage from the break-in was still plainly visible.

'What the hell are you doing here?' said Mike, taking one step up. He wanted to be close enough to jump the man if he pulled out a gun from his pocket.

The man reached inside his coat and took out a card.

'My name's Harry Waterman. I'm doing some research for the Centre for Disease Control, research on a company called Mendelhaus.'

He handed the card over. Mike didn't look at it.

'I really came to see the lady of the house, but I gather she's out of town.'

Mike eased himself onto the landing. This must have been one of the people Cathy had told him about, the ones who followed her, frightened the hell out of her. In all likelihood he'd carried out the break-in as well, only he hadn't found what he was looking for. The CDC shit was just a lie.

'That's right,' said Mike. 'She's out of town.'

'In Europe, in fact. At least that's what her employer told me.'

208

'Right. So what do you want with me?'

The stranger cleared his throat.

'Just a little information, Mr Varela. That's all. I can assure you – '

'Sorry, but I can't help you. You seem to know it all already.'

Mike pulled out the keys to Cathy's apartment and walked over towards the door.

'I wish I did,' said the stranger. 'But certain information has come to light which suggests an investigation is justifiable. The public interest – '

'If your investigations are in the public interest, Mr . . .'

'Waterman.'

'Then I suggest you make an appointment to see Miss Ryder yourself. I'm sure she'd be only too happy to co-operate, if she were here. You can always leave a message. Doubtless you already know the number. Now, if you'll excuse me.'

'Listen,' said the stranger, 'I don't think you understand exactly what's at – '

'Good night.'

Mike turned the latch and opened the door. The man stepped back.

'Have it your way, Mr Varela,' he said. There was menace in his voice. 'Only let me give you some advice. If you or your girlfriend know anything about this Mendelhaus company, anything at all, you'd be better off telling it to me. A lot of funny things have been going on lately. A lot of things which seem to point to Mendelhaus. Now I don't want to worry you, but if there is anything *unusual* about your friend's absence, anything which might have something to do with Mendelhaus, I think she might be in real danger.'

Mike turned on him.

'What do you mean?'

'My worry is that, in the normal course of her work, she may have found something out about the company, something which they want to keep quiet. I believe I know what that something is, and if I'm right it is a matter of direct concern for my organisation.'

Mike hesitated for a moment. He wanted to tell this guy everything, and to find out what he already knew, but there was something about him which made Mike uneasy. He needed time to think, if it was only a couple of hours. Seeing him hesitate, Waterman stepped forward and handed him his card.

'You can contact me here in New York on the number written on the back. If I were you I wouldn't take too long thinking it over. Quite apart from the Mendelhaus angle this whole Erixil business has caused a lot of people a lot of pain. They want that pain to stop. I'd start with the locks if I were you, and make sure you don't lose that card.'

Mike watched the stranger disappear and then went inside. The noise from the TV below was coming up through the floor. He took off his coat and went over to the answering machine, just in case there were any more calls. Then he noticed that, as well as the normal red light, there was another, a green one which he had never seen on before. The label below the light said: WORKING.

Mike flipped up the lid which concealed the two cassettes. The wheels of the incoming cassette were going round. Some one was ringing up to hear the recorded messages. But only Cathy knew the code. *Cathy!* He snatched up the receiver.

'Cathy, it's Mike! Cathy, I've been waiting for you. I had to explain. It wasn't the way it seemed. I . . .'

There was a click, then the moan of a dead line. She had hung up on him. It was just as he had feared. She would do anything to avoid him. The thought took all the strength out of him. His hands were trembling like he had a fever. *Maybe it wasn't her . . . Maybe she just didn't hear me . . . Maybe the phone doesn't work.*

He stayed that way for several minutes, holding his head in his hands, before he noticed that the message counter had changed from six to seven. Slowly he reached out and pressed the replay button.

'*Number of messages received: seven.*'

He skipped through the first six messages and played the last. There was always a chance that the message was from Cathy.

'Mr Varela. Perhaps we had a misunderstanding earlier.'

It was Krystal's voice, Mike recognised it. He sounded calm, almost friendly. 'It so happens that I *have* had word from Miss Ryder recently. In fact she has asked me to give you some correspondence. I'm flying to Zurich tomorrow morning, but if you want, I can meet you for breakfast at the Café de Lyon on William Street at eight. I shall be at table number ten. Good night.'

27

Manhattan. February 10th, 1996.

Mike woke at six after two hours dozing on the sofa. He had decided to stay at the flat rather than go back to Queens, reckoning that the time needed to go back and forth across the East River would be better spent catching up on sleep. But then he had started going through old photograph albums, looking at Cathy's childhood and adolescence. Even in the early photographs she had those dark, hypnotic eyes. The pictures kept him awake until four, the pictures and the scrapbook which contained twenty years' ephemera including stories she had written for a high school magazine, and a series of newspaper cuttings about time she had spent in hospital at the age of twelve, just after her father died in an automobile accident.

She had never hidden the scrapbook, but she had never shown it to him either. It was only since she had disappeared that he had really looked at it. The newspaper cuttings, dated between June 3rd and June 10th 1978, told the story of 'little' Cathy Ryder who had been cured of a type of kidney cancer – a nephroplastoma, they called it – after spending several months in Maine Central Hospital undergoing chemotherapy. There was a faded halftone picture of Cathy squinting into the camera, the darkness of her narrowed eyes in stark contrast with the paleness of her strange, hairless head. The title on one story read 'MIRACLE CURE'. For a long time Mike had considered the picture, tears pricking at his eyes.

Thoughts of the Cathy he knew, the Cathy with the heavy fragrant hair and the full woman's body, filled his short, troubled sleep. When he woke up he found the scrapbook across his chest open on a photograph of Cathy playing the violin to a small dog in what looked like a suburban back yard. There were marks in the top left-hand corner as if something had been written on the other side. He peeled the corner back to see Cathy's round girlish script in blue ball-point – *Me, age eleven.*

He stood up and went through to the kitchen where a security light somewhere outside threw a lozenge of orange light onto the ceiling. Standing at the sink he washed Cathy's Schubert mug and then spooned in the instant coffee. It had been just over two weeks since he had last seen Cathy. It felt like two years. *Maybe today will bring her back.*

He came through to the lounge and sipped at his coffee, looking down at the street. He was deep in thought, hardly conscious of the early risers going about their business and the small man coming out of the phone booth on the other side of the street.

He played the last message on the answering machine for the fourth time – *it so happens that I have had word from Miss Ryder* – listening to Krystal's voice, trying to judge from the tone whether it meant something good or something bad for him. Then he looked at his watch and stood up, almost spilling his coffee. It was a quarter to seven. He would have to hurry if he was going to be on time.

He rode the elevator down to the basement, where he had parked the car. He had washed but was still unshaven, wearing faded jeans and a coat over the cashmere sweater Cathy had given him at Christmas. He hoped that the

213

Café de Lyon didn't have a tie-only rule at breakfast time. He knew plenty of places that did.

It was cold in the basement car park. He walked along the line of cars to Cathy's Peugeot hatchback. It had become his point of reference in the last couple of weeks and he always tried to park as close to it as possible. The Toyota was three cars down, almost lost in the shadows. Mike stopped. For the first time he noticed that two lights, one over a fire exit and another fixed to a cement pillar, were broken. The exit sign looked as though it had been deliberately smashed. It was odd. There was no graffiti in the basement and he had always thought it was safe from that kind of thing.

Then, as he was walking into the darkness where he could just make out the gleam of the old Toyota's body-work, his scalp tightened. He slowed down. The words of the stranger he had met on the stairs came to him: *They want that pain to stop*. He had a feeling that somebody was waiting for him in the dark, waiting for him to put the key in the door before giving him a tyre tool across the back of the head. He went cold, standing still and looking into the darkness, trying to make out what was there. He gave himself a shake. Why would anybody want to hit him over the head? It was just the darkness that had spooked him. He took a step forward, telling himself that in another moment he would be driving up the ramp and out into the dawn light towards Krystal, towards Cathy.

His shoes crushed broken glass, and again he struggled with the idea that something was wrong. There seemed to be glass on the floor, yet he couldn't see any damage. He took out his keys and bent forward to find the right one on the ring. His hands were shaking and he could feel the hair standing up on the back of his neck. In another second he'd be on the ramp, driving up towards the sun. Feeling for the lock in the dark, he inserted the key, opened the door and lowered himself into the driver's seat. Even as he sat down, he realised he was in trouble. There was glass on his seat and the dim interior light showed where the off-side window had been shattered. Someone had gotten into the car. He looked at his hand on the key, his heart thumping, waiting for the blow to fall. But nothing happened. Then he looked down and saw the gaping hole where the Blaupunkt had been and he gave a deep sigh.

'Thieves!' he exclaimed, his voice booming with relief in the interior.

'Just a sideline, lover-boy.'

Mike froze, his hand on the ignition key. He felt the cold touch of the gun at the base of his skull. Then there was the voice again, a hard voice with a real edge of meanness.

'Put your hands on the wheel, Mister Varela.'

Leaving the key in the ignition, Mike put his hands up on the wheel.

'Good.'

There was an odd pause in which the gunman said nothing. Then, speaking closer so that Mike could feel his breath on his neck; 'Now we are going to take a ride.' Mike glanced at the mirror, but all he saw were his own staring, bloodshot eyes. The mirror had been twisted over. The pressure of the gun at his head increased and he heard the hammer click back.

'I don't want you *looking*, friend.' There was fear in the man's voice, fear and violence. Mike gripped the wheel. 'Look at me again motherfucker and I'll open your fucking head!' He stabbed at Mike with the gun.

There was a long silence. Mike heard the man move on the seat behind him. Then, his voice calmer now, he went on,

'You don't need the fucking mirror to drive, Mikey. Nobody in this stinking city looks in the fuckin' mirror. So I don't want you touching that mirror. *Entendido?*'

There was another silence. The gun left the back of his neck. Mike felt the man behind him was smiling. His heart hammered and he tried to control his breathing. His palms were wet on the wheel.

'Should I start the car?'

Instantly the gun was back at his neck.

'Don't smart-talk me, college boy. Don't smart-talk me, Mr Miguel Taco Wetback!'

Mike felt his face burn. He was scared, but he was also angry. He kept his eyes fixed on his hands.

Fifteen minutes passed. People came down to their cars, half asleep. They didn't even look at the Toyota in the dark corner. Then, at a quarter past seven, a fat guy wearing a cardigan came along the line of parked cars. He paused for a moment in front of Cathy's Peugeot, looking down at the number plate. In the silence, Mike heard the stranger move and felt the barrel of the gun touch his neck. After a moment the fat guy got into another car and drove off. Mike felt hot breath as the gunman let out a big, almost comical sigh. His breath smelt bad – cigarettes, and something sweet, vegetable, tomatoes. *The guy stank of tomato soup!*

'So start the car, you fucking hump.'

Mike turned the ignition key. The engine turned over once, coughed and then started. Mike put it into first and pulled slowly out of the parking bay.

The car nosed out of the shadows and moved slowly towards the exit. Mike tried to think. Maybe he could stall the car on the ramp. Maybe someone would come into the basement and call the police. Maybe he could run into another car. But then the gun was at his neck again and instinctively he speeded up, moving towards the ramp and the greyish daylight which was filtering down into the basement.

'That's right Miguel, just drive the fucking car.'

But as they reached the ramp the man stabbed with the

216

gun and told Mike to go round once more. So, turning the wheel Mike brought the car back into the darkness and followed another line of cars until they were at the other end of the basement where a ramp led down to the second level.

'Stop the car. Okay. Take me downstairs nice and easy.'

Mike turned onto the ramp, his mind racing. Things were starting to look bad. He felt that the man behind him was improvising. Killing time. And what happened when the time was up?

There were fewer cars in the second basement, parked mostly in ones and twos. Mike drove past until he came to a big space.

'Drive over to the far side and park.'

It was dark, but the faint glow of the security lighting coloured Mike's hands with a dead orange hue. Again they sat. They were waiting, but for what? It came to Mike that what the guy wanted was to stop him from seeing Krystal. Krystal was going to lead him to Cathy and for some reason they didn't want that to happen. It had something to do with the old guy on the stairs, something to do with Mendelhaus. His hands dropped from the wheel.

'Put 'em back up there, you dumb fuck!'

The man behind struck into his neck with the barrel of the gun, sending a pain through his skull. Mike gripped the wheel as if it were the guy's neck.

He knew he had to get out of the car but how? How lucky was he feeling? He didn't think the guy behind him was going to shoot. If he had come to kill him he would have done it a while ago. He wouldn't have sat there risking discovery. No, he was there to keep him away from Krystal. But how did they know about the meeting?

Another five minutes passed. Mike glanced at his watch. It was almost seven-thirty. Krystal would be making his way to the café. Then a noise brought him upright in the seat. It was the sound of elevator doors opening somewhere near where they were parked. As the doors came open a hard white light was thrown across the cement floor. Then, from behind one of the buttresses two men appeared, one dressed in a beige trench coat and carrying a briefcase, the other in a sports jacket, some kind of document wallet under his right arm. Mike felt his heart quicken. The gun was no longer at his neck. His eyes cut across to the door handle. Could he get out in time?

There wasn't time to think about it. The two men had reached a car parked ten metres away. In another moment they would be gone, and Mike would be left in the dark. And Krystal would be on his way to Switzerland. *I told Mr Varela about your letter, Cathy, but he didn't bother to come and collect it*. It could be the last chance.

He made his move.

It seemed to take for ever before he was on the ground rolling over and over away from the car, rolling and calling out to the two guys who were just getting into the red Lincoln saloon. As he got to his feet, Mike saw the gunman trying to climb past the front seat of the Toyota coupé. He had the gun in his right hand. He looked stupid, his trousers riding up his extended left leg, showing a strip of pallid flesh. Mike didn't wait to see him get out. Running with his head down, he made for the ramp.

The street was full of cars moving slowly towards the junction with Amsterdam Avenue. Mike ran down towards the corner, running with a steady jog. It was fifteen minutes before eight. Just time to take the subway down town if he was lucky. He shook his head, hardly able to believe what had just happened. He relived the moment in which he had reached for the door handle. It seemed crazy to him already. He wanted to tell Cathy what he had done. He wanted to tell her that he would look after her now.

From the subway station he ran. By the time he reached William Street at ten past eight he was pouring with sweat. His coat was covered with dust from the cement floor in the basement and he had oil on his jeans. When he entered the Café de Lyon a couple of the guys standing at the bar in immaculate suits turned and looked at him. He looked down at himself for the first time and was shocked by his appearance. Brushing himself off, he made his way through the group of men to the tables which gleamed with white napery. Several groups were already seated. At one table a young guy in braces was drinking champagne with an old woman. The tables were discreetly numbered and as far as he could make out, number ten was the one by the window, lit by a small spotlight fixed in the ceiling.

What Mike saw then stopped him in his tracks. Sitting at table ten, drinking orange juice from a tall glass, was the man he had seen in the Irish bar the night before. There was no possibility of a mistake. The distinctive scars and the thick grey moustache identified him immediately. Could this be Krystal?

A sudden flush of understanding darkened Mike's face. *They had heard Krystal's message!* This guy had come to meet Krystal in his place. He would call himself Michael Varela and Krystal wouldn't know any better. *So you can get to Cathy before I do!* The sonofabitch was sipping his orange juice and looking at a copy of the *New York Times*. Mike set his jaw and had started towards the table when the barman shouted across the room.

'Call for Michael Varela!'

Mike stopped in his tracks as the other man rose in his seat. Before he could speak there came a loud crack from somewhere behind him, like someone cracking a whip. The man at table ten sat down again abruptly, his powerful hand bursting the unfinished glass of orange juice. Somewhere in the room a woman was screaming. Then

219

Mike saw the neat black hole punched into the stranger's forehead, the dark rivulet of blood trickling down the side of his nose. He slouched forward onto the table. The back of his head was all blown away, the wall behind him bright with blood.

Mike fell, pushed from behind, understanding flooding his consciousness. The bullet had been meant for him! *Krystal wanted him dead.* All around was a mass of grey-suited bodies, diving for cover behind the tumbling furniture. Broken glass and ice cubes skidded around on the floor and Mike's nostrils filled with the smell of spilt orange juice and cordite. He covered his head with his hands.

PART TWO

The Annunciation

1

Near Alleinmatt, Switzerland. January 30th, 1996.

Cathy's grip tightened on the arm of her seat as the chopper crested a line of snow-laden mountains and plunged down the steep slopes on the other side. For an instant she glimpsed a cluster of skiers near the top of the ridge, looking up at her with their hands over their eyes, but then they were gone. The aircraft swept down towards the shadows of the valley floor, passing so close to the trees that Cathy felt she could almost reach out and touch them. Half a mile away to the north she saw two cable-cars passing each other above a deep precipice, their huge steel arms gleaming in the morning sun. Down below, the village of Alleinmatt was hidden beneath a blanket of grey mist, all but the church spire, which stuck up through the blanket like a needle, sharp and black.

Without warning the pilot put the chopper into a steeply banked turn, skimming over a rocky bluff on their right. Cathy felt like her stomach had broken free inside her and was rolling around, colliding with her heart every time they changed course.

'*Da vorne ist der Heulendthorn!*' shouted the pilot, pointing up ahead of him.

Cathy steadied herself and leaned forward to get a better view. There before them was the mighty Heulendt-horn, standing at the southern end of the valley, a vast granite sentinel, its sheer faces barely dusted with snow. To its razor peak clung a single wisp of cloud, reaching out across the valley like a long white pennant. At its feet lay the sprawling trail of a glacier, the surface scored with countless blue crevasses. Cathy had never seen anything so beautiful or so overpowering. As they flew towards the mountain, closer and closer until nothing else was visible, she began to feel as if she were shrinking, she and the little fibreglass bubble that carried her. Soon they would be just another white speck against the towering immensity that already seemed to engulf them. She felt fear and exhilaration. There was not room for anything else.

They began to climb again and then slowly the Heulendthorn slipped out of view. As the horizon appeared ahead of them Cathy began to relax again. The mechanical beat of the chopper blades, the coolness of the pilot, the array of technology in front of him, all of it added to a sense of reassurance. Her first ride in a chopper and she was a wreck! She sat back in her seat and took a couple of deep breaths. She was in good hands.

The pilot was looking out towards the southern sky where a mass of dark clouds were gathering.

'*Es sieht so aus als ob wir bald Schnee bekommen*,' he said.

Cathy didn't know what he was saying except that *Schnee* meant snow. They were going to have snow. She thought back to the reception she had attended the night before in Zürich, and of the conversation she'd had with Pierre Lambert, the head of the Mendelhaus cosmetics division. He had remembered her from the Erixil launch in November. He had told her how great the skiing was at Alleinmatt, especially off-piste, and that she should take time off to do some while she was there. In fact, he had even said he would be her guide if he could get away.

224

He had his own chalet in the village. Something had told her that he had more than skiing in mind.

She had hesitated to accept at the time. It wasn't just that she didn't trust him to behave – she didn't, but she knew she could handle that. It was more that she hadn't wanted him to think she wasn't serious about her work. But now she felt different, exhilarated by the idea of a real break. She hadn't had one for many months, and she needed one, especially after everything that had happened. Why shouldn't she take a few days off while she was here? It would help her to keep her mind off Michael. After the initial explosion of anger, she had come to think that maybe she should have listened to his explanation. It was just that in the midst of all the pressure at work and the wheedling and scheming of people like Steiner, Mike's betrayal, if that's what it really was, had pushed her over the edge. She had come to expect so much from Michael. Whatever his reasons turned out to be, he should never have lied to her.

'For most of us on this side of the Atlantic,' Lambert had said, with a quizzical expression on his suntanned face, 'work is just a means to an end. It seems to me sometimes that many Americans think it is the end as well.' Up here, surrounded by the majesty of the Alps, Cathy could see that he had a point. How could anyone exchange all this for a stack of Manhattan skyscrapers?

She disliked Pierre Lambert. In spite of his looks he had an oily charm which made her shudder sometimes. However, it was convenient to have someone attentive around, otherwise she would have felt completely alone. Ernst Krystal was still in New York. And Lambert could be quite witty. In fact talking to him had been the high point of an otherwise awkward evening. She had arrived early that morning from New York and had been taken to the Baur au Lac, a sumptuous old-world hotel of the kind you weren't supposed to book into on expenses, at

225

least not until you were a really big fish. Only this time, it was all courtesy of Mendelhaus. She had received the invitation just three days earlier, from Ernst Krystal, and had accepted at once. At last here was a chance to get more information about Mendelhaus, something Mike Paine had been demanding for weeks.

Ernst Krystal had called it an informal 'get to know you' visit, but it had sounded to Cathy as if something was about to happen at the company – a partial flotation of stock maybe, or some new joint venture. Even at such short notice there was no question of turning the offer down. Her knowledge of Mendelhaus had been her trump card, the very basis of her credibility in the market and at Webber Atlantic. If anyone else came up with new information on the company before she did, that credibility would be gone.

She had assumed that other analysts would be invited to Switzerland at the same time as her, but when she turned up at the reception in the elegant glass dome of the orangery she soon discovered that she was the only American there, the only foreigner in fact. She was introduced to a couple of brokers and people from a number of banks, but, as far as she could see, they were all Swiss, all part of the local scene. What made her most uneasy, however, was the fact that among forty or fifty guests she was virtually the only woman. There were three or four wives of Mendelhaus executives as well, but, as far as Cathy could see, most of them barely said a word all evening.

The pilot began talking on the radio: *'Phönix eins kommen.'*

The radio hissed for a second, then a voice came back: *'Hier spricht Phönix eins. Identifizieren sie sich.'*

'Hier spricht Adler eins. Wier landen jetzt.'

The chopper turned slowly northwards. To the left Cathy could see a steep ridge, capped with spines, a sloping expanse of virgin snow beneath it. The ridge was shaped like a horseshoe, the highest point lying at the western end, opposite the Heulendthorn. On the eastern side the ridges became gentler, disappearing beneath the snow, opening out into the next valley. They drew closer to the granite walls, following them around to the south. Then they began to descend. They were only a hundred feet from the ground when Cathy caught sight of a building, crouching on the edge of the tree line, its back to the sheer rock face. The austerity of the structure surprised her. It looked almost military. The building was protected from avalanches by several lines of steel barriers drawn up at the foot of the cliff. As they neared the ground the view vanished behind a fog of swirling snow.

Cathy's heart took another jolt as they landed with a heavy thud. The pilot leaned around and smiled. Cathy could see her reflection in his sunglasses.

'*Es tut mir leid*,' he said.

Then through the fog two figures in white jackets and fur-lined hoods appeared running towards the chopper. They peered in through the perspex window for a second and then slid back the door. The noise from the blades was suddenly louder. One of the men outside shouted something to the pilot and beckoned for her to come out. She fumbled for a moment with her seat belt, and then scrambled towards the exit. She pointed to her suitcase which sat strapped in on the seat beside her but the two men outside simply beckoned to her again.

'*Viel vergnügen im Phönixlager!*' said the pilot as she was about to step out onto the ground.

'Thank you,' she said, although she did not understand him.

'*Bitte schön, Fraülein.*'

As soon as her feet touched the ground one of the two men in white jumped into the chopper and emerged carrying her suitcase. The other man shook her hand

227

and without saying anything led her away towards a big building at the end of a driveway which had been carved out of the snow. The building looked much like a modern alpine hotel, except for the plain rectangular windows which reflected the pale blue light of the sky. All around the grounds were tall fir trees, their branches heavy with snow, but just beyond them Cathy could make out a high perimeter wall made of granite.

They were half way to the building when Cathy heard the sound of the chopper lifting off behind her. It climbed almost vertically towards the craggy summit of the ridge and disappeared. As the regular beat of its blades faded away, Cathy stopped and listened: her own breathing and the muffled footfalls of her two companions were now the only sounds. Everything else was shut out by the walls, smothered by the heavy blanket of snow. The silence was like a weight upon her. It seemed unnatural. She didn't want to stir, to stop listening, until she heard it broken – by the call of a bird perhaps or the stirring of the trees. But there came no sound at all.

On the slope above her the two men in white had stopped too. They stood together watching her, waiting.

2

The Phönixlager. January 30th, 1996.

To Cathy it seemed more like an expensive country hotel than a clinic. In the entrance there was a long counter made of dark wood heavily carved in the rustic Swiss style. Vases full of lilies stood on either end of it. The floor was of a rough grey stone with a huge Persian rug in the middle, and there were lanterns suspended from the heavy oak beams. An ancient grandfather clock stood in one corner. On the walls hung tapestries depicting hunting scenes.

'Miss Ryder?'

A stranger stood waiting at the bottom of a short flight of stairs, his hands behind his back. He was in his late forties, had neat grey hair and glasses with rectangular lenses and fine gold frames. He was wearing a business suit.

'My name is Egon Kessler. I'm the chief surgeon here and the deputy research director. It's a pleasure to meet you at last.'

They shook hands. For a moment he went on looking at her, as if he wanted to be sure he had the right person. His eyes were blue.

'I have been given the honour of guiding you around our facilities here. I hope you had an enjoyable journey.'

229

'It took my breath away,' said Cathy. 'It's a fantastic location you have here.'

'I'm very glad you think so. We hope you have a chance to explore it. For the moment, if you would please follow me . . .'

Cathy had come across Kessler's name before. She had heard it at the reception in Geneva, and she had read it in the research documents Ernst Krystal had given her. He was responsible for the technological breakthrough involved in the Erixil system. It was remarkable that he should be prepared to give up his valuable time for *the honour* of being her tour guide. She felt embarrassed by it all. What did they imagine she could possibly do for them in return?

'This is so kind of you,' she said. 'I had no idea that all this would be laid on just for me.'

Kessler waved away her thanks.

'It is nothing, I assure you. Your work in the United States has been a great help to us. Let me introduce you briefly to Felix Gaechter, one of our senior researchers, and then we must show you to your quarters. When you are ready your tour of the facilities can begin.'

The man who had escorted her from the chopper, and who was standing just behind her, pulled back his hood and smiled. He was young with very short hair and a bony face. The other man, who had taken her suitcase, was nowhere to be seen.

'This floor is where we lodge our patients,' said Kessler. 'But since our research work will be of greater interest to you, we have decided to put you in the Research Centre itself. It is quite comfortable. We have special quarters there for visitors and executives of the company.'

'It's beautiful,' said Cathy, looking around her. 'Not at all what I expected.'

'We like our patients to feel as relaxed as possible,' said Kessler. 'And for this reason we like the non-medical areas of the clinic to be as private and homely as possible. The very last thing we want is an institutional atmosphere.'

As he was talking he led Cathy across the hallway to a door marked *Privat – Private*. The door led into a long corridor. It was slightly colder than in the clinic and there was a bad smell of sulphur. They turned a corner at the end of the corridor and were immediately confronted by a large riveted metal door.

'Have you ever stayed in a hospital, Miss Ryder?' Kessler went on.

'Yes, a long time ago,' said Cathy.

'Indeed?' said Kessler. 'Then from your own experience you know how anxious people usually are to get out. Not just because they want to be well again, but because they feel alienated and vulnerable – at the mercy of strangers. I believe that much of the company's success in the treatment field has been based on its respect for the patient as an individual.'

Cathy could not help listening to his words with a touch of cynicism. In this branch of medicine success was measured in dollars. And if you wanted to fill your clinics with the richest patients in the world, it made sense to lay on every possible luxury. She remembered the hospital where she had lain ill for months as a child. It had been a little institutional, but she hadn't minded. The nurses and doctors had all been kind to her. That was what she remembered most.

'What sort of medical treatment do you carry out in this clinic, Doctor Kessler?' Cathy asked as they went through the door.

'Of the main Mendelhaus facilities, this is the most general,' said Kessler. 'Our other four clinics, although they are much larger in terms of the number of patients they can handle, each have areas of special medical expertise. Here, however, we like to think we can carry out any form of treatment. And if we lack the necessary equipment or medical staff for a particular patient's needs, we have it brought in.'

The heavy door closed behind them and they proceeded along another corridor.

'So you have five clinics?' said Cathy. 'From your literature I got the idea there were only four.'

Kessler and the younger man looked at each other. Then Kessler smiled.

'One forgets what a keen interest you have taken in our company, Miss Ryder. And of course you are right. We don't publicise the existence of the Phönixlager clinic to the same extent as our other facilities. But that is in the nature of the place. From the patient's point-of-view, the principle attraction of the Phönixlager – apart from the first rate treatment available – is its absolute seclusion and privacy.'

They came to a double fire door and went through into an area that was lit with bright neon lights. From all around came an electronic hum and the faint rushing sound of air conditioning.

'It will surely not surprise you to learn,' Kessler went on, 'that there are people, often highly important people, who may have good reason to keep their medical needs as secret as possible. We spare no effort to ensure that the presence of such patients is, and remains, a fact known only to them and to us.'

'And yet you've allowed me to come here,' said Cathy, smiling in case her words should cause offence.

Kessler smiled too.

'Indeed we have, but I do have to confess that one of the reasons we are confining your visit to the research laboratories is to better guard the privacy of our patients in the clinic itself. I hope you will understand. As for the existence and approximate location of our facilities here, we are trusting to your discretion on that point. I need hardly say we would not even have considered a visit had not Mr Krystal assured us of your complete trustworthiness.'

'That was very kind of him,' said Cathy. 'You may rest assured . . .'

'Of course, of course. Mr Krystal's judgement of such matters is beyond challenge.'

Cathy gave an involuntary shudder.

'You have noticed the drop in temperature? We are inside the mountain here,' said Kessler, pointing up ahead of him. His voice, like their footsteps, reverberated around them. 'Our laboratories are as well protected as any on earth.'

'You mean you carved the whole thing out of the rock?' said Cathy.

'Not exactly,' said Kessler. 'The excavation was originally done by the military – back in the 1960s, I believe. The place was intended as a strategic storage centre, for munitions and the like. In any case the generals decided some time afterwards that the site wasn't suitable – you know the way they are – and Mendelhaus were allowed to lease it in perpetuity.'

'But why did you want it?'

'Well, it has some very important practical advantages. At this altitude we are relatively free of pollutants in either water or the atmosphere. In addition, this particular site gives us almost complete protection from any unwelcome radiation, whether from the sun or from some kind of nuclear accident. That was probably the main reason why the site was excavated in the first place. Of course, there is a certain low-level radiation from the rock itself, but it is not significant and is easily screened out. And, I could add that the site even fulfils our legal obligation to provide a fall-out shelter for staff and patients in case of war. Altogether I should say it was a bargain.'

'I'm sorry for asking you all these questions,' said Cathy. 'But it's all so interesting.'

'Please don't apologise for your curiosity,' said Kessler. 'That's something that we all understand very well here. Without it,' he added with the trace of a sneer, 'we should still be worshipping stones.'

All she could see through the window were eight yellow points of light arranged in an uneven circle. She could not tell how far away they were or what they were meant to indicate. She put her hands over her eyes and leaned against the perspex so as to cut out the reflection, but that only made the darkness more impenetrable.

Kessler stood a few feet away going through some kind of check-list with Gaechter and another assistant, an oriental called Chen. They both wore jeans and sweat-shirts. Around them on a series of benches and shelves was an array of metal boxes, some with dials on the front, others with switches and counters. One of the assistants sat in front of a computer terminal. Cathy didn't ask any questions because she didn't know where to begin. She knew she was about to witness something, but she could not begin to guess what it was.

'All right, run the ASC,' said Kessler.

The oriental began typing at the computer keyboard. Kessler came over and stood at Cathy's side.

'You must forgive me,' he said. 'But these preliminary checks are absolutely critical. A little carelessness at this stage could destroy years of work. That's why we run all our procedures in parallel. The humans keep a check on the computers and the computers keep a check on the humans. Only if everyone agrees do we proceed.'

'What's out there?' said Cathy. 'What am I looking at?'

'Felix, give us some lights out there,' said Kessler. 'What you're looking at is an anechoic chamber – one of three we have here.'

Cathy could not help letting out a short gasp as the lights went up beyond the window. What she saw was a forest of huge black teeth, rising out of the floor, hanging from the ceiling, protruding from the walls. They were many different lengths, some just a few inches long, like needles, others much longer. As she looked more closely she saw that they were really cones and that they were arranged around the inside of a large square box, about thirty feet in each direction. The face nearest to them had been opened out, like a pair of barn doors, affording them a view of the inside. In the middle of the box stood a long cylinder, like the bottom of a submarine's periscope, with several circular windows in it. Pointing into each of the windows from a distance of several feet were other metal and glass tubes, from the inside of which came the points of yellow light.

'The walls of the chamber are designed to absorb energy or deflect it away from the centre,' said Kessler. 'What are we trying to avoid are reflections.'

'Reflections of light?' Cathy asked.

'Reflections of anything: light, sound, in this case microwaves.'

'You mean, like in a microwave oven?'

'Indeed,' said Kessler. 'The chambers are all equipped with eight microwave lasers – masers as they're usually known.'

He took a handkerchief from his top pocket and began to polish his glasses. Cathy sensed a touch of impatience in the way he spoke, as if he saw no point in explaining his work in this way, or did not think it advisable. When talking of other things – the clinic, for example – he was perfectly forthcoming, but when it came to his own work in the Research Centre he seemed a lot less comfortable. Perhaps, unlike Ernst Krystal, he feared that she might betray them somehow. But she had to come away from the visit with some hard information, the kind that she could use in her reports, information Ben Steiner and all the other analysts didn't have.

'And what do they do, these masers?' she asked.

'Why, much the same as a microwave oven, in principle, only with the reverse effect.'

'So it cools things down?'

'Better than that, it freezes them, at least down to temperatures at which no chemical reactions can take place. In dealing with organic matter our target temperature has been minus one hundred and ninety-five degrees centigrade, the boiling point of nitrogen. We achieved that for the first time almost two years ago. Now we go down to below minus two hundred.'

Cathy looked again into the centre of the chamber.

'So cold,' she said, almost to herself.

'How does that work?' she asked. 'What's the principle?'

Kessler glanced round at his two assistants, and then turned his back on them again, as if he did not want to see their reactions.

'The principle is simple, the application is not. All particles – atoms, molecules – can be thought of as resonating systems. Like the strings of a violin they each have their own natural vibration frequencies, which they move between depending upon their state. For years physicists have been anxious to study these transitions so as to understand better the behaviour of atoms and the sub-atomic particles of which they are made. The problem has always been that the atoms are normally too excited – in effect moving too fast – for close study. But with the advent of sticky light technology in the late 1980s, it became possible to freeze atoms instantaneously.'

Cathy heard Gaechter laugh.

'You didn't know light could be sticky, Miss Ryder, did you?' he said.

They were the first English words he had spoken.

236

'No, I'm afraid I didn't,' she said. 'It's an odd idea.'

'Sometimes they call it optical molasses.'

His bony face arranged itself into a grin, but then he seemed to become self-conscious and went back to his work. Kessler did not turn round.

'It is simply scientific short-hand,' he said. 'As I explained, particles vibrate at their own frequencies. The hotter they are, the more violent the vibration and the faster the movement of the particle itself. If, then, you introduce another source of vibration to the particle, one that exactly counteracts the vibration of the particle itself, you can hold that particle still – in effect frozen. Imagine two identical stones thrown into a pond: if you adjust the distance between them you can ensure that one small area of the surface of the pond remains motionless because the peaks of one set of ripples coincide, at that point, with the troughs of the other, and vice-versa. Since the two forces are equal, they cancel out. In freezing atoms and molecules, lasers are used because the range of frequencies is appropriate. They are synchronised in such a way as to counteract the natural vibration of the atom, rendering it still and easier to study.'

'But why are you freezing molecules?' asked Cathy.

'We are not. We are using the masers for something quite different. And that is perhaps our greatest technological advance,' said Kessler. 'For in doing so I believe we may have forged the most important tool for biological research since the electron microscope.'

He looked around at Cathy and added: 'In the right hands.'

'You're saying that you've adapted this sticky light technology for biological use?'

'Precisely. Instead of freezing atoms for study, we have been freezing organic materials – cells, to be exact. For that, lower frequency radiation is needed. This is because, as with all organic matter, the most prevalent substance

237

is water, and water molecules vibrate at a much lower frequency than free atoms. You can understand the vibration of the water molecule if you think of a tuning fork, with the oxygen atom as the base, and the two hydrogen atoms as the arms.'

Kessler was speaking rapidly now. Cathy just wished she could take some notes, but after all the talk of secrecy, she did not know how her hosts would react.

'You mentioned microwave ovens,' Kessler went on. 'They work by producing microwaves whose frequency is chosen to resonate with the natural vibration frequency of the water molecule. The amplitude of the molecule's vibration is thus increased. This movement creates heat. In fact, water is exceptionally susceptible to this type of excitation, thanks to its hydrogen–oxygen bonds. Carbon–hydrogen bonds, such as are found in oils for example, barely respond at all to this treatment. In any case, what we have done is reversed the process, all but freezing the molecular movement of the water in our cell cultures. This produces the kind of temperatures at which no chemical reactions can take place.'

'Has your technique been made public yet?' Cathy asked.

'Not quite yet,' said Kessler. 'We wish to be completely satisfied that we have arrived at the optimal arrangement. It took us years to arrive at the basic techniques, and without the advanced wave analysis programmes developed by the director I am certain that we could never have produced an area of radical temperature reduction – what we call a freeze zone – large enough to be useful.'

'And how big is that freeze zone?' asked Cathy. 'Could you freeze a glass of milk?'

'Unfortunately not. But a large cluster of human eggs would be no problem at all. We can already cover almost half of one cubic millimetre.'

Chen pushed himself back from the computer terminal.

238

'The ASC says okay, Doctor Kessler,' he said.

Kessler nodded. 'Go with the alignment check.'

Chen punched some more commands into the computer and suddenly a series of red lights began to flash on and off on two of the masers, which were opposite each other. Then for a second the lights went green. After a moment the sequence was repeated with another pair of masers, and then another, until all eight had been tested.

'We are checking here that the masers are correctly positioned,' said Kessler. 'We run another check when the anechoic chamber is closed.'

Cathy sat back in her chair and folded her arms. So far, what Kessler had told her sounded fascinating, important. But it wasn't the sort of thing she could use in a report, even a confidential one. She could not see for a moment where it fitted into the world of cosmetics, or even the world of health care. She *had* to have something to say when she got back to Webber Atlantic, something that would make Mike Paine sit up and listen, something that would make them happy in Sales. She hated herself for thinking that way, for being in this position. Here was a man of science, pushing forward the frontiers of knowledge, laying before her the results of many years' work, and all she could think about was whether meatheads like Brad Matthews could deal on it! But then again, she was head of European Research and she had to act like it. There was no soft landing from a job like that. If you were down you were out. She decided to head straight for the point.

'What exactly are you using all this for?' she asked. 'What kind of products are you aiming for?'

As she spoke she saw Gaechter and Chen exchange glances, as if her questions were bound to be unpopular with their boss, but Kessler merely removed his glasses and massaged the flesh around the bridge of his nose.

'You will recall that I described this apparatus as a

239

tool,' he said at last. 'I have not yet described the task for which it is used. But you may be sure of one thing. The products that you have seen thus far, the products that have brought the name of Mendelhaus to your attention, are no more than trifles along the way towards far greater achievements. With the body of knowledge this system has already enabled us to amass, we are on the verge of practical applications that may revolutionise the practice of medicine.'

Cathy could not help blushing.

'I should love to hear about them,' she said, 'if you can spare the time.'

Kessler looked down at her.

'You shall,' he said. 'But that can wait a little. And besides, I know that the director himself will be anxious to explain our future plans to you in person. He is American himself, you know.'

'An American? I didn't know. I'd always assumed that you were the director.'

Kessler shook his head. 'I'm surprised no one told you,' he said. 'Our director of research is Professor Edward Geiger.'

3

The Phönixlager. January 31st, 1996.

At just after two in the morning the main ventilator shut
down and for the only time in the diurnal cycle there was
almost complete silence inside the mountain. The generators for the heating plant which maintained a steady sev-
enteen degrees centigrade in the clinic were located at the
surface, a short distance from the main building. Once the
main access door to the laboratories was closed even the
barely audible hum of the heating system was lost. Under
the mountain the hum was replaced by the soft rush of
ventilation. But now there was nothing.

Two men moved through the laboratory, their perspiring
faces lit momentarily as they passed a green security light.
The taller man carried a black medical bag, his companion
pushing a steel trolley on which a piece of apparatus the
size of a portable television lay buried under coiled cable.
At the door leading through to the cryogenic store they
turned right and went through the double fire doors which
opened into the main corridor. The cable slipped from the
trolley and for a moment they both stopped as the shorter
man bent down to pick it up. Neither of them spoke. At
the end of the corridor they came to an elevator. The door
slid back filling the corridor with white light. The second
man wheeled in the trolley. The doors closed and the man
carrying the bag pressed the button marked level two.

'Micturition – '

'Induced. Though it was hardly necessary. Like most American women she has a remarkable appetite for carbonated mineral water. She urinated before going to bed as I already told you.'

The shorter man shook his head once. The sweat stood in beads on his upper lip.

'As I already said' – he repeated the phrase under his breath – 'there is nothing to worry about.'

He blinked as the doors opened onto another, darker corridor. Level two was still inside the mountain but was mostly residential. It also housed the director's library. There was a smell of the white lilies which were everywhere in the clinic. They wheeled the trolley out of the elevator, turned right and moved along the thickly carpeted corridor.

When they reached the door the taller man took a plastic pass-key from his top pocket and pushed it into the slot over the handle. Without a sound the heavy door rode back on its newly oiled hinges. The shorter man's breath came short and rapid through his nostrils.

There was a dim light coming from behind the heavy velvet curtains. The two men stood for a moment breathing the young American's perfume. Cathy had pulled off the covers and lay naked in a twisted sheet. A nightdress, unused, lay crumpled across the bed beside her. She was breathing steadily through her open mouth, lost in heavy, sedated sleep. At first neither of the men moved, both stilled by the beauty of her sleeping form. Then, giving himself a shake, the taller man came forward, placing the heavy bag at the foot of her bed. Leaning forward, he took a corner of the sheet and pulled. There was a sibilant, unravelling sound and then he was standing with the warm sheet in his hands looking down at her. His eyes moved from the mass of black hair spread on the pillow to the dark nipples, then along her stomach to the dark mound

242

of her pubis. Withdrawing the sheet had released more of her scent into the air. This he breathed, his lips slightly parted. Never in his dreams had he figured her as beautiful. He was a rational man, but somehow her beauty increased the significance of what he was about to do.

A movement from the other man brought him back to the task in hand. Slowly he kneeled before her and opened the black bag. Out of its shadowy mouth a faint antiseptic smell mingled with her subtler odour. Taking a last look at the dark cleft between her pale thighs, he withdrew from the bag a light steel instrument.

In spite of endless rehearsal it was still unfamiliar to him and he held it for a moment, trying to bring together in his head her soft secrets and its cold, chrome-plated hardness. It looked like a duck's bill, the two blades of the beak being attached by a hinge. A steel grip ran down from the lower bill where it was linked to a long screw which ran through another handle attached to the upper blade. When the screw was turned, the blades parted, and the duck gaped.

'I am recording.'

The voice of the other man broke in on his thoughts. He looked at the micro cassette which was placed next to him on the floor.

'Yes. Yes, of course.'

He placed the instrument on the floor. Then he removed a small surgeon's lamp from the bag and lowered the strap over his head, fixing the lamp in the centre of his forehead.

'Abdominal examination first.'

'Yes, yes!' He was growing impatient with the other man's relentless practicality.

He looked at the smooth belly for a moment, looking for any deformity or swelling. Then he placed the flat of his hand below her ribcage and began to work the flesh, looking for anomalies, tell-tale knots, subcutaneous cysts,

243

inflammation. Cathy closed her lips and for a moment there was a pause in her breathing.

'Michael.'

The kneeling man turned and looked up at his companion. He leaned back and removed a stethoscope from the bag. He placed it above her navel slightly to the left. Frowning, he began to listen.

'Auscultation. Yes . . . Yes. Normal aortic pulsation. Nothing else. Nothing foetal. If she is pregnant the foetus is less than 24 weeks old.'

Once again he leaned back. He wiped the sweat from his forehead. Then he removed a pair of gloves from the bag. So close the smell of her sex roused him. His eyes wandered involuntarily to the pale swelling of her breasts, and the darker petallic teats.

'Standard lithotomy position,' he said, speaking down towards the red light of the cassette, his voice charged.

He turned abruptly to the other man, who had been preparing the electronic apparatus.

'Well, Herr Doctor, you must leave your machine for the moment.'

The other man came forward. Together they drew the drugged body to the end of the bed until the buttocks were at the very edge of the mattress. Then the smaller man, standing beside the bed and reaching forward, lifted and parted the legs, bending them at the knees until they were doubled over her abdomen. There was a breathless silence as they watched for any sign of her waking. Her breathing remained steady. Then the man on the floor switched on the electrical equipment.

Out of the dark her genitalia flamed into sudden colour and detail. There was complete silence. The kneeling man looked at the dark, puckered flesh of the labia majora shading a deeper brown in the cleft of the buttocks. Reaching forward with both hands he gently separated the outer lips of her vagina.

244

'Traces of vaginal discharge, scanty, viscid. Maybe the beginning of bleeding. No sign of candida albicans or trichomonas. But we'll have to wait for the smear. Urethra fine. No sign of infection. If it is the beginning of a period she will ovulate around the middle of next month. But let's not get ahead of ourselves.'

He reached down for the steel instrument and then applied a thin layer of transparent lubricant.

'Inserting the speculum . . . wait a moment.'

He slowly withdrew the tip of the duck's beak.

'What is it?'

The man holding Cathy's knees leaned forward, trying to see what it was that had silenced his partner.

'She's not sick is she?'

The kneeling man let the instrument come to rest in his lap. He was shaking his head.

'No,' he said. 'No, she's not sick.'

He shook his head once more in disbelief. Then he turned to the other man.

'She's intact. She's a virgin.'

There was a silence of several seconds. The other man frowned.

'You're sure?'

The kneeling man nodded.

'Does this change anything?'

'It does make it more difficult. And she may also experience a little soreness in the morning, but there is no fundamental difficulty.'

'Then let's carry on.'

The kneeling man looked down at the red eye of the micro-cassette. His voice had a new urgency.

'Bimanual palpation.'

He inserted the index finger of his right hand into the body and pressed down with his right hand, feeling for the size and disposition of the inner organs.

'Position of cervix, normal. Uterus is anteverted. Also perfectly normal. Now.'

He leaned back for a moment and touched the perspiration from his forehead with his sleeve.

'The smear.'

Reaching into the bag he removed a plastic spatula from a cellophane wrapper. His hands were trembling.

With extreme care he inserted the spatula until it was deep inside.

'Taking material from the external os for exfoliative cytology.'

There was another minute's silent work. Frowning with concentration, he spread the cells on a microscopic slide and fixed the smear with a mixture of ethyl alcohol and diethyl ether. Later the cell nuclei would be stained with haemotoxylin.

At just after half past two the kneeling man closed the mouth of his bag. His face was bathed in sweat and his hair stuck to his neck and forehead. He stood up, the light from his lamp throwing shadows across the room. The other man lowered the woman's legs until they were extended on the floor. They both looked down at her naked body. The taller man wiped the sweat from his face, talking in a low reflective monotone.

'It worries me that she has had no sexual intercourse. It may indicate some kind of neurosis. She's too beautiful not to have had any offers.'

'What difference does it make?'

'If her sexuality is a difficult issue she is less likely to be in favour of the project.'

'Director . . .'

The taller man looked up from the naked body.

'Yes?'

The other man tapped his watch.

'Time. We must go on. We must be finished before five. We don't want to have to deal with those idiots in security.'

'Yes. Yes, of course. We must go on.'

The taller man kneeled as before, this time holding a probe attached to a thin cable which was connected to the apparatus. His partner raised the woman's knees until her genitalia were fully exposed.

'Ultrasound examination. I am going to take a look at the endometrium and then the ovaries.'

Pushing and twisting the probe with extreme delicacy, he watched the blue image on the screen shift and turn. For a while nothing was clear. The man holding Cathy's knees compressed his lips, trying to make sense of what he was seeing.

'It's difficult to . . . Wait. Yes.'

The kneeling man froze, his eyes fixed on the screen. He twisted the probe with the slightest movement of his fingers.

'Yes. The uterus. The endometrium. We can get an exact measurement. Taking a picture.'

He pressed a button on the machine and the apparatus on the trolley began a low ventilating sound.

'It is as I thought. She is at the end of a cycle. Leucocytic infiltration. Vasoconstriction of the arterioles. She is about to start bleeding. With the results of the smear and the endometrium measurements we should be able to pinpoint ovulation pretty well.'

He glanced up at the man holding the woman's knees.

'If you can hold on a little longer I am going to take a look at the ovaries.'

For another twenty minutes the two men worked; observing, recording. When they were finished the woman's legs were again lowered, and she was lifted back onto the bed and covered with the sheet. The taller of the two men took a clean handkerchief from his pocket and wiped the lubricant from between her legs.

247

At four o'clock they were sitting in the laboratory drinking coffee. Outside the wind had picked up. It gusted plaintively in the ventilation ducts. Their faces, lit by a single desk lamp, looked tired. On the desk next to a pile of notes were the slides of material taken from the woman's cervix. The taller man looked into the black round of his coffee as he spoke.

'It is all very promising, Herr Doctor. No carcinoma, and no sign of cervical or corporeal cancer. No trichomonas or candida. She is immaculate. According to the ultrasound measurements and the hormone levels she is about to menstruate and will ovulate on the fifteenth.'

'If we assume a twenty-eight-day cycle.'

'Of course.'

The taller man sipped at his coffee, regarding his colleague's face.

'Whatever happens, we must begin the treatment as soon as possible.'

Up in her room Cathy stirred, the effects of the drug beginning to wear off. Another gust brought her out of sleep. For a moment she didn't know where she was and tried to find the familiar wardrobe and desk in her own apartment. She felt a tightness behind her eyes and when she moved her head a dull pain began to throb in her temples. And there was something else. An unfamiliar sensation inside her, between her legs. Then fragments of a dream came to her, but she was unable to remember. But it was something terrible, some violence or rape. Suddenly thirsty, she slid her legs over the side of the bed and sat up. For a few moments she felt unsteady, her vision clouded. Then she stood up and went into the bathroom. She turned on the light over the sink and stood looking at herself for a moment. Then she drank a glass of water and went back into the room. Her watch said five o'clock.

4

The Phönixlager. January 31st, 1996.

It was the telephone that woke her.

'Miss Ryder, your breakfast is ready. Shall we send it up?' It was a man's voice.

'What time is it, please?'

'Eight o'clock in the morning.'

'Thank you. Yes, send it up.'

She pulled back the covers and sat up on the edge of the bed. A stab of pain ran through her head from the top down. She felt like she had been out drinking all night: her mouth was dry, and she felt dizzy. And yet the whole of the previous evening she had not had more than two glasses of wine. She wondered if it was the jet lag catching up with her. As she stood up she felt stiffness in her thighs and something else: a strange cold ache in her groin. Maybe she was getting sick, she thought, and then she smiled at the aptness of it: she might get to sample Mendelhaus's medical care for herself. She decided to take a long hot bath. The tub was about the biggest she had ever seen.

She walked unsteadily across the room and pulled back the heavy velvet curtains. There was no window behind them, but a big nineteenth-century painting of a stag in the mountains, lit from above by a small strip-light. Cathy had forgotten that she was inside a mountain herself, and

249

the realisation brought her a tremor of claustrophobia. She had to switch on all the lights in her three big rooms to dispel it.

By the time Kessler knocked on her door she felt better. The aches in her body had almost gone, and the breakfast had taken care of her head. Kessler was at least as friendly as he had been the previous day, but he was somehow less relaxed. He smiled at her a lot, in a forced, unnatural way, as if making a conscious effort to put her at ease. He also looked as if he had not slept very well.

'I miss not having a view,' Cathy said, as she closed the door behind her. 'Especially knowing how beautiful it is out there.'

'I know what you mean,' Kessler replied. 'But we are regrettably restricted by the terms of our lease. In any case you would not see very much from a window this morning: we are engulfed in low cloud, and blizzards are expected later.'

'I had no idea,' said Cathy. The thought of fog outside brought the claustrophobia back for a moment.

'Neither had I,' said Kessler, 'but one of our directors was planning to fly in today, and he has had to postpone his trip. You can't use a helicopter in these conditions, of course.'

'Which director was that?' Cathy asked.

'Mr Lambert, the head of our cosmetics division. Ever since we developed Erixil here, he has been coming up here quite regularly. Still, it seems we shall not be troubled with him today.'

'I've met him,' said Cathy. 'As a matter of fact, he offered to take me skiing.'

'Skiing?' said Kessler. He looked surprised. 'Did he?'

Cathy had the feeling Kessler disapproved. Perhaps it did seem a little philistine to be thinking of recreation when important advances in medical science were being shown to her, advances very few others had seen. Or then again, perhaps Lambert had a reputation for abusing his position of authority. It would not surprise her.

'Of course,' she added, 'that's only if there's time. I'm very anxious to see what you've achieved here, and to understand it.'

Kessler smiled again.

'I have given the matter some thought,' he said, 'and this morning I thought we would visit the computer centre. There you will be able to see in graphic form the sum total of the data we have amassed. I have also spoken to the director, and hope he will have time to join us later. He can explain our ultimate objectives far better than I.'

They walked together along a succession of long corridors, every twenty paces or so passing another door. Although she had no way of knowing, Cathy had the impression that she was just below the surface of the rock because there always seemed to be a cool breeze blowing. High up on the walls she noticed a series of big ventilation shafts covered with metal grilles.

They took a lift up a level and entered a large, half-lit room with an array of computer terminals along one wall, and data storage units along another. Instead of normal monitors the computers had huge flat screens, about three feet square. Four people, all men, were working, their faces lit up in a bluish light. From where she stood, Cathy could just make out patterns of spheres and lines moving back and forth across the screens. Kessler led her to the furthest corner of the room where they both sat down in front of a terminal.

'All the information we gather is stored on computer,' he said, 'not only for convenience's sake, but so that it can be subjected to the range of numerical analyses which we have developed. I say *we*, but really the director alone is the author of our analysis programs. His hand has been evident in every stage of our advances. Only in such

251

practical areas as the physical exploration and manipulation of cells have others, such as myself, made any original contribution.'

He tapped a few keys, and then something appeared on a screen: a long, fuzzy line with a big 21 beneath it. The line was superimposed on a grid, with more numbers running along the bottom and the left-hand side of the screen.

'This,' he said, 'is a diagrammatical representation of the DNA strand in chromosome 21, the most thoroughly studied chromosome to date. Perhaps I had better explain what that means exactly.'

'If you wouldn't mind,' said Cathy, and privately she hoped that Kessler would take her back to basics, if only so that she herself could sound more convincing when she explained to her colleagues what Mendelhaus's research was all about.

'Well, it is like this,' said Kessler. 'Inside every animal cell lies a complete set of blueprints for the whole of that organism – in other words all the information that might be needed by every different type of cell in the body from fertilised egg to adult. In all, in a human being there are about 250 different types of cell, all of which must occupy and function in its proper place – the kind of cell you might find in your liver, for example, would be no use at all in your brain. That information is stored in the nucleus of the cell, on pairs of units called chromosomes. Human cells have twenty-three such pairs. The chromosome is composed of a single strand of a complex molecule called DNA, together with molecules which hold that strand in position. What you see here is a computer model of the DNA in chromosome 21, neatly laid out in a line. Close up you may recognise the structure of the DNA.'

Kessler tapped some more keys and the strand enlarged again and again until a tiny fraction of it filled the screen. It was made of two spirals wound around each other, with

252

rungs between them, like a ladder twisted round and round. The rungs were all made of two halves: either one half black and the other white, or one half red and the other green.'

'It's the double helix,' said Cathy. 'I do recognise it.'

'It is within the double helix that the pieces of information physically exist. The information is expressed in a chemical alphabet, two letters of which are found on each of the rungs you see. Together those chemical letters make chemical words or commands. The letters are what we call chemical bases, and there are only four different ones: A for adenine, T for thymine, G for guanine and C for cytosine. On the screen we have given each of the four its own colour. It is links between pairs of these bases that make up the rungs in the DNA molecule, A always linking with T, and C always linking with G. That is why the rungs are usually referred to as base-pairs. To read a piece of DNA, you pull the double helix apart, breaking the rungs in half, and then read the letters down one side. You only need to look at one side because you always know exactly what the opposite side will look like: if one side spells A,C,C,T, then the other side must spell T,G,G,A. Groups of these letters, sometimes thousands of them, contain the necessary information to produce one useful molecule – a protein – that the cell can make. Such a group we call a gene.'

'And how many base-pairs are there?'

'In all something over three billion, divided between the DNA in the forty-six chromosomes. But the majority of these base-pairs are simply structural – the blanks between words, as it were. The number of genes, that is functional groups of base-pairs, is estimated at around 75,000. However, the word *gene* is a functional, not a physical definition. Individual genes may often use some of the same base-pairs, just as different words may share components. For example: the word *standard* contains

253

the information to make *stand, tan, and*, as well as *standard* itself, depending on where you start to read.'

'And you've been working on identifying these base-pairs, is that right?'

'Half the genetics laboratories in the world have been working on that,' said Kessler. 'The Human Genome Project, which began seven years ago, involves the collaboration of some two hundred and twenty research groups in twenty-three countries. Each one of them, with some differences in method, have been painstakingly cutting up pieces of DNA and noting down the sequences they find. And they will be doing it for a good many years yet. The size of the task is immense, and the interpretative problems even more so, not least because the genetic code of every individual is different. It is no simple matter to work out which pieces of genetic code describe the essentials and which the minor variations, which genes make the iris and which determine whether it is blue or brown. In fact, it is an immensely laborious process trying to identify where one gene begins and another ends, or even which base-pairs are part of genes and which are just the padding between them.'

'You mean the project will identify the sequence of letters in the code, without knowing where each word begins or ends?'

'Initially, yes. And unless some legal restrictions on human embryo experimentation are lifted, it may be many decades before all the individual words – the genes – are identified. You cannot be certain what many genes do unless you alter them and see what results.'

'But you do collaborate with the Human Genome Project?' Cathy asked.

Kessler folded his arms and smiled. There was pride in the way he spoke, and vigour. Until then Cathy had always believed that he had been explaining his work to her because he had been told to, and that he really thought of it as an intrusion on his time. But now she sensed his eagerness to make her understand, to infect her with his own enthusiasm, to feel the triumph of what they had achieved.

'Nominally, yes,' he said. 'We contribute whatever information on base-pairs we can. Most of the data you see here has been provided by the project: results of sequencing are pooled. But the thrust of our research is different, and, I believe, infinitely more rewarding, at least for the time being. That was why we wanted you to see our work with the microwave lasers. Without it we would be as blind as all the others.'

'I'm afraid I still don't see the connection,' said Cathy.

'You shall,' said Kessler. 'But first consider this: a cell is like a highly complex machine with a computer built in, the computer being the nucleus with its chromosomes. Like all computers, it is programmed to respond to certain pieces of information which it receives from the external environment, and which it recognises. When an organism is growing from egg to adult, for example, cells migrate within the body in complex patterns, changing their form and eventually coalescing into specialised tissues. All this has to be organised by the cell's on-board computer, responding to signals from its environment. Now, the man-made computer we have in front of us here will also perform some immensely complex tasks at the touch of a few keys. It is simply waiting for the right signal to go into action. We do not have to know precisely how every part of those tasks is performed, to know every line of the program the computer is following. All we need to know is which signals are appropriate. The computer will do the rest on its own.'

'But inside a cell what form do these signals take?'

'Man-made machines and man-made computers all use electricity to perform their tasks: everything from powering conveyer belts to conveying information inside a microchip. Inside a cell the job is done by proteins and other complex molecules. Proteins are what genes describe. When a particular protein is required the part of the DNA where the relevant code is found unwinds. A chemical impression of the gene's code is formed by a complementary molecule called RNA. This process is called transcription. After transcription the short strands of RNA, carrying the chemical imprint of the gene, then pass out of the nucleus into the cytoplasm – the space between the nucleus and the cell wall – where they are read by factory units called ribosomes. The ribosomes construct the necessary protein from food particles in the cytoplasm.'

'But these signals, they're proteins too?'

'They are specific combinations and concentrations of proteins, often highly complex ones. Certain genes – "smart genes" we call them – respond to combinations of these signals sent from one gene to another, within a cell or from one cell to another, and then switch on and off the other genes as required. The smart genes, if you like, give the orders to other parts of the cell computer. They are like the Central Processing Unit in a man-made computer, if you like.'

'So what do they indicate? What do these signals say?'

'They convey, so we believe, all the essential information the nucleus needs. For example, the presence of certain protein signals, as opposed to others, tells a smart gene that it is time for a cell to change its shape somehow. The smart gene then switches on and off all the necessary functional genes to achieve the shape in question by activating the enzymes that perform transcription. When an individual is developing from fertilised egg to adult, such signals tell the smart genes in which way the cell should differentiate, the structures it should adopt, when to begin manufacturing particular substances and when to stop. From the moment a cell is created there is a steady turn-

256

around of information from the smart genes in the nucleus back and forth, via the cytoplasm, to the nuclei of other cells, conveyed by the many different proteins. All these proteins can be manufactured artificially.'

At last Cathy was beginning to understand. The information on the Erixil system that Krystal had given her had talked in just such language: of certain proteins educating the cells in the epidermis to behave as their younger predecessors did, and, presumably, to produce the substances lacking in older skin.

'So if you know which proteins trigger what responses, you can get your cell to do anything, right?'

'Anything it *can*. All cells have one common ancestor – the original fertilised egg – but they differentiate as the foetus develops. Differentiated cells carry the information for all types of activity, of course, but the structures they adopt may be incapable of alteration. In other words certain genes may be switched off permanently.'

'But you know about the proteins? You know all the signals?'

For the first time since Cathy had met him, Kessler laughed out loud. Her excitement pleased him.

'Give us a few more years, and we may have most of them. So far we have only a very small proportion, but as with all our research, Professor Geiger has directed our efforts towards the most useful areas. It is part of his . . . of his cleverness. We have concentrated on the first hours, days and weeks of life – in other words the early stages of cell differentiation. It is there that the work has the greatest medical value.'

'And you use the maser technology for this?'

'It has made this whole line of research possible. As I said, there is a constant traffic of proteins through a living cell. If you open up a cell, inevitably killing it in the process, you can extract and identify some of those proteins, but that will not tell you what their function was.

257

If you have a whole culture of cells at the same stage of development, and you study just one cell, you will face the same problem, for in the time it takes you to identify the proteins in that cell, the other cells may have passed on to quite a different set of operations. You may never be able to marry cause and effect. *But we can*, Miss Ryder. Our cell cultures are instantaneously frozen in their entirety in the anechoic chambers, while a handful are studied. We look for RNA strands in the cytoplasm, to see which proteins are being manufactured, and we can even get inside the chromosomes to look at the proteins binding to the smart genes that we have identified. When our investigation is complete we instantly unfreeze the cultures, and let them continue developing for a fixed period. Then we repeat the process. Our first cultures we stopped every twenty-four hours. Then we narrowed the time to twelve hours, then six. The cultures were divided in an early pre-differentiated stage and run in parallel so that errors in freezing or unfreezing did not jeopardise the whole series. With the director's programs analysing the data, we began to perceive patterns, cycles. We concentrated on the beginnings of these, to uncover how they were triggered. We discovered that some of these cycles coincide with the times when cells must decide which of two different development routes to follow. Until recently this was where the bulk of our work was done.'

Cathy glanced over her shoulder. Two of the other men were watching her, but they went back to their work as soon as she saw them. Kessler did not notice; he was tapping at the keys of the computer. The double helix vanished from the screen, and the letters *I. D.* appeared in its place.

'Here is some of the raw data on the culture we were about to freeze yesterday,' he said. 'It is our most mature culture to date.'

He hit some more keys and a column of yellow numbers

filled the screen. Kessler moved the cursor to the bottom of the screen and pressed *Enter*. This time three columns appeared. In the first were long groups of chemical symbols arranged into groups, in the second names like *cytokine 14* and *oncogene erbB*, in the third column dates and times.

'One day,' said Kessler, 'we shall have a complete understanding of the information and regulatory systems of all human cells. We shall have the ability to artificially manipulate a cell from fertilised egg, right the way down to any of the specialised cells in the adult body.'

'But you mentioned medical applications,' said Cathy. 'Where are they?'

Kessler had just begun to reply when he suddenly stopped speaking and stood up. Cathy realised that someone was standing behind them. The moment she looked round, she knew who it was.

'I hope Dr Kessler's lectures haven't confused you,' he said. His voice was gentle but precise. 'You mustn't worry if it all means nothing to you.'

'Miss Ryder, may I present Professor Geiger,' said Kessler.

'How do you do?' Cathy said, holding out her hand. 'It's an honour to meet you, Professor.'

He was tall and almost athletic looking. He had a high forehead and dark hair, which had begun to recede from the temples. His eyes were brown and deep-set. If you looked at them he appeared to be frowning, even when the rest of his face was animated or smiling. It was almost as if he were looking out from behind a mask. Perhaps it was just the contrast with Kessler that did it, but Cathy sensed that there was something courtly about him. There was nothing of the absent-minded professor she had come to expect. He was younger than Kessler by a few years – about forty-five, she guessed – and handsome in a cold, distant kind of way.

259

'The pleasure is mine,' said Geiger. 'I'm only sorry I wasn't able to greet you when you arrived.'

'Not at all,' said Cathy. 'I've been looked after wonderfully. I must say I'd no idea your researches were so extensive, or that they'd been going on for so long.'

Geiger smiled. 'Most people in the financial world, so I have observed, regard three or four years as a long time. So I suppose fifteen years must be an eternity. But the human genetic code has evolved over several hundred million years. Millions of centuries growing more and more complex, more elaborate, more indecipherable. To unravel such a puzzle then, is a few thousand days so much to ask?'

Cathy shook her head. She knew Geiger was correcting her, criticising her naivety, but she was not embarrassed. The way he spoke, with calm confidence, gently but without a trace of hesitation, did more to convince her of his genius than anything Egon Kessler had said. She felt like a child before him, with no more need to be ashamed of her ignorance than a child has. She only wanted to hear more.

'But if I understand Dr Kessler correctly,' she said, 'you've already made enormous advances.'

'In research terms we have made some headway,' he said. 'But although it may not be a fashionable thing to say, in the end I believe we must weigh such advances in terms of their benefit to humanity. As yet we have little to show for our efforts in that sense.'

Kessler looked at his shoes.

'I was just asking Dr Kessler about the medical applications of your research,' said Cathy. 'I understood that they were pretty exciting.'

'Potentially, that's true. Since I was a student I have always believed that this branch of cell biology would have the greatest impact on medical science, on the treatment of disease and the prolongation of life. That's why

260

I've chosen to spend more than twenty years on it, one way or another. Compared to an understanding of the human cell, the exploration of the galaxies, even of our own sun, is an irrelevance.'

He grinned, as if to apologise for being so serious so quickly, and then shrugged his shoulders. 'But, unfortunately, in any field, between pure research and practical application there are always more obstacles than one expects. After more than two years of clinical trials we are still finding them.'

'That must be frustrating,' said Cathy, not sure what she should say. Suddenly she no longer felt at ease. The other men in the room were all back at their work, but she sensed that they were listening to her every word.

'Yes, frustrating,' said Geiger, 'but worse than that sometimes. For example, when you have a patient whose time is running out.'

'You mean patients here?' asked Cathy.

Geiger did not answer. He seemed to sense Cathy's discomfort, or even to share it.

'Perhaps it would be better if we moved on,' he said. 'If you will excuse me for saying so, Egon, I think Miss Ryder is primarily interested in the practical application of our work, not so much in the pure research. Isn't that so?'

'I suppose so,' said Cathy, 'but I'm glad to have heard about it. I do want to understand.'

'I felt sure you would,' Geiger said, and showed her towards the door.

They went down to the level her room was on, but this time to a part of the Research Centre Cathy had not seen before. Here it looked more like an extension of the main clinic building, except that there was no antique furniture or tapestries on the walls. In fact it looked more like an ordinary hospital. Cathy saw two male nurses in white jackets walking along one of the corridors.

'We keep special patients here,' said Kessler, 'the ones that we are most anxious about.'

They went into a big office with television monitors and other electrical equipment all along one wall. In one of the monitors Cathy could see a man lying in bed. He was an oriental.

'This man,' said Geiger, 'is Kazuo Hiraizumi. You will have heard of him, perhaps. At twenty-five years old he survived the American bombing of Tokyo, which killed the rest of his family. He went on to found the Hiraizumi Corporation, which today is one of Japan's largest companies.'

Cathy looked at Kessler, remembering what he had said only the day before about the need to conceal the identity of patients, but he did not react. Again she felt uncomfortable. Instinctively she looked around the room. It was perfectly ordinary. What had she expected? She saw the two men looking at her, and flushed, trying to come up with a question as if nothing had happened.

'He's still the chairman, isn't he?'

'Yes,' said Geiger. 'But not for much longer, I fear. He has a diseased liver, caused by a build-up of iron. Two attempted liver transplants have failed through rejection.'

Cathy looked down at the monitor. The man looked thin and drawn, a frail figure with the sheets pulled almost up to his chin. He was sleeping.

'Can you treat him?' she asked.

'Eighteen months ago I would have said yes,' Geiger replied. 'Then I would have been confident of an operation that, if you will forgive my lack of modesty, would have changed the course of Western medicine.' Cathy looked at Geiger's face, feeling her heart beat starting to pick up. She felt as if whatever she was going to say had already been said by her in the same room to the same listeners. The moment seemed to be out of time. Jet lag and being stuck in the mountain were playing tricks on her mind.

'And why not now?'

Geiger leaned back against the edge of his desk, his hands behind his back. Kessler sat down on a sofa opposite.

'Egon has, I believe, explained to you our progress in identifying the chemical signals within human cells, the signals that direct their development during the early stages of life.'

'Yes,' said Cathy. 'In outline at least.'

'Good. The point is we have reached the stage where we can mimic many of those signals artificially, and so manipulate an undifferentiated cell into becoming something more specialised. The types of cell we have concentrated upon are those which make up the constituent parts of the vital organs: heart, liver, brain and so on. In Kazuo Hiraizumi's case, we would use our knowledge to create a small culture of foetal-type liver cells – at precisely the right stage of differentiation – which we would then introduce into his body, into what's left of his liver. Provided the correct protein regulators were present in the right concentrations – and some such proteins would be there naturally – those new cells should multiply and develop, eventually creating a new, healthy liver in place of the old.'

The two men looked at Cathy, as if waiting for some reaction. She lifted her hand to her forehead. Then Kessler said: 'Organ regeneration, Miss Ryder. That is the revolution I told you of. In time we should be able to treat almost any part of the body in this way: a man-made resurrection. We will not have to count on the gods any longer.'

Cathy said nothing. She was trying to come to terms with what she was being told and why she was being told it. A feeling inside her was becoming more focused, a feeling of displacement, *déjà vu*. Her mouth was dry.

'It may surprise you to learn that the basic idea of such operations did not originate here,' said Geiger, calmly. 'In the late 1980s, in the United States, there were attempts to treat Parkinson's disease with implants of foetal brain matter. It was hoped that the primitive brain cells would pick up the right kind of protein signals from the environment and produce some of the substances necessary to promote a better functioning of the surrounding tissue – in the case of Parkinson's disease the ones that control the motor functions in the body.'

'They used the brains of human foetuses?' said Cathy.

'They began to have some success in the early nineties,' said Kessler, 'but they lacked information on the optimal age of the foetal brain cells, and on the types of protein signals that were required for the desired path of development. This is information we will acquire in the near future.'

'But,' said Geiger, turning from Kessler to Cathy, 'we have a problem. It cost two lives for us to realise it.'

Kessler suddenly became agitated. He stood up and spoke in a harsh whisper. 'Edward! Do you really think . . .?'

'It's all right,' said Geiger firmly. 'There's no harm.'

Cathy looked from one to the other. The disclosures were no longer simply indiscreet. She felt as though she were being drawn into knowledge which was dangerous for her. Geiger looked at Kessler who had remained standing, then he said: 'I think I can take it from here, Egon. They'll be needing you in the labs.'

Kessler nodded.

'I hope to see you later, Miss Ryder,' he said, before closing the door behind him. 'Thank you for your patience.'

As Geiger turned back to her, smiling gently as before,

Cathy felt frightened for the first time, frightened for herself. She did not know why. In spite of his smiling face, she felt the stern concentration of his deep-set eyes. He looked down at his hands for a moment and then carried on.

'We performed our first operation almost two years ago, on a patient with a dangerously weak heart. Actually I didn't think we were ready, but there were pressures from various quarters. In any case it seemed a great success. The new cells performed well, the heart showed every sign of getting stronger. About six months later we felt confident enough to repeat the operation.'

'Were you using foetal cells as well?' Cathy asked. Perhaps it was unscientific, but she could not dismiss the idea from her mind.

'No,' Geiger replied. 'We used cells from the patient's own body, the most primitive we could find. We'd performed tests on such cells and successfully brought them to what seemed like the right condition for transplant into the heart.'

Cathy did not say so, but she was glad of that at least. If the cells belonged to the patient himself, what harm could there be in using them?

'If we'd used cells from any other individual the patient's immune system would have recognised those cells as alien and attacked them. Almost all cells exhibit sugar structures on their surfaces that identify them as belonging to that particular individual. To stop the immune system attacking alien cells we would have had to use immune suppressants, just like in a conventional transplant, and that was something we wanted to avoid. They're dangerous in themselves, and they expose the patient to an enormously increased risk of infection. What we didn't realise was the degree to which genetic damage had built up in the cells we used.'

'You couldn't tell that the cells were damaged before-hand?'

'How? The damage would have been done to the genes inside the chromosome. Even if we could have looked at them, the chances are we wouldn't even recognise the damage if it was staring us in the face. You must remember that the cells in question weren't using any but a tiny minority of the genes in their chromosomes – not until we began to play around with them. In any case the damage showed up too late, in the form of cancer. Some of the implanted cells wouldn't stop multiplying, and the cancer was so virulent in the second case, it killed in a matter of weeks.'

Geiger got up and went over behind his desk. Cathy noticed that he was sweating. He looked uncomfortable, as if there was something he had to say, but did not know how to begin. It gave Cathy a trembling feeling in the pit of her stomach. Suddenly she had to know where *she* fitted into it all. Before she could stop herself the words came out: 'Why are you telling me this? Why *only* me?'

Geiger sat down slowly. He brought the tips of his fingers together as though about to pray. The room was absolutely silent. She would remember this for ever.

'Because you can help us,' he said.

Cathy said nothing. Suddenly the pressure of the mountain all around them seemed to press in on her. She did not want to think what Geiger meant. She didn't want to hear. She sat frozen, hoping that she had misunderstood; that she had heard it wrong. Geiger watched for a moment, then he sat back in his chair and folded his arms.

'I am sorry Cathy. I have frightened you, and really there is no reason for fear. These past few weeks I have run this meeting, our conversation, through my head a number of times, without ever finding a satisfactory way of saying what I must now tell you. But it seems to me that if I can explain how I have arrived at the conclusion

that, I know you will agree, is inevitable, you will understand me better; you will see that this' – he gestured at
the room, at their relative positions, he on the chair,
Cathy on the couch – 'is about science, about reason.
There are no shadows to be afraid of.'

Still Cathy said nothing. Her eyes remained fixed on
the man in front of her. Geiger sighed and looked away
from her, compressing his lips.

'Cathy, when those men died – the heart patients – I
thought I was finished along with them. I thought twenty
years of research, of real progress, was for nothing. And
all because of a simple problem that I could have envisaged at the very beginning. I needed cultures of cells
without gene damage. But how can you get young cells
from an old man? Genetic damage occurs all through life
and is replicated at cell division. Cultivating cells from a
patient – unless the patient is very young – produces an
enormous risk of cancer. The only answer was to find a
source of young human cells, foetal cells. But there, with
the cells from another human being we would come up
against the problem of simple transplants: rejection. I
needed cells that could escape attack from the immune
system. A histo-compatibility complex that. . . .'

'I don't understand,' Cathy said. She wasn't sure she
wanted to hear any more.

'Cells carry a sugar structure on their surface, a structure unique to that individual. The killer cells of the
immune system recognise that structure and do not attack.
Anything they do not recognise in that way they attempt
to destroy. But if you could find cells with a universal
key, a structure that all key cells thought they recognised,
then you could transplant at will.'

'That's impossible, you'd never find . . .'

'I thought so too. I was not even hoping I would find
it when I did the research.' He gave his head a single,
impatient shake. 'But let me finish the story. After the

267

failure of the operations I turned to the only source of data available that might have some bearing, however oblique, on what I was trying to do: data compiled in the world's cancer research centres.'

Cathy ran her tongue over her lips. It was as if something had opened in her head. She could see everything now. She shook her head almost defiantly.

'I don't understand you,' she said again.

Geiger's eyes never wavered.

'Cancer cells are just cells that go on multiplying after they should have stopped, because of some genetic damage. For forty years now different types of cancer cells have been removed from patients, artificially bred, and then distributed to cancer laboratories for study. The oldest strain was derived in 1952 from cultured tissue taken from the cervix of a woman called Henrietta Lacks.'

Cathy could hardly hear what he was saying. She felt as if she was watching them talk from outside the room. She had a sharp recollection of her father sitting by her bedside, holding her hand. He couldn't bear to see her lose her hair. He held her hand, tears streaming down his face.

'Until the late 1980s consent was not even required by the patients. In many of those labs the cancer cells are introduced into rats, to see how they behave, and how the animal's immune system deals with the invasion.'

They had thought she was going to die. It had seemed very simple at the time. She used to lie looking up at the ceiling waiting for an angel to come into the room. Everything she had done since ravelled back to that time. It had been the beginning of her life.

'I looked everywhere for the most virulent, the most unstoppable of the cells that had been studied, hoping to find some that, like red blood cells, could escape most immune systems. The cells I found – '

'Were mine.'

Cathy put her head in her hands. A sudden rush of vertigo made her sit back. She felt as if she was going to vomit. It had all been planned: the meeting with Krystal, the tips, the reports, the invitation. She saw it now. It had all been done to secure her co-operation, to make her need them as much as they needed her.

'Though you probably never knew it,' he said, 'the nephroplastoma from which you suffered as a child – and which you were very fortunate to survive – sent your cells to cancer labs all over the world. Except for the damage to the genes controlling cell division, they were no different from most other cells in your body. They all carried the same identification.'

Geiger stood up, pushing back the chair as if he didn't want to disturb the young woman who was still holding her head in her hands. He looked for a moment as if he were going to sit down beside her, but then he hesitated, leaning against the side of the desk instead.

'Cathy, when I was searching the records of those labs, I was acting out of desperation. All I was hoping for was some evidence as to whether the kind of cells I needed existed to any degree, cells that could fool most immune systems. I never expected to find cells that came from a person who was not only still living, but female, and young enough to reproduce. It was then, and not for the first time in my life, that I felt . . . something, call it the force of destiny if you like. I felt part of a greater plan. My years of scientific practice did nothing to dim that belief – rather they strengthened it. I could sense a purpose, as clear and logical as my own. I continued my search through the records to learn if there were other examples, other cell cultures that exhibited the same extraordinary quality: *I found not one.*'

He stopped talking and waited for the woman to look up. When she did finally, she saw that he was smiling benignly.

269

'Cathy, to us you are unique. Perhaps a freak of nature even. You are the only universal donor known to modern science. In that respect your role in this project is far greater than mine.'

'Stop!' Cathy shouted, and then, struggling to control her voice: 'You tricked me. Don't start telling me how important I am. Just tell me what you want.'

Geiger's voice hardened.

'I want to be able to create a colony of undifferentiated cells, a stock from which I can draw when – '

'What do you want from *me*?'

Cathy had pushed herself into the furthest corner of the sofa, her hands gripping the leather. Geiger looked at her, and this time she could see his displeasure. He paused.

'Oocytes, Cathy. Ova. Eggs. Your eggs. Selectively fertilised they will form the basis of the colonies I spoke of. With them I . . .'

Cathy was on her feet.

'I think I've heard enough, Professor Geiger,' she said, fighting back the panic that was welling up inside her. 'I'm leaving now, if you don't mind. It's been very interesting.'

'Miss Ryder' – his voice was calm again, and he was almost smiling, but she could see the stern determination of his eyes – 'I would ask you to consider the scale of the contribution you can make to the advancement not only of medicine, but of mankind. I count my own position in that respect a great privilege. I urge you to think of yours in the same way.'

'I'm far from convinced that the benefit of mankind is what's at stake here,' said Cathy. 'Judging from this company's record, it's commercial benefits that are the top priority.'

Geiger stood up and pointed with an outstretched arm at the television monitor where Kazuo Hiraizumi could be seen asleep.

'That, Miss Ryder, is a dying man! If you help me he may live!'

Cathy had her hand on the handle of the door.

'You can't blackmail me that way. Your patient must be nearly eighty. I'm sorry he's ill, but at his age it's hardly unusual, is it?'

'No, but . . .'

'What *is* unusual is his wealth. Isn't that what this is all about, Professor Geiger?'

Geiger looked away, speaking to himself, it seemed, more than her.

'You understand nothing of what is happening here.'

'I understand very well. I understand that most of the research you've been doing here would be illegal almost anywhere else, certainly in the United States, and for all I know in Switzerland too.'

'Only a fool or a fanatic would seek to hinder the work we have done here,' said Geiger, genuinely angry now. 'And doesn't it strike you as paradoxical that the countries where the abortion of near fully-developed foetuses is most readily available are the very same ones that now prevent life-saving research on embryos a small fraction of their age?'

'You may have a point,' said Cathy. 'I don't know. But I can't be part of your research. I could never . . .'

'All I ask is that you give the idea some thought,' said Geiger. 'As you become more familiar with our work, you will come to see its value. I am certain of that. And more, you will come to realise that the role we offer you is nothing less than a place in history.' He smiled as he shook his head at her. 'You have already sensed this, Cathy. You have been waiting for it to happen. You have always known that you were different.'

Cathy shook her head. This was the most terrible thing. She knew there was some important truth in what he said.

'I don't know what you mean. I never felt that way.'

271

Geiger laughed, a big surprising laugh, and for the first time Cathy thought he might actually be mad.

'If that's so, then why have you never let a man make love to you? Why have you kept apart?'

'How . . . ?'

The blood drained from her face. She remembered the pain that morning, in her head, in her groin. They had drugged her and . . . She staggered for a moment, weakened by the horror of it. *She was a laboratory rat!* In the next moment she was struggling with the door handle and then running, running along the harshly lit corridor in the direction of her room.

It seemed to take for ever to find. She was blinded by her tears. She could hardly breathe she was so terrified. It felt like the bottom of the deepest nightmare. Once inside she pulled her suitcase out from under her bed and opened up the wardrobe where she had hung her clothes the night before. They were all gone. In their place hung one simple grey dress on a plastic hanger.

5

Zürich. January 31st, 1996.

The snow had stopped, but if anything it was colder. Hans
Klein – Herr Klein to everybody at the hotel – looked
out across the gardens to the brightly-lit quays beside the
lake. It was a quarter past six and still the new boy hadn't
arrived. Flecks of snow were drifting past the Nordfinanz
Bank building to his left, obscuring the sign over the shop
on the ground floor: A.C. BANG BY APPOINTMENT FURRIERS
TO THE ROYAL DANISH COURT SINCE 1817. Herr Klein
shivered.

In the old days, he reflected, in the old days the boy
would have been sacked on the spot. He looked around
at the wood-panelled reception area of the Baur au Lac
and compressed his lips, making his magnificent moustache bristle. The hotel wasn't what it used to be. The
old American couple who had taken the red suite on the
third floor were asleep on the ottoman after what must
have been a particularly heavy tea. No doubt waiting for
their daughter to come down, Herr Klein thought. He
looked at his watch and shook his head. For the last
twenty years the change of staff in the reception area at
the Baur au Lac had taken place smoothly at six o'clock,
allowing him to be home in time for the news at seven
o'clock. But this new boy . . .

Herr Klein came to attention, one of the few remaining

indications of his military past, and walked back through the heavy bronze and glass doors. Ulrich Schroder, a weasel-necked boy with an ill-fitting uniform, had just turned the corner from Talstrasse and was making his way across the forecourt.

'What time do you call this?' said Herr Klein in an enraged whisper as the boy came through the door.

'Sorry Herr Klein, I had a little trouble . . .'

'No excuses, thank you, just get behind the desk and do your job.'

The boy made a move towards the reception desk, but the heavy hand of his immediate superior caught him by the scrawny shoulder.

'And if you are late again there will be trouble. That's not a threat but a promise. Do you understand?'

The boy clicked his heels and bowed his head, knowing that such behaviour was worth a thousand conciliatory words with Herr Klein, whom the bellboys called the *Kaiser*.

After another glare, Herr Klein went out through the door, almost bumping into the tall, dark-haired woman, dressed in a beige raincoat.

'Room 203 please.'

Ulrich Schroder caught a whiff of expensive perfume as he passed the keys across the desk, and watched appreciatively as the woman walked over to the lift. With a practised gesture he flipped open the register and looked at the entry for room 203.

'Ryder, hmm, yes, a very agreeable lady.'

He spoke under his breath, in what he considered to be a sinister, lecherous manner. A heavy key fell on the desk, bringing him sharply back to his duties. Another guest was checking out.

The woman closed the door behind her and waited for her eyes to grow accustomed to the dark. Everything had

274

gone very smoothly. She had entered the hotel just after the change of desk staff. The street light filtered in through the closed wooden shutters. She switched on the light and walked across to the desk where she opened the drawer. It was empty. She looked around the room. There were some magazines on top of the television, and a copy of the *Wall Street Journal*. She opened the wardrobe and took out the suitcase which was on the second shelf. She opened it on the bed. There were a couple of pullovers and a slim leather case in which she found a string of pearls and a gold chain with a locket.

She dropped the raincoat off her shoulders, and put the locket round her neck. Then she walked over to the mirror and looked at herself. She smiled, liking, as always, what she saw. They had insisted she change her haircut, giving her specific instructions as to length and shape. It made her look less of an Amazon, more businesslike. The clothes too made her look like a banker. She thought for a moment of the woman who owned the clothes and she frowned. She had an idea that something bad was going to happen to her, but as Madame Beauvais had said, the client wasn't paying (and paying well) for curiosity. She shook herself and looked at the locket. There was a small figure engraved on the back of it – a treble clef.

She closed her hand over the locket and looked at herself again. Then she turned, picked up the magazines and dropped them into the suitcase. Finally she checked the bathroom, but found nothing there. She left the room and went back down to reception.

Herr Schroder looked up from his magazine and swallowed. The American was leaning towards him and asking for the bill. He slid her passport across the marble counter and then took her American Express card.

It was dark in the street. The girl pressed the buttons

on the street door keypad and the heavy door clicked open. She went up to the fourth floor. Once inside her own kitchen, she felt a rush of relief. It was the first time she had done anything so . . . so odd. Normally it was a question of spending an evening with an overweight businessman, listening to how the wife did not understand. To go to an empty hotel room in another woman's clothes, this was more difficult somehow. Then again, she reflected as she undressed, leaving the strange clothes in a heap on the floor, it was quite amusing too.

She ran a bath and soaked for a long time, not answering the phone which rang several times. From time to time she looked down at the locket suspended between her tanned breasts.

An hour later she put the clothes into a bin liner along with the magazines. The leather case too and the pearls. *Everything must be destroyed* they had said.

When she had closed the bag she realised that she was still wearing the locket. She held it in her hand, admiring the rich colour and the fine engraving on the back. She wanted to keep it. Not just because it was beautiful. She felt that she was maybe the only person who was thinking of the woman who owned it – whoever she was – the only person who would remember her.

6

The Phönixlager. February 5th, 1996.

No light or sound. Then light. Light under the bed shading
to thick darkness above her where there were . . . what
looked like instruments – a camera maybe. Something
caught the light. A lens. Then the light was gone. She
was playing the violin to her father in the garden in Maine
in brilliant sunlight, but it wasn't a violin she was holding.
She was holding something alive. Was it her cat, Sergei?
Then there was a light. Something was suspended over
her head. It caught the light. Something turned with a
low whine. Struggling against the drugs, Cathy blinked,
trying to focus. There was light under the bed. No – under
the door. Someone was in the next room. But it wasn't
her father. A vision of Michael walking along the street,
his hair wet with rain. She pointed at the towering office
blocks and he laughed. She touched the inside of her lip
with her tongue. The pain brought her flooding into the
moment, into the dark space and time in which she was
alive, her heart beating in her head, her lip stinging from
a recent blow. She tried to concentrate. It felt as if the
skin on her scalp would come apart, as if her skin were
too tight now. Gently, hardly daring to move, she turned
her head to look at the light under the door. Someone
was there. She could see feet come and go almost without

sound. Slowly she turned back to the ceiling, everything coming back, filling her eyes. She blinked the tears away.

She had tried to run. When she had seen the single dress in the wardrobe she had made a sound she would never have thought possible, an animal sound. Immediately they were behind her. They were speaking softly. Speaking to her as if she were a child who had fallen over and hurt itself. Their voices were soothing. She remembered a story she had once read by H. G. Wells, *The Time Machine*; she remembered how the *morlocks* had spoken in soothing voices to their victims, to the gentle creatures they were about to eat. Above her in the half dark something moved. It sounded like a camera. She knew that somewhere she was on a screen; her face blown up like a flickering grey balloon, her swollen lip dark, like a wound.

She tried to stick out her tongue, but it was too painful. What had they done to her mouth? In a sudden rush of panic she tried to sit up. There was a moment of frenzied twisting, wrenching effort and then she screamed, her voice sounding dead, muffled, small. She breathed, blinking away the tears which welled up endlessly, coursing down her cheeks, running into her ears.

Then the door opened and Geiger entered, carrying his micro-cassette.

'Cathy, Cathy, Cathy.'

It was the same voice, the voice of the morlock. She looked at his face. His deep-set, dark eyes were in shadow.

'My mouth.'

She tried to raise her hands, but she was strapped down. Geiger's face came nearer.

'You . . . you lost control, Cathy. We had to restrain you. You are very strong.'

Watching his face so close to her own, hearing his soft voice, Cathy felt the anger welling up in her chest.

'Bastard! You fucking – fucking son of a bitch! Let me off this . . . this fucking bed!'

She could hardly breathe, anger and panic suffocating her. The pain in her lip filled her head. She felt herself drifting away. She struggled to focus on the dark head suspended over her own. Geiger stepped back from the bed. His voice came to her from a great distance, as if she were deep under water.

'Cathy, I want you to understand what is happening. What I am doing. Why I am doing it. Until you can control yourself, your anger, you will remain strapped to the bed. There was a danger that you might hurt yourself, and I can't let that happen. You are too important.'

Cathy struggled back to full consciousness, following her throbbing pain back into the present. She looked across at Geiger. He said nothing for a moment.

'I didn't want it to be like this. You must believe me. I hoped . . . I thought you would understand, that you would help me.'

His words were calm and level, as if he had prepared them in advance, was reading them from a card.

'What are you going – ' The pain in her lip was too much. She formed the words with infinite difficulty. 'What are you going to do to me?'

'In ten days you will ovulate. We will take the ova.'

Cathy closed her eyes tight shut, trying to control her hammering heart. She twisted against the leather straps. Geiger's voice hardened.

'Instead of flushing the eggs into the sewer with a sanitary towel, we will take the eggs for our work. We – '

He paused, stilled by the expression of anguish in the woman's staring eyes. Her mouth was twisted as she spoke. The cut on her lip had opened up and there was fresh blood on her chin. She was spitting out the words as if they were real things, things from inside her.

'You . . . can't . . . take . . . what's . . . *mine.*'

279

Ben Steiner was sitting opposite her, laughing at something she had said – no, laughing at something on her plate. She looked down. There was a perfectly formed foetus with its candy striped umbilicus in a pool of red. She started awake, her face bathed in sweat. There was a light filtering in under the door. She touched the swelling on her lip. There was something, a new dressing attached to her chin with sticking plaster. The smell of antiseptic ointment filled her head.

'No, no, no.'

The room blurred through her tears. She felt herself drifting into sleep, but the thought of the dream that was waiting for her, made her open her eyes wide. She hung on to the reality even if it was little better than the nightmare.

The door opened. Geiger came in with Kessler. Kessler avoided looking at her. A panel opened next to the bed and the room glowed with the green light of an oscilloscope, tracing the steady tick of her heartbeat. Kessler looked at the instruments in the wall for a while. Geiger was preparing a hypodermic syringe. Cathy watched them both, her mouth dry.

'This is nothing to worry about, Cathy. Nothing at all.'

Geiger turned to face her. He pulled down the crisp sheet which was tucked under her chin, revealing her body in its simple grey smock. He patted the vein in the crook of her left arm.

'I am going to give you something to stimulate the development of the Graafian follicles, the egg-making follicles in your ovaries.'

He leaned towards her. She watched his bowed head, her eyes staring in horror as she felt the needle go in.

'It will not affect this cycle. But in a month's time we may start to see results.'

Then Geiger stood up. For a moment his lips flickered into a smile.

280

'The human reproductive apparatus is singularly parsimonious. It is estimated that there are two million primordial follicles in the ovaries at birth. Think of that. Two million. Of course many of these degenerate even before puberty – when those that are left get a chance to mature, to produce eggs. But out of these hundreds of thousands only one a month actually produces an egg. Why make a machine with such capacity only to produce one egg every thirty days?'

'What did you put into my arm?'

Kessler was adjusting something on the oscilloscope. Cathy saw him hesitate for a moment. Geiger smiled.

'It was nothing special. It is something quite commonly used in cases of infertility.'

'Am I infertile then? Am I sterile?'

'No, I don't believe you are.'

'Then why give me the drug?'

A faint look of puzzlement crossed Geiger's face.

'As I explained. It was to stimulate your ovaries into producing more eggs.'

'So what did you put into my arm?'

'Human pituitary gonadotrophin. HPG.'

'So what *is* it?'

Geiger placed the syringe in a cellophane bag and took a chair from the far corner of the room. Kessler closed the panel in the wall.

'We have a meeting at three, director. We cannot . . .'

'Thank you, Dr Kessler,' said Geiger, not taking his eyes from Cathy's face. Kessler closed the door behind him as he went out.

'Doctor Kessler sometimes allows the . . . the business side of things to get in the way of what is more important. I was – '

'What is HPG? What's in it? I have a right to know what is being put into my body.'

Geiger put his hands behind his back.

281

Yes, of course.'

He leaned back in the chair and looked Cathy in the face for a moment.

'HPG is a mixture of two hormones: follicle stimulating hormone or FSH and luteinizing hormone or LH. FSH causes the formation of Graafian follicles in the ovary. Luteinizing hormone causes the release of the egg on about day 14 of the menstrual cycle. In the early part of the cycle about fifty follicles start to mature, but as I said before, in most cases only one follicle goes on to produce an egg for reasons known only to nature. With a daily injection of HPG followed by an injection of HCG or human chorionic gonadotrophin on the tenth day it is possible to stimulate the ovaries into maturing more follicles – more eggs.'

'How many eggs do you hope to get?'

Geiger pushed back his hair.

'That depends on you, Cathy.'

Cathy looked up at the ceiling.

'And if I promise not to tear out my ovaries will you untie me?'

Geiger looked at her for a long time.

'Yes.'

Cathy's eyes drifted across to Geiger's face. She stifled her rising anger, and tried to smile.

He rose to go.

'I have to talk to Dr Kessler now. But I will be back in an hour. We can talk then.'

He closed the door, and the room became dark again. Cathy felt the hot tears fall onto her cheeks. She sobbed in deep gasps, her mind racing, looking for some kind of solution, some kind of escape. First thing was to get free, get Geiger to untie her. Then . . . what?

She listened to the sounds outside the door. Apart from the rush of ventilation there was nothing. For the first time she noticed a large mirror fixed against the wall on the other side of the room. They would stand behind that mirror and watch her, she was sure of that. Then someone went past in soft shoes. She imagined the injected hormones moving through her body, cheating her own system into doing something unnatural. In a month or so they would have a dozen little eggs to do whatever they wanted with. Then she thought of what might happen if they were fertilised – they might develop into foetuses to carry out their experiments. She imagined her children, locked in darkness, wired to machines, drugged.

She rolled her head from side to side, moaning softly. What would become of these children? What would become of her? Then in an ice-sharp moment of perfect clarity she understood. They would never let her leave, not now. How could they? The Phönixlager was where she would die. They would empty her and then incinerate her body.

'Michael,' she said.

7

The Phönixlager. February 5th, 1996.

The boardroom was located two levels above the main
body of the research centre, and looked out over the roof
of the clinic towards the distant valley floor. Across the
horizon, on the Italian side of the border, stretched a
range of ice-blue peaks, their outlines softened by a thick
covering of new-fallen snow. But Dietmar Hoffman, the
managing director of Mendelhaus, was not admiring the
view. He was waiting to see who would emerge from the
white helicopter that hung now just a few feet off the pad,
throwing a cloud of snow up around it.

Already seated round the expansive boardroom table
were Gustav Denzler, the head of the Medical Services
Division, Hans-Joerg Bruggman, the finance director, and
Egon Kessler, who beside the role of chief surgeon and
deputy research director, also sat on the executive committee as a 'special adviser' – a position that did not yet
entitle him to a vote. That still left three members to
come: the chairman, Oswald Hunziker, his deputy Karl
Moser, and the head of the Cosmetics Division, Pierre
Lambert. Hoffman, a slim figure in an immaculately
pressed grey suit, looked at his watch and put his hands
behind his back. Bruggman turned over another page of
The Financial Times. Denzler lit a cigarette. No one
spoke. It was always that way.

At last the chopper put down and the door was opened by two of the security staff. One of them helped Hunziker slowly down onto the ground, and tried to do the same for Karl Moser, but was irritably brushed aside. No one else emerged. The two men, both carrying briefcases, began walking slowly up the gravel-strewn path.

'It seems that we shall be without Monsieur Lambert again,' said Hoffman, emphasising the word *Monsieur* as if to mark his disapproval of his colleague's French-Swiss background. 'I wonder what he can be doing this time.'

Denzler exhaled a long plume of smoke.

'He's in Rome, I believe. Italian campaign.'

Hoffman turned round. He had a square clean-shaven face, and a full head of neat grey hair, parted down the left-hand side. He was fifty-three years old but looked younger. His skin in particular had a youthful smoothness which was interrupted only by the deep dimple on his chin.

'That's next week,' he said. 'Pierre said he'd be here today.'

'I suppose we could get him on the telephone.'

Hoffman frowned. 'I hardly think so, Gustav,' he said. 'Not this time.'

'No, I suppose that would be a risk,' said Denzler, 'this time.'

While they waited for the others a servant, who was dressed in a uniform with an embroidered blazer and white gloves, served them with fresh coffee from a big silver pot.

'Just leave it here, Celio,' said Hoffman. 'We're in a hurry today.'

The servant bowed, and did as he was asked, depositing cups and saucers in front of the two spare places at the head of the table. He was just leaving when Hunziker and Moser came into the room.

'Good morning, gentlemen,' said Hunziker. 'I hope we

haven't kept you.' There was a business-like jocularity in his voice, the kind that established immediately who was in charge. 'How are you this morning, Celio?'

'Very well indeed, thank you sir,' replied the servant, who was the same age as the chairman, but who seemed much older: a slight, wizened figure with a wrinkled face. Hunziker, for sixty-nine years old, was a picture of health. He had wavy silver hair, a gently sun-tanned face, and wore glasses with rectangular brown frames. Although not tall he was in good shape, thanks largely to his daily tennis practice with a one-time Italian professional, who now held down a sinecure at the Zürich office. He was also a good skier, although these days he only ventured out onto the mountains when conditions were perfect, and when the helicopter that served as his personal ski-lift could be sure of a safe landing.

'That's good to hear, Celio,' he said. 'I hope your coffee's good and hot.'

The servant waited for Hunziker and Moser to take their places, and poured out two more cups. Hoffman folded his arms as the ritual, which involved the careful addition of fresh cream and half a teaspoon of raw cane sugar, was played out. Only when the servant had gone, closing the door behind him, did the chairman speak again.

'Is Herr Lambert not to join us?' he asked, looking at the one empty chair.

'He's in Italy apparently,' said Hoffman, 'on the new launch.'

'Of course he is,' said Hunziker. 'Then let's proceed. Dr Kessler, do you have some news for us?'

Kessler cleared his throat. His cup of coffee sat in front of him, untouched.

'So far everything is going according to plan,' he said, being careful to look the chairman full in the face. 'We've run all the fertility tests and we're confident that in ten days from now we shall be able to begin amassing our preliminary stock of ova.'

'Of eggs, you mean?'

'Yes, of eggs.'

The chairman nodded slowly.

'And you're certain they will prove suitable for our purposes?'

'We can't be absolutely certain of that yet, but our preliminary results are favourable.'

'What results are those?' said Hoffman.

'The results of our histo-compatibility tests,' said Kessler. 'We took a sample of living cells during our preliminary examination of the donor . . .'

'The Jewish woman?'

'Yes. So far most of those cells have successfully survived transplants into laboratory animals. This is only a rough guide, of course. Until we test our cell cultures on a human immune system we won't be sure the donor cells are safe from attack. But I'm more than confident that our faith in the existing data is justified.'

An expression of concern crossed Hoffman's face.

'Are you saying, Dr Kessler,' he said, 'that more of our patients must play the role of human guinea pig before we can be sure of any benefits at all?'

'With every new method of medical treatment there is always someone who must go first,' said Kessler. 'Even the most theoretically perfect procedures can fail in practice.'

'Nevertheless, Egon,' said Hunziker, looking at Kessler over the top of his glasses, 'the patients at this clinic have not paid to be experimented upon. I'm sure you understand that. If there is any question of danger, you must carry out your tests on members of the public. I'm sure that could be arranged. What we must avoid at all costs is any repetition of what happened eighteen months ago.'

Kessler sighed through closed jaws. He and Geiger had only made one serious error since the whole genetics programme had begun, but these people never passed up an opportunity to remind him of it. Not even the Erixil triumph had wiped away that sin. He was only glad Geiger himself had never sought a seat on the executive committee. He might have found their carping too much to bear.

'I think it's only fair to point out,' said Moser, speaking for the first time, 'that the first of those operations was carried out against Professor Geiger's advice. And the patient was fully apprised of the risks.'

'Not fully enough, unfortunately,' said Hoffman.

Moser ignored the remark. He was the oldest member of the committee and was only a year or two away from retirement, or so Hoffman reckoned. He certainly did not look as healthy as the others: although tall he seemed frail, and the fatigue was etched into his face. On the other hand, he was the only member of the committee who did not spend at least a few days every month taking advantage of the company's most advanced health and body care programmes. He almost seemed to despise such things. And yet he had been from the beginning the most enthusiastic supporter of Geiger's research efforts. Hoffman never understood that. If Moser was so happy to grow old, why was he so anxious to help others live on and on, beyond their natural span?

'I should like to add,' said Kessler, 'that this time the risks should be significantly smaller. If the implanted cultures are rejected, the patient should suffer no more than a mild fever. If not, then it is simply a question of whether we can set in motion the necessary messenger protein sequences for the cycle of development we are looking for. I am confident that by using foetal material – material that should be genetically pristine – the problem of uncontrolled growth will not occur again.'

'Are you certain?' demanded Hoffman.

'There is no such thing as certainty,' said Kessler, the impatience beginning to show through his carefully measured speech, 'as any scientist will tell you. Especially not at the forefront of research that may quite possibly turn out to be the biggest step forward in the history of medicine. But given what we know from our last trials, I would say the chances of the same problems occurring again are small. Apart from anything else we shall be looking out for them.'

Denzler put out his cigarette with a series of rapid, staccato stabs against the polished jade ash-tray. He was a thick-set, stocky man with big pores and big hands.

'How long before you'll be ready to treat someone?' he asked. 'There's one priority patient I think we'd all be very anxious to help.'

'Kazuo Hiraizumi, you mean?'

Denzler nodded.

'I believe we'd only need a week or so after the first ova became available.'

'A week!' said Denzler. 'Last time it took nearly six.'

Kessler smiled.

'That was eighteen months ago. Since then we've run trials on hundreds of embryos, and our basic data has been improving all the time. We can now bring a colony of cells to the right stage of differentiation in a fraction of the time it takes nature – but then, we aren't trying to grow a whole foetus, are we?'

'So you could operate on Hiraizumi in, what, two and a half weeks?'

'I believe so. In fact he'd be a very good starting point – from a medical point of view I mean.'

Denzler looked at the chairman. He did not look happy.

'I'm sure I don't have to point out how valuable a contact Mr Hiraizumi is to this company,' said Denzler.

'You're right, Gustav,' said Hunziker. 'You don't.'

'Then consider how useful it would be if we were to treat him successfully. There could be no better advertisement for our services.'

'Nor a worse one if he were to die,' said Hoffman.

'He will die anyway,' said Denzler. 'He has a few weeks to live at best. His relatives have already been informed. If we save him we can write our own cheque.'

For a moment there was silence.

'There's no other treatment that might work?' said Hunziker.

'Only a conventional transplant. And in his condition he'd never survive it.'

Hunziker looked first at Moser, then at Hoffman.

'In which case he might agree to take the risks. If it's his last chance.'

'He'd be foolish not to,' said Denzler.

'Then I suggest we put it to him. Apart from anything else, the support of his corporation in the Far East would be invaluable. With Hiraizumi's influence behind us we could wipe out the competition in six months.'

'I'd go along with that,' said Bruggman. 'The costs of a big campaign out there could be astronomical, and the normal rules of the market-place don't apply. If we trod on the wrong toes we'd be lucky to get our products into anything bigger than a corner-shop.'

'Very well then, that's decided,' said Hunziker. 'Egon, you'll put the idea to our patient as soon as you can.'

Kessler nodded. He knew Geiger didn't want to rush into another operation too soon, but they had to show results and quickly. Besides, Kazuo Hiraizumi was an unusual patient even by Mendelhaus's standards. The economic power he wielded made him the most irresistible of allies. To save his life was an opportunity they could not afford to pass up.

Hoffman leaned forward in his seat, placing his palms on the surface of the table.

'I should like to make one proviso,' he said, looking at Kessler, 'if I may. And that is that we do nothing to draw attention to the work of the clinic, especially not on the research side. Under present circumstances too much public interest in our affairs could prove highly embarrassing. I would personally prefer it if our advances, as far as the public are concerned, were confined to the realm of cosmetics.'

'Isn't it a little late,' said Moser, 'to be worrying about the ethics of genetic manipulation? Especially now, when we're on the verge of a breakthrough.'

'That's not what I meant, Karl. I'm referring to the presence of this Jewish woman, our donor as Dr Kessler calls her, right here in the Phönixlager. Because I've heard that her co-operation has not been as complete as he had wished.'

Kessler felt the blood rising to his face. Hoffman had been keeping this in reserve, and he wasn't ready for it.

'I . . . we were always prepared for that. Steps have already been taken to ensure that nothing can be detected.'

'I know,' said Hoffman. 'Mr Krystal is very effective. But there are always risks involved in kidnapping, to say nothing of murder.'

'Murder?' said Moser. 'No one said anything about murder! Egon, what the hell is all this?'

'I don't know what Mr Hoffman is referring to,' said Kessler. 'But I would remind you that I obtained the committee's permission to use coercion over a year ago, so long as appropriate steps were taken to prevent the company from being implicated. Those steps have been taken.'

'I recall no such meeting,' said Moser.

'Karl, it was agreed in principle,' said Hunziker, soothingly. 'There was a quorum. I believe you were away at the time.'

'Ill,' said Hoffman.

'Well, I should like to make up for my absence by declaring right now that I am completely opposed to the idea. The risks involved are simply enormous.'

'Hardly *enormous*,' said Hunziker, 'not for us. This *is* Switzerland.'

Hoffman suppressed a smile. Moser's outrage at being left out of a key decision was a pleasing sight.

'In any case,' the managing director went on, 'it is surely disingenuous to suggest that we can release this woman once we have finished with her. She could destroy us all.'

'What is your point, Dietmar?' said Hunziker. 'You supported this decision, as I recall.'

'My point is simply this: that as long as this woman is alive she poses a threat to the company, and to us. As soon as we have what we need, every last trace of her existence must be wiped clean from the entire establishment. We mustn't wait a day longer than is necessary. Every day the danger of unwanted attention grows greater.'

'I must insist that all decisions of that kind be left to the research director,' said Kessler urgently. 'This woman is the only one of her kind ever located. The chances are we will never find another. If we were to act prematurely the entire project will have been for nothing.'

'I must disagree with you there, Doctor Kessler,' said Bruggman. 'The skin-care products have already helped our financial position a good deal. In all probability the research costs will be paid off in eighteen months or less. Compared to mass-market products like Erixil, your egg factory may be of marginal financial benefit.'

'I have explained many times that these mass-market products you refer to are merely spin-offs, detours on the way to something far greater, medically *and* financially. And for this reason I must insist that the fate of the donor be left entirely to Professor Geiger and I. Until we are sure we can clone the ova perfectly, the egg factory, as you call it, must be kept running.'

Hunziker shook his head.

'I'm sorry, Egon, but we cannot leave such a decision in your hands alone. Dietmar is right: this woman can destroy us. Nothing, not even your precious project, could be worth that. Nevertheless, there is no need to be hasty. While you are still extracting what you need we shall simply redouble our vigilance. With our contacts we should receive plenty of warning of any enquiries. But I must ask you when you think we may rid ourselves of this danger.'

'If all goes well,' said Kessler, 'after the second ovulation. With the stimulants, we should have a larger batch.'

'The staff tell me you've cloned successfully before, using other eggs,' said Denzler. 'So once you have your next batch of ova you should be able to produce a renewable stock in just a few days, isn't that correct?'

'It isn't quite so simple,' said Kessler. 'We have to be sure we can reliably fertilise the ova while retaining the donation characteristics. What's more the existing methods can often rupture and kill the ovum. That's why we must gather a reasonable stock of them.'

'I see no problem with waiting a couple of weeks or so,' said Hunziker, 'do you, Dietmar?'

'No, I don't, Oswald,' said Hoffman, looking once again at Kessler. 'So long as we are vigilant. We cannot gamble where the interests of the company are at stake.'

Hunziker smiled at Hoffman, a fatherly, indulgent smile. 'You can count on our support for whatever is necessary,' he said, 'as always.'

8

The Phönixlager. February 6th, 1996.

They removed her watch. There were no windows in the room and a weak light was always on over the door to make it easier to watch her, or so Cathy thought. They asked her if she wanted anything to pass the time – books, videos. Live television was not permitted. Strapped to the bed she screamed and wept, falling asleep with the tears wet on her face. On what she assumed to be the first night she bled more heavily. It woke her up. At first she thought she had wet herself, but then she realised what was happening. She was too embarrassed and angry to call out. When they came in several hours later they found a plume of blood on the sheet beneath her. Kessler cleaned her. Rather than risk another violent struggle – she was burning with shame and rage and shouting obscenities – he did not give her clean underwear, but dressed her in a sort of diaper, fixed with tapes on either hip. She became hysterical, and he administered tranquillisers. Hours passed. Sometimes Kessler, sometimes Geiger came into the room to talk to her. Again Geiger asked her if she wanted anything to pass the time. If she promised no violence he said he would undo the straps. She asked for a Stradivarius violin and then laughed, still delirious in spite of the medication. She dreamed. She thought of Mike Varela. She tried to imagine what he

294

was doing at that moment, but then she realised that she no longer had any sense of time. There was only the continuous presence of the weak light and the silent progress of her body, manufacturing the eggs for Mendelhaus's New World.

She began to recognise sounds in the building around her: the rush of ventilation at what she thought must be an early hour of the morning, the sound of people going past outside. The hum of cleaning machines fading into the distance in the evening. She tried to imagine the surface of the mountain and the wind on her face. Sometimes she would lose control and start shouting for help. She feared for her life and she feared for the eggs her body was making. What were they going to do with them? Maybe there were other women like herself in the clinic, confined like battery hens. One morning – she assumed it was morning – she woke up and saw a violin standing on a chair on the other side of the room. The case on the floor with what looked like a bundle of music on it. The same day Geiger let her out of the harness. *You understand now that violence is senseless*, he had said.

It was a Stradivarius. It would have been worth hundreds of thousands of dollars. Money was no obstacle to these people. Her first impulse was to smash it against the bed once Geiger had left the room, but she couldn't resist playing it for a moment. She played a long plaintive note on the E string and then played a passage from 'Death and the Maiden'. Tears welled up, but she kept on playing. In the semi-dark on the other side of the mirror Geiger smiled and looked up at the ceiling.

She played for several hours and then got back onto the bed, exhausted. Time passed. Each day she was given hormone injections. Each day she played the violin.

A moment always came when Geiger's face changed and

he looked down at his black bag, placed discreetly under his chair as he came into the room.

'Time for Cathy's medicine I suppose?'

Geiger brought the bag onto the table without replying. Cathy rolled up the arm of her smock and slapped the vein like a junkie. She was no longer restrained, but whenever the moment arrived for the hormone injection she had a flash of defiance, expressed in bitter irony.

Geiger stood and she stood, revealing her pale inner arm where the needles went in.

'Hit me, Doc.'

Holding her lightly at the elbow, Geiger cleaned the area of skin over the vein.

'I've been thinking, Professor. What happens to Miss Ryder when she has filled the company's egg box?'

She blinked as the needle went in.

Geiger looked her in the face as he put the used syringe into a cellophane bag.

'What do you mean?'

Cathy smiled.

'You know what I mean.'

Geiger shook his head.

'What I mean, Professor Geiger, is once I have given you what you want, what are you going to do with me? You're not just going to let me walk out of here, are you? With what I know about your work I could have you closed down in a week.'

Geiger closed the black bag and sat back down. Cathy stood looking down at him for a moment and then sat herself.

'Well?'

'First, I think you exaggerate the threat your eventual indiscretion represents. You would have no proof to offer to the authorities, and anyway, by the time the police got round to paying us a visit, any evidence would have been removed. Second – ' He raised a hand to interrupt her objection ' – second, and this is perhaps more important to you, Cathy. Nothing I do to you, I am doing to you – nothing I do will be irreversible. I promise you that.'

Cathy looked into his eyes, trying to take in what he was saying, trying to believe it. After a moment, she went on. She spoke in a quiet voice.

'And my eggs, my children.'

Geiger looked down at the floor and moved his feet.

'Don't think I don't understand when you say things like that. You just . . . you just have to understand that these, these eggs, they are just cells, like any other. It's the same as if I took cells from the end of your finger. They are just at a different stage of development.'

Cathy brushed the tears from her face. She was shaking her head slowly.

'Are you saying there is no plan to fertilise my eggs, doctor?'

Geiger felt his face burn.

'Why would we fertilise them?'

He was looking her in the face. The corners of his mouth twitched.

'I don't know, doctor. You might need developed foetuses, you might need babies.' A thought flashed through her mind. She began to smile.

'Who's going to be the donor?'

'Donor?'

'Who's going to give the sperm? You need sperm to fertilise the egg, right?'

'Yes.'

'It's you, isn't it?'

She had stood up. Geiger remained in his chair, his hands on his knees.

'So why go to all this trouble, why not just rape me like any other animal?'

She was breathing through her open mouth, her heart thumping.

'Cathy, Cathy. Your imagination. You torture yourself with these ideas. There is no sinister side to what I am doing here. It is a question of advancing the frontiers of knowledge, of human potential. Look at the world, Cathy. Knowledge is what it needs. Look where ignorance and superstition have brought it.'

Cathy turned away from him and walked across the room to where the violin was on the chair.

'But where will it stop?'

She picked up the violin and plucked a string.

'It will stop as soon as we have enough material – '

'No, I mean where will your research stop? Let's forget about me for a minute. I'm just a means to an end.'

She turned to face him, holding the violin loosely by its delicate neck. She was frowning, a deep vertical fold dividing her black, compressed brows.

'What you are doing – it's wrong.'

Geiger shook his head.

'Wrong. Right. What has that got to do with science? Don't misunderstand me. It's not that I share your view. I don't. I believe that the work I am doing here will be a force for good, but I have never allowed questions of morality to cloud the issue for me.'

He stood up.

'For me ignorance is wrong. Knowledge is right.'

'But life. The gift of life. What right do you have to . . . to tamper, to twist life to your own ends?'

'But a gift implies a giver, Cathy. Which giver are we talking about here? God? There is no God, Cathy. No God. No heaven. No hell. No eternal punishment. *We live in an old chaos of the sun* as Wallace Stevens so aptly put it. We live and die in disease and failure. The body fails us, our genes fail us. We grow wise just in time to die. Why *should* we simply accept that? Maybe three score years and ten was good enough when life was simpler, when we lived little better than animals. But the

298

world we live in now needs better than that; it is too complex, and the pace of change accelerates remorselessly. We cannot wait for evolution. Humanity must be prepared to adapt itself.'

'I'm not against finding cures for disease, but when it comes to taking life, taking the seeds of individuals – '

'What's the difference? A seed is not the plant, Cathy, an egg is not the animal. These are just cells, Cathy, cells, like the cells in your teeth, in your hair.'

'But given time. Given time to grow they become people.'

'And the cells in your teeth, given time, manipulated in the right way, they too could become a person.'

'But not naturally. Naturally they would never do that.'

'But that word *natural*, what does it mean? Life itself, organic life, is unnatural, Cathy. If all matter tends to maximum entropy, then organic systems, life, is unnatural. And if you want to put that little trick down to divine will, to God or Allah or whatever you want to call him, that's fine, but it has nothing to do with science, Cathy. Besides, if God can reorganise the natural order, why shouldn't we? If I do it with this' – he put a finger to his temple – 'and these' – he showed her his hands – 'why should I not? Nobody *gave* God this prerogative, Cathy. He took it.'

Geiger left the room and went along the corridor to his office. He sat at his desk, holding his head in his hands. After a while he looked at the papers scattered on his desk. Two computer printouts had been put on top of Cathy Ryder's papers. He picked up her diary and removed a photograph from inside the cover. It was a passport photo of a young man, an Italian maybe. He wondered who it was.

9

Zürich. February 11th, 1996.

The roar of the engines grew suddenly louder as they began their final descent towards the snow-laden runway. Looking out over the wing Mike could see traces of cloud streaking over the flaps, lit up by the warning lights and the yellow glow of the cabin. The wind was strong. He could feel the aircraft struggling against it, rolling first one way then the other, accompanied by the rattling of the overhead lockers. He had always hated landings, especially at night, in the fog, when there were mountains all around. He knew they did everything by computer these days, could fly the plane with their eyes shut, but that did not reassure him. Suppose there was a bug in the software? He could never feel easy trusting his life to a fistful of microchips.

But then it was absurd to get nervous about the one-in-a-million chance that the plane might crash when a man who had already tried to kill him was sitting just a few rows away in the business class cabin. If he leaned out into the aisle Mike could just make out the back of his head, and his right hand planted squarely on the arm-rest. And Mike did lean out, just as he had done every ten minutes or so since they left New York. Even inside a jetliner at 40,000 feet he did not feel safe. It was less than twelve hours since their promised meeting at the

Café de Lyon on William Street. The memory of it was so fresh in Mike's mind, he still couldn't think of it without a shudder.

Although he had no clear recollection of hearing a shot, Mike knew that the gunman had been behind him. But when he had looked round, half expecting to find a rifle in his face, he had seen nothing, just confusion: people yelling, diving for cover behind their tables, and a waiter who had dropped a big tray of breakfast all over the floor. Table number ten was just beside the frosted-glass doors, perfectly situated for a killing. A gunman could be back on the street before most people even had time to register what had happened. Then Mike understood: he was the one they had wanted to kill. Krystal had set him up. The man who got killed had taken his place in the hope of finding something out. And the creep in the underground parking lot, his only job had been to keep the real Mike Varela from showing up.

After that he had not hesitated. He could have waited for the police, queued up to give a statement along with a dozen other people, and told them what he knew. But in the meantime Krystal would have been on his way to Switzerland. Even if he could have convinced the police to arrest him at the airport, there was little chance that they could have held him. Mike had nothing for evidence but a message on an answering machine, and he was fairly sure that no one else had even heard the killer call his name. Officer Bales already had him down as a possible basket-case: a jealous spic who couldn't take it when his up-town girlfriend walked out on him. Worse than all that, if Krystal thought they were on to him it could only add to the danger for Cathy – if she was still alive . . .

He had called the airport from a call-box at the end of the street. There was a direct flight to Zürich at 10.45am, and not another until late in the afternoon. He made a reservation there and then with his gold card and raced

301

back to Cathy's apartment, just in case he were wrong, just in case Krystal had tried to ring up and cancel their meeting. But there was nothing new on the answering machine. He decided to leave a message beside it in case the police showed up again, but when it came to it he couldn't think what to say. He understood nothing, only that he couldn't sit back and wait for things to work out, that his only chance of getting Cathy back was to find her himself. So he wrote: *Cathy Ryder is in Switzerland. I've gone to find her. If you have questions, put them to Ernst Krystal.* Below it he added the telephone number he had found on the matchbook.

He'd thrown some things together at Pop Varela's house and made it to JFK fifty minutes before the flight. By then he had already decided what to do. Just before emigration there was an airport information desk, manned by a group of bored-looking women in printed polyester blouses. Mike had gone to a pay-phone a few yards away and called the desk, asking for Ernst Krystal and mentioning the flight number. It was urgent, he'd said. They put Krystal's name out over the PA system. Several minutes went by without anything happening, but then a man appeared, a tall man, carrying a briefcase and a grey overcoat which was slung over his arm. He stood looking around for a moment, as if to check that nothing was wrong, and then went to the desk. When the girl handed him the phone, Mike hung up. Krystal had not shown much reaction. He handed back the phone and stood there looking around, as if he knew what had happened. Mike turned away and began talking. When he glanced back Krystal had gone.

Since then Mike had kept that picture of Krystal's face at the front of his mind. He wanted to be sure he could recognise it once they were on the ground. He had seen him again at the departure gate, but he did not get too close, in case he was recognised. He reckoned Krystal

302

could not know what he looked like, but there was always a chance. Cathy had kept a little photo of him in her wallet. Maybe Krystal had seen it.

The aircraft put down with a jolt just after midnight local time, and taxied towards a gate at the far end of the terminal building. Inside the cabin jolly Alpine music came over on the loudspeakers, interrupted by the standard set of announcements from the cabin crew. *Welcome to Switzerland. We hope you have a pleasant stay. Thank you for flying Swissair.* The other passengers seemed subdued, stultified by eight hours of in-flight music, complementary alcohol and lack of exercise. Wearily they reached for their belongings and stood waiting in the aisles for the doors to open. Mike did not feel so relaxed, but he tried to look like the others. He didn't want to draw attention to himself.

The business class cabin emptied first. The way from the economy class cabin was politely blocked by a steward. The front sections were deserted by the time Mike walked through. As he stepped out of the aircraft a freezing blast of wind made him shiver. It was colder than New York. He did not waste time putting on his coat.

It was a long way to the arrivals area down neon-lit passageways decorated with back-lit advertisements for credit cards, cigarettes and Swiss banks. Mike walked quickly along the moving walkways, brushing past other passengers, almost colliding with an old man who stopped too suddenly to adjust a strap on his suitcase. Someone protested to him in German, but he hardly noticed. He could not afford to let Krystal get away. It might be his only chance. He had not thought of it before, but if there was a hold-up at Immigration . . .

The airport was not busy, but most of the immigration desks were closed. As he stood waiting with the other foreigners, Mike caught sight of Krystal in the other line, just as he was going through. Most of the Swiss nationals were being let past on the nod, only having to hold up their passports in front of them; but the foreigners were having their papers inspected carefully by a skinny young man with a big Adam's apple and a beginner's attention to detail. Mike was still a dozen places from the front of the line when he heard one of the carousels in the Baggage Reclaim Area start up. The young official began asking questions of an American woman at the head of the line. His accent was so thick she could barely understand him. Mike could do nothing but stand and wait.

When he got through there was already a crowd of passengers standing around the carousel, which carried the bags around in a twisting circuit a few inches above the ground. Overhead an electronic sign read: NEW YORK. Some people already had their bags and were loading them on to big metal trolleys. A group of teenage kids were struggling with a large cardboard box tied up with string. Mike moved to a space on the far side of the carousel and scanned the faces on the opposite side. Krystal was not there. He moved around and tried again, searching for the face he had seen at JFK. He began to feel the panic rising up inside him. Maybe Krystal had gone out a different way, maybe he hadn't brought a suitcase. Maybe he hadn't even got on the plane. Maybe it had been someone else . . . He searched the faces again, and still Krystal's wasn't among them. More passengers were coming through Immigration, filling up the few remaining spaces round the carousel. Mike's own suitcase, a black one made of woven nylon, went by beneath him, but he ignored it. Maybe Krystal was in the bathroom, he thought. After a long flight . . . A second carousel at the far end of the hall started moving. Another flight had just come in.

Then Mike saw him. It was just the same as at JFK, only this time Krystal was the one on the phone. There was a row of little cabins just around the corner from the

304

exit. He hung up and then walked over to where the other passengers were standing. Mike moved around the back of the crowd and stood just a few feet behind him. Krystal waited with his right hand buried inside his overcoat pocket. Mike saw his own bag go round a second time. Again he ignored it.

Half a minute later Krystal took his hand out of his pocket and edged closer to the carousel. Mike did the same. And as he saw Krystal reach down for a big grey Delsey case he too made to pick it up.

'Excuse me, sir,' he said, in his dumb Dixieland accent. 'I think that's my case you have there.'

Krystal looked at him as if he were some kind of madman.

'I'm afraid you're mistaken,' he said.

'No sir, indeed. That there is my case. It's got my name on it. Right there on the label.'

Krystal looked around. A guard by the exit was watching them. Krystal smiled a tight, irritated smile.

'I think you'll find,' he said, 'that the name *and* address on it are mine.'

And he reached down and opened the flap on the black plastic tag. Mike bent right over to read it.

'Sixty-two Bergstrasse, Hottingen. Hell, mister, I sure don't live there! I'm really sorry about that. Damned if this ain't the exact same case as mine, though.'

'That's all right,' said Krystal drily, and walked away towards Customs. He was almost there when he stopped and looked back for a moment. Mike just kept his eyes on the carousel, folding his arms impatiently. Beneath him his black bag went past for the third time.

10

Zürich. February 12th, 1996.

He stripped the cellophane from the plastic beaker and looked into the mirror.

'Good morning, Herr Varela.'

He tried to smile, but again a sense of unreality broke over him in a wave and he had to steady himself against the sink. He opened the faucet and watched water turn into the plug-hole. Then he looked back up at his reflection, soothed by the sound which made the empty, antiseptic space easier to bare. Holding on to that sound he walked across to the bidet. He sat down, holding his head in his hands. He tried to think.

He had woken up several times in the night, disturbed by traffic on Silstrasse, and each time he had lain there reminding himself of what was happening to him, of what had happened. Only six months ago he had been leading a regular life in New York: making money, seeing friends. He had felt at that time – not that he ever had to think of such things – that his life was made up of a past and a future. Each reservoir – one opaque, dark, the other luminous, full of detail, of things he would acquire – flowed through the present moment. Now his life was reduced to a strange hotel room. His past had disappeared into the moment he had seen the bullet open the stranger's head. He knew that the bullet had been meant

306

for him. He knew that the same violence was directed at Cathy, that somewhere she was suffering at the hands of the same violence. His present, the clean emptiness of his bathroom, was filled with the idea of Cathy.

He frowned and looked down between his legs into the ceramic bowl. Cathy filled his present – his whole existence since the killing in the cafe – she filled his present and yet he felt he hardly knew her. They had been together such a short time. The thought that she had got him wrong, had mistaken his intentions, this was almost as bad as the idea of her suffering somewhere. He brought his hands together, twisting them together in his frustration. He looked at his wrist. He had forgotten to adjust his watch. It seemed appropriate somehow. There was no time for him now. All that was left to him was an interval. It was as long as it took for his money to run out and for American Express to block his card. It was as long as it took him to find Cathy. It was a precious interval. Time bled from the moment like the water running into the sink.

He closed the faucet.

'You need a shave, Herr Varela.'

Out on the street, he looked at the address scribbled on the cheap tourist plan he had been given in reception. The US consulate was on Zollickerstrasse, above the lake on the south-eastern side. A forty-minute walk, the girl in reception had said. It was cold in the street and he turned up the lapels of his coat. He had another address scribbled down. The paper was folded in two and pushed deep into his back pocket, but he no longer had to refer to that. It was fixed in his mind.

Zürich was a weird town. All the Swiss bankers he had come across in New York had seemed like regular guys, friendly, outgoing. And they all spoke an English you could understand. But here the few people he saw making their way on foot in heavy winter clothing looked almost hostile, cold and haughty. He could not make himself understood. It was a relief to talk to an American.

'Certainly, Mr – '

'Varela. Michael Varela.'

'If you would like to take a seat Mr Varela, Roy Calhoun will be through in a moment.'

Mike looked around at the office. There was a small reproduction of a Modigliani portrait on the wall. He noticed that his wet shoes had made a dark patch on the beige carpet. Consular staff came in and out of the room. They smiled at him as they came into the room. As the minutes passed this began to irritate him. *They tried to kill me* he wanted to say to the smiling faces, *time is running out*.

Finally Roy appeared. He was a big blond guy, receding at the temples. He wore a grey suit with a waistcoat. It gave him an avuncular look.

'Mr Varela.'

His handshake was firm and he gave off a faint smell of soap.

He took down the details with a fountain pen, nodding every now and then and looking up.

'Have you checked with the company she visited here? Maybe they . . .'

'Her boss did. I know that. Apparently they said she left them almost two weeks ago.'

'Well have you reported this to the local police?'

Mike shook his head.

'I thought with her being an American citizen, I should come to you first.'

'I see.'

Roy wrote something in his notebook.

After a moment, he looked up, surprising Mike with a big friendly smile.

'My advice to you, Mr Varela, is to go along to the

police headquarters and to report Miss – he looked down at his notes – Miss Ryder to them as a missing person. You say she should have been back in the States about two weeks ago?'

Mike nodded.

'The thing is they have the facilities to investigate this kind of thing. I'd like to help but we are only a small team here, and I think you'll find the Swiss police very efficient.'

As Calhoun spoke a sound of chanting slowly grew until it was too loud for him to go on.

'Demonstrators,' he shouted with the same affable smile. 'Greens. They're always complaining about some factory or other ruining the environment. Some companies have their headquarters up here.'

He laughed although his laughter was drowned by the shouting. Mike watched his shoulders shaking.

'What would they think if they saw Detroit?' he shouted, rising from his seat.

'I don't know Detroit,' said Mike. He was beginning to find all the smiling a little false.

Outside he watched the demonstrators move off along the street. The women wore army surplus and some of them had their hair brushed into orange spikes. They looked dirty. They were carrying different banners which he couldn't understand, but the message was clear from different symbols painted around the words. There were crude pictures of factories belching out smoke and dead trees. He hated militant types and he hated dirt. There would be a faint odour of patchouli and sweat. He wrinkled his nose and turned back towards the middle of town.

In the police headquarters there was less smiling, but he couldn't get them to understand what he wanted. A fat guy sitting at a counter filled in a form as he spoke. After fifteen minutes of watching the policeman make his slow words, his red tongue pushed into the side of his cheek, Mike was surprised when he looked up and said,

'Reason for your visit here, Herr?'

Mike steadied himself against the counter.

'Look. I just explained what the fu . . . what the problem is. I'm looking for a woman, an American. She came here and she . . . she disappears. *Disappears.*'

'Was she skiing?'

Mike looked around the office to see if anyone was in on the joke.

'Skiing?'

'Yes.'

The man pushed back his chair and made movements with his arms negotiating a difficult slope.

'I know what skiing is, friend.'

'Yes we have many accident. People ski our mountains but they don't see the. . . . the danger.'

Mike passed his hand over his face. The fat man looked up at him, his tongue resting on his lower lip.

'An American woman. A professional person, a stock analyst. You know, invested funds.

'Fun?'

'Funds!'

The fat man sat back in his chair, startled by the stranger's tone.

'Okay, okay. Calm down now, Herr – ' he squinted at the paper, 'Herr Ryder.'

Mike shook his head. It was beginning to seem like a nightmare.

'I am not Mr Ryder.'

'Then who are you?'

'Varela. Michael Varela. I am an American. An American.'

'Yes, yes. Land of the brave.'

The man began to cross out what he had written on his

form. Mike was about to say something when another man came to the counter. He was scrubbed so clean his face shone. He said something in German to the fat guy and then looked up at Mike.

'Papers please.'

Mike handed him his passport. He looked at it for a moment, turning the pages crisply.

'When did you last see the woman?'

'In New York. She went missing here in Switzerland. She visited the Mendelhaus clinic and then . . .'

'Mendelhaus?'

'Yes. She visited the clinic.'

The young man nodded. He tugged at his scrubbed red earlobe. He frowned. Mike began to feel he was getting somewhere.

'Is there something you know?'

'Something? No, no. I know nothing at all. But I can make enquiries for you if you wish. Have you been to the consulate?'

'Yes, they sent me to you.'

'Mr Calhoun, I suppose. A very nice man. Very helpful, and always smiling.'

Mike reached into his back pocket and pulled out the folded scrap of paper.

'Here,' he said. 'This may be of some help.'

He handed it to the young man. He looked at it for a moment, and then looked up. His face had become serious, or it seemed to Mike that way.

'Krystal?'

'That's right, Ernst Krystal. I think he may know something about where the woman went. That's his address.'

The man folded the paper and went to put it into his pocket.

'Hey, I need that. I just gave it to you so you can copy it down.'

Without taking his eyes off Mike, the young man

pushed the piece of paper in front of the fat guy. He said something crisp in German and it might have been a dime in a slot by the way the fat guy started scribbling.

'And where are you staying, Herr Varela? In case I hear of anything.'

'I'm staying at the Hotel Edelweiss. Room 207.'

The fat guy pushed the piece of paper across the counter.

'Enjoy your stay in Switzerland,' he said, his face finding a smile for the first time. Mike wished he hadn't bothered.

11

Alleinmatt. February 13th, 1996.

Kessler took the call in his office.

'I'm sorry, Ernst. I wanted to take this on my own line. I'm sure you understand.'

'Of course, Herr Doctor. I wouldn't normally bother you with this kind of thing, but I know that the arrangements for the girl were your responsibility, and so I thought it best to come to you first; unless of course – '

'No. no. You were absolutely right, Ernst. And I appreciate your discretion in this matter. There's really no reason to bother the board with such details.'

There was a pause as both men waited to see what would come next. It was Kessler who spoke first.

'And so what is the problem exactly?'

'It seems that an American, a Michael Varela, is in Zürich asking . . . inconvenient questions. For some reason he has got it into his head that I have something to do with her disappearance.'

Kessler frowned, but his voice remained even, calm.

'Why should he think that?'

'Just before I came away from New York, I received a call from this same person. He claimed that the girl had given him my name and number.'

'Very unfortunate. And?'

'Well of course I told him I couldn't help him. But then

he said something which worried me; something about the girl. He said, *I don't think we are talking about the bank's business.* Those were his words.'

'Yes.'

'He implied that my interest in the girl had something to do with her being *special.*'

'But that could mean . . . anything.'

'I agree. It could. Including that someone else has discovered – '

'Good God. No, I can't believe that. Our whole line of enquiry has been unique. No one else – '

'I heard that scientific breakthroughs often occur almost simultaneously in different places. It's just that we only hear of the ones which come first. Wasn't that the case with the invention of the telephone? With the discovery of the double helix itself?'

'What did you do?'

'The morning after our interview, I arranged to meet this man. I felt it was better for all concerned, given the importance of the programme, given what is at stake, given the months of work and preparation – '

'What did you do?'

This time Kessler couldn't help sounding alarmed.

'I arranged to have him silenced.'

'Silenced?'

'Definitively.'

Kessler took the phone from his ear, and looked at the opposite wall. He shook his head slowly. Krystal's voice buzzed in the earpiece.

'And this person who was *definitively* silenced, why is he in Zürich asking questions now?'

'I'm afraid there was some confusion. The wrong man turned up. He must have been hoping to find out something. He has been identified as the kind of person we have to fear.'

Kessler stood up. He was beginning to lose his temper.
'You shot the wrong man?'

'It hardly matters. Nothing can be traced. These things are easy in America. All that is needed is money.'

Kessler slowly lowered himself back into his chair.

'So what do you suggest happens next, Ernst?'

'I think Varela is dangerous, unpredictable. His methods are unconventional, certainly – it is as if he wanted to draw attention to himself – but he is making progress. Nor can I believe he is working alone.'

'So what do you suggest we do?'

'I know where he is staying. I know someone who is ready to pay him a visit.'

'No more killing!'

Kessler was up on his feet again. He took a moment to get control of himself.

'No more killing, Ernst, not here. We are not murderers.'

Krystal marked a pause. It came to Kessler in a flash that the other man was playing with him.

'As you wish, Herr Doctor. Although I wonder if the board would feel comfortable about the situation if they knew how it stands – how it might develop.'

'They may not be happy with *you*, Ernst. They do not like mistakes, not when they threaten to bring us unwelcome attention. What you propose is too dangerous, too close to home. Zürich is not New York.'

Kessler could hear the other man draw a slow breath, as if he were dragging unsteadily on a cigarette.

'What then?'

'*I* will make the arrangements. All I want from you is to know where I can find this Michael Varela.'

Kessler wrote down the information and hung up. He stood by his desk for a few minutes, looking down at the ground. Then he leaned over and switched on the intercom.

315

'Karen, bring me some coffee. Fresh. I don't want reheated. And get me Madame Beauvais on the line will you?'

12

Zürich. February 13th, 1996.

Mike's head started to sing. Just the one note. High and far off. He recognised it. It was the first sign of a process which would end the next morning with a colossal mother and father of a hangover. He sipped at his whisky. In spite of the drink, the memory of the day was still there. The music in the bar was almost deafening, but even so, inside his head, Mike could hear perfectly the quiet voice of the young man at the police station telling him to pack his bag and go home.

Mike frowned trying to recall exactly what the young man had said. *We are investigating this matter now, Mr Varela. The best thing you can do is go straight to the airport.* He took a big bite of the numbing whisky and looked at the barman's talking face.

Out in the street, Mike touched at his jaw. The ringing in his ears had stopped. He watched a Mercedes go past. A face watched him out of the back window. For a moment he had an idea it might be Krystal or someone working for Krystal. He couldn't explain it, but since his second interview with the police he felt more exposed. Were they in league with Krystal, did he pay them? He regretted having given them his hotel room number.

He shook his head. What did the police have to do with Mendelhaus? He was getting paranoid. He felt for the scrap of paper in his back pocket. It was still there. He knew what his next move had to be. He would go to Krystal's house. Have a look around. Maybe learn something. Then he realised that he had left his map of Zürich back at the hotel. He didn't know where Hottingen was, and he wasn't about to go back into the bar to ask the barman.

He turned up the collar of his coat and walked back to the hotel.

By the time he got there he had almost completely sobered up. He stopped outside the door of his room. Again he had the feeling of being an easy target. He looked along the silent corridor to the fire exit. The elevator doors opened and two old ladies came out, one with a pekinese. As they came towards him he opened the door, staying where he was and pushing back the door with a little shove. The light was on. It had been off when he left. The old ladies were getting nearer. They had gone quiet, watching him, he was sure of it. He could hear their shoes on the carpet. When he looked round he met their little yellow smiles.

'Hi.'

They went on past, pausing at the room two doors from his. Still he didn't enter his room. For the first time he realised that what he needed was a gun. Reaching forward very slowly, he took the door handle and pulled the door shut. He went down to reception.

'Herr?'

The young woman behind the desk was leafing through a motorcycle magazine. Mike didn't know what to say at first. Then he found himself talking.

'It's the TV in my room. It won't work.'

'You could have used the phone, sir. There was no need to come down.'

Mike shrugged.

'I'll send someone up straight away, sir.'

When Mike didn't move from the desk, she frowned. Then she picked up the phone. She said something in German. Immediately a sleepy-looking man in overalls appeared. He smelt of drink. The girl looked at Mike.

'Reiner will go with you and look at the television.'

'Good, fine.' Mike tried to sound officious, exacting. He turned on his heels, followed by Reiner.

The TV worked first time. Reiner sighed and looked around the room, but the American was peering into the bathroom, as though he expected to find someone there.

'Iz vorking now, Herr.'

Mike withdrew from the bathroom and looked at Reiner who was standing under the overhead light, a tuft of black hair sticking up on his head.

'Good, good.'

There was another silence, and then Mike realised Reiner was waiting for a tip. He reached into his pocket for some change.

When Reiner had gone he stood in the empty room listening intently. Upstairs someone flushed the can. The room had been tidied and the cover on his bed turned back. Mike guessed one of the maids had left the light on.

'Paranoia,' he said with as much conviction as possible. Then he went over to the desk and looked at the map. He stared at it for a long time. Then the network of streets began to blur, and the sorrow and despair welled up inside him, heightened by the alcohol.

'Cathy, where are you? *Where?*'

He squeezed the tears from his eyes and went into the bathroom. He threw water on his face, but did not look in the mirror.

'Need a gun, need a gun,' he said. Then he went back into the bedroom and sat down to look at the map. Hottingen was a suburb on the eastern outskirts of town. He would take a taxi to the next street and then walk. What would happen then he didn't know. If he could somehow get hold of Krystal maybe he could force him to talk. The map began to tremble in his hands. The restaurant with the dead man sitting at the table came back to him. It seemed so unreal, yet he knew that his hands were shaking because it *was* real. The danger was real. He had to learn to live with that idea if he wasn't going to end up with a hole through his head.

He stood up. To his surprise he found that his legs were shaking.

'I need to eat something.'

His voice sounded small in the empty room. It was seven thirty. They served dinner in the restaurant until eight thirty. He went into the bathroom, took a quick look in the mirror, and then went down to eat.

There were very few people in the restaurant. The first bite of his steak told him why. But after a few mouthfuls of food he began to feel better. He tried to think how he would go about getting hold of a gun. In the States it wasn't a problem, but over here in Europe: what did you have to do? Then the idea of carrying a gun around, the thought he might have to shoot somebody or get shot himself terrified him. Here he was, Mike Varela, investment banker, behaving like he was James Bond or something. He had ordered a bottle of burgundy and to his surprise when he put down his knife and fork the bottle was almost empty.

'What the hell,' he said, emptying the rest of the bottle into his glass. Krystal could wait until morning. He didn't feel like going out to Hottingen in the dark without a gun. Get a gun then go see Krystal, that was what he would do.

'Would you like a *digestif* in the lounge, sir?'

The waiter was at his shoulder.

'A what?'

320

'A cognac sir, or a whisky perhaps. There is a beautiful fire in the hearth. Just a suggestion, sir.'

Mike looked at the waiter. There was a kind of knowing look on his face. Mike nodded.

'And a damn good suggestion, my friend.'

The waiter smiled broadly.

'Make it a nice big cognac, and I'll have a cigar with that.'

'Certainly, sir.'

There was quite a crowd in the lounge, which had a bar at one end and a big log fire at the other. Mike took one of the armchairs near the fire and waited for his drink. Now that he had decided not to go out to Krystal's he felt himself relaxing in the warmth. He thought of Reiner trying to fix his perfectly functioning television and smiled . . . a smile that froze on his lips. From where he sat he could just see over a display of flowers to where a girl was sitting at the bar. She had her back to him. *It was Cathy*. He sat up straight, almost knocking the glass from the waiter's hand.

'Your cognac sir, and a selection of cigars.'

'Yes, yes. Thank you. I'll take one of these.'

'Dutch, sir. Henry Wintermans. An excellent choice.'

Mike kept his eyes fixed on Cathy as he bent to the flame offered by the waiter. Then he thanked him and stood up. He made his way across the lounge between the chairs and tables to the bar. As he reached her, she turned, and he felt his heart jump.

'Cathy?'

But as he said it he knew it wasn't her. The girl had the same hair, the same kind of clothes, but she was more glamorous somehow, sexier, with a harder look in her eyes.

'I'm sorry?' She was smiling at him. The smile spread slowly showing her perfect teeth. She was fondling a

321

locket which Mike knew without looking – he didn't dare look – was nestled between her tanned breasts.

'Excuse me, I thought you were someone I knew.'

There was a pause, two beats of a conductor's baton, and then she said,

'She must be someone special.'

For a moment he didn't know what to say. Her eyes were mesmerising. He could feel his own being drawn to the shadowy perfumed area where the locket nestled, but with an effort which was almost physical he kept looking at her face. She drew her fingers along the chain until they closed on the medallion.

'I mean, she must be someone special for you to cross the room like that.'

'Like what?'

'Like you were walking on water or something.'

She laughed and tossed back her hair as if it were long and heavy, although it was cut to shoulder length, exactly like Cathy's.

'Do you mind if I sit down?'

Again her slow smile seemed to open inside him somewhere. He looked at the top of his untasted cigar embarrassed.

'Go ahead. I can't say this is a free country, but if you have a little money things can loosen up.'

'You're not from here?'

'Do I look Swiss?'

Mike laughed with her this time and again she threw back the long hair which she didn't have.

'I like your new hairstyle.'

For a moment he thought he had said something wrong. A flicker of anxiety crossed her perfect features.

'What do you mean?'

'Your haircut, I like it.'

She watched him, trapping her full lower lip with brilli-

322

ant teeth. Her dark eyes had hardened. They were black like volcanic glass.

'You keep tossing your head back as if you were used to a lot more hair. I just guessed you'd had a haircut.'

She touched at her hair delicately. She was smiling again.

'My, my. You *are* observant, Mister . . .'

'Varela. Mike Varela.'

She smiled.

'I'm Pascale,' she said. 'Charmed to meet you.'

They had a cognac together, and then another. She tilted back her head to empty her glass and Mike admired her beautiful throat and for the first time let his eyes drop to the dark shadow of her cleavage. The locket caught the light, and flashed like a semaphore with her heart-beat. She breathed in, her breasts filling Mike's vision. He looked up at her smiling face, embarrassed.

'What would your special lady say?'

Mike felt the colour rise in his cheeks.

'You're an incredibly beautiful girl.'

She looked down at the locket and twisted it around her finger.

'But where is she, your friend? She is your friend, I take it. I mean your lover.'

Mike didn't answer for a moment, his eyes held by the locket. It reminded him of something. His head felt thick with all the alcohol and the cigar. He looked up at her dark angel's face.

'I don't know. She disappeared. I know people don't just – '

'It happens all the time. People see things they shouldn't. Hear things they shouldn't. Do things they shouldn't.'

'No, but Cathy – '

'Cathy?'

'Cathy, yes. That's the girl's name. Cathy Ryder. Have you heard it before?'

She appeared to think for a moment. Mike's eyes drifted back down to the locket, but it was trapped in her fist now.

'No, never.'

She was smiling again.

'So what do you intend to do to find her? How will you go about it?'

Mike looked into her dark eyes. It unsettled him to be talking about Cathy to this woman, who was in many ways much more . . . exciting. It wasn't that he felt he was spoiling his chances, but it made him feel vulnerable somehow. He didn't want to think about it. Not now. He sipped at his drink, feeling the presence of the cognac, a buzzing behind his eyes.

'So?'

'Oh, I don't know. Tomorrow I have to take a decision.'

'Manyana.'

Mike stiffened. 'You know the song? Mañana, mañana, mañana is good enough for me.'

'You have a nice voice.'

Suddenly the whole situation seemed to come into focus. Here he was sitting in a bar with a beauty queen, who was giving him her undivided attention. What did it look like? Things like that didn't just happen. What was in it for her?

'What do you do for a living?'

The crudeness of his tone made it perfectly clear what he thought she did for a living.

And then they were making their way up to his room. He couldn't believe what he was doing. He was walking behind her, watching the smooth roll of her hips under the tight black skirt.

His room looked small, sordid. She went into the bathroom and he crouched down, peering in at the mini-bar trying to understand what was happening. It occurred to him that he would have to pay her in cash. He didn't even know how much he had in his wallet. And how much did you pay a high-class, a *very* high-class, Zürich hooker?

She came out of the bathroom smiling. Under the smile she felt bad. It wasn't the sort of thing she liked doing. Yet the money, the money was so good. She glanced slyly at her watch. Four hours and she would be flying out of Zürich – for good this time. No more Switzerland, and no more Madame Beauvais.

'Champagne?'

She laughed at Mike as he crouched by the mini-bar, the champagne bottle in his hand.

'Only if you promise not to say the bubbles go up your nose.'

They drank for a while, he sitting on the bed, her in an armchair. They talked about Zürich and how appalling the Swiss were, and then he felt he had to go to the can. He put his glass down on the chest of drawers and went into the bathroom. She touched him as he went past, letting her slender hand brush against his groin. He felt his scalp tingle.

In the bathroom he urinated as discreetly as he could and then looked in the mirror. His eyes were red and his tongue looked like it had been pulled out of an old base-ball boot. There was still time to throw her out.

When he came back into the room, she was sitting on the bed, her legs crossed in the full lotus position. Her clothes were on the chair. Mike swallowed, looking at her brown muscular body, and her beautiful smile. He loosened his belt and let his slacks drop to the floor. Then he approached the bed and was about to get in when she said: 'I'd like to propose a toast to all the bankers in Zürich.'

Mike smiled, puzzled by her expression. She was completely naked except for her jewellery. On her left wrist she had a heavy gold bangle and round her slender neck she still wore the locket. His eyes rested on this for a moment. In the light of the bedside lamp he saw it clearly for the first time. It was engraved with an initial or something. Then he took his glass from the chest of drawers and raised it to the woman sitting on his bed.

'To Zürich and its bankers. God bless their souls and may they sleep soundly in their waterbeds.'

He tossed back the champagne. She drank hers slowly and then threw the glass at the wall on the other side of the room. This sudden violence stirred something in Mike. He felt his sex harden, as he pulled his shirt over his head.

He sat on the bed next to her, and kissed her shoulder. There was a rich smell of amber from her fine skin. Then, as he was reaching forward, to kiss her breast, he felt as if someone immensely strong had taken his head and squeezed it tight at the temples. He blinked, hardly able to believe the pain. He tried to focus, gripping the strange woman by the arm, and as the full weight of the drug started to draw him down into darkness, he recognised, with a drowning feeling of terrible remorse and anger and fear, the treble clef engraved on the dissolving gold.

13

Zürich. February 14th, 1996.

They were sitting together at a bar, facing each other, holding hands. They were very close. Mike could smell the familiar perfume of her hair. She looked more beautiful than ever, and she was smiling. He didn't have to say anything. He knew everything was all right now: she was safe, and her love for him was alive again, renewed. He felt as if a heavy weight had been lifted from his shoulders. The happiness made him giddy. He would be everything for her. He would never let her down again. *Cathy*. He was about to put his arms around her when the barman slid two fluted glasses of champagne towards them. They took the glasses and raised them in a silent toast, but the champagne did not taste right. It was flat and bitter. Mike held his glass up to the light, but it fell from his hand and shattered on the floor with a deafening crash, like a brick going through a window. When he looked up, he saw that the woman opposite him was not Cathy at all, but someone he had never seen before. He asked her where Cathy was, but the stranger just smiled at him and raised her glass again. Then Mike saw the gold locket around her neck, the one he had bought for Cathy at Christmas. He tried to reach forward and take it, but the ground seemed to be giving way beneath him. He was falling, and as he fell he could hear the angry voices of people in the bar shouting after him. He looked down just in time to see the marble floor of the hotel reception hurtling towards him. He felt sure the impact would shatter his skull, but as he opened his eyes he realised that the floor was soft. He was lying in his hotel bed, and there was light coming in from behind the curtains. The red digits on the radio-clock read 10:04. He could still hear the shouting, but it came from outside: the chanting of young voices, a crowd . . .

He sat up. It hadn't all been a dream. Pascale had been real – and the locket? He wasn't sure. Ignoring the splitting pain in his head, he crawled over to his jacket, which lay draped over an upright chair. He felt inside for his wallet and pulled it out. The credit cards were all still there, and the money. His passport was still there in the other pocket too. Perhaps, he thought, with the booze and the jet-lag, he had just crashed out. But no: he was lying there in his shirt and his pants. The bitch had drugged him for sure. But why?

He got to his feet and pulled back the curtain a few inches. At the far end of the main street a group of maybe a hundred and fifty people were standing and shouting in unison, taking their cue from a bearded man with a megaphone. Some in the crowd were carrying placards, but Mike couldn't understand what they meant. Two cars and a pick-up truck were trying get through, but the crowd wouldn't move. From a couple of blocks away came the high-pitched wail of a police siren.

Mike pulled his shirt off and went into the bathroom. He splashed some water onto his face and turned on the light above the mirror. His eyes were little more than slits, and his whole face looked puffy as if he'd been in a fight. He started the shower running, slowly pulling off the rest of his clothes as the water heated up. He would sit cross-legged in the tub until his head felt clear enough to think with. Then he would go back to the police and tell them what had happened. Maybe this time they would take a little more notice.

He opened the cupboard behind the mirror, looking for a fresh cake of soap. Inside he found an array of toiletries in black paper sachets: bath oils, body milk. The maid had put his sponge-bag in there too, on the top shelf. He took it down to get his razor and found a lot more sachets, pink plastic ones this time, lying inside. The plastic was slightly opaque, but it was impossible to see what lay behind it. Maybe it was some kind of soap or shower gel. There was nothing else around that you could wash with.

He climbed into the shower and let the warm water flow over his body for a few seconds. Then he reached over to the sink and grabbed one of the sachets. With his eyes shut he tore it open with his teeth and tried to squeeze out the contents. What came out was neither soap nor gel, but a fine white powder that stuck to his skin, forming a crumbling paste in the palm of his hand. It wasn't like talcum powder either; there was no perfume. Ducking away from the jet of water, he tried to get a better look.

Then there were two men standing in the doorway. One of them had a scar over his right eye which broke his eyebrow up into a zigzag. Both of them were carrying revolvers. Mike stepped out of the shower.

'What the hell?'

'Stay where you are and put your hands on your head!'

Naked and dripping wet, Mike stood watching as the man with the scar came towards him. He pushed Mike flat against the wall and twisted his right arm behind his back. The other man said something in German and they both laughed. Then he pulled Mike round and marched him through into the bedroom. He was a big man and strong, with grey staring eyes and short-cropped hair.

'What the fuck are you doing?' Mike yelled. 'What's going on here?'

The man gave a vicious twist to Mike's arm and threw him onto the bed.

'What are you doing . . . ?' he yelled again.

He was silenced by a punch in the stomach. The pain was so bad he thought he would vomit. The man with the scar leaned over him as he twisted on the bed.

'*Polizei*, Herr Varela. Narcotics.'

Again the men exchanged words in German and then the second one went into the bathroom. He was younger than the man with the scar, but he had the same staring, emotionless expression on his face.

'Listen,' said Mike, still gasping for air, 'I've been set up. I'm the victim of . . .'

The man with the scar lifted his revolver until the barrel was just a couple of inches from Mike's throat.

'You will be silent, Mr Varela,' he said. A moment later the second man reappeared carrying the washbag and the pink plastic sachets.

'I don't know anything about that stuff!' said Mike, as the younger man carefully opened one of the sachets with a penknife. He tasted the powder inside with the tip of his finger and nodded at his partner.

'*Heroin, höchste Qualität.*'

The other man handed Mike a towel.

'You can begin getting dressed now, Herr Varela. And I told you to be silent.'

The younger cop began searching through the bedroom, rummaging through Mike's suitcase, opening all the drawers. In a recess beneath the telephone lay another batch of sachets in a black plastic bag.

'Look,' said Mike. 'The person who tipped you off is the person who planted this stuff. She doped me and I . . .'

It was the excuse the older cop was looking for. He

330

swiped Mike full in the face with the revolver, knocking him on his side, so his head smacked against the head-board. Blood ran down his cheek and dripped onto the white pillow case.

'I told you to get dressed,' said the cop. 'Unless you would prefer to ride to headquarters as you are. Of course no one will care if a drug dealer freezes to death.'

He picked up Mike's shirt and thrust it at him. The younger cop began putting his things into the suitcase. Slowly Mike pulled on his clothes. There wasn't anything else he could do.

They didn't go out the front way. The cops escorted Mike down the back stairs which led down to the kitchens. A small group of the hotel employees stood watching as they went out through a door at the corner of the building – two men in dark suits, police almost certainly, and a dishevelled American with wet hair and a bloody bruise on the side of his face. The older cop smiled at them and said: '*Guten Morgen,*' to which they all replied in kind.

Out on the street the demonstration had got bigger and noisier. The crowd were chanting at the tops of their voices, the same thing over and over again: *HÄUSER, KEINE BULLEN!* They were moving slowly towards the hotel and the police car parked outside it. About thirty yards further down the road two white police vans stood in their way. More policemen, armed with batons and perspex shields, were jumping out. Mike stopped and looked into the crowd: the demonstrators were all young, an assortment of mean-looking kids with half-shaven heads, earrings and bad complexions. They were just the sort of people he had always despised: lazy, trouble-making, blame-the-system losers.

'Keep moving!' said the big cop and shoved him hard towards the car.

Mike stumbled forward, slipping on the icy sidewalk, and fell to the ground. In spite of the snow it felt as hard

331

as concrete. The two cops ran over and grabbed him by the arms. They were hauling him to his feet when the older cop let out a yell of pain. Something had struck him on the side of his head.

'*Diese Schweine!*' he roared, pulling out his revolver. There was yellow paint all over his face and his coat.

From the other end of the street came the sound of the police loud-hailer: '*Bitte, räumen sie sofort! Räumt die Strasse!*' But the crowd were surging forward now under a barrage of missiles. The younger cop tried to bundle Mike towards the police car but the way was no longer clear: a group of demonstrators were already around them, jeering and pushing. One kid jumped onto the hood and began hitting the windscreen with a piece of wood. Others rushed past them, towards the riot police, who were hastily trying to form up in a line.

A few yards away, Mike saw the older cop running back towards them, holding his gun over his head. '*Aus dem Weg! Aus dem Weg!*' he was shouting. A third cop appeared from out of the police car and threw the kid off the bonnet. In another few seconds Mike knew they would get him away. And then what? Prison maybe, deportation at best. He would never find Cathy that way.

He didn't wait any longer. With all his strength he swung a punch at the cop who was still holding him by the arm. Without looking to see the result, he ran stumbling into the heart of the crowd that was still moving slowly towards them. He could hear the older cop shouting behind him, but he kept going. They couldn't shoot with so many people around.

He was near the back of the crowd when the water-cannon opened up from a narrow side-street. With all eyes fixed on the riot police no one had seen it coming. The power of it knocked a dozen people clean off their feet, others ran for cover on the opposite side of the road. Suddenly everyone was yelling, scrambling in different directions to avoid the freezing cascade. Mike saw a woman with long red hair scoop up a small child and carry it screaming to another woman who stood forlornly in the midst of the confusion. Mike ran too, but his shoes wouldn't grip the ground. He went stooping, grabbing on to other people for support, sometimes crawling on all fours.

The crowd was mostly back where it had started now, except for a handful of people crouching behind parked cars near the hotel. The riot police began marching towards them, banging their batons against their shields. Then the big green truck carrying the water-cannon swung out onto the road, and began driving everyone even further back. One desultory paint-bomb burst against its mesh-protected windscreen.

Then Mike caught sight of the woman again, the woman with the long red hair. She was being helped onto the back of a pick-up by the bearded man with the megaphone, and a couple of others. It had been there from the beginning: Mike had seen it from his hotel window. It started to move off, away from the trouble.

'Wait!' he shouted, running towards it. 'Wait!'

One of the men saw him and pointed him out to the others. The bearded one beckoned towards him.

'*Schnell! Los steig auf!*'

As the pick-up began to accelerate, they reached down and pulled Mike aboard. They turned a corner onto a big road just as a fleet of police cars, their sirens wailing, came speeding the other way.

14

The Phönixlager. February 15th, 1996.

They watched her on their hidden screen. They took her temperature. They took her blood for analysis. For all she knew they analysed her shit, her urine. Geiger gave her the daily hormone shots.

Under the dim persistent lights, switched off altogether during what she assumed were the hours of night, Cathy lost all sense of time. She tried to work out exactly when she had bled, to try to get a rough idea of where she was in her cycle, but it was impossible. She knew that her imprisonment had begun on the thirty-first. She knew that some time after that she had bled but it was difficult to be precise. She usually began menstruating in the first week of the month, which would mean that she would be ovulating around the middle. But when was the middle?

She lay awake listening to her body, trying to guess what was happening inside. She had never taken an interest in gynaecology. Her twice-yearly examinations were ordeals that she went through without ever asking too many questions. She knew that her different hormone levels changed through the month, that her body responded every step of the way, but she had no way of recognising the signs. She tried to get information out of Geiger and Kessler, the only two people she ever saw, but neither of them would talk about it.

334

It seemed to her that the only way she would know would be by looking at the reactions of the two men. They knew exactly what was happening to her, she was sure. They had her insides mapped out like the New York subway. But they were bound to reveal their understanding if she only looked carefully enough. At some point they would show their hand, and then she would act.

Time passed. Repeatedly they took her blood. She tried to imagine how it would be. How would they take her eggs? Would they knock her out? Yes, yes that was how it would be. She would come round from a deep sleep and it would have been done. They would rob her in her sleep. The thought filled her with panic, the thought that they would grow her children in a jar for their experiments. It was inhuman. Like pickled foetuses, but living, they would be suspended in incubators, wired, taped, smeared with sterile oils. But what could she do? When the time came they would give the drug that would send her into a long sleep. Then they would give her another drug to make her forget the pain. But deep in her soul, deep in her subconscious the whole thing would be enacted with total lucidity. Later, if there was to be a later, she knew Geiger's glass pipette would surface in her dreams, a frozen, transparent, perfectly sterile, phallus; not giving: taking.

Then there was a sign. Geiger came into her room in an unusual state of intense concentration. He tried to joke with her, but his hands trembled when he took the sample of her blood.

'What's the matter?'

He looked up, startled out of his thoughts.

'You're trembling.'

He looked at his hands holding the blood-filled syringe.

'We are making progress with some important work. I get as excited now as when I was a student in . . .'

'Cut the shit, Professor Geiger. Don't give me your shit.'

Geiger stood away from her, injecting the blood into a sealed bottle. Cathy stood up.

'We are excited because our little goose is ready to drop her golden egg.'

Geiger frowned. He removed the needle from the syringe and placed the used syringe in a cellophane bag.

'Or is that just my imagination?'

Finally he turned and looked at her.

'Cathy, I'll tell you exactly when you are going to ovulate, if that makes you happy. I understand your desire to know what is happening. I respect that, and you will be the first to know.'

'I will be the first to know? No, doctor. I will be the second to know, or maybe the third.'

'It was just an expression.'

At that moment Kessler came to the door. His face was flushed. He was about to speak, when Geiger cut him off.

'I will see you in my office, Doctor Kessler.'

The door closed and Cathy picked up her violin. She played a long plaintive chord and then tossed the violin into the corner. As it left her hand, time seemed to slow down. She watched it as it drifted through the air towards the wall. It struck the ground with a resonant knock, undamaged.

'Yes, yesterday's blood tests confirmed it.'

Geiger's voice was constricted, intense. The two men stood close together in Geiger's observation room, in which he had installed recording equipment. They looked at a list of figures and a chart. Then Geiger looked up at Cathy who had climbed back onto the bed.

'A surge in the output of the luteinising hormone,

beginning here – ' he pointed at the chart with his pen, 'and ending here. A burst of about thirty-six hours.'

'And the FSH?'

'Yes, as normal, a slight increase shadowing the LH.'

'So we operate?'

Geiger continued to look at the charts, his mind aflame with the raw data. It was the closest he had ever felt to the woman. He felt he understood her in every way, the layers of impression, her dark eyes and beautiful mouth, her cleverness, her insight, and further in – her blood sugar, the squeezing of her cardiovascular system, the rush of her blood.

'So we operate?'

Geiger blinked and looked at Kessler's smooth, pale face.

'Yes. This afternoon. Four o'clock. Make sure the theatre is ours.'

15

Zürich. February 15th, 1996.

'Leaflets, leaflets! What we want is *confrontation*. It's the
only way the media ever takes an interest.'

Sitting outside the kitchen, leafing through a trilingual
ecological magazine, Mike looked up as he heard the
male voice raised in anger. Even if he had been able to
hear what was being said he would have understood
nothing of the *Sweizerdeutsche*. But he had a good idea
of who had spoken: it had to be Fleischman, the most
volatile of the small group of activists which gathered
at Anna's apartment to discuss demonstrations, sit-ins,
leafleting and the full range of 'protest techniques', as
they called them.

Fleischman was the least friendly of the group and had
spoken little to Mike in the two days since he had been
there. He had thin fair hair, and strangely enough, thick
dark eyebrows which almost met across his nose. He
was bearded and looked very strong. Yet in spite of his
surliness, Mike liked him best. He was the only one in
the group who didn't roll and smoke dandelion leaves,
preferring Marlboro instead, and he had a business-like
manner which Mike understood and respected. With the
others Mike felt uncomfortable. Even Anna, who had
effectively taken him under her wing, made him uneasy.
She was too nice somehow. Even though he wasn't

allowed to sit in on meetings. Anna had allowed him to stay in her house almost without question. It was a little too cosmic.

After the riot, they had driven straight back to the house and Anna had rooted out some warm, dry clothes. He looked down at his hand which held a clumsy stone-ware mug of camomile tea. He was wearing a banded red, yellow and brown hand-knitted sweater – Anna had made it for her brother who had refused to wear it – a coarse collarless shirt and jeans held up with string. He couldn't help smiling. All his life he had distrusted people who dressed like he was now dressed. In New York, he sniffed a little coke every now and then to be sociable and smoked marijuana like everyone in Congress, but these people, people who dressed like these, he assumed they never sat down to eat without frying up a plateful of hallucinogenic mushrooms. They were constantly high on one thing or another, one idea or another – constantly raving about reform, the dawn of some new age.

He had always thought of it as part of the white man's guilt trip: they have their industrial revolution, fuck up the planet with millions of tons of packaging, poison gases, toxic waste, and then want you to stop using aerosol in the privacy of your own bathroom when you *knew* the Chinese, the Africans, the Indians, all the teeming millions of the struggling semi-industrialised nations were now belching out enough shit to finish the planet by the end of the century anyway. Spray your armpits and face Armageddon smelling sweet was the way Mike saw it.

He was shaken out of his thoughts by the sound of Anna's voice. He recognised the tone, but not the words.

'The trouble with confrontation, Hans – '

'Is that people get hurt. I know, I know. But it helps if the public see the police laying into unarmed protesters. It gets us on the seven o'clock news.'

'But it's *not* so good when they see Etienne Louvois security guards – '

'*That* was an accident.'

Anna looked down. She was unable to face Hans when he was so worked up. His eyebrows met in a bristling line. He looked mad.

There was another silence. In the kitchen Mike sipped at his tea and breathed the smell of rolled tobacco. He would have given his Rolex for one of Hans's Marlboros. Suddenly he was looking up into Anna's pale round face, framed as always by her long red hair.

'We are going to take a break for a few minutes, Michael. Is there anything I can get you?'

Mike showed Anna his mug of untouched camomile tea and shook his head.

'No, I'm fine thanks. How's it going?'

He pointed to the open door of the lounge with his chin.

'We won't be much longer.'

Anna shuffled off along the passage to the distant kitchen. Mike found himself looking at Anna's trodden-down slippers and her skirt, apparently made from a piece of sacking. He bit his lip and looked down. Here he was finding fault with these people when, without their help, their house, their clothes, he would be in a Swiss jail facing drugs charges. He had ingratiated himself with them, pretending to be interested in their activism because he needed their help, and now he sat apart listening to their funny German with a sneer on his face.

He sipped at his tea and tried to think of what he should be doing to get to Cathy. He had got Anna's sympathy, he realised that, but he had yet to define exactly what it was he was doing in Zürich. He worried she would lose interest if he told her the truth.

The meeting was breaking up. Mike let people go past him out of the room and then went in to talk to Anna.

She was opening a window to let out the smoke. Freezing late-afternoon air made Mike shudder.

'Sorry,' she said, half-closing the window again. She turned and smiled at him. Her face improved when she smiled. She looked less careworn and her brilliant, even teeth were her best feature.

'No, don't apologise,' said Mike, taking a seat. 'I don't know how you put up with all the smoke, not smoking yourself.'

'Unfortunately not even people fighting to clean up the atmosphere necessarily want to breathe fresh air. At least it's not smoke from some multinational cancer maker like Marlboro or Benson & Hedges.'

'Right,' said Mike and looked down at his full cup.

'Did you have a chance to look at the cuttings?' she asked.

Mike looked up. He had told Anna he was interested in what was happening at Mendelhaus. She had produced a file with a number of cuttings on different Swiss pharmaceutical companies. Animal experimentation was one of their big concerns. But Mendelhaus was only ever mentioned in passing in the articles which were for the most part about companies such as L'Oreal, Ortega-Petercam, or Lorenzo Versacci.

'Yes. Yes, they're interesting, but I can't see any reference to the laboratory.'

'And you are sure Mendelhaus has a laboratory?'

'They must have. They need a laboratory to develop new products.'

'I've only ever heard of the clinics. Mendelhaus is not on our list.' Anna began to gather papers together with her bitten fingers. 'If they were hurting animals to develop cosmetics that would be different, but we've never heard about that.'

'Would you have heard? If they were doing something wrong, I mean.'

341

She sat down next to him. She smelt faintly of perspiration. There was a dark down on her upper lip. She spoke to him with her grey eyes, moving from his eyes to his mouth to his glossy dark hair.

'It depends on so many things. We comb the press for stories. There are some journalists who are very sympathetic to our cause. Sometimes we get a call from a worker who has seen something . . . something upsetting. But I'm sure there are companies where discipline is so strict that nothing leaks out. Laws against disclosure of company secrets are very harsh in Switzerland, you know? We know of a number of people who are in prison on charges coming under Article 273 of the law governing disclosure, simply because they told the European Community that certain safety norms were not being met.'

Mike nodded understandingly. He never knew how to react when Anna got polemical.

'Looking at it from the American standpoint, it must be pretty shocking to you.' – again Mike nodded – 'But the oppressive nature of the ruling hegemony is not only restricted to industry you know. Outsiders tend to think of Switzerland as the perfect democracy with almost all big decisions being taken by national referendum, but in reality fewer than one hundred people actually run the country through a close-knit mesh of key jobs in politics, business and the professions.'

Mike felt his eyes glazing over. But Anna, fired up by whatever had been said at the meeting, was not about to stop.

'Police archives hold 900,000 secret files on Swiss citizens and foreigners. Can you believe that?' Mike shook his head, manifestly unable to believe it. 'It was only after we took to the streets that they agreed to put the secret police under parliamentary control.'

At last Mike saw his chance to respond.

'You don't have to tell me about the police,' he said, tapping at the cut on his temple.

Anna stopped talking and looked at him for a moment, as if only now realising how little she knew about him. Mike became uncomfortable under her gaze.

'But why are you so interested in the Mendelhaus laboratory?' she said after a moment.

Mike looked into her grey eyes, searching for something to say. Up to now she had been satisfied when he had said it was a personal thing. How would she take the truth? If he told her he suspected Mendelhaus were scooping the brains out of monkeys or some crazy thing like that maybe she would help him find Cathy. He hesitated.

'If you don't want to tell me . . .'

She stood up and crossed the room.

'No, I do. I mean . . .'

Mike stood up, holding his mug with both hands.

'Anna, you've been incredibly good to me. These clothes, letting me sleep in your friend's room. You've never asked me any questions.'

She looked at him across the table on which there were still some scattered papers from the meeting. There was a photograph of some kind of chemical plant. She waited for him to go on.

'I have reason to believe that Mendelhaus – '

'Mike.'

The tone of her voice surprised him. It gave her a dignity which her heavy grey pullover and greasy red hair seemed to deny.

'Don't expect me to believe that you are interested in all this.' She gestured at the scattered paper.

Mike felt his face burn. He smiled sheepishly.

'I'm not saying you don't look the part in those clothes Brigit found but . . .'

She covered her mouth with her hand and began to

343

laugh. This surprised him too. Out of this careworn, unkempt woman rose bright, spontaneous laughter. She had a nice laugh. Mike was laughing too, partly in relief. Just when he thought she was going to turn nasty on him, she relaxed, backed off. He realised in a flash that he really liked her. He stopped laughing and waited until she was listening to him again.

'No. You're right. Politically I am not the world's *numero uno*.' He looked down at his pullover. 'Though I think I could grow into it.'

He waited for her laughter to subside and then went on. 'No. I am looking for a woman.'

Anna sat down on the other side of the table. They faced each other across the papers.

'Her name is Cathy Ryder. She is a financial analyst from New York. She came to see Mendelhaus about a month ago and then she disappeared. Nobody has seen her since.'

He sat back in his chair. His mouth was dry.

'And why do you think finding the Mendelhaus research labs will help you find her?'

'She was working on some products they have produced. You know, the Erixil skincare products?'

Anna shook her head.

'They're busy wiping out the US cosmetics industry with these new products and somehow Cathy knew all about it before anyone else. If she was visiting Mendelhaus she would have been most interested in seeing their research facilities. She would have wanted to know what they were going to come up with next.'

'She was analysing the company?'

'Yes, but there was more to it than that I think. There was something else. Some strange things happened in New York.'

'Strange things?'

'Bad things. She was scared. I got scared too.'

344

'So why don't you just contact the Zürich police?'

'I already did.'

'And?'

'The morning I came running out of the crowd and jumped on your van? That morning the Zürich police were trying to put me in prison for drug peddling. It was a set-up. That's why I share your views on the Swiss police.'

Anna shook her head in disbelief.

'I know. It sounds pretty half-baked, doesn't it? But I just know they're involved in all this, and Cathy . . . Cathy . . .' He felt his voice going out of control. He looked down at his hands and took a breath. Anna touched him on the shoulder.

'But why?'

He looked into her face.

'Why any of this?' she said. 'It doesn't make sense.'

'Unless in her research Cathy found out something she wasn't supposed to know. Something about Erixil, for example.'

Anna sat back and was quiet for a moment. Then she looked up and gave her head a little shake, resolved it seemed.

'I believe what you say, Michael. Other people in our group are not so trusting.'

'Like the guy Fleischman. He doesn't – '

Anna stopped him in mid-sentence with a raised hand. 'We worry about infiltrators,' she said. 'We have to. To a lot of big business here we're a real threat, you know? They don't want it to be like the rest of Europe – all the restrictions, the public access. They think it will destroy their special advantages. And we know they've put their people in the movement before, to watch us, to find out what we know and what we're planning. But don't worry. This is my house. You can stay here. For a short time at least. My room-mate Amalie is going to be away for a couple of weeks. You can stay in her room. You'll be safe there.'

'Anna.'

She shook her head and blushed.

'Please don't tell me I'm good and kind. It infuriates me.' She flashed him her white smile. 'And as for your friend I think I know how we might find out about the lab. I have a friend who works for the *Zürichzeitung*. They have a good collection of cuttings. We are – '

She looked up towards the door.

'Sorry, am I interrupting?'

It was Fleischman. He was standing in the doorway, his powerful torso filling the entrance. He smiled at them both. There was a large gap between his front teeth.

'I was just wondering about the rendezvous point for this weekend's action. It seems to me we could be much more . . . confrontational if we go directly to the main square.'

Anna sighed and leaned back against her chair as if Fleischman's presence alone was too strong for her.

'*Ja*, Hans. As always you are probably right.'

16

The Phönixlager. February 16th, 1996.

They had lied to her as she knew they would. She came out of the anaesthetic with a metallic taste in her mouth. Emerging consciousness felt like a condensing of her body, a solidifying, and a coming into focus. She kept her eyes closed, feeling the barely perceptible movement of the conditioned air on her face. Above her, suspended in the shadows, she sensed the watchful eye of the camera. She didn't want them to see that she was awake. She was restrained again. She felt the slight pressure of the straps across her ribcage and on her wrists. But she didn't struggle this time. Things had changed. They had lied to her. Geiger had lied. He had said she would be informed all the way, and yet it had turned out exactly the way she had thought it would – a drift back into consciousness with a sense of loss, of violation. She tried to control her breathing, to suppress the rising anger in her chest. She knew that her only chance of escape was to stay calm, and to think rationally. Why was she restrained? They must have assumed she would have a violent reaction, that she would hurt herself in some way. Then it came to her that she had been operated on; opened up like a treasure chest. Without moving she tried to feel where she might be cut. There was a dull, drugged feeling in her abdomen. It felt like paralysis. She clenched the muscles in her buttocks, and far off, as if from another body, she felt an unusual pressure in her left side. What had they done to her? They had taken her egg or eggs, of that she felt sure. But what was to happen now? She knew she could no longer trust Geiger with her life. She had to wait for an opportunity, even if it only meant cracking his skull with something and taking her chances outside. She had to do *something*.

'Cathy.'

The soft voice startled her. She opened her eyes. Geiger was standing over her, smiling.

'I was asleep.'

'Not according to our ECG readings.'

Cathy looked into the man's eyes with a deep feeling of hatred.

'I was thinking.'

'Thinking?'

'Thinking about how you lied to me.'

The smile went from Geiger's lips. He opened the panel in the wall and looked at the different indicators.

'You said you would let me know about every development.'

He turned and looked down at her. He was shaking his head.

'Sorry, Cathy. I just didn't believe I could trust you.'

'You trust *me*. You don't have to trust me. You've got me tied up like a Thanksgiving turkey.'

Geiger smiled.

'I had to do that. I didn't want you to hurt yourself after the operation.'

'After you stole my eggs.'

'One egg. There was just the one egg.'

'Oh, I'm sorry to have been such a disappointment to you.'

'Don't worry, there is plenty of time.'

Cathy strained against the straps with her fists.

'You think so?'

'You don't?'

'You can't believe you can just take an American citizen off the shelf like that. People are looking for me, you can bet your bottom dollar.'

'Your boyfriend, perhaps?'

Cathy became quiet. The thought that Mike might be looking had never occurred to her. She wondered what Geiger knew about it. Maybe he had heard news of Mike's coming to Switzerland. But why would Mike do that? It didn't make sense.

'The young man in the photograph.'

Cathy felt a rush of understanding, of disappointment. He was just making wild guesses. Mike was still in New York, getting on with his life. He probably hadn't even called after their argument, after she had hit him in the face. She looked at Geiger with a contemptuous smile.

'Who knows?' she said. Geiger looked at her for a long time. Then he turned to go out of the room.

'How long do I have to be strapped down?'

He turned on his heels and faced her.

'That depends on you, Cathy.'

'I can't bear being restrained. You know that.'

She smiled at him, her eyes stinging with rising tears and hatred.

Kessler waited until the doors of the C Lab were sealed behind him before starting to remove the special protective clothing. In spite of the new materials they were still uncomfortably warm, the priority in design being to prevent bacteria from entering the laboratory environment. Knowing that Geiger had been watching his every move from the observation gallery had not helped him stay cool. Fortunately the operation of introducing the ovum into the growth medium was routine, and there had been no complications.

349

Geiger was still staring out into the lab when Kessler came in. He did not bother to enquire how things had gone, but then, thought Kessler, he would have been able to judge that for himself.

'Egon, I want you to ensure that the ordinary lab staff don't come in here,' he said after a moment. 'The other cultures can be transferred to other labs.'

Kessler frowned.

'You think that's necessary? There's never been contamination in . . .'

'It's needless risk. Accidents can happen. We can handle all this ourselves.'

Kessler nodded. 'Very well. Although I don't think we need worry about Chen.'

'Chen, yes. Keep Chen. But that's all.'

Kessler went and fixed himself a cup of coffee from the machine at the back of the gallery. Geiger stayed silent. Kessler sat down.

'Is something worrying you, Edward?' he said at last. 'You don't envisage any difficulties do you?'

'We must always envisage the difficulties. How else can we be prepared for them?'

He turned around.

'We have been lucky, Egon. Luck can change.'

Kessler studied Geiger's face for a moment. Luck was not a word the Professor used very much, not usually. It was a factor that rarely entered his calculations.

'Time is not on our side perhaps,' he conceded. 'But then it never has been.'

Geiger did not respond.

'You think we should accelerate the programme?' Kessler ventured. 'Is that what you mean? It would certainly be desirable from a practical point of view. We did discuss this idea some time ago, before . . .'

'Before Miss Ryder came here. And I ruled out the

super-oestrogen treatments you suggested because of the likely side-effects on the donor.'

'You've changed your opinion?'

'The circumstances have changed.'

Kessler took a sip of coffee. He had wanted to suggest that they attempt to boost egg production further, especially after what Krystal had told him, but the right moment had not presented itself.

'The circumstances are not entirely as we had envisaged, I must admit that,' he said. 'But the programme is not in jeopardy so long as we are able to accumulate the necessary stock of ova . . .'

'In the time available. That time may be running out.'

'You're not confident that the HPG treatment is sufficient?'

'Are you?'

Kessler folded his arms. Geiger had not asked his opinion in days.

'Most of the clinical data relates to women with infertility problems. Since our donor doesn't appear to be one of these, we cannot be sure of the results. But I would guess that we may get as many as three ova next time, possibly four. A sufficient number, if not a comfortable one.'

'We shall never be able to repeat this part of the programme again, Egon.'

'No.'

'So we need more ova than that, and quicker.'

'Then we must reconsider the alternative. We begin with the super-clomiphene and then move on. Is that your suggestion?'

Kessler waited for a reply. Several months before, when the good news had first come over from the States, they had discussed how the donor would be exploited. The accelerated treatments Kessler had developed, based on existing oestrogen and progesterone stimulants, had been ruled out by Geiger as 'inappropriate' although he hadn't explained what he meant. The short-term side-effects – pleural and abdominal effusions – could be dealt with, but the longer-term risks of thrombosis were far more serious. Blood clots could form, most likely in the deep veins of the legs, threatening to break away into the bloodstream at any time – perhaps many months or even years later. They would travel unimpeded into the right half of the heart and from there into the smaller vessels of the lungs where they would lodge, sometimes breaking open the vessels themselves. Then the victim could suffer a pulmonary embolism, unable to draw breath, slowly drowning in her own blood. Kessler had not been able to develop the conventional stimulants without at the same time increasing the risks of thrombosis. He was only sorry he had not been able to give the question more time.

Geiger looked up slowly.

'The programme demands that we maximise ova production. As I said, the circumstances have changed.'

He opened the door and walked away down the empty passageway. Kessler listened as the sound of his footsteps slowly faded away, and then drained his cup.

17

Zürich. February 17th, 1996.

After four hours in a Volkswagen dormobile that belonged to Anna's flat-mate, Mike was cold right through to his bones. He sat behind the steering wheel with his arms folded, rocking back and forward, occasionally beating his hands together to keep his circulation going. Almost everything he had on had been borrowed from Anna: a red woolly hat with a pink bobble on the top, shapeless ethnic sweater, unfashionably bulky ski jacket, hairy alpaca gloves. They fitted him pretty well, but they weren't enough. His cold, like his swollen cheek a memento from the Zürich police, was getting worse. His nose was red and sore, and it hurt to wipe it. He knew he should have been in bed, but how could he rest when every day his chance of finding Cathy got smaller and smaller?

He wiped the condensation from the window and peered out across the quiet suburban street. Like most of the houses round about, Krystal's was set back about forty yards from the road and mostly hidden by a thick evergreen hedge. It was a big place, tall and grey with sloping slate roofs and white shutters. The driveway went round to the side of the house, and from where he sat Mike could just make out the front of the garage with Krystal's jade green Mercedes parked outside. The

353

entrance to the driveway was secured by a heavy wooden gate.

Mike had to come there because he felt sure Krystal knew where Cathy was. At the same time Anna had promised to check through the newspaper files at the public library, and look for anything about Mendelhaus that might help. Mike reckoned if Cathy's trip to Switzerland had begun as a professional visit she would have wanted to know about future products in the company, and that meant a trip to the laboratories. But in the public records, beyond the head office in Zürich, there was nothing listed but the addresses of the four big clinics at Geneva, Lausanne, Rorschach and Davos. Anna had put in a call to the head office that morning, but was unable to find out where the main laboratories were located. Mike's own recollections of the Raeburn take-over were no use either. His main concern at the time had been the strength of Mendelhaus's financial situation.

In the meantime Krystal was the only certain link to Cathy. For sure he had played a part in Cathy's leaving for Switzerland, and he might even have arranged the whole thing. There was at least a chance that Cathy had been to his house at some time or other. He couldn't approach Krystal directly, but someone who worked for Krystal – his driver maybe – might be more co-operative. Mike's own experience in the underground parking lot below Cathy's apartment block had given him the idea. He would wait for the guy to drive home for the evening and follow him. After that he would do whatever was necessary to get information.

The idea of using violence didn't really worry him any more. The conventional channels had yielded nothing, and he was a fugitive now in any case. He could imagine what had happened in the time since his escape from the Zürich police. They would have been checking his record with the US authorities. That didn't matter if they were just looking for previous convictions – he had none – but if someone had been able to identify him at the Café de Lyons, had heard his name called even, then any kind of conclusion might be drawn. The cops were probably looking for him already, worrying his dad, checking on his friends. How would he ever explain it all? He tried not to think about it. All that mattered was finding Cathy. Find Cathy, and it would all work out. He thought back once again to the good times they'd had, to the mistakes he'd made. It seemed like a lifetime away, except that he missed her now more than ever.

He banged his hands together one more time and switched on the radio. Synthesised euro-pop filled the van, the kind he hated, but he turned it up loud all the same, bouncing up and down in his seat and waving his arms in time to the music. *When we go out danzing and you hold me ti-yight, oui je l'aime! Oui je l'aime!* Gradually he began to feel warmer.

The song was just fading out when he heard an engine start outside Krystal's house. It was five thirty, already dark, just the time when a driver might be off home if his boss wasn't going out for the evening. Mike switched off the radio and reached down to the ignition key as a white Fiat Tipo appeared on the other side of the gates, its headlamps lighting up the parked vehicles opposite. The driver climbed out. Mike couldn't see his face. He opened the gate, drove through, and then got out a second time to close the gate behind him. When the Mercedes had gone through the other way two hours earlier the gates had opened automatically, but the driver's own car clearly wasn't equipped with the necessary remote control.

'A good sign,' said Mike to himself. 'His boss doesn't trust him.'

He waited for the driver to get back into the car and then turned the ignition key. The Volkswagen engine made a series of hollow wheezing noises but didn't start. The Fiat was pulling away. Mike pulled out the choke and tried again. The vehicle began to lurch back and forward, but still the cylinders wouldn't fire. He pushed the choke half way in again.

'Move, damn you!' he yelled, turning the key again and stamping on the throttle. 'MOVE!'

The red lights of the Fiat were fast disappearing in the distance. Mike made one last desperate attempt to start the dormobile, tickling the throttle with his foot, easing the choke back in. There came a series of agonised groans from the engine, and then suddenly it kicked into life. Mike turned on the headlights and pulled out into the road without looking in the mirror. He heard the angry blast of a horn as another car pulled up sharply behind him, skidding on the icy surface.

The Fiat was no longer in sight. Mike urged the dormobile along Bergstrasse, sounding his horn at a BMW coupé that swung out of a right-hand turning and roaring past it to the annoyance of the driver who shouted something at him.

As he reached the lights at the end of the road he caught sight of the Fiat again, just moving off from another set of lights on a bigger road at right angles to his. Mike pushed his way into the right-hand lane and followed. The traffic was much heavier here and it was difficult to make up ground. People sounded their horns at him each time he tried to overtake, but he ignored them, keeping his eyes fixed on the car he was following. In the darkness it was getting difficult to tell it from the others.

A minute later he was about five or six cars behind the Fiat, waiting at another junction. Craning his neck he could just make out its polished white roof, and in it a reflection of the red light suspended above the road. The light changed to green, and slowly the line of vehicles

356

began moving off again. Mike could see the cars ahead of the Fiat crossing the junction, and then the Fiat itself.

The car in front of him, another BMW, was just approaching the same spot when the lights changed again. Suddenly it stopped dead, blocking Mike's way. Mike hit his horn and then saw that the lane on his left was momentarily free. He was just about to swing out and run the red light across the junction when he saw why the driver in front of him had been so cautious: there was a police patrol car right behind them. It slid up beside the dormobile and came to a stop. Mike saw the policeman in the passenger seat look up at him. He was talking on his radio.

Mike did nothing. He didn't even look round. In his wing mirror he could see the cop's face: he was looking up and down the length of the dormobile, like it was a piece of shit on wheels. Then he said something to the cop beside him and laughed. When the time came Mike moved off slowly, following the other cars, not attempting to overtake anyone. The police car coasted along beside him for a minute and then sped off ahead and disappeared. By then the white Fiat had disappeared too. Mike's long cold wait had been for nothing.

A few kilometres on he stopped at a gas station. In his efforts to catch up with Krystal's driver Mike had lost all track of where he was. He took the name of the road and called up Anna from a booth opposite the pumps.

'Mike, you sound terrible,' she said in her funny Swiss accent, drawing out the words. 'Are you okay?'

She was really concerned, Mike could tell. Even shivering there in the cold, he was touched. She was the first person he had met since Cathy disappeared who really seemed to want to help him. And all because she'd seen a couple of cops giving him a rough time outside his hotel. That was all she needed.

'I'm okay, Anna, thanks,' he said. 'I just screwed up

this . . . this thing. My man got away. I couldn't start your friend's van!'

'I'm sorry, Mike. I should have told you. You have to know how. It's a little bit cranky, her car.'

'Forget it, forget it. My fault. Listen, did you have any luck at the library?'

'I don't know. Maybe.'

Mike put another half-franc coin in the slot. A big truck rolled onto the forecourt.

'Tell me.'

'You sound like you are going to freeze to death, Mike.'

'It's so *cold* in this damn country! Tell me what you got.'

'Well there wasn't much. But there was this one short article from a local paper in the Valais. It's about a man that died at a Mendelhaus clinic – an American.'

'What man?'

'He was an actor. His name was – I have it written down here – Matt MacArthur. Actually, I think I remember him, but I don't go much to American movies, you know?'

'Matt MacArthur died at Mendelhaus? No kidding.'

'About a year and a half ago. It says cancer.'

'I see. Well, is that it?'

'No. You see, it's a Valais paper. The article was written by a reporter in Brig.'

'So?'

'The story says that after receiving its death certificate in Brig, the body will be taken to the American consulate and flown home.'

'I don't get it.'

'Mike, there aren't meant to *be* any Mendelhaus clinics in the Valais. And for sure not at Brig. MacArthur must have died somewhere in the area or his body would not have been with the Brig authorities, and the report wouldn't come from there. You see what I'm saying?

358

There has to be another clinic. A clinic they don't talk about.'

'And you think the labs might be there too?'

'It would make sense. They like to keep all that stuff where no one can see it.'

'Anna, you're a genius!'

He heard Anna laughing on the other end of the phone.

'If you want to know what's going on in Switzerland, you have to be pretty sharp! We don't have a right to know like you do.'

'But how are we going to get closer? If we go to Brig, what then?'

'I don't know, but I have a good friend up there. Her name's Tania. Maybe she can help.'

'She lives in Brig?'

'No. She teaches skiing in Alleinmatt. That's a resort in the area, just by the border. Very exclusive!'

'Well let's call her.'

'I don't think she has a phone at her place. She calls me from the ski school. Mike, there's someone at the door. I must go. Are you coming back here or what?'

'Yes, sure, if I can find . . . sure.'

'Okay, I'll be here.'

Mike hung up even though he knew he'd forgotten to ask the way back to Anna's house. He got some barely comprehensible instructions from the man behind the counter, filled up the tank, and set off across town.

Flecks of snow were hitting the windscreen by the time he got to Anna's part of town. He'd gone wrong several times on the way and it had taken him almost forty minutes to get there. Every time he stopped and asked someone for directions they told him something different, or barked a few hasty words in German, as if they wanted nothing to do with him. Mike didn't let it worry him. He reasoned that it was just too cold to stand around.

359

Besides, he wasn't on his own any more, he had help: Anna, her protester friends, now this girl in the mountains; they were on his side and they knew the ground. It made him feel better. Getting arrested began to seem like the best move he'd made yet. They were OK these people – a little strange some of them, maybe naive when it came to their politics – but hell, they were on his side when no one else was.

He turned the corner into Anna's road and slowed down as he approached the house. There were no spaces to park. It was six thirty and everyone was back from work, their cars lining the street. Mike cursed and dropped into second gear. He cruised along looking for a space. Finally he was able to squeeze the dormobile in between two cars, but he was almost at the end of the street. He turned off the engine and got out. It was freezing outside, and sleet had started to fall. He pulled the bobble hat down over his ears and made his way back up towards the house.

He rang the front doorbell and squeezed in under the porch to get out of the rain. He dabbed at his streaming nose, consoling himself that in another few minutes he'd be climbing into a hot bath. An old woman walked past the house, huddled under an umbrella. After a few seconds he rang again. He peered in through the frosted glass of the front door. There was a light on at the end of the passage coming from the kitchen. But he couldn't see any sign of movement.

'Come on, Anna. I'm freezing out here.'

Then he remembered that he had a key of his own. Anna had popped it into one of the innumerable pockets of his ski jacket. He gave another stab at the doorbell and started fumbling for his own key. It took him at least a minute before he found it and still no one had come to the door. He felt a flutter of fear as he inserted the key in the lock. He told himself that Anna was already in the bath and had put the radio on. She hadn't heard him, that was all. In another moment he would be in the warm kitchen. Everything would be OK. He gave his key a turn and pushed open the door.

'Anna?'

For a breathless moment he listened, hoping to hear the radio. The house was completely silent. There was a smell, like newly baked bread. Mike carefully closed the door behind him. He knew that there was no way any one could know that he was staying at the house; no way anyone would want to hurt Anna, but the killing on William Street came back to him again and he felt uneasy.

A movement drew his eyes to the floor. A ball of hair rolled towards him along the passageway, carried by a draught he could not feel. It was Anna's hair. She was always brushing it and then cleaning out the brush over the bin in the kitchen. Making no sound, Mike started to move along the passage towards the light from the kitchen. The door was half open. He could see the toaster and the electric kettle through the gap. Steam rose from two mugs of Anna's camomile tea.

'Anna? Are you . . . ?'

Mike pushed the kitchen door with stiff fingers. Something was blocking it. He took a deep breath and pushed again, squeezing through into the kitchen which was full of the hot smells of new-made bread and camomile tea.

It looked as if someone had taken a litre of red paint and thrown it across the room. Anna was slumped against the kitchen door, her green eyes staring up, the pupils drilled points of terror. There was a deep, rough-edged gash just above her left collarbone. Her cheese-cloth shirt was soaked in blood. Other deep wounds formed a star shape on her chest. A heavy army knife with a serrated edge lay in a pool of blood next to the loaf of bread Anna had baked for their supper.

Mike, suddenly a seeing machine, suddenly only able

361

to see, to absorb, stood against the wall hardly breathing. His eyes moved slowly over the dead girl, taking in the red hair matted with congealing blood, the cut hands which had struggled against the plunging, tearing knife. It seemed to go on for ever, this seeing. He wanted to close his eyes, to turn away, but nothing could stop him from taking in every detail.

Then he was suddenly free again. He staggered towards the sink, hardly able to control his shaking legs, and he was vomiting.

He turned on both taps and watched the water flush the vomit away. After a moment he tried to calm himself, taking deep breaths through his mouth. Why? Why Anna? *Because she tried to help me.* The thought brought him upright, hands gripping the sink. Whoever it was who had come to the house had surely hoped to find him there. If he hadn't got lost he would have been there forty minutes ago. It was then that he remembered what Anna had said on the telephone. Someone had come to the door. Who? Who?

Then the lights went out.

For a moment Mike could see nothing. From along the hallway he heard a foot press a creaking floorboard. Light filtering through from the back garden lit the knife which glistened on the table. Mike took it up, squeezing the sticky hilt in fear and anger and disgust. He crouched in the middle of the kitchen facing Anna's dead body, ready for her killer to come through the door. He seemed to wait for ever.

Then he heard soft laughter. Whoever was in the hallway was enjoying the game. A voice, familiar somehow, but muffled by a mask or something, began to drift through from the other side of the door. It was singing a little phrase over and over, quietly, taunting him to make a move.

'*Ich weiss wo du bist, Amerikaner. Ich weiss, ich weiss, ick weiss wo . . . du . . . bist.*'

Mike blinked perspiration from his eyes. He gripped the knife so hard it hurt his hand. The singing stopped. There was another step in the hallway.

'Come in here and you're a dead man.'

It was his own voice. It sounded loud, stupid. It frightened him to hear himself sound so weak. On the other side of the door he heard a short, scornful laugh. His fear flashed into anger.

'Why Anna, you bastard?'

He backed across the kitchen until he came against the garden door. Then he froze. Slowly the handle to the hall door started to turn. He knew that in the next instant the killer would come through the door. Maybe with a gun, maybe with a knife like the one he was holding. He reached behind him for the handle to the outside door. It turned in his hand.

Then he was running, forcing his shaky limbs to work, shutting out everything else. He ran hard against the fence at the bottom of the garden. There was a muffled thud from behind him and a section of fence next to his hand exploded into fragments, causing him to drop the knife. He clambered over the fence and ran across another rain-soaked garden. Somewhere a dog started to bark. He ran against a trash can, scattering its contents across a path. A porch light came on. Then he was in the street, running heavily under the freezing drizzle, picking thick splinters from the back of his hand.

18

Alleinmatt. February 18th, 1996.

It was a strange kind of noise: whining, electrical, but faltering. It rose and fell and rose again, drawing closer towards him through the freezing dawn fog. Mike stood with his back to the parking lot, staring uneasily along the snow-laden road that led to the village. He was all alone. Behind him the neat rows of German cars waited in silence, an inch of snow on their hoods. Everything in the parking lot was automated, and after you had left your car there all you had to do to summon a taxi was press one of the big yellow buttons beside the pedestrian exit. There were no attendants. Mike began to wonder whether the cab wasn't going to be just a machine too, with a robot for a driver.

The whining noise got louder and then the taxi came into view. It was a small white vehicle, a bit like a milk float, with a moulded fibreglass body and a single head-lamp in the front. From the noise Mike realised that it was powered by battery. Behind the wheel there was no robot, but a bearded man wrapped up in an old-fashioned black overcoat, a long scarf and a hunting cap.

'*Guten Morgen.* American?' he said as he drew up.

Mike jumped. Were they waiting for him here as well? It was impossible. He had driven all night.

'You, American,' said the man again, pointing at Mike

with a gloved finger, and then he shook his head and drew it back inside the cab.

'Yes,' said Mike. 'Yes that's right, American.'

The man nodded and pointed over his shoulder.

'Go in back, please.'

Mike climbed into the back of the cab, which was decked out with two padded benches facing each other. Over the benches were No Smoking signs. The driver slowly steered his vehicle away and headed back the way he had come.

'You got reservation?'

'No,' said Mike. 'I'm looking for . . .'

'No problem,' said the driver. 'Bad weather, many peoples not coming. Where you want to go? Hotel?'

'Maybe. But I'd prefer something private. A house that takes visitors maybe?'

'*Gasthof* you want?'

Mike leaned forward towards the driver.

'A *private* house, if possible. You know one?'

'Ah *ja*, private,' said the driver, nodding. '*Ja*, I know a place. House of my sister. *Sehr gut, sehr sauben*. You like.'

'Sounds fine. Let's go.'

A few minutes later they were in the village, passing a row of cafes, banks, and elegant boutiques with the latest ski-wear in the windows. Around the main square the buildings – the town hall, the post office, a big, old-fashioned hotel – were mostly of grey stone, with carved wooden balconies on each floor and big colourful flags flying over the doorways. Just above the square stood a church with a tall black spire, as sharp as a thorn. It wasn't at all like the resorts Mike had been to in the States, where nothing except the mountains and the woods looked any older than the customers. Alleinmatt had heritage; it was no mere product of the skiing boom. The rich had been going there for a hundred and fifty years to admire the scenery, to skate or toboggan, or just to take the mountain air. And it showed. The wealth and self-assurance were visible in every street. Even the old cowsheds had been transformed into tasteful expositions of rustic charm, serving now as ski hire shops or taverns.

They drove on, past rows of big chalets, to a cluster of houses two or three hundred yards outside the village, just where the road began to climb again. The houses were modern: simple white-washed constructions, their windows square, without shutters, and fake brass lanterns by the door. A dirty orange Volkswagen Passat stood outside a garage.

'Very easy for ski lift here,' said the driver, pointing somewhere up the hillside. 'You can walk even.'

Thirty feet over his head the huge red cable-car swung from the gaping mouth of the lift station and climbed noiselessly into the misty sky. There were only a handful of diehard skiers on board, big men with day-glo jackets and untidy blond hair. Mike had seen them go in. It was too early still for the smart set or the weekenders, and too cold. Below the lift station, at the foot of the nursery slopes, the ski school was just opening, and a group of young kids were being led inside by a woman who looked like their teacher. They chattered excitedly and jabbed each other with their little ski poles. Mike got in the queue behind them.

Inside, behind a counter, were a couple of men dressed in red instructors' uniforms. They worked efficiently, filling in forms, taking names from the teacher, and then punching the information into a computer. Other instructors could be seen coming in at the back, talking in loud voices, laughing as they pulled on their ski boots and their woolly hats. There were no women among them. As he waited, Mike looked at the walls, which were covered with big aerial pictures of the valley, with the trails marked in different colours according to the degree of difficulty: green for easy, through blue and red to black for the most difficult. Mike knew that in a lot of resorts trails were designated as black even though they were not especially challenging, simply to give the resort the impression that it catered for all standards: experts as well as beginners and intermediates. But Alleinmatt was not one of those. Its black runs were said to be as difficult as any: narrow, twisting and steep.

The kids eventually shuffled off with a couple of instructors leaving Mike in front of the counter. He'd had time to shave and take a shower, but he felt conspicuously ill-dressed in Anna's old clothes.

'*Ja bitte?*'

The instructor got up from behind the computer terminal and came towards him carrying a clipboard. He was maybe thirty years old, with very short black hair and a weather-beaten face. Mike tried to sound as calm as he could.

'I'm looking for an instructor called Tania. Do you know where I can find her?'

'Tania? Tania Schaffner?'

'I guess so. I don't know her second name.'

The man hesitated for a moment. Mike wished he'd just said yes.

'You want lessons?'

'No. I have a message for Tania from a friend of hers. It's important.'

The man turned over a page on his clipboard. Mike could tell he was suspicious already.

'You can leave a message here, sir, of course. What is your name please?'

'My name . . .' He thought about lying, but that was dangerous too. '*Miguel*. Miguel Diaz.'

The guy didn't look like he knew how to spell it.

367

'But listen, I really need to speak to her. I mean do you have her phone number so I could call?'

The man shook his head.

'She does not have phone. She lives up . . .' – he gestured over his shoulder – 'High up the valley. No lines. But you can leave a message here. She will have it today, or tomorrow maybe.'

'That's no good,' said Mike. 'This is urgent . . .'

Another instructor, a tall blond man, came over. The two of them started talking in German, and Mike knew they were talking about him. He heard Tania's name several times.

'You're looking for Tania?'

The blond man spoke almost perfect English, with an American accent and a deep voice. There were something in the way he asked the question that made Mike feel uncomfortable.

'Yes. Do you know where I can find her?'

The guy nodded. *What is he, her boyfriend or something?*

'You got a message for her?'

'It's a bit more complicated than that. Listen, are you gonna tell me where I can reach her or not?'

There were more people in the school now, queuing up for registration. One of them, a middle-aged woman, said something, but Mike couldn't understand what it was. The first instructor went back to work.

'Okay,' said the boyfriend, 'but if you want to see her in a hurry you'll have to find her on the mountain. She's got classes all day.'

Mike looked again at the maps on the walls. The valley was vast and there were at least three separate skiing areas.

'She usually meets them below the Hornberg, at the top of the main cable car. Her first class should be at ten thirty. After that I don't know.'

368

'The Hornberg? Okay. Thanks.'

Mike made to go. The blond man called after him: 'Where are you staying? In case she comes in.'

Mike shouted back: 'With friends.'

It was five minutes past ten by the time Mike got back to the cable car station. It had not taken long to get equipped – the ski hire shop was huge and efficient, and the boutiques were only too pleased to off-load their expensive goods on a hurried customer – but there had been another line of kids at the lift company's office, and he had spent almost twenty minutes waiting to get a pass. There was another line for the cable car, snaking its way around a steel cattle grid, but the cars carried a hundred and twenty people at a time, and it didn't take long to reach the front. At a quarter past ten Mike was watching the resort of Alleinmatt slowly disappearing into the distance.

The clouds were starting to break up as they climbed up the western side of the valley. Looking out to the south Mike could just see the outline of a huge grey mountain – he guessed maybe six or seven miles away – although its peak was still hidden. Down below lay a dense forest of pines through which a few wide ski trails had been cut. After a few minutes they passed over a tall cliff, on the top of which stood a big steel pylon, leaning out precariously over the precipice. Above the cliff the trees were fewer and fewer, giving way to a bleak white wilderness interrupted only by outcrops of dark brown rock. The wind was stronger there: forced up the mountainside, it whipped the snow off exposed faces and carried it in clouds towards the summit. As Mike looked out at the snow-covered rock he remembered what he had seen the night before. He saw again Anna's staring dead eyes. He had to blink and shake his head to get rid of the image. He could feel the cable-car slowly swinging from side to side but he felt no fear. Surprised at his own

369

calm, he realised that events were changing him. If he had anything left to lose he couldn't see it, couldn't feel it anyway. He had to win, that was all that mattered. And he would do whatever was necessary, without hesitation, regardless of the cost. He watched disinterestedly as the operator slowed the car down as they passed the other one coming down, just to be sure of not hitting it.

The cable-car stopped four hundred metres below the Hornberg, at a station called the Hörnlihütte. From there you could either ski down to the bottom of the valley or continue up the mountain in a second, smaller cable-car which travelled over a wide expanse of marked trails, most served by chair-lifts. Pressed up against the perspex window, Mike stared down at the handfuls of skiers carefully traversing the wind-blown slopes. He had always liked skiing, although he hadn't started until he got to college, and since he started on Wall Street there hadn't been time for more than a few days at once, and that mostly in Vermont. But none of it felt like recreation to him now. The mountains, the snow, the clouds, all of it was just a barrier between Cathy and him, an impediment to be overcome as quickly as possible. *Find Tania, find the lab, find Cathy*; that was all he could think of.

It was twenty-five minutes before eleven as they approached the top station. Just below Mike could see several groups of skiers gathering beneath the Hornberg, a shapeless mass of rock and snow with a big radio mast on the top of it. Some of the skiers had red jackets on.

Mike grasped his skis and hurried down the steel stairways to the exit. Outside he found the snow carpeted with skis, and scores of people getting ready to move off: testing their bindings, tightening their boots, adjusting their clothes, even doing warm-up exercises. Mike stumbled his way past them, scanning the area ahead of him for a class, a class being led by a girl called Tania. About twenty yards away, down a gentle slope, was a big board with signs pointing down the different numbered trails. It was an obvious meeting point, but there were only a couple of skiers there looking at the coloured arrows and consulting their maps. Mike looked at his watch: it was ten forty.

He threw his skis down and snapped into them. Maybe, he thought, the class had arranged to meet round the other side of the lift station. He pushed off and headed down to the signpost, hoping for an better view. A figure in red, a man, went past him on his left. It was an instructor.

'Hey, excuse me!' Mike shouted, still moving.

The man looked over his shoulder. He wore sunglasses with silvered lenses.

'I'm looking for Tania's class! Tania Schaffner!'

A couple of skiers overtook him, laughing. The instructor put his hand to his ear.

'Tania Schaffner!' Mike shouted again.

The instructor slid to a halt at the side of a traverse cut into the deep snow by a plough. Then he pointed with his ski pole down a route marked 21 in red, and shouted: '*Sie fuhr dort entlans, vor circa Zwei Minuten!* Two minutes gone.'

He'd missed her by two minutes, but she had a whole class with her. If he was quick he could catch her. He headed off down the trail, pushing with his sticks to gain speed.

The run was a mix of gradients: one minute gentle, the next steep, but it wasn't crowded, and the recent falls of snow meant that there were no big bumps to contend with. At first the skis felt awkward and unfamiliar, but Mike kept his mind on Tania, on Cathy. The icy wind tore into his eyes. He tried to lower his goggles with one hand and almost lost his balance. In a minute he was skiing faster than he had ever done before, without so much as a minute's preparation. Each time he tried to

371

slow himself, carving a sharp turn through the powder, his thigh muscles burned with the effort.

Then he caught sight of a chair-lift away to his left. The wires and pylons reached back up towards the cable-car station, but Mike couldn't see if it was running or if anyone was on it. The next moment he felt a violent jolt, and for an instant he was airborne. He landed again with a lurch that knocked the wind out of him, but he was still on his feet. And there, a few hundred yards ahead of him, was another chair-lift, running up towards a range of granite needles, with a small line of maybe fifteen people waiting to get on.

Mike covered the remaining distance without bothering to turn, almost colliding with the wooden fence at the bottom. He reached the end of the line just in time to see an instructor – a woman – being lifted off the ground accompanied by two other people. For an instant she looked back . . .

From his place five chairs back, Mike could see her, catch glimpses of her whenever the angle of ascent steepened. He could see blonde hair spilling out from under a big blue hat, sun-glasses. It had to be her. He reached into his pocket and pulled out the piste map they had given him with his ski pass. He reckoned he was on the lift below the Höllenspitze. He noticed that from the top all the runs down were black, in fact all but one of them were marked with a dotted line which meant they weren't really trails at all, just suggested off-piste routes. But what did that matter? Once he found Tania he could take the chair back down if he had to.

As he approached the top of the lift the air suddenly became still. The granite towers above seemed to screen them from the wind. Mike lifted the bar on his chair and got ready to climb off. As he did so, sliding down a short path, he saw the girl and her class disappearing off ahead of him again. He shouted her name but his voice seemed to get lost in the vastness of his surroundings. He turned to the lift attendant who sat in the doorway of a little wooden hut, listening to the radio.

'Was that Tania?' Mike shouted. 'Tania Schaffner?'

But the attendant didn't seem to understand.

Mike moved off again down the slope, only this time he didn't feel like pushing. Down below him was a steep, narrow trail, already churned up into an untidy pattern of moguls, and bounded on both sides by rocks. Looking down it almost gave Mike vertigo. He tried shouting and waving, but the line of skiers were already a hundred yards ahead of him, weaving and bounding athletically over the uneven surface. Tania wasn't taking a class; she was just acting as a guide for a group of experts. Mike took a deep breath. His heart was pounding like a drill.

You can do it Mikey . . .

He took the first part well, keeping his legs relaxed, anticipating each bump as it came, but the snow was heavy, the consistency uneven. It seemed to want to force his skis apart. He tried planting the ski pole more firmly, to bounce through the snow, but he found himself leaning too far back at the end of each turn, accelerating, losing his balance. With all his strength he forced himself to a halt, gasping for breath, his legs trembling from the effort. He looked down. The trail wound around some rocks on his left, steeper than before, with what looked like a long drop on the far side. Tania and the others were no longer in sight. *Come on, damn you . . .*

He pushed off again, urging himself on, driving out the fear. Around the turn he hit a bump so badly it almost knocked him on his back, but without stopping he pushed himself up again. It felt like free fall, out of control, but out of the corner of his eye he could see Tania's group ahead of him again. He hurtled over a vast, razor-backed mogul, plunging down into the deep powder on the other

373

side, his knees almost colliding with his chest. One of the skiers was waving at him with his ski pole . . .

The next second one of his skis hit something just below the surface of the snow. With a noise like a muffled shot it came clean away from his boot and, for a heady moment, Mike was flying down the slope on a single ski, one leg drifting free from the other as if on a space walk. Then he slammed, chest first, into the snow. His vision went brilliant red, but he could still feel his body rotating through the air. He opened his eyes in time to see the ground still coming towards him.

The second impact hit him on the shoulder. It hurt worse than the first: his body twisted, he felt his other ski come free. He thought of the drop by the side of the trail and tried frantically to stop himself falling any further, clawing at the snow with his hands. Then his boots hit something solid, and his whole body was pitched upwards so that he was almost standing again before . . .

He was lying on his back looking up at the grey sky, which seemed to slide about, like it was going to tip over and land on top of him. There was snow in his mouth and a salt taste of blood. He spat it out, coughing. He didn't want to move. He didn't want to find he had broken his neck.

In his ears there was a loud, high-pitched whine, like the white noise from a TV. Then the noise subsided a little and he realised that someone was talking to him.

'*Sehr Sie OK? Können Sie Ihre Beine fühlen*?'

It was a woman's voice. She was bending over him.

'Tania . . . Schaffner,' he said, lifting his head a couple of inches. 'I have to find her.'

19

Alleinmatt. February 19th, 1996.

The fire burned his face, but the back of his neck felt cold and exposed. It was good to sit still listening to the occasional crack from the pine log burning in the grate, and beyond that, the silence of the mountains. Mike looked around at the sunlit room. The house was a bit like a log cabin in a Walt Disney movie. There were two leather armchairs and a low wooden coffee table. Against the far wall there was a single bed which served as a sofa. An oak buffet stood next to the door which went through to the kitchen. It was a big, heavy piece of furniture, at least five feet long, but there wasn't an inch of space on the top. Tania had covered the wood with an embroidered linen cloth but even this was hardly visible under the mass of cups, and trophies, photographs and medals.

Tania was moving around in the kitchen. Since he had told her about Anna's death she had been very quiet. But he could see from the framed photographs on the buffet and on the wall that she usually had a smile on her face, a big, winner's smile.

Set in the middle of the display there was a black and white portrait of her as a young girl holding a trophy. She had set the statuette in a ball of snow which she held in her gloved hands. As he looked, the flames of the fire moving on his tired, unshaven face, the features of the girl dissolved and he was looking at Cathy, Cathy with her violin. *Me, age eleven.*

'Here is your chocolate, Mike. I hope I didn't make it too sweet.'

She sat in the armchair opposite him and drank from her mug, saying nothing for a while.

'That's quite a collection of cups you have.'

Tania half turned in her chair.

'Yes. I don't know what to do with them really. There are so many.'

'I'm surprised you could get them all up here. It seems so isolated.'

She turned back and faced him, squinting in the hard sunlight which came through the small window.

'You came up by the lift, and then the path through the fir trees, the pretty way. But there is a road about fifty metres from the chalet on the other side. They would not have built the chalet if there hadn't been a road. It is not always passable mind you, especially in winter.'

'If I'd known I would have driven up.'

Tania frowned, puzzled.

'After yesterday, I wasn't in such a hurry to put the skis back on.'

For the first time Tania smiled. The smile spread slowly, revealing her perfect white teeth. She covered her mouth, laughing.

'Yes. Yes, it was quite a fall.'

'Quite a fall! I nearly killed myself.'

Tania was laughing, shaking her head.

'No, no. Not as bad as that. You tumbled very fast. It is worse when you stop, how do you say that, when you stop sudden.'

She clapped her hands together to illustrate the point.

'I lost consciousness!' said Mike, hoping to see her smile some more, but the smile began to fade as she

376

recalled the scene from the day before, the moment in which he told her Anna was dead.

'For a moment perhaps. You were dizzy more, I think.'

She sipped at her chocolate. Her blue eyes cut across to the fire. She was withdrawing into herself again. Mike looked down at the chocolate. He was tired. The effort of coming back up the mountain in the rigid plastic boots after a cold night in the *Gasthof* had taken its toll. He had taken the cable car up to the Hörnlihütte and then skied down carefully, very carefully, to the beginning of the fir trees as Tania had instructed him to do the day before. There was a group of chalets at the end of the winding path. Tania's was the only one that looked inhabited. The others were used for animals.

He took a deep breath and tried to fix his mind on the reason for his being there. He thought of Cathy, in a room somewhere, maybe nearby. What did they want with her? He thought of the photographs he had seen at Anna's house. The shaved cat with the tube grafted into its skull. He looked up at Tania who was watching him over her steaming chocolate.

'You must have known Anna very well.'

Tania shrugged.

'I did know her well. We went to the same school in Zürich for a time, but then I came back to the mountain. I trained hard. Really hard. For years I lived only for the skiing.'

She indicated the trophies with a nod.

'I skied as a child, you see. From very little. For me school was just an, *Ich weiss nicht*, an obstacle. Anna was not like that. She too was from a small village but she was drawn to the town, and to the problems of the town. In Switzerland you know we are not always as liberal as our western neighbours, and so there was plenty for her to get upset about.'

She shook her head, and looked down at her chocolate.

377

'But to hear that . . . to hear that this has happened. I cannot believe it. *Tot*. It seems impossible that Anna should get involved in something so serious that someone wanted to kill her.'

Mike began to feel uncomfortable. He hadn't got round to explaining exactly what he believed had happened to Anna nor what he wanted from her. All he had said was that Anna had told him to come to her, that maybe she could help him. He hadn't said what with. She was watching him again.

'Do you know why, Mike?'

'What?'

'Do you know why someone wanted to kill Anna?'

Mike drank the last of his chocolate. He tried to think of a way to start. There was no question of lying. What would he say? He needed Tania to help him find the clinic. He had to get her on his side. He looked into her pale blue eyes.

'Yes. I think so. I think . . .'

Tania shuddered. She stood up and walked around the room.

'I'm sorry, Michael. I'm sorry.'

She walked across to the trophies and touched a brilliantly polished silver medal in a leather case. Then she turned to him.

'I'm sorry. You frighten me. I get the feeling that by talking to you I am in danger. That what you are going to tell me is bad news for me.'

Mike watched her, unable to think of what to say. He watched her from where he sat. Eventually she smiled, only faintly this time, and came back to her chair.

'Tell me why.'

'I don't know if I should, Tania. You're right. Maybe it *is* bad news for you.'

She said nothing, waiting for him to go on. He looked around at the brightly lit room.

'Do you mind if we go outside? At least then I won't feel like I'm putting a curse on your house.'

It was crisp outside. The sun was following its low trajectory just above the tree tops, flinging long blue ribbons of shadow across the snow.

'Let me show you my mountain,' said Tania, clipping into a pair of battered white boots.

Mike hesitated, looking at the skis he had left leaning against the wall.

'Don't worry, Michael. We will take it very slowly.'

They drifted down through the trees on a winding path which carried them onto a part of the slopes which Mike didn't recognise. The sunlight glared on the snow.

'You follow me, okay?'

And she was gone, sweeping away from him in a wide traverse of the pristine slope. Mike swallowed once and then turned to face downhill.

They skied for about ten minutes, making shallow sweeps across the slope which nobody else seemed to have discovered. Then Tania pulled up at the edge of an unmarked drop. Mike came to a halt beside her, slowly falling over as he lost his balance at the end of the stop turn.

'You're getting better,' said Tania, smiling.

Mike climbed to his feet.

'Why is there nobody else on this slope? It's perfect.'

'We are on a part of the mountain which is very danger-ous to ski in certain conditions. There are some very big rocks.'

'Now you tell me!'

'You are safe with me. I know the ground and I know which parts to avoid. But conditions can change quite quickly and so it is not open to the public. But look.'

She pointed out into the blue air beyond the ledge on which they were standing. There was a breathtaking, unbroken view along the valley. In the distance they could see Alleinmatt, and suspended high above the town three bright sails slowly turning in the blue.

'Hang-gliders,' said Tania, squinting up at the sky.

'Tania.'

Mike's voice was serious, almost sad. Tania removed her sunglasses and looked Mike in the face. Her breath came and went in little puffs. She was ready to listen.

'There is a girl called Cathy Ryder, a girl I met in New York. She was doing some research into Mendelhaus, that's her job; she is an analyst for a securities house on Wall Street.'

He looked down at his feet, trying to sort out in his mind the best way to present the facts.

'I don't know if you know anything about Mendelhaus, but they make cosmetics and they run a number of clinics here in Switzerland. They do a lot of medical research apparently.'

He set his ski poles into the snow and squared himself on his skis. Tania was watching him.

'A few months ago Mendelhaus launched a new cosmetics range in America, Erixil.'

'Yes, of course. I have heard about that. It is supposed to be revolutionary.'

'No. It *is* revolutionary. I'm no expert in this, but it's based on some whole new kind of bio-technology. It has turned the industry upside down. People have made, and lost, a *lot* of money. Somehow Cathy was involved in all this. She seemed to know a lot about what was going on in Mendelhaus and I think she was getting inside information from someone; a guy called Krystal, I think. But something went wrong. Cathy was invited across to Switzerland, to look around I suppose, and she just disappeared.'

'But . . .'

'I know. She could have just disappeared, right? Happens all the time. She could have been knocked over crossing the road. She might be in a hospital somewhere right now with nobody knowing who she is.'

Tania nodded.

'But I don't think so. You see, since I started trying to talk to Mendelhaus, to Krystal, things have happened.'

Mike moistened his lips.

'In New York I tried to fix a meeting with Krystal at a restaurant. But you know what? When I showed up someone got their head blown off right in front of me. Someone who was sitting in *my* place, pretending to be *me*.'

Tania closed her eyes, and then opened them again.

'And Anna?'

'I don't know, Tania. How can I know? All I'm saying is that Anna was helping me look for Cathy and then she got killed.'

Mike stopped and looked down at the snow. A gust of wind lifted particles of ice into his face. He moved his skis back and forth. He thought for a moment and then looked up.

'Now I've told you. I told you because I wanted you to know what happened to Anna. But I am not asking you to help me. Anna said you could help me if you wanted to. But if she had realised the dangers, then maybe she wouldn't have given me your name.'

He looked away towards Alleinmatt.

'If you tell me how to get down the mountain I'll just ski off into the sunset.'

'And what about your friend?'

'I'll find out where they're keeping her and then I'll get her out. If she's still . . .'

He didn't finish the sentence. Tania looked back up the slope towards the trees which hid her home. She lifted her ski poles and then set them lightly in the snow.

'Mike. Nobody knows you're here, yes? Nobody. How can they know? But what I don't understand is why you don't just phone Mendelhaus and ask them where the clinic is?'

'We tried that. There are four clinics that are listed, and none of them are in this area. Anna believed that a fifth clinic, a secret clinic with a laboratory maybe, is somewhere near Brig, maybe near Alleinmatt.'

'I have many friends here, Michael, and I know the place. If there is some kind of installation here somebody will know.'

Mike spread his arms.

'What can I say, Tania?'

But Tania was looking down towards Alleinmatt.

'Come, follow me down,' she said, and she pushed away from him, quickly gathering speed as she went down into the shadow below the ridge.

20

Alleinmatt. February 20th, 1996.

'No one's heard of this place,' said Tania, shaking her head. 'The Town Hall was a complete waste of time.'

They were sitting opposite each other in a rustic kind of bar called Rudi's, with old wooden skis hung up on the walls and a huge log fire in the grate. It was three o'clock.

'I went through the phone book, and then I checked the list of businesses in the Brig area . . .'

'They won't be on that kind of list,' said Mike. 'Not one that the public can get to.'

Tania shook her head. She was staring down at the surface of the table.

'That's all the records there are,' she said. 'All the businesses have to pay the local taxes, and that's the list they use. Maybe Anna made a mistake – or you did.'

'No. She said Brig. She saw it in the newspaper article. There has to be another clinic up here somewhere.'

The waitress came by and put two steaming glasses of *Glühwein* in front of them. Tania didn't look up.

'Well it seems stupid to me,' she said. 'I mean, I can't see how Mendelhaus could avoid getting themselves on the public registers. Apart from the taxes, you can't get permission to build anything without approval from the

383

local authorities. They're very strict about that kind of thing.'

'Maybe so,' said Mike. 'But the records of an application could be kept separate couldn't they, with the connivance of the authorities? Someone could pay, and then – '

Tania sighed impatiently.

'That's just the sort of stupid thing Anna would say. All this talk about conspiracies. This is a modern country. I mean why would anyone *want* to keep something like that a secret? What's so sinister about a clinic?'

'I don't know. Maybe we'll find out . . . I mean maybe *I'll* find out.'

Tania didn't say anything. She looked sullen, unconvinced. But then how could he expect her to trust him so soon? The day before she'd seemed so willing to help that he had taken her for granted. He had persuaded her to give up a class and spend all morning searching the local records, while he bought as many maps as he could find of the area and waited for the newspapers to come in. There'd been plenty of time for Tania to change her mind, to tell someone, to get suspicious. Maybe she was thinking she should go to the police. Maybe she had decided he was just a madman.

He leaned across the table towards her, his palms flat on the table, speaking softly: 'I know it seems crazy, Tania. I know it doesn't seem possible. Sometimes I lie in bed myself and think: this isn't happening. I'm an ordinary guy and this kind of thing doesn't happen to ordinary guys. This is just a bad dream. But you know what? Every time I get close to convincing myself that this whole thing isn't real, that I've just let my imagination run away with me, *someone gets killed.*'

There were tears in her eyes, but he couldn't stop himself. He had to let it out.

'Then I know it isn't a dream. It's real, and it's right

384

here in beautiful Switzerland. Well I'm gonna get to them, Tania, I don't care who their friends are. I'm gonna get to them and I'm gonna make them pay!'

Tania covered her face.

'Please stop,' she said. 'I can't bear thinking about it. Poor Anna. She never hurt anyone in her life.'

Mike sat back and picked up his glass.

'I know,' he said, looking into it. 'I'm sorry.'

'I can't believe anyone would want to . . .'

She looked up at him.

'You can't be sure it's anything to do with you or your girlfriend. And anyway the police will find out who killed her.'

'No,' said Mike. 'You're right. I can't be sure.'

For a few moments they were silent. Then Mike took a rolled-up copy of the day's newspaper from his coat pocket and slid it across the table.

'Have you seen this yet?'

Tania picked it up.

'The report's on page five. I don't read German but I think they for one have a different theory.'

Tania looked at him, and turned over the pages. Then she read the report. It only had five column inches. When she looked up again her expression had changed.

'This isn't true. The bastards! How can they print this?'

'What do you mean?' said Mike, although he was sure he already knew.

'I can't believe it. It says: "According to the police information, Anna Norden was a political extremist, and was closely associated with a number of militant anarchist groups. There is speculation that her death may have been the result of divisions within the anti-democratic alliance over policy or leadership." That's not true! Anna wasn't into that kind of thing. She used to go on demonstrations about vivisection or . . . or pollution, that's all. She liked *causes*. They make her sound like a terrorist!'

'They must have reckoned she was bad for business.'

Tania read on: ' "In particular, the police are anxious to question a dark-haired man, aged about thirty, who was believed to be staying at Miss Norden's house the night before she was murdered." '

'That was me,' said Mike. 'They think it was me.'

Tania looked at him. Suddenly she was calm.

'Is that what you are then, an anarchist?'

Mike wanted to laugh.

'To tell the truth I'd planned on voting Republican. I haven't given it much thought lately.'

For the first time that day Tania smiled.

'Let's get out of here,' she said. 'It's too hot with that fire.'

They walked along the main street towards the ski school. The bad weather had cleared up that morning, and everything was bathed in golden yellow sunshine. A stream cut the village in two, and from the main bridge Mike could see almost the whole valley: the granite peaks, the distant snowfields, even some of the bigger lift stations high up on the western side. And in the distance, alone, the cold grey Heulendthorn. He stopped to look at it. *Is she there? Somewhere up there?*

'Tania, if you had to build a clinic, a clinic for the richest, most exclusive clientele in the world,' he said, sheltering his eyes from the light, 'and you had to build it somewhere near Brig, where would you put it?'

Tania leaned on the rail and looked down at the boulders on the bed of the stream, still covered with snow.

'The most exclusive clientele in the world?' said Tania. 'Then I guess it would have to be right here. At Alleinmatt. There are other resorts in Switzerland that are more famous, you know, for film stars and things – St Moritz, Gstaad – but they're not close to Brig, and anyway, Alleinmatt is more – how do you say? – discreet.'

'Aren't there other places like that around here?'

386

'There are other resorts, sure. But Alleinmatt is where the real money comes: the bankers, the old Swiss families. You don't see them much. They only come when the weather's good and they spend their evenings in each other's chalets. You should see some of the ones they have up behind the church. Inside they're like palaces. They pretty well own the whole valley, and almost everything in it.'

'But why would any of that matter to you, if you were setting up this clinic?'

'I don't know. Prestige, I suppose. Also if I was the director of the place or something, this is where I'd want to live.'

They walked on in silence until they stood at the foot of the gondola lift that Tania took to reach her chalet. It was cold in the shadows.

'You've helped me a lot,' Mike said. 'I appreciate it. If you think of any way to find that clinic . . .'

She began to walk up the steps ahead of him, but then she stopped and looked round.

'Mike,' she said. 'It only took them a few days to find you in Zürich. How do you know they won't come looking for you here? Someone might have reported you already.'

Mike looked at his feet.

'Maybe they have. But maybe I'll be ready this time.'

She looked at him for a moment and then walked back down the steps.

'You're talking like a crazy person. If what you've told me is true you must be very careful, Mike. You can't just wait for them to find you. Look, go and get your things now and then you come and stay in my house. That way no one will ever know you're here, okay?'

'Tania, I don't know, it could be . . .'

'That's what we're going to do. Besides, I've got an idea about how we could find that clinic.'

The mountain rescue helicopter was a red Arospatiale
Gazelle, fitted with skis instead of wheels, and it stood
waiting on the freshly swept tarmac, its blades already
spinning. Tania slid back the door and they climbed in
behind the pilot.

'Mike, this is Wolfgang. He's an old friend.'

They shook hands. Wolfgang had short blond hair and
wore sunglasses, just like all the ski instructors.

'I appreciate this,' said Mike.

'Okay,' said the pilot and showed him a thumbs-up
over his shoulder. 'Let's go.'

He spoke into his radio: '*Hier ist Rettungswache Eins.
Abflugbereit.*'

Then the craft lifted slowly off the ground. Mike put
on his seat belt and eased himself away from the door
which seemed ready to slide open any moment. Anna
took out the collection of maps Mike had bought and
began folding them on her lap.

'Okay,' she said, shouting over the noise of the engines.
'We're going to check the western side of the valley first,
right down to where it meets the Rhône. That's about
twenty-five miles. Then we come back again on the eastern side. Then, if we don't find anything, we can try
another valley maybe tomorrow.'

'But how will we recognise it?'

'Like I told you, normally you have to have permission
to build or enlarge anything, permission from the local
authorities. The work for these maps, the original survey
using aerial photography, was done more than twenty
years ago. But since then they've been updated every
couple of years to put on new buildings and roads and
things, using the administrative records. The maps are
prepared by the authorities themselves, you see?'

'So?'

'So if anyone *has* got around the system, has arranged
for their new buildings not to appear on the records, then

those buildings won't be on the map. So all we have to do is find a big site somewhere that shouldn't be there. That shouldn't be so hard up here. Outside of the main villages the biggest buildings are mostly lift stations.'

They were drawing closer to the head of the valley, dominated by the Heulendthorn, its craggy blue glaciers just catching the morning sun. Below them the forests and winding ski trails lay in blue shadow.

'There's nothing up here or we would know about it,' said Tania. 'Some of the best off-piste skiing is just below the Heulendthorn, only you have to be careful of avalanches. Especially now. They couldn't build anything up there.'

They cleared the tree-line and then after a few more miles turned west, heading back down towards the smaller peaks of the Höllenspitze and the Hornberg.

'You see where we are?' said Tania, pointing away to their left. 'See the lift station? That's the one that serves the whole southern skiing area.'

'Right, I got it,' Mike said, trying to keep from feeling giddy. 'It says here three thousand three hundred metres altitude.'

'That's the one. And can you see my house now?'

Mike looked out to his right. Running up the western side of the valley he could see a series of lines and cables, made easier to spot by yellow and red spheres strung out along them like beads. Below one of these lines passed a slow procession of gondolas, carrying skiers up to the snowfields south of the Höllenspitze.

'There!' shouted Mike. 'That's the mountain restaurant we went to. And that's your house further down by the trees.'

'Okay. You've got it. But I don't think they would put their clinic all the way up here. It's too exposed, and there are no roads. More likely it would be nearer the northern end, lower down, somewhere among the trees. It would be much more convenient.'

Mike wondered if that was the sort of convenience Mendelhaus would be concerned about. But at this end of the valley it would be difficult to hide away. There were ski runs all over the place, and above the tree-line everything was visible.

'Okay, let's take a look.'

Half an hour later they were still travelling along the western side of the valley. There were scores of small settlements in among the trees, and they grew more numerous the closer they got to Brig. Mike felt dizzy from looking back and forward from the map to the ground and back again, twenty times a minute. So far everything he had seen had been on the map, or too small to worry about. He was beginning to wonder whether it wouldn't be easier to hide a laboratory and a clinic in a town – perhaps in Brig itself – than out here where such a complex would inevitably stand out, at least from the air.

Tania was talking to Wolfgang, pointing down into the forests ahead of them. The mountains were much lower at this end of the valley, and only their rocky spines were visible above the tall trees.

'Mike, do you see that clearing up ahead? It looks like trees have been cut down. Can you find that on the map?'

Mike checked.

'I don't see anything here. Is there a building?'

'I think so. I can see a roof – and there's a road coming out further down, joining the main road.'

They banked to the left and then descended rapidly towards the clearing. Mike could feel the pressure change in his ears. They were less than a hundred feet over the trees. He scanned the map again. There were no side roads marked where Tania had pointed.

390

'This will give them a shock!' she shouted. 'They won't see us until we're on top of them!'

She seemed so confident Mike began to take heart. He unfastened his belt and leaned against the window. If this was really the clinic it might only be minutes before he saw Cathy again. Her face, her hair, her eyes. But she would be guarded, and they had no guns. How could he get to her without them . . . ?

'There it is!' Tania shouted.

Mike looked down as the chopper drew up. For a moment Mike couldn't see anything over the swaying of the trees, then a building appeared, a big building, like a chalet only bigger, with rows of neat windows. Behind it were other small buildings, arranged in a square. And there in front, in a messy area of mud and snow were men, men in white. One of them was running. Among them stood machines: a cement mixer, a portable generator, a roller. The men were working. It looked like they were making a driveway.

'You want me to set it down?' said Wolfgang.

The men had stopped work and were looking up at the chopper, shielding their eyes from the sun.

'Wait a minute,' said Mike. 'This place doesn't even look finished. Some of those windows up there don't have glass in them.'

Tania stared at the building for a moment and then slumped back in her chair with a groan.

'I know what this is, Mike. I should have remembered. There's a big sign on the road.'

'What is it?'

'The Nikolai Hotel. It's going to be a convention centre or something. It's supposed to open in the summer. I'm sorry.'

The men below started waving. One of them threw a snowball.

'Let's get out of here,' Mike said.

Fifteen minutes later, on the opposite side of the valley, just above the river, they found another site which wasn't on the map. It turned out to be a new pumping station.

'I didn't realise there was so much building going on,' Tania said. 'But at least we're picking up the new places, right?'

'Right,' Mike said, trying to sound positive. 'There's still plenty more places to look.'

Tania looked over her shoulder and smiled at him.

'If it's not here then we can – '

She was interrupted by Wolfgang: '*Die Arbent ruft! Ein Unfall in der Nähe des Heulendthorn!*'

'Mike, we've got to go,' said Tania. 'There's been an accident somewhere. Maybe we can try again later.'

Wolfgang put the chopper into a steep turn and headed towards Alleinmatt. Mike had to grip the back of Tania's seat to keep from rolling over. In a few minutes the village was directly below them. Mike could see smoke rising from the chimneys.

'*Irgend ein Idiot hat eine Lawine gestartet.*'

'It's an avalanche,' said Tania. 'Opposite the Heulendthorn, on the eastern side. There isn't time to drop you off.'

Wolfgang looked round: 'They were skiing below the Phönixlager.' He tapped his temple with a gloved finger. 'Crazy people.'

They were close to the Heulendthorn now, flying over the great curved glacier whose deep, ocean-blue crevasses were mostly hidden below a tempting expanse of virgin snow. Opposite the mountain, and a little further south, stood a towering ridge, beneath which lay a broad skirt of powder at least half a mile wide, descending for a thousand metres to the edge of the tree line. As they drew closer, Mike could make out the curved tracks of skiers running from about half way up the slope, where

392

a small head of rock jutting out from the ridge made for a convenient platform.

'They got up there by helicopter,' said Tania. 'They should check with us first, but often they don't bother. They see the sun and the powder and they just go. Mind you no one skis over here unless they know nothing about the area.'

'Italians!' shouted Wolfgang. 'They come from the other side. And no passports!'

Mike could see figures by the trees. About three hundred metres above them a great slab of snow was missing from the slope: Mike could see traces of rock and ice, and below that an untidy mass of snow where the avalanche had come to rest. The people – there were three of them – started waving.

Wolfgang had been talking on the radio again. He seemed to be arguing.

'Ah, I don't believe it!'

Mike leaned forward.

'What's happening?'

'Nothing,' said Wolfgang. 'They don't need us.'

'Why not?'

'False alarm,' explained Tania. 'Someone saw the ava-lanche from below the Heulendthorn and called us. But those people have radios and they say nobody got hurt.'

'Not *absolute* crazy people,' Wolfgang added, with a smile. 'Italians. Well, you want to go to Italia?'

'To Italy?'

Tania pointed out towards the ridge.

'Just the other side of the Phönixlager: that's Italy. Almost the whole of that valley is in Italy, but there's nothing in it.'

'We take a little look,' said Wolfgang. 'They come to Switzerland, we go to Italia.'

He put the chopper into a climb, passing just over the ridge into a horseshoe-shaped area of rock and ice. The

393

ridge continued in an arc both to the north and south, and opened up into a narrow valley to the east. They headed towards the south.

'Just down here we can – *Jesu!*'

From nowhere a white chopper appeared dead ahead of them, barely a hundred yards away, hovering over the southern ridge. Wolfgang banked steeply to the right, throwing Mike against the side of the cabin. Mike saw rocks ahead of them. He closed his eyes.

'*Kretin! Idiot! Das ist der letzte Scheis!*'

They cleared the ridge by a few feet. Wolfgang was swearing at the top of his voice, shaking his fist at the other craft, which slowly turned east and headed off up the far valley.

'Where did he come from?' said Tania.

'I don't know,' said Wolfgang. 'Down there.'

Mike fastened his seatbelt again and looked. They were at the top of a great cliff that went all the way down to the tree-line. In the distance stood another range of mountains.

'More helicopter skiers?' he asked.

Tania shrugged.

'Maybe, but there's no skiing this side. The terrain is too difficult. Maybe they just . . .'

'Wait a minute, what's that? Just above the trees.'

He could see a building as big as the hotel at the other end of the valley, crouching with its back to the cliff, protected from avalanche or rock-falls by a series of steel barriers fixed in the granite above it. He picked up the map again.

'Where are we exactly?'

Tania took the map and pointed.

'Just there. Right on the border.'

'But there's nothing marked!' said Mike. 'And surely there can't be a new hotel here if there's no skiing.'

'No, nothing,' said Wolfgang.

'I never knew there was a place here,' said Tania, shaking her head. 'It's incredible. If there's a road it must go in and out of Italy.'

'Tania, I think this could be it. There's a wall around the whole site, look. If it wasn't for the Alpine charm it could be a military installation.'

'How can we be sure?'

'By landing,' said Mike. 'I'm going in there. If I don't come out in ten minutes, radio the police.'

'Mike, wait a minute. You can't just go in there and demand – '

'What else can I do? Ring up and make an appointment?'

Tania thought for a second and said: 'Yes. That's exactly what you can do. You can ring up and make an appointment.'

21

Los Angeles. February 22nd, 1996.

Waterman was still thirty yards down the street when he heard his phone ringing. He tried to pick up speed but after jogging for two miles he could not run another step. His lungs were screaming. He could barely walk. At the gate he managed one last desperate spurt, tugging the doorkeys from his pocket as he went. Halfway up the yard they slipped through his sweaty fingers and fell to the ground. As he bent down to pick them up he felt sure he was going to be sick. Finally, almost passing out, he stumbled into the kitchen and grabbed onto the receiver with an outstretched hand.

He didn't have enough wind left to speak. All he could do was pant.

'Harry? Hello?'

'Yuh,' he replied between gasps.

'Is that you, Harry?'

Waterman tried holding his breath for a second. He couldn't do it. There was barely enough for another. 'Yuh.'

'Harry?'

'Yuh, it's me.'

'Jesus, what's the matter with you? You sound like some kinda sex maniac, or something.'

Waterman recognised the voice. It was Lieutenant

396

Bernie Logan, of the New York City Police Department, one of his few good contacts over there.

'Hi Bernie. I . . . I just went jogging. Still gotta . . . catch my breath.'

Logan broke into his sarcastic New York cackle.

'What's gotten into you Harry? Got tired of bein' a slob or something? And I thought that kind of lifestyle was just coming back in.'

Waterman ignored the jibe. Bernie Logan was always making them. It was his substitute for wit.

'Yeah, well. You gotta . . . gotta try and hold the line somewhere, right? How's it going over there?'

'The heating's broken down in the office and I'm having my ass frozen off, if you really wanna know.'

Waterman pulled up a stool and wiped the sweat off his eyelids with a paper towel.

'Sounds good to me,' he said.

'Yeah, yeah. I'll bet. Anyway, before you go cool off in the pool, I got a word from Homicide on that chick you were looking for.'

'Homicide?'

'Yeah, but maybe it don't mean nothing. I'm just telling you 'cos you asked me to keep a lookout, that's all.'

Waterman reached for pen and paper.

'So . . . so what happened?'

'You okay, Harry? You sound like you're gonna have a heart attack or something.'

'I'm okay. Just tell me what happened.'

'Well ten days ago some guy got his head blown off in some fancy restaurant on William Street. Professional hit, no question. Guy turns out to be called Chaney, Sam Chaney.'

'Hey, I think I heard that name.'

'Yeah, I reckoned you might, you goddamn sleaze-ball. He was in the same kind of business as you: security, surveillance, industrial espionage – '

'Bernie, you know I don't do that kind of stuff, I'm strictly – '

'On the side of the angels. Sure you are, Harry. Just don't ask me for a character reference when you find yourself in front of a jury. Anyhow this Chaney character runs quite a pretty serious outfit out of Boston.'

'Was he working on something?'

'That's the news, Harry. The other creeps in his organisation say they didn't *know* what he was working on, but they found a notebook on his body. That's where your girl comes in. Her name was there, her address was there, a whole load of stuff. Even the name of her boyfriend.'

'Did they manage to figure out what he wanted it for?'

'I don't think so. Homicide ain't sure she's got anything to do with the killing. Guys like that get their noses stuck in all kinds of nasty business. Mind you, if *you* got any ideas, Harry, I think the guys in Homicide would like to know – through me that is.'

'Well sure, Bernie. You'll be the first to hear. But so far no police leads on the hit?'

'They're checkin'. But the girl ain't showed up though since that break-in she had. They tried to call her and she still ain't in. And this is the really interesting part: she ain't showed up at work during the past couple of weeks neither. She went to Europe an' she ain't come back.'

'And they haven't been able to reach her anywhere?'

'She took care of her business for the bank, checked out of her hotel in Switzerland, and vanished. Her boss's already got her listed as an official missing person over there.'

Waterman thought back to the picture of Cathy Ryder on the cover of *Fortune*. It was all he had ever seen of her. An icon of someone he had searched for but never found, searched for without really knowing why. She was the key somehow, but to what?

'Harry, you thinkin' what I'm thinkin'?'

'What's that, Bernie?'

'That this lady's got the same treatment as Chaney some place?'

'Hell, I don't know. She was just a goddamn stock analyst. It doesn't make sense.'

'Yeah well, that's just what they said in Homicide. Listen Harry, I gotta go. You find anything big an' illegal, you let me know first, okay?'

'Okay, you can count on it. Thanks for the call, Bernie. I appreciate it.'

'See ya, Harry. Oh an' Harry, don't go joggin' too often, okay? I hear the earthquakes is bad enough as it is down there.'

'Sure Bernie, sure.' Harry replaced the receiver and sat down in the breakfast nook. Chaney dead. Why had he been carrying Cathy's name? Cathy's and the boyfriend's name? If it was what he had originally thought, that the girl had found out something the company didn't want her to know, then her disappearance made sense. But what had she found out? Did it relate to Bladon and McArthur? And where did Chaney come in? Harry peeled off his T-shirt and sat looking at his stomach, deep in thought.

The first set of skeletons wouldn't turn the lock. There were two tumblers that weren't moving. Crouching under the dim light of the landing, Waterman selected a different combination from the folding leather pouch. He had never been very good at this kind of thing and these days he didn't get much practice, but the dead-lock was old and the latch had been damaged in the break-in. It would have been a simple matter for a pro. From the floor above he could hear voices, somebody laughing, a door slam. He waited, listening. He thought for a moment he heard something on the stairs.

He tried the lock again. This time he could feel four pin

399

tumblers obediently rolling back. Only one still wouldn't budge. He reached in with a third hook and moved it around. The latch was already held back by a plastic phone card. Then he found the fifth tumbler. The door jolted and swung open, almost pitching him into the hallway.

Inside he used a torch, sorting through the papers that lay now in piles around the coffee table and the fireplace. Bernie Logan had told him that Homicide had tried to call Cathy Ryder again. But as yet they hadn't bothered to go back to her apartment. They were following other leads. That gave Waterman time to get what he could before it disappeared into the black hole of police evidence. He didn't like to think what would happen if Logan ever found out what he was doing, but he had already made up his mind about all that. The link with Chaney had confirmed what he had already begun to suspect: that, one way or another, this whole business was steeped in serious money. Maybe Chaney himself had been ahead of him, but maybe Chaney had been stupid.

In the kitchen he found a stack of newspapers and magazines, but nothing more recent than the beginning of the month. Nothing, in fact, since Chaney's death. That suggested that the boyfriend had finally cleared off around the same time. He hadn't liked that guy a bit. He sure acted like he had something to hide, but he also acted like an amateur: ducking around alleyways and all that shit. He couldn't see him taking someone's head off in a crowded restaurant and then just walking away. That took nerves of blue steel and an immaculate sense of timing. Judging from their last meeting, Michael Varela didn't have either.

What he wanted most was a diary, a notebook: something that might help him make connections. He could barely afford it, but he had already decided to follow his leads to Switzerland. It meant turning down some handy

400

insurance work, but he was going to play for bigger stakes than that now. He was tired of people treating him like a joke, or worse than that, like some poor relation with embarrassing habits, people like Bill Miller and Bernie Logan. Even on the phone to the CDC these days he could sense what they were thinking: *What can we give him to keep him going, to keep him from bugging us? Poor old Harry.* And it would be the same year in year out, until one day Bill Miller or someone else would say: *What are we running here, a charity?* And then that would be that. Unless he could stop depending on them, get some capital behind him and set up his own business: security consultant or something. You could do very well out of that on the West Coast.

And besides, he had to *know*. He had to know what Edward Geiger had been doing all these years. He didn't want to wake up one morning and see it on the breakfast news, or read it in the papers. He wanted to get there first. And he was ahead of the field, he was sure of that. He was really on to something, was finally making the connections. He would never forgive himself if someone else beat him to the truth. Maybe this was his once-in-a-lifetime chance, the chance he'd waited for for so long.

So he was going to follow every lead until it went dead. And if it really was to be nickel and dime stuff the rest of his life, then at least he would always know that he'd tried for something better and given it his best shot. Something *had* gone wrong at Mendelhaus, he was sure of it, and it had cost Bladon and McArthur their lives. Maybe Chancy or Cathy Ryder had found out about it. Whatever the truth, there were people out there willing to pay – either to hear it or to suppress it. And somewhere in the middle of it all was Geiger. The exact importance of this was less clear, but Waterman's gut told him that it was crucial. A leading light of the scientific establishment had

401

disappeared, and for ten years it had been as if he had never existed . . .

He searched through the desk, finding nothing of interest but an old address book. Lastly he turned to the answering machine which stood winking at him from the little mahogany card table beside him. He took out the incoming cassette and replaced it with another from his pocket. Then he saw the note in front of it: *Cathy Ryder is in Switzerland. I've gone to find her. If you have any questions, put them to Ernst Krystal (212) 623 9111. Michael Varela.*

Waterman tore the piece of paper from the pad, folded it in half and put it in his pocket.

22

Oswald Hunziker was ushered into the dimly lit room by the white-gloved servant. He was wearing a blue track-suit with a pristine white towel around his neck.

'Sorry to interrupt your workout, Oswald. You know I wouldn't have done it if I didn't think it was important.'

Dietmar Hoffman was sitting on the elephant hide sofa. He was wearing a double-breasted blue suit. He gestured to Hunziker to sit beside him and then turned his cold green eyes on the servant, still standing in the doorway.

'Thank you, Celio, you can leave us now. Ask Maria to bring in – tea all right with you, Oswald? Yes. Orange Pekoe then, Celio.'

The servant left the room, the door closing silently behind him. Hoffman began to apologise again, but Hunziker silenced him with a gesture.

'It really is of no consequence Dietmar. I don't normally work out in the afternoon. It was a way of dealing with the tension.'

'Yes, everyone is a little on edge at the moment. What time is the operation in fact?'

'Kessler tells me they will be starting at ten o'clock.'

'And is everything okay with the patient?'

'Apparently, apparently. Though he is very old, you know. Very sick.'

Hoffman frowned. He stood up and went across to a walnut drinks cabinet on the other side of the room.

'You start early, Dietmar.' Hoffman looked back over his shoulder at the other man seated on the sofa. 'The tension must be getting to you too.'

Hoffman shook his head.

'No, it's not that, Oswald. I mean, I am worried about that, naturally. One never quite knows what to expect from our resident scientists. No, there is something else.'

At that moment the door opened and a beautiful, dark-haired girl came in with the tea. Again a frown flickered across Hoffman's brow. The tea things were set on the low coffee table.

'Thank you, Maria.'

The girl turned to go, and Hoffman touched her lightly on the shoulder. She smiled up at his tanned face. She was about eighteen.

'Make sure no one disturbs us, would you?'

She nodded and left the room.

Hoffman sat beside Hunziker on the sofa. He turned to face the older man, resting a brilliantly polished shoe on his knee.

'I asked you to come up because there is something I wanted to tell you. Something I didn't want the others to hear.'

'It sounds serious.'

Hoffman nodded.

'It may well be serious, I'm afraid.'

Hoffman reached forward and poured tea into the two china cups.

'It concerns our donor.'

Hunziker nodded.

'I thought it might be something likc that.'

Hoffman watched the other man's face for a moment, trying to read his thoughts.

'I got the impression at our meeting that you were sympathetic to my, my position on this . . .'

Hunziker nodded, his steaming cup raised to his lips.

'I too am worried about the girl, Dietmar. You know that.'

'Yes. Well, things . . . things on the outside seem to have taken a turn for the – they are if anything more worrying.'

Hunziker raised his eyebrows. His lips were moist with tea.

'Yes, I am afraid so. In spite of Herr Kessler's assurances regarding arrangements, I have reason to believe, I have no reason to doubt, that someone is looking for her.'

'But there were bound to be some questions. A young American comes to Switzerland and goes missing. There are bound to be some questions to answer.'

Hoffman sipped and set his cup back in its delicate saucer.

'No it is more than that. I understand that a person is in Switzerland, and he is looking for the girl.'

'Then surely the source knows what to do.'

Hoffman gave a little irritated shake of his head. He picked up the heavy glass which was half full of whisky and looked at it against the light.

'Unfortunately, it is not quite as clear as that, Oswald.'

'What do you mean?'

'Well, I don't quite know how to put it, given the long years of admirable service of the person in question; long years characterised, I may say, by faultless execution of any service demanded.' Hoffman paused and sipped at the whisky. Hunziker watched his face, his mouth open. 'But it seems that our friend has recently made a number of mistakes.'

'Mistakes?'

'Yes, Oswald, mistakes. It appears that somebody was killed in New York.'

'My God.'

Hoffman set a perfectly manicured hand on the older man's shoulder.

'No traces. No possible connection, I am assured.'

'By our friend.'

'Yes, by our friend. And I am inclined to believe him. I do not believe he has started to lie to us yet. But that is another matter. There was another unfortunate incident a few days ago in Zürich. Once again nothing that can be traced to us.'

Hunziker sat back against the sofa and dabbed his face with the towel.

'However – '

Hunziker stopped dabbing and watched Hoffman's face.

'However, while there is little or no chance of the authorities concerned making the connection between these different accidents, it must be becoming abundantly clear to the person in question, let us call him the intruder, it must be becoming perfectly clear to him that the accidents *are* connected, and that we are somehow involved. In short, this person must have a fairly strong suspicion that we are hiding something, and I mean by that of course, the Jewish girl.'

Hunziker sat in silence for a long time. In spite of his tan and the years of treatment in the clinic he looked old, tired. Hoffman sipped at his drink and waited. Finally Hunziker looked up.

'How do we know that the intruder is looking for the girl? He might be . . .'

'We know he is looking for the girl because our source has concrete, irrefutable evidence of the fact. It appears that the intruder was involved with the donor somehow, emotionally I mean.'

'The boyfriend comes to Switzerland to find his lost love.'

'I don't know if we can put that gloss on it, Oswald. There is some suggestion, according to the source, that the intruder had or has an ulterior motive. It is also by no means clear that he is working alone.'

'What?'

'Apparently, the accident in New York would not have happened, could not have happened, had he been alone.'

Hunziker was shaking his head.

'Yes, Oswald, it is by no means clear to me either.'

Again there was a minute of silence.

'So what do you suggest?'

'We do? It seems to me there are two things we can do. In the first place I have already given the source instructions to do whatever is necessary on the outside.'

'But . . .'

'And I have his assurance that there will be no further problems. In the meantime I have deposited a certain amount of cash in the appropriate account.'

'But what about the girl?'

'That is the other thing about which we can do something. I seem to recall that Herr Kessler said there would be a sufficient stock of ova for cloning after the second ovulation. I am of course no expert on these matters, but it seems to me that if Kessler and Geiger are ready to cut open Mr Hiraizumi today, then the donor must have given up some of her treasures at least a couple of days ago if not more. This means that the second ovulation should occur by the twentieth of next month at the very latest.'

'We could get clarification on that point from Herr Kessler.'

Hoffman guffawed dismissively.

'In my experience, Oswald, Kessler is remarkably unclear when it suits his purpose.'

Hunziker looked down at his cold tea. Hoffman went on.

'By the twentieth of next month we will be in a position to take a decision about the donor's future.'

Hunziker looked up.

'Now, Oswald, I called you in here because I didn't want to air this with the rest of the board. I am afraid we may not be able to count on Karl, for example, to back us up. We may have to take an initiative, on our own I mean.'

Hunziker replaced his cup on the silver tray. He looked at his watch.

'It's nearly ten o'clock, Dietmar.'

Hoffman raised his whisky, and then tossed it back, his green eyes fixed on the ceiling.

Sitting in the dimly lit room, the two green-clad surgeons looked at the colour monitor which was the only way to see what was happening in the theatre. The image was grainy and whenever a surgical instrument caught the powerful overhead lights a luminous trail was made, fading only after a couple of seconds. The head of the patient was clear above the green, sterile sheet, although his mouth and nose were covered with a mask.

'David looks worried,' said one of the surgeons, indicating the anaesthetist with the unlit cigarette he held. The anaesthetist, his face pink and shiny on the screen, was frowning down at what was happening out of sight under the glare of the lights.

'I'd be worried too,' said the other young man, squinting up at the monitor. At this his colleague lit his cigarette and looked down at his hands.

'You don't think Geiger can do it?'

He knew what the other man would answer. There was a lot of bad feeling among the surgeons at the clinic about Geiger's excluding them from the developments he was making in their field. The emphasis, as they understood it – Kessler was never very forthcoming on this matter, and Geiger was unavailable – was on placing cell cultures in the right place at exactly the right time, the whole process being imaged through fibre-optics, the applications themselves requiring tools Geiger had designed. Cutting was reduced to a minimum. After the operation the only sign that they had been inside the body was a small cut on the surface, a straight line about two inches long, which healed quickly afterwards. This much they had been able to verify with the American film star who had subsequently left the clinic feet first.

'I'm just saying that any anaesthetist has got to be worried when he sends a geriatric under. Did you see the Jap before they wheeled him in? He is not a well person. Look!'

He pointed at the screen. For a moment they both watched in silence. Kessler, who was the only other person in the theatre apart from Geiger and the anaesthetist, had moved to the left to attend to a flickering screen, and the patient's torso was exposed. It was difficult to make out the detail, but what looked like a steel tube ran into a vivid, though small, red cut in the yellow flesh. Another tube, more like a wire, looped out of the torso.

'Fibre-optic imaging.'

Kessler moved back and the view was blocked.

'Fuck!'

The surgeon with the cigarette stood up and ran his fingers through his hair. He had been at the clinic for three years and had never had any reason to complain. His huge salary was paid into a numbered account, and he had a relatively easy workload. However most of what they did at the clinic was no different from what happened at ordinary hospitals, even if there was a rather heavy emphasis on skin grafts, nips and tucks, ossature modifications, and the full panoply of cosmetic surgery. The prospect therefore of doing something at the forefront of medicine excited everybody. Expectations had been raised by the rumours about what Edward Geiger was cooking up in the labs – labs to which they had no access. And then they had found themselves shut out. All Geiger needed was an anaesthetist. The rest he could do himself. Everyone understood that the bottom line was secrecy, and understood also that secrecy in Switzerland meant money. They were never going to know what exactly was happening to Geiger's patients because that knowledge was worth too much, because if they did know even the fat salaries paid by the clinic would not be enough to keep them inside the mountain. So they were kept in the dark.

Inside the theatre Geiger frowned down at the screen which relayed a perfect image of the failing organ. Perspiration stood on his brow, and there was no nurse to wipe it off. He had been working for almost three hours and now it was finished. He looked at the screen for a long time, his eyes fixed on the three points in which he had injected the material with its stimulating proteins. He went back through the process step by step, making sure that he had forgotten nothing. He blinked and looked at the yellow face under the mask. Now it was up to the patient.

23

Alleinmatt. February 22nd, 1996.

As he climbed Mike tried not to look down. He wanted
to check his feet, to be sure that they were secure in the
thin steel brackets, but he didn't want to see how far from
the ground he was. So he gripped each handhold with all
his strength and concentrated on going up. He wasn't
sure, but he had the impression that the pole was swaying
very slightly back and forward, working its way looser
and looser. He stopped for a few seconds and took some
deep breaths. There wasn't far to go now, just six or seven
more steps. He was out of breath and the freezing cold
wind made him shiver.

Until he'd come to Alleinmatt he'd never had to face
it before, not even in high-rise Manhattan: he was scared
of heights. In an aircraft, in a cable-car, even in a chopper,
he could contain the fear by using reason. The odds were
tiny that anything would actually go wrong, that he would
look down and see nothing but thin air between the distant Earth and him. But halfway up a telephone pole on
the side of a mountain, that argument didn't apply. Why
shouldn't he fall? It seemed only too likely, especially
with every limb shaking like a jelly.

When he reached the top Mike took the harness that
was around his waist and attached the end of it to the top
of the pole. Then at last he looked down.

'How is it going?' Tania shouted.

'Okay,' Mike shouted back.

The telephone pole stood on the edge of a wooded area about three-quarters of a mile northeast of the Phönix-lager. From the chopper they had been able to trace a line of them from the clinic, beside the road that led to the Italian border, and then northwards along the lower slopes of the valley towards Brig. Tania reckoned they had installed their own telephone lines because radio communication was often difficult in the mountains, especially in bad weather, and was more private than the airwaves. The mountain rescue sometimes did survey work for the phone company, checking on lines that were damaged, and it wasn't hard for Wolfgang to get hold of a testing set and enough rudimentary information to do the job. He had spent the previous evening explaining to Mike how to tap into the line, and now here he was, a telephone engineer with vertigo.

The junction box was just below the cross-piece. There was a lock on it, but the lock hadn't been turned. Maybe the engineers liked to make these easy for themselves; locks could freeze up after all. Inside the box were rows of terminal blocks, each one carrying the different wires needed for each phone line. Mike reckoned in all there were maybe ten lines going up to the Phönixlager.

He took off his gloves and with one hand carefully unzipped the nylon bag around his waist and extracted first the headphones and then the testing set, which was just a rectangular grey box with a numbered keypad on one side and a series of wires coming out of the side, each one ending in a crocodile clip. Then he connected two of the clips to what he hoped were the voice-bearing lines on the nearest block. Through the headset he heard a loud crackle followed by a voice speaking in German. Even with the wind blowing it seemed uncomfortably loud. There were two men: one speaking quickly, sternly, the other in a subdued, monosyllabic way. It sounded like someone was getting a roasting for something. *So far so good.*

He took a piece of wire from the bag, and connected one end of it to the red terminal at the top of the block. Then he waited for the conversation to end. He knew he could try another line, but he couldn't help feeling lucky having found the right terminals on this one. He checked his watch: it was ten minutes past nine. In a few minutes the chopper would be back, and he didn't want to keep it waiting. It was far too conspicuous.

Two minutes later his hands were going stiff with cold, and Tania was beginning to look anxious. Up ahead, just over the tops of the trees Mike could see the bleak face of the Phönixlager and the tip of the building below it. It felt too close for comfort.

'Come on, come on,' he said under his breath, and then remembered too late that his voice could be heard.

There was a pause on the line.

'Hallo? Wer da? Hans?'

'Ja.'

They talked for a little and then hung up. Mike didn't waste time. He connected the red terminal to the yellow one at the bottom of the block, creating a short-circuit that boosted the voltage on the line carrying the ring-tone. Through his headset he could hear the phone buzz at the other end.

'Güten Morgen.'

It was a woman's voice, a receptionist maybe.

'Hello. Do you speak English?'

'Of course, sir.'

'Good. My name is Miguel Diaz. I'm calling to make an appointment for some minor surgery.'

'I'll connect you, sir. Just one moment.'

He couldn't believe it. He said *surgery* and she hadn't even blinked. This was really the place.

413

'Hello. This is the appointments office. May I have your name, sir?'

'Miguel Diaz.'

He spelled the name out slowly.

'I want something done, cosmetically,' he said. 'I hear your clinic is the best there is.'

The voice at the other end hesitated.

'All our clinics work to the highest standards, sir, of course. However, cosmetic surgery is normally performed at the Davos clinic. I can give you the number.'

'Yes, I know that. But the Alleinmatt clinic was especially recommended as suiting my particular needs, recommended by Hans-Jorg Bruggman in fact. He gave me this number.'

Mike remembered the name of Mendelhaus's finance director from the days of the Raeburn deal. Bruggman had been his most senior contact. The tone of voice at the other end of the line changed at once.

'I see. Well I'm sure we *could* meet your requirements here, if that were desirable. It is cosmetic work you require?'

'Yes. Nothing too radical.'

'I'll check our schedules, sir, and call you back. Where can we reach you?'

Mike could hear the chopper coming up the valley. He was sure it was audible on the line.

'I'm gonna be moving about for the next few days. I'll call you. Okay?'

The voice adopted a knowing tone.

'Of course, sir. Just give us a day to sort things out.'

'You got it,' said Mike. 'Goodbye.'

PART THREE

A sacrifice

1

Brig. March 1st, 1996.

Tania parked the Opal Corsa about a hundred yards from the entrance to the Brig heliport. Mike looked across to her. He was pale, nervous.

'What's the problem?'

'We can't exactly park this next to the limousines, can we?'

Mike nodded stiffly.

'I guess you're right.'

He was uncomfortable in his new clothes bought in the expensive shops in Alleinmatt. He was wearing a Burberry raincoat over a sports jacket and cavalry twill pants with a little cuff that sat perfectly on the heavy brown brogues. The whole outfit had been astronomically expensive. When the assistant in Bally had run a check on his Amex card he had expected it to burst into flames. Then he realised that it was nothing compared to what he was going to be spending up at the clinic; a thousand dollars per day maybe. Could they ask for more than that? He still had some money in his account from the sale of the apartment, but at some point that would all be gone.

'Are you ready, Michael?'

He looked into Tania's face. She looked beautiful, her cheeks slightly flushed from the cold. A blonde curl

417

escaped from under her bobble hat. The thought occurred to him that it might be the last time he saw her.

'I'll call you as soon as I get a chance. Tania . . .'

She smiled.

'Good luck, Michael.'

The mountains looked menacing, deadly. Once inside the Mendelhaus chopper the attractive escort who introduced herself as Brigitte insisted he put on an enormous fur coat. Fortunately she didn't insist on talking to him as they flew up the valley towards the looming Heulendthorn. Ski trails twisted beneath, white threads traced through the trees. As they climbed higher he tried to see Tania's chalet nestling against the great barren mountain, but the weather was deteriorating, and swathes of wind-blown snow shrouded the slopes.

It was only now coming home to him what he was about to do. He had no idea what would be waiting for him at the clinic. If Mendelhaus had been behind the planting of the drugs in his hotel room then there was a chance that they knew exactly what he looked like. He pictured the door of the clinic swinging closed behind him and Krystal emerging from the shadows with a gun. He pulled the heavy fur together, as if in that way he was better protected. He thought of Cathy. He tried to picture what she was doing at that moment, but he couldn't; it seemed like a bad omen.

'Don't worry, everything will be fine.'

The girl Brigitte had to shout to make herself heard over the noise of the rotor. He looked at her heavily made-up face. He realised she thought he was nervous about the treatment he was going to receive. A flush rose in his cheeks. It embarrassed him to think that she thought he had something wrong with him, something he was ashamed of, some terrible birthmark or something, or even worse that she might think he was there for some

418

kind of face lift or nose job. The chopper banked and he
looked down at the barren, sheer rock faces, dusted with
blown snow. A nose job. That *was* what he was there for.
He and Tania had worked out that this was the only thing
he could convincingly ask for. He had always liked his
nose, but it was true: when you looked at it objectively
it was a little on the big side. 'They won't operate straight
away anyway,' Tania had said. 'You will probably be out
of there before they get their knives out.' Knives! Mike
touched his nose. It was sensitive around the nostrils from
where he kept blowing it. He still hadn't shaken off the
cold he had caught in Zürich. Maybe he could delay them
a little bit by pretending to be sick. If he ever got that
far. The pilot's harsh German broke in on his thoughts.
'*Phönix eins kommen.*'
Immediately the radio rapped back.
'*Hier spricht Phönix eins. Identifizieren sie sich.*'
'There, Mr Diaz. There's the Phönixlager.' He followed
Brigitte's manicured fingernail where it was pressed
against the bubble of the chopper. A gust of snow surged
across the face of the rock and then he could see the
building he had spotted with Tania. As he looked, he saw
cold white lights blink on in two windows. A plume of
vapour issued from a place above the building itself, as
though coming directly from the mountain. Suddenly it
was there, and then it dissolved in the wind. A few
moments later and they were down on the ground,
Brigitte leaning past him to open the door.
A blast of freezing air opened his fur coat as he stepped
out onto the helipad. Two men in white padded jackets
took his suitcase and a bag of what looked like mail from
the chopper. He followed Brigitte towards the light of the
main entrance, his heart pounding against his ribs.
Once inside, Brigitte helped him out of the coat and
walked him towards a long wooden counter in a heavy
rustic style. He had expected some kind of reception, but

there was nothing; a discreet nod and smile from the girl behind the counter, and that was all.

'Welcome to the Phönixlager, Mr Diaz.'

Mike handed her his passport and she looked at it as though it were hardly of any interest and handed it back to him immediately. Then, magically, a door behind her opened and a young man in a grey uniform appeared to take him to his room. Brigitte explained that someone would come to his room to welcome him properly. Mike said goodbye and followed the young man along the carpeted corridor.

The complete absence of sound was like noise to Mike's ears after the thwack-thwack of the rotor. He looked for signs to orientate himself. There were numbers on the doors, which stood at irregular intervals along the corridor, all of them on the left-hand wall, and from time to time a painting or a plant. It seemed to him they were walking parallel to the exterior wall, not going towards the mountain itself. Then there was a larger, slightly wider door let in to the right-hand wall. It didn't have a number. Finally they reached a door marked 23 and stopped.

'Here we are, sir.'

The boy pushed a plastic card into a slot and turned the handle.

The room was enormous. There was a large oriental rug in the middle of the floor, the rich reds and blues in stark contrast with the pale walls and drapes. Freshly cut white roses in tight buds stood in an opaque Lalique vase which had been placed in the centre of a glass coffee table. Trying to feel like a multimillionaire, Mike dropped his coat onto the white sofa. The boy took his suitcase through to the bedroom. Mike followed him through, taking in the heavy drapes, and the king-size bed. When he came out of the room the boy was standing by the door ready to leave.

'Someone will be along in a moment to welcome you to the clinic, sir.'

He clicked his heels and was gone before Mike could get the bill out of his pocket. Straightaway, Mike went over to the desk and took some writing paper from the top drawer. He drew a rough map of the reception area and the corridor along which he had just walked, trying to place the unnumbered door in what he assumed to be the interior wall. Then he sat for a moment in thought.

It was the silence that brought him back to the present. Even in Tania's house there had always been a little noise, but here it was totally silent, like a tomb. He got up and walked across to the window. The light was fading fast and all he could see was his own reflection. Then he went across to the desk and switched off the lamp. The room drowned in deep blue twilight. He could see snow being blown against the window, and imagined the noise of the wind outside, though he could hear nothing. From time to time a strong gust cleared the swirling snow and he could see the shapes of mountains, but then the snow changed direction and large flakes swirled in eddies against the glass. He tapped the window with his finger-nail. There was absolutely no resonance. It sounded like stone.

There was a quiet knock on the door. He crossed the room and opened it.

'Mr Diaz. My name's Schindler, Katya Schindler. I am here with the medical staff. I wondered if we might talk for a moment.'

Mike stood back and gestured for her to pass. She hesitated for a moment, seeing the room in near darkness. Mike snapped on the wall lights with a sheepish smile. She went on past him. She was tall with short blonde hair and was wearing a grey suit, a feminine version of the uniform the boy had been wearing. Under her left arm she carried a leather document wallet.

421

'I hope the room is suitable, Mr Diaz.'

She sat down on the sofa and Mike sat opposite her in one of the armchairs.

'Yes, it's fine. I was surprised by the amount of space. Actually, I feel a little lost in it.'

A look of concern flickered over her perfectly symmetrical features.

'Would you prefer to change?'

Mike started to shake his head, but then paused.

'Well, what else is there on offer? I imagine the place is pretty full, right?'

'Well, there are only two floors and the first floor is being refurbished at the moment so none of those rooms are available. We are not the Intercontinental, but if you would like to see some other rooms on this floor I'm sure there would be no problem.'

'Maybe something looking onto the back. I get a little agoraphobic looking at all that space out there.'

'Ah, in that respect, I don't think we can help. You see the rooms in the Phönixlager all face the valley. The back, as you put it, is solid rock.'

Mike put his head on one side, as though puzzled.

'You mean the clinic is built right into the rock?'

'Yes, that's right.'

He gave a little theatrical shudder. Maybe that was where the laboratory was hidden.

'I see. Oh well, I guess I can always keep my curtains drawn.'

'Absolutely. Now.'

She removed some papers from the leather wallet and pushed them across the table to him.

'I didn't want to drown you with our literature as soon as you arrived, but I know that most of our guests don't want to draw things out any more than necessary.'

She pointed to a paragraph on the second page of a brochure.

'But if you could just find time to look this through, we can talk about choices in the morning.'

'Choices?'

'Yes, the kind of profile you have in mind.'

Mike turned the page and was surprised to see a series of noses shot from below, above, and from either side.

'There are three-dimensional models too, but this may help you in thinking about what you want to achieve.'

Mike nodded. The noses were world-beaters. His eyes fixed on a straight WASPy-looking nose that Napier Drew would have been proud of. He wanted to ask why there was no Chink, no Jew, no wetback.

Miss Schindler was standing up.

'Tomorrow morning we will take photographs and X-rays and there will be a complete medical check. In the meantime' – she extended a manicured hand – 'you will find everything you need to know about the clinic in the booklet.'

'Really, oh that's great.'

Mike looked around the room and realised as he did so that he had left his sketch of the corridor on the desk. Miss Schindler was already crossing the room, a frown on her face.

'Excuse me, somebody must have overlooked this.'

She glanced at the paper for a moment, and then tossed it into the wastepaper basket. Then she snapped open the drawer and removed the booklet which contained the secrets of the Phönixlager.

'What do I do about dinner?' said Mike as she crossed the room. She showed him the booklet.

'It's all in here, Mr Diaz. You can either eat in the restaurant where dinner is served from seven until ten or, if you prefer, you can have it sent to your room at any time – provided it is not against doctor's orders. There is a choice of menus here.'

She opened the booklet and indicated a list of different dishes.

'And now I wish you a pleasant evening and look forward to seeing you in the morning.'

She squeezed his hand and left him standing in the middle of the room with his nose brochure and the introductory booklet.

It was a moment before he moved. He looked down at the pictures of the noses and felt a rush of panic. He had never been into hospital in his life and the idea of surgery made him feel sick. Then the idea that Cathy was in the building swept over him. He put his hand to his forehead and sat heavily in the armchair. He had to think. He had to work something out. He didn't even know if there *was* a laboratory.

Sitting upright, he opened the booklet on the coffee table and started to work through the glossy pages. *Welcome to the Phönixlager, the most exclusive* . . . In the centrefold there was a plan of the clinic with the dining room, the gym, the swimming pool, different areas for treatments, but nothing to indicate what might be inside the mountain, if there was anything. Then he remembered the unnumbered door. He looked at his watch. It was six thirty. He had time to walk around. If he was asked what he was doing, he could say he had gotten lost. He had only just arrived and was looking for the dining room. He went into the bathroom and washed his hands and face. Breathing the soapy smell of the clean towel, he looked at his nose and frowned.

There was no sign of anyone in the corridor. The same silence lay on everything like a suffocating blanket. He pulled his door closed and slipped the plastic card into his back pocket. As he made his way towards the reception area at the end of the long corridor, someone came out of their room further along, but they didn't look his way. Then he was at the unnumbered door. There was a handle, and unlike the other doors no slot for the card. Looking at the receding figure moving towards the lighter area of reception he pressed down the handle and the door opened.

Inside it was completely dark. Rather than fumble for a light switch while standing in the corridor, he stepped through the door and waited, trying to control his breathing. To his surprise there was a faint rushing sound as of air conditioning. Looking up he could feel a draught of slightly cooler air. Still he could see absolutely nothing. He felt for a light switch, but the wall was blank. Then he reached out his hands and slowly moved forward. In two strides he came up against a wall, and what felt like a coat hanging on it. *A broom closet!* He almost laughed with the sudden relief and absurdity of it. Then he turned and made his way back towards the door. He listened for a moment, and then went out into the corridor, shaking his head like a person that was lost.

He started along the corridor towards the reception area, and then the thought that he might be recognised brought him up short. He turned and made his way back to his room. Like most of the Phönixlager's exclusive clientele, he imagined, he would stick to room service.

2

Zürich. March 1st, 1996.

The interior of the consulate on Zollikerstrasse was like corporate America on a reduced budget. Waterman sat opposite Roy Calhoun in a chair that was too soft and too low, balancing a cup of coffee on the end of his knee. The cup was plastic with a kind of brown holder that saved you from burning your fingers. As he explained what he wanted Calhoun, a big blond man with broad shoulders, listened with his hands folded on the blotter in front of him, smiling and nodding like the host at a Manhattan dinner party. From one of the adjoining rooms came the sound of a TV tuned to CNN.

'What we're hoping to find out,' said Waterman, 'is if the things that killed these two men had a common origin: a virus someplace, a type of treatment maybe. That's why I'm anxious to take a look at the full medical reports on Matt McArthur. We still don't have enough information about his death.'

Waterman waited for Calhoun to say something, but he just carried on smiling and nodding slowly, earnestly.

'So what I want is to see any medical reports you were given by the Swiss authorities prior to his body being flown home. You did take care of that, right?'

'Yes we did. We did indeed. Always a tragic . . . kind of thing.'

426

'So . . . have you got any records?'

Calhoun frowned.

'I'd have to check that. On the other hand I should say we don't *normally* release that kind of material without due clearance. I believe we have procedures that we're supposed to follow.'

Waterman got the strong impression that if there were procedures, Calhoun didn't know what they were.

'Of course,' said Waterman. 'And normally we'd have gone through the State Department, but given the possible danger to the public we've had to cut a few corners. You know how it is. When something important comes up you can't always wait for the bureaucracy.'

Calhoun did some more nodding. Then he said: 'The thing is, Mr Waterman, the Matt McArthur . . . thing . . . wasn't an ordinary sort of situation. Obviously someone with such a – ' he paused, searching again for the right words ' – high profile, might be the object of undesirable attention.'

'Of course,' said Waterman, 'and I'm fully aware of that. But we're only interested in medical details. You have my word there'll be no question of publication, or anything in the press.'

Calhoun seemed to have run out of objections. He nodded a couple more times just to round off the series and stood up. With his broad shoulders and thick neck he looked wrong in his plain grey suit, like a linebacker in a tuxedo.

'Okay then, let's take a look.'

He led Waterman out of his office and into a long neon-lit room full of metal filing cabinets. His assistant, a Texan lady with permed hair and a smile like her boss's, followed behind holding a bunch of keys.

'Let's see now,' said Calhoun. 'This is . . . uh . . .'

'Temporary passports,' said the assistant. 'A through F.'

'Right, and we want . . .'

'Deaths and Deportations, G through M.'

The secretary passed ahead of them and opened one of the drawers with a key. She watched for a moment while Calhoun rummaged around inside and then announced that she had something to take care of and left.

'This must be it,' said Calhoun at last, pulling out a yellow cardboard folder. 'This must be the report from the coroner. Yup, August 29th, 1994. That accounts for it.'

'Accounts for what?' said Waterman.

'For the fact that I don't recall much about it. I'd only just got here then, and my predecessor was still in charge.'

'Right, can we take a look?'

They went back into the office and spread the papers out on the top of the desk. There was a photocopied report on official paper with stamps and seals all over it and a couple of black and white photographs.

'These were sent by the police, I suppose?'

'Right,' said Calhoun.

'And this is the full report from the coroner?'

Calhoun picked up the papers and flicked through them. A look of doubt crossed his face.

'I think, well maybe not. It looks a little short. This is a photocopy of the *summary* of the report – and the first page. Usually they're longer than this.'

'What does it say?'

'Well, let's see. Yes, it says the cause of death was cancer of the heart . . . and that the cancer must have been there for some time judging from its size. There's some technical stuff, but it looks pretty much like you said, Mr Waterman.'

'Did the police say why they weren't sending you the whole report?'

'Well, I don't know. Perhaps that's all they were asked

for. I mean if the relatives didn't want the whole thing . . .'

'So they don't send a full report as a matter of course?'

Calhoun went around to his side of the desk and sat down.

'Well, *normally* we're not dealing with cases like this. Mostly it's accidents we have to deal with – road accidents. In those cases, with insurance to worry about and that kind of thing, we do need all the details. But with this, maybe . . .'

Calhoun finished his sentence with a shrug. Waterman picked up the photographs and looked at them. One was taken from beside the slab, one from above it: McArthur lay there on his back, naked and pale, paler still around his groin where his swimming shorts had always covered him. His face was drawn and bony, but there was no doubting who it was. Waterman couldn't help thinking of all the times he'd seen the guy up there on the big screen, smiling his sly kind of smile as he came out with those sharp one-liners. In the films you always knew he was going to come through; life was something he just had licked. That was just how Waterman had wanted him to be. Even now he couldn't believe this was really how the star had ended up: so cold and so mute.

Perhaps what made it seem worse was the quality of the prints themselves. At one of the corners and on the backs there were pale brown marks, as if the printer hadn't kept them in the fixer for long enough. The prints weren't very clear either. The face was okay, but the main trunk of the body was washed out and partly out of focus. There was barely any detail visible on the skin.

Calhoun didn't look like he even wanted to see them, but Waterman stuck the pictures under his nose.

'Are they always this rough and ready? They look like they were taken by a real amateur.'

Calhoun picked them up, holding them at arm's length.

'Well, they came from the mortuary at Brig. That's not a big place. They probably don't have the same facilities.'

'Brig? Where's that?'

Calhoun pointed over to a big coloured map of Switzerland on the wall beside him. He suddenly sounded more confident.

'It's in the south, near the Italian border. It's got some of the best skiing in the country round there. You should go if you get a chance.'

At last Waterman understood the attractions of a place like Switzerland to a man like Calhoun.

'Mind if I borrow these for a few days? I'd like some of my people to look at them.'

Calhoun looked doubtful.

'Well I . . .'

'Don't worry,' said Waterman, picking the papers and the folder off the desk and opening up his briefcase. 'I'll keep them safe. But since the guy was cremated well over a year ago this may be all we have to go on.'

'Well I guess . . .'

Waterman stood up.

'You've been very helpful, Mr Calhoun. I'll be sure to mention your name if we come up with anything big – provided you agree, of course.'

Calhoun got up and followed Waterman towards the door.

'There is just one other thing,' said Waterman. 'I'm anxious to talk to an American who came over here about two or three weeks ago. His name's Michael Varela.'

Calhoun looked uncertain for a moment, then his expression changed.

'I thought you said this was just a medical matter, Mr Waterman.'

'It is. I simply have reason to believe . . .'

Calhoun shook his head.

'That guy's in a *lot* of trouble. I mean fourth down and long. God knows what the hell he's mixed up in.'

'You've seen him then?'

'Once, yeah. He came in here with some story about his girlfriend disappearing, and then a couple of days later the police turn up and say he's probably a narcotics dealer and ask a lot of questions. And *then*, about a week after that, they come back and say now he's got himself mixed up with a lot of terrorists and is wanted in connection with a murder.'

Waterman put down his briefcase.

'You reckon it's true?'

Calhoun shrugged.

'Well, the authorities here can be a little . . . a little harsh sometimes. I mean they just aren't used to the kind of trouble we see back home, and they do tend to assume the worst. You learn that out here. But that guy's in a *lot* of trouble, you can bet.'

'Sounds crazy,' said Waterman. 'A murder? You got any details on that?'

3

The Phönixlager. March 2nd, 1996.

There was another flash, and Mike blinked. He felt like a convict – left profile, right profile, face on. Miss Schindler said encouraging things from the far corner of the room, a blue file clutched to her chest.

Just after breakfast, taken in the room as was the meal of the night before, Miss Schindler had come to see him, wanting to know what he had decided. He had spent the whole night tossing and turning, the thought that Cathy might be somewhere nearby giving him no rest. He had given absolutely no thought to his new nose.

'It's funny, picking a nose should be easy enough.'

He watched for a smile, but Miss Schindler had only blinked.

'I can't seem to make up my mind. Maybe you could give me some advice.'

There had followed a long discussion in which his bone structure was discussed, Miss Schindler pressing her fingers under his cheekbone, and feeling at the cartilage in his nose. For her it seemed there were only three possibilities unless he wanted to take a risk on 4C, the nose he had picked out as perfect for Napier Drew.

'The danger with that is that you might change the character of your face.'

'But isn't that the idea?'

432

Miss Schindler sighed. Apparently he hadn't given it enough thought. She suggested that while a slight change might improve his profile, too radical a departure from the present line might draw embarrassing attention. The three options she suggested didn't look too hot to Mike. He pointed to the one that looked the least silly.

'Yes,' said Miss Schindler, 'a good choice I think. Slightly straighter on the bridge and less weight in the tip.'

She looked at his face and squinted as though picturing the new nose in place.

The technician was removing the film from the camera.

'Now for the X-rays, Mr Diaz.'

Mike was brought back to the present by Miss Schindler's hand placed lightly on his shoulder.

'Structural information,' she said, reassuringly.

The day seemed interminable. At a quarter past nine Mike heard someone come to his door to collect the trolley on which his dinner had been brought to him. On the other side of the room the television flickered, the sound turned down. He went across to the door and turned the handle silently. Looking through the crack he watched the uniformed figure receding in the dimly lit corridor. As always there was absolute silence in the clinic. He went back into his room and sat down at the desk.

The sketch of the clinic had gained in detail since the previous evening. His visit to the photographic studio and then, at Miss Schindler's suggestion, to the gym and the swimming pool in which an old woman in a floral swimming hat was floating on her back, had given him the opportunity to look at the way the building fitted together. To his sketch of the reception area with its central elevator, which went, he presumed, to the first-floor rooms, he had added the two arms of the corridors which seemed

433

to run along the face of the mountain. On his side there were rooms, and on the other side there were the facilities. He had not been able to look into all the rooms on the far side, but he didn't think the laboratory, if there was one, would be so accessible. As for what went on up on the first floor, he had no idea. But it seemed to him that if there was anything to find, anything that took place inside the mountain, there was probably access from somewhere in the clinic. Somewhere there was a door, hidden or otherwise, that led into the rock.

He sat looking at the sketch for a long time, the shifting light of the television dancing on his face. Suddenly an idea made him sit up in his chair. He pressed his hand to his forehead as if to get a grip on his thoughts. The smoke or vapour he had seen coming out of the mountain; where did that come from? He closed his eyes trying to visualise it. It had appeared well above the line of windows, he was sure of that. It had come out of the rock unexpectedly. It could just be some kind of duct from air conditioning in the clinic, or maybe some kind of laundry facility. But if there was something inside the mountain, it too would have to be ventilated. He looked across to his panoramic window. All he could see was himself reflected in the black glass. It would be useless to go outside now, and anyway what excuse could he give? *I just want to have a stroll in the sub-zero wind in the pitch dark.* No, that would have to wait. He looked back down at the plan. The two wings of the hotel sprawled out like the wings of a giant bird, with the reception area and the elevators as the body. He looked up at the ceiling.

'What's on the first floor, Cathy?'

It was slightly cooler in the corridor. His shoes made no sound on the carpeted floor. He almost wanted to hum or whistle. On his right, numbered doors slipped past. He had no idea what was happening behind him. He had seen very few people in the clinic, but that only made him feel even more exposed.

As he approached the reception area the light intensified. There was a young woman sitting behind the dark wooden counter looking down at a magazine. She was not there to welcome guests. Clients went in and out by helicopter. Nobody was just going to walk in off the mountain. No, she was there to answer queries from the silent rooms, to relay requests to the appropriate people, to deal with calls to the clinic from the outside, to keep watch.

Mike stopped behind a group of plants and looked at the girl's head. The elevator doors were ten feet away. If he moved into the open she was sure to look up. Or if she didn't look up immediately, she would hear the elevator doors opening. What could he say? Suddenly the idea that there was someone at his back made him turn. The corridor funnelled darkly to the distant rubber plant which he recognised as being the one just before his room. He wanted to go back; shut the door behind him and think things through some more. *That's what you've been doing all day.* He pressed his nails into his sweating palms, angry with himself. *Think!* The girl was still reading her magazine. Maybe he could win her confidence. Maybe she had seen Cathy come into the clinic.

At that moment the doors of the elevator opened. One of the grey-uniformed staff emerged pushing a trolley with the remains of a dinner under a crumpled napkin. Mike froze. The boy turned to the left, calling out something in German to the girl as he went into the far wing. The girl grunted an answer without looking up. Mike felt himself walking forward on stiff legs towards the open elevator. Just as he reached the brightly-lit box the door began to close. He had to twist sideways and thrust himself forward. Then he was inside, the doors closing. Had the girl looked up?

435

Mike blinked, taking in the panel of buttons, his thoughts racing. Two floors were marked and then below that there was a small keyhole. Miss Schindler had said that the rooms on the first floor were closed. If this were true then where was the bellboy coming from? The floor that was accessed with a key? He stabbed at the second button. There was a moment's silence, in which he noticed for the first time the smell of raw fish, a sharp, tangy smell. Silently the elevator rose.

The second floor looked exactly the same, except that where the reception area stood on the first floor here there was some kind of terrace. Peering out through the dark Mike could see what looked like sun-loungers stacked in a pile. Not knowing where to go, he started along the corridor.

After a couple of paces he halted. Further down the corridor two orientals emerged from one of the doors. They were both dressed like businessmen, but they looked more like Sumo wrestlers. They appeared not to have noticed him at first, and he hesitated between going on and turning back. But there was no time, they were coming towards him now, the wall lights moving on their oiled hair. Instinctively Mike stopped at one of the doors, showing the two men his back. He knocked as they passed behind him. One of them said something in Japanese and the other laughed. If there was someone in the room he would pretend he had made a mistake. He knocked again. Nobody answered. It was as he thought: the clinic was almost empty. He looked along the corridor at the backs of the two giants. Their faces were illuminated as the elevator door opened. Then they were gone.

Mike swallowed hard and walked on to the end of the corridor. Outside the room from which the two men had emerged he paused, listening. A politician, he thought. The men would be his bodyguards. Then it came to him that the fish smell in the lift was sushi – that was what the bellboy had been carrying on his trolley. The politician or his guards had had some nice fresh fish flown up the mountain. No expense spared. But why did Schindler say there was no one on this floor? Maybe the Jap had paid for the whole floor. He had met guys on Wall Street with that kind of cash.

He started back towards the elevator, noticing a door on his left in about the same position as the one on the ground floor in which he had found the cleaning materials. He tried the handle. It was locked.

He walked on past the elevator, moving more quickly now. He didn't like the idea of the Sumo wrestlers coming up to find him again. He could hardly try knocking on another door.

At the end of the corridor there was a door of glass just as there was downstairs. There it led through to the gymnasium and swimming pool and the treatment rooms. He was trying to see through the glass door into the darkness on the other side when he heard the lift doors opening again. He froze, watching what was happening in the reflection of the glass. Two men in white coats came out, the smaller of the two carrying a bag. They made their way along the corridor to the other end. Hardly daring to breathe, Mike turned. He watched them go into one of the rooms. He couldn't see, but he had a feeling it was the same room that the two wrestlers had come out of. In spite of his fear, he started to make his way back along the corridor. Where had the guys in white coats come from? He stopped in his tracks, an idea forming in his mind.

He almost ran to the elevator. The doors slid back noiselessly.

In the reception area he strode across to the girl behind the desk. She didn't look up from her magazine until he put his hands on the counter.

'Excuse me. I'm Mr Va – Mr Diaz. I'm staying in

437

room twenty-three. I wondered if you could give me some advice.'

The girl listened as he went into a long explanation about his desire to do some skiing once he left the clinic.

'I wondered if there was any way of hiring choppers for some off-piste skiing away from the crowds.'

She was a pretty girl, with reddish hair and green eyes. Her teeth protruded slightly over her bottom lip which she moistened as she spoke with little whisks of her tongue. All the time she was speaking, Mike was listening for the sound of the elevator. If the doctors didn't come out of the lift it was because they had not finished with the mystery client, or because they were going to another floor, the floor that was accessed by the key maybe. If he listened hard enough he might hear if the elevator went past without stopping.

'Mr Diaz?'

Mike looked into the girl's face.

'I'm sorry, I was thinking about something else.'

'That's all right. I was just saying that the helicopter skiing is best arranged during the day. If you like I will leave a message for Maria to do it. I know she has already organised that kind of thing for our directors.'

Mike felt the hair lift on the back of his neck. He could hear the elevator doors opening again. Moving as casually, as naturally as he could, he turned to look. The elevator doors were closed. Emerging from a door beside the entrance to the small swimming pool was the old lady. She returned his look with a little wave and made her way along the corridor to his left, leading back to the rooms.

'Heat treatment.'

Mike turned to look at the girl's confiding smile.

'She's been coming here for years.'

At that moment there was a distinct swish as the elevator doors slid back. Mike turned just in time to see the

438

two white-coated men go into the door that he had only just discovered existed. It was a moment before Mike realised the girl was still speaking to him.

'Not one of our most popular treatments. They smear her with bad-smelling mud. Black. Hot.'

Mike kept his eyes on the door.

'I see. And it all happens in there, does it?'

'Yes.'

'But why isn't that facility in with the other rooms, the swimming pool and the gym?'

The girl smiled and held her nose.

'Because of the stink.'

Mike nodded.

'Could I take a look?'

The girl looked surprised. She looked him up and down. Then she leaned forward conspiratorially.

'But that is for the really old people,' she whispered. 'People with aches and pains.'

'Just out of curiosity,' Mike insisted.

The girl sat back in her chair. She looked slightly annoyed.

It was noticeably colder once Mike was behind the door. The change was accentuated by the white walls and the blue lino on the floor of the corridor before him. It looked as though they made less of an effort with the decor in this part of the clinic. He had expected a bad smell, but there was only a faint smell of sulphur. The door to the treatment room was clearly marked. He listened outside the door, hoping to hear the two men in conversation. Suddenly the door opened and stinking hot air belched out. A small, withered man came out of the room, struggling to hold back the door which was on a spring. As he went past, the door sprang shut. Without acknowledging Mike's presence, the old man went back into the main clinic.

In the split second that the door had been open, Mike had got an impression of the white interior. A woman standing with her back to him was washing her hands in a sink. The men were not there. His heart quickening, Mike made his way further along the corridor. In four strides he came to a bend which led him into a darker space. Behind him he heard the spring creak as the door to the treatment room came open, and he heard the footsteps of the woman. He froze. She said something quietly in German and then he heard her going away along the corridor. Then the lights snapped off and he was plunged into complete darkness.

For a moment he stood there breathing the egg-smelling dark. Then, reaching out with his hands, he started to inch forward.

The door was massive, and riveted all around the edge. It looked like a piece of a military installation. Before the light went off, he had noticed a steel panel set in the wall on his right. It was like the panels he had seen at Swift and Drew; like the panel he had slotted his ID card into every morning for three years. He felt certain he had found his door. He pressed his face against the cold metal.

'Cathy,' he said, his whisper sounding harsh, dangerously loud in the black silence.

4

The Phönixlager. March 3rd, 1996.

Kessler knocked at the door and went in without waiting for an answer. Geiger was sitting in an armchair, his head resting against the back, listening to music: a Bach partita for solo violin. Away on the far wall the lights of the graphic equaliser rose and fell. The sound was turned up loud.

The chair faced away from the door, towards where a window would have been in any ordinary building. The company had set aside rooms for the professor in one of the wings of the clinic, but these days, especially since the arrival of the donor, he rarely bothered returning to them. Most nights he spent inside the mountain. He checked over equipment in the laboratory or stood in the observation room watching the girl through the mirror. It was almost as if he were afraid to stray too far from the laboratory complex for fear that someone might break into it during the night, and steal away with his prize.

Kessler walked around to the side of the chair.

'Edward, I have the data . . .'

Geiger held up his hand for silence. His eyes were closed. Kessler could only stand and wait.

'She plays well,' said Geiger after a minute. 'Better, wouldn't you say?'

Kessler hadn't realised who was playing, but now he

understood that it was the woman. Geiger had taped her at practice, but then he recorded most of what she did one way or another. Kessler listened.

'A considerable improvement. There is more power. Perhaps more . . . conviction.'

Geiger smiled.

'I have set up recording equipment in the observation room. The acoustics are remarkably good. She finds her humanity in the music. Thanks to us it's the only place where she can look for it; so she looks hard. You can hear how she searches.'

The music went on. Every note was charged, intense, as if the player was intent on shutting out the world, leaving nothing but the sound of bow on string. Then suddenly there came a series of crashing discords and the music stopped. After a moment's silence there followed the unmistakable sound of a woman crying.

Kessler cleared his throat.

'All told, the violin is clearly excellent therapy. In these circumstances it is essential to keep the patient occupied, and . . .'

'Egon, please,' said Geiger. 'Why tell me what I already know?'

Geiger pressed a button on his remote control and the cassette deck stopped with a clunk.

'What do you want, Egon?'

'I have the data on Hiraizumi's latest tests.'

'I've seen them,' said Geiger. 'They're what I expected, more or less.'

'More in my case,' said Kessler, 'I have to say. There is no rise in temperature, the rate of cell replacement is optimal, and there is clear evidence of self-directed differentiation. A third treatment may not even be necessary.'

'We shall know soon enough.'

'In any event it is not too early to tell the board of our

success. Hunziker and Denzler are here. We're due to meet them at five.'

'What about Hoffman?'

'I saw no need to request his presence.'

'He'll be there, rest assured.'

Geiger stood up and went over to the cassette player. He removed the digital cassette and replaced it with another.

'I think you should be the one to tell them this time,' said Kessler. 'These should answer their doubts. If Hoffman is there, all the better.'

'You go,' said Geiger. 'It will sound better coming from you. I have no skill when it comes to presentation.'

'Edward, this is our moment as far as Mendelhaus is concerned. This man is of the greatest importance to them, and we – *you* – have saved his life. This means money, far more than just the fee. In return for his support commercially I shouldn't be surprised if they waive it altogether.'

Geiger turned and looked at him.

'And therein lies a problem, don't you think? How many Hiraizumis can there be in the world?'

'More than you might think, Edward. And don't forget the board themselves, and their circle. When they've seen what we can do, what we *could* do with further development, believe me they'll be first in the line. They don't want to die at seventy-five, any more than the next man – perhaps even less. They have that much more to live for.'

Geiger turned the tape recorder on.

'You see? You *are* much better at presentation than I am. You tell them.'

The music started. It was Cathy again, playing something by Fritz Kreisler, only slowly and less expertly than before. Kessler sighed.

'Very well. I will tell you about their reaction. I'd rather thought you might want to see it for yourself.'

'A year or two ago I would have done. But their money and their facilities are all that should interest us now. You know, Egon, sometimes I think you're a lot more sentimental than you look.'

Kessler nodded.

'You are right about this, of course.'

He went back to the door. As he reached for the handle Geiger said: 'However pleased they might be, Egon, they'll still be very anxious to tie up this stage of the project. They'll be worrying about our donor. Whatever happens, don't let them interfere until it suits us. I don't have to tell you how important that is.'

He turned back to the tape recorder and adjusted the volume.

'Apart from anything else, there are some more recordings I want to make.'

Oswald Hunziker rose to his feet and clapped his hands together triumphantly. Kessler hadn't seen him looking so excited for years.

'Well, gentlemen, good news at last: results! My congratulations, Herr Doctor Kessler. Our faith in you has not been misplaced. I think this calls for a celebration.'

He reached across his desk and pressed a button on the intercom.

'Maria? Send Celio in with champagne.'

'You're quite sure, Doctor, that the old problem has not recurred,' said Hoffman from the sofa where he sat, smiling also so as not to spoil the mood. 'As I recall, your initial results with the Americans were equally promising.'

'Naturally we shall have to wait and see,' said Kessler. 'But there is every reason for confidence. The source of the cell colonies is entirely different and from a much safer source. Furthermore, the rate of cell replacement is

444

much more linear than it was in either of the other cases. There is no sign of what one might call runaway growth. Cell multiplication is taking place only where it should, only where the appropriate concentrations of the appropriate chemical stimulants are present. We were originally prepared to introduce artificially a number of these substances to ensure that multiplication was inhibited where necessary. However, these tests strongly suggest that the cells in the surrounding tissue are producing these substances themselves. In effect, the body is now organising the regeneration of the liver itself. If so, the patient should recover fully in a month or so.'

Celio knocked and entered pushing a trolley. On the trolley were four fluted glasses and a bottle of Dom Perignon in an ice-bucket. The servant filled the glasses and served them from a silver tray.

'A toast, gentlemen. To . . .'

Hunziker paused.

'To Kazuo Hiraizumi. Long may he live – with our help!'

They all laughed appreciatively and drank. Celio refilled their glasses and left on a nod from the chairman.

Denzler lit a cigarette and exhaled a plume of smoke.

'I think it can safely be said that Mendelhaus was the only organisation in the world that could have saved him. He must be made to realise that if he doesn't already.'

'I believe he does,' said Kessler. 'You can imagine the kind of facilities that were available in Japan, and the expertise. But he was written off as a dead man – understandably, from the conventional medical point of view. He has already expressed his thanks.'

'He has?' said Denzler. 'I thought he was far too ill to speak.'

'And so he was. But he has been able to sit up, talk and read for the past three days. He even ordered his favourite sushi yesterday evening. Not at all convenient for the catering people. He is still very weak of course, but . . .'

Hoffman looked unhappy.

'We should have been informed. The moment he was well enough to hold a conversation you should have told us.'

'I didn't want to raise false hopes. At that time we still had no positive data that . . .'

'Nevertheless, the opportunity to speak to him, to let him know that everything was being done, was one . . .'

'We fully apprised him of all that before the operation,' said Kessler. 'He understood well enough. Professor Geiger and myself attended to him personally, after all.'

Hunziker drained his glass and smiled.

'Don't worry, Dietmar. There'll be plenty of opportunities to get down to business. I'm sure Mr Hiraizumi will be in our care for many weeks to come, isn't that right Dr Kessler?'

Kessler cleared his throat.

'He shall have to stay for another week at least, but he has expressed a desire to be returned to Japan as soon as it is practically possible.'

'A week?' said Hunziker. 'You propose to let him leave in a week?'

'Since we hope that no further operations will be necessary, all that remains to be done is to keep him under close observation. That can be done anywhere. Special transport can be laid on easily enough. And he has his own team of doctors waiting in Zürich.'

'Why is he so anxious to leave?' said Hoffman.

'I can't say,' said Kessler. 'But he's always been a reluctant traveller, as I'm sure you're aware.'

'But a *week*?'

'Perhaps I was mistaken. But I didn't think it would be in the interests of the company to detain him without good reason. His own doctors are highly competent.'

'Quite right, Egon,' said Hunziker. 'Ill or not, this is one man one should never play for a fool. I shall pay him a visit myself, first thing in the morning. In the meantime I don't think we should keep this piece of good news all to ourselves. We should make sure the whole board knows about it straight away.'

'Everyone should be here tomorrow in any case,' said Hoffman, 'for the monthly meeting.'

'Of course, of course,' said Hunziker. 'And I hope we'll have Pierre this time? I'm sure we'll want to take a look at his plans for an Asian campaign in the light of recent events.'

'He's said he'll be here. I'm sure he won't fail us.'

'Excellent. Will you pour, Dietmar? All this excitement has made me thirsty.'

Hoffman got up off the sofa and refilled the glasses, all except Kessler's which was still almost untouched.

'Now that your programme has reached the stage of practical application,' he said, 'I take it you will soon have no further need for your new donor.'

Kessler deliberately took a sip of champagne before answering: 'I'm afraid that is not the case just yet. We have begun preliminary cloning of ova, but we cannot be sure the cloned stock has been replicated without damage. In short, we risk everything if we do not have a larger stock to work with.'

'Egon, we cannot wait indefinitely,' said Hunziker quietly but without a trace of compromise. 'We are all at risk here.'

'I realise that,' said Kessler. 'And we are doing everything possible to speed up production. The next ovulation should produce a cluster that is sufficient for our needs: we have applied some very effective fertility drugs, which the Professor has himself developed.'

'So I hear,' said Denzler. 'One of the staff was telling

me that you expect the whole cycle to be shortened to as little as three weeks. Is that correct?'

'No,' said Kessler loudly. 'I mean . . . It's . . . There's no clear evidence about that. It may be so, but I would say it's highly unlikely. What is affected is the number of eggs produced, not the speed of the cycle.'

'I must insist on knowing when you think we can proceed, Mr Kessler,' said Hoffman.

'I should say in about two weeks from now, if all goes well.'

Hunziker and Hoffman looked at each other.

'That is longer than we would like, Egon, but we will try to accommodate you. When the time comes, your full co-operation – and perhaps that of Professor Geiger as well – may be needed. You understand that?'

'Of course,' said Kessler. 'We have already drawn up our own procedure. It will be taken care of.'

'Very well then,' said Hunziker. 'We shall turn to other matters. Another bottle, gentlemen?'

5

Zürich. March 3rd, 1996.

The old woman looked at him like he was some kind of criminal. She had been walking along the pavement, wrapped in furs and a Russian-style hat, with a small dog on the end of a lead. Waterman had gone up to her because there was nobody else around. He asked her which house was Anna Norden's, but she shook her head, pretending she couldn't understand him.

'I'm from Satellite Television News,' he went on, saying the words slowly and deliberately. 'And we're hoping to do something about what happened here. You know, the murder?'

The woman stopped and looked at him.

'The television is coming here?' she said.

'Yes ma'am. It's for part of a documentary.'

'With cameras?'

'Yes,' said Waterman. 'Next week. You know which is Anna Norden's house?'

The dog was pulling on its lead, its little paws sliding on the ice. The woman brought it to heel with a sharp tug.

'Yes, I know it. My house is opposite. I was there when it happened. When the police came.'

'No kidding. Which house?'

The woman pointed back the way she had come. She

had a lot of make-up on and red lipstick. Up close it wasn't a pretty sight.

'The big one,' she said, 'the fourth house before the end. The Norden girl was on the other side. I knew her, you know.'

'You did?'

'Of course. We were neighbours. She was not here very long, but I met her. She was not a happy girl.'

Waterman nodded eagerly.

'Did she live alone?'

'No, there was another girl living there too, and,' – she drew closer, putting her gloved hand on Waterman's arm – 'there were men coming and going all the time. I don't know who they were, but I didn't like the look of them.' She tapped a finger against her temple, and added: 'I sensed all along that they were criminals.'

'Is the girl still there, by any chance?'

'I haven't seen her for weeks. I think maybe she left. Her name was Amalie, and I think she took drugs.'

'Well that's very helpful,' said Waterman. 'We may want to interview you when the cameras get here. Would you mind that?'

The woman shrugged.

'No, I wouldn't mind,' she said. 'My name is Openhoff, and my house is number seven. Do you want my telephone number?'

'We'll be sure to look you up, no question,' said Waterman, and headed back up the street. Belatedly the small dog yapped at him.

Anna Norden's house, like the whole neighbourhood, was more expensive-looking than he'd thought it would be. With the newspaper reports talking about anarchist groups and left-wing extremists, he had been bracing himself for a Swiss equivalent of the Bronx, if such a thing existed. This wasn't the richest part of town by a long way, but the houses, most of them about twenty-five years old he reckoned, were neat and solid-looking, with white or grey walls and tiled roofs. To American eyes all they lacked was space in between them. If Anna Norden really had been an anarchist, he thought to himself, she must have been the Patty Hearst type.

Waterman was just crossing the road when the front door of the house opened and a man appeared. He was stocky, with a beard, and wore a camouflage jacket. He crossed the small tarmac driveway and got into a car, a white Fiat hatchback, which was parked a few yards away. Waterman watched him drive off and then went over to the house.

The girl who answered the door was small, with short, mousy-coloured hair. She was almost pretty, Waterman thought, but her skin was pale and there were dark circles under her eyes. She was holding a cigarette.

'Good morning. Are you Amalie by any chance?'

The girl looked at him blankly.

'*Ja.*'

'You don't know me. My name's Waterman and I'm a reporter. I'm trying to find out what really happened here. To Anna Norden. Can you spare me five minutes?'

The girl didn't answer. She looked back at him, just the same as before, and then slowly stood back from the door to let him in. As he crossed the threshold, he thought: *the old woman opposite knew what she was talking about.*

'I didn't know about it until a couple of hours ago. Hans just told me. I've been away for three weeks in England. I didn't hear anything about it. I just . . . I still can't believe it all. It's horrible.'

They were sitting in the lounge, the girl still smoking, talking rapidly, nervously, Waterman opposite her with his coat on. The kitchen area where Anna Norden's body

451

had been found was still taped off and an opaque plastic sheet covered the floor. The house was cold.

'I'm sorry,' Waterman said. 'I thought you'd have known weeks ago.'

She shook her head.

'I don't think anyone knew where to reach me. I just told Anna which flight I'd be on so she'd meet me at the airport. Hans showed up instead. I guess she must have told him before . . . before it happened.'

'Who is Hans? The guy I saw coming out of here?'

Amalie nodded.

'Was he Anna's boyfriend or something?'

She exhaled slowly, staring down at the floor.

'Anna didn't have a boyfriend,' she said. 'She had a lot of men friends but not . . . She was very, you know, *involved* – in movements and things. Hans is one of the people she met through that. They used to talk politics all the time. I thought it was a drag actually. And I think she only did it because it was a kind of – '

'Substitute?'

'I don't know. Maybe. You want some coffee or something?'

'Yes, if you've got some.'

She stubbed out her cigarette vigorously and went out into the kitchen. She called out to him.

'No milk yet. Sorry.'

'Black's fine.'

Waterman watched her as she came back into the room.

'The newspapers said she was mixed up with some bad people,' said Waterman. 'They implied she was some kind of anarchist.'

'I know,' said Amalie. 'Hans told me. He said the police were just using her death to discredit the Green movement here.'

'What do you think?'

'I don't know. I wasn't here. To tell the truth, I didn't

452

really see very much of her. I only moved in with her a few weeks before Christmas. All I know is she wasn't what the papers said. I didn't get too involved in her political things, but I do know she was completely against violence – all violence. She would never have got involved in anything . . . really bad.'

'Then why did it happen? You think it was just a break-in or something?'

'Hans says he thinks she was killed by someone the authorities tried to plant inside the group. He says they want to intimidate everyone, to make them behave.'

'Did he say why he thought that?'

'He said there was a man. An American. He stayed with Anna at least one night, and he wasn't there when the police showed up. He was on the run from the police or something. Now no one knows where he is.'

'Do you have any idea where Anna might have met this guy?'

Amalie shook her head.

'Hans didn't say. But it's just the sort of thing Anna would do. If someone was in trouble, she would help. She wouldn't ask questions. She wouldn't try to find out if they were a murderer or a madman first. She would just feel sorry for them and help them. She was stupid like that. She didn't think about herself. She was so *stupid*.'

She brought her feet up onto the sofa and put her hands over her face. Waterman looked away as she struggled with the tears, her shoulders convulsing. He stood up and went across to the front window. The street looked desolate and empty. By the time he sat down again she was drying her eyes with a crumpled white handkerchief.

'I suppose this doesn't really help you very much does it, Mr Waterman?'

'Well, it kind of confirms what I already heard.'

He looked out into the hall. He wondered how Anna Norden had been killed. The guy at the American consulate hadn't told him. Was it a bullet in the head, perhaps, like Sam Chaney, or something more improvised? Either way her room-mate was going to get a shock when the police lifted the plastic sheet in the kitchen.

'Listen, have you spoken to the police yet?'

Amalie shook her head.

'Not really, no. A woman told me not to touch anything in the kitchen. They didn't want me to stay in the house, but I have nowhere else to go.'

'Well they'll probably come by pretty soon. They'll have been wanting to interview you, just in case you know something.'

'I suppose so, but I don't know anything. Anna isn't – wasn't – the kind of person who made enemies. She was a nurse, for God's sake. And she was nice, you know?'

'Sure.'

Waterman reached inside his coat pocket and took out a pack of cigarettes. He took his time taking off the cellophane wrapper.

'Let's suppose for a minute that this guy Hans was on the right kind of track. Let's say this isn't just the act of a passing criminal or a casual acquaintance.'

He offered her a cigarette and she took it. Waterman reached over with the lighter, and waited for her to take a couple of drags. He noticed that her hands were shaking.

'Let's suppose someone killed . . . did this for a reason. And let's say it was something to do with her politics or something.'

The girl didn't say anything. She seemed to be shivering, but then it wasn't cold enough for that.

'Maybe we could get a clue about that from her work. I mean, did she have a study here, somewhere she might have written letters or something?'

Amalie took another deep drag on the cigarette.

'Just her room. She kept her books there and her personal things.'

'Could we take a look?'

She exhaled.

'Hans said the relatives had already gone through her possessions. I don't know how much they took. They weren't all that, you know, close. But I suppose they'll have her letters and her scrapbooks at least.'

'That's a pity. They might have turned up something.'

'I'm sorry. But if you're really interested in what she was doing you should talk to Hans or one of Anna's other friends. Why don't you take his number?'

'All right, I will.'

'It's up there by the phone. Anna had most of her friends' numbers at the back of the pad.'

The phone was hung on the wall, with a big all-in-one calendar and notice board beside it. The calendar was decorated with characters from Walt Disney. Waterman took down the telephone number opposite Hans's name.

'Thanks,' he said. 'This is a real help.'

The girl smiled faintly and shook her head.

'I don't think so. It was just some thief that did it. The American or someone else. Why else would they steal my car?'

Waterman turned round and looked at her.

'Your car?'

'My van. My old Volkswagen. It's missing and the keys are gone. Maybe Anna lent it to someone – I said she could use it – but if so they haven't brought it back, have they?'

'And do the police know about this?'

She hesitated.

'I don't know. I suppose not unless they noticed.'

'Well,' said Waterman, 'I think you ought to tell them, don't you? The sooner we find it, the sooner we can nail the sonofabitch that took it.'

6

The Phönixlager. March 4th, 1996.

Just after seven o'clock in the evening, the three Japanese doctors filed out of Hiraizumi's room. Kessler, his assistant Chen and the deputy chief surgeon were waiting for them, together with two bodyguards in neat grey suits. The Japanese doctors were not smiling, but then they never smiled.

'Have you completed your examination, Doctor Hamada?' said Kessler. 'Is there anything else you need?'

The eldest of the three, a small, bald man with a wrinkled forehead and sour expression, shook his head.

'The preliminary examination is complete. That will be all for the present.'

He handed a bulging clipboard to one of his colleagues, who placed it inside a black briefcase. Kessler waited for him to say something else, but the Japanese simply took off his glasses and placed them in his top pocket. There was nothing to suggest that he had seen anything at all remarkable.

Chen and the Mendelhaus surgeon exchanged glances.

'And do you find your patient in good health?' said Kessler.

Hamada squinted up at him.

'So far we find nothing to contradict your data, Doctor Kessler,' he said. 'The essential purification processes

456

seem to have been restored. We shall conduct further tests when Chairman Hiraizumi is returned to our care.'

'I see,' said Kessler, putting his hands behind his back. 'Then allow me to conduct you down to the ground floor. As I mentioned earlier, it was decided to mark Chairman Hiraizumi's recovery – and your visit – with a small celebration.'

Hamada made a very slight bow, the kind one only made to subordinates. His two colleagues followed suit, except that their bows were slightly lower. As Kessler led them out along the passage and into the main lift, he wondered whether they were jealous of his success, or worse: humiliated by their own failure? Was it some deep-seated sense of superiority that had been offended, or were Doctor Hamada and his team just afraid of losing their meal-tickets?

In the salon, which was especially set aside for entertaining, the rest of the board were gathering, together with most of the top people from the Medical Services Division. Hunziker had insisted on a celebration, ignoring Dietmar Hoffman's obvious lack of enthusiasm. The two non-executive directors from Union Bank of Geneva had been invited, and, like Denzler and Bruggman, they had brought their wives with them. The chairman of the bank was expected too. The waiters served champagne cocktails and extravagant canapés.

Hunziker welcomed Hamada and the others to the gathering and began talking at once, in slow, deliberate English, about what an honour it had been to treat Hiraizumi, and what a remarkable man he was. The Japanese listened without saying much, unused, Kessler felt sure, to discussing either the virtues or the faults of anyone so far above them in rank. Nevertheless, they appreciated the cocktails, judging from the speed with which they drained their glasses.

Kessler excused himself and went to a telephone outside in the reception area. There were more bodyguards there, Europeans this time, in plain clothes, standing together by the main door with their arms folded. They turned and stared at him without saying anything, and then went back to their conversation. The girl at the desk, seated in a leather armchair at the far end, looked up from her magazine and gave him a nod. Kessler dialled Geiger's extension and waited. Half a minute passed before there was any answer.

'Yes?'

'Edward? They're finished now, finally. But they don't seem very convinced.'

'Did they say that?'

'No, but they didn't exactly hail their man's recovery as a miracle.'

'It isn't a miracle, Egon. It's simply progress. That's what galls them. We got there first.'

'You don't think they could spoil things?'

Kessler could hear Geiger laugh; his breath across the mouthpiece.

'Don't worry about that. Hiraizumi's health will speak a lot louder than they can. So long as he's happy, everyone else is ecstatic.'

From outside came the sound of another chopper. One of the security men opened the door and peered out into the twilight. A powerful beam of light swept across the front of the building.

'I still think it would be an idea to come down here, Edward. The whole board is arriving.'

Geiger paused.

'I know. If there are more questions it will be better if there are two of us to deal with them. I'll be there directly.'

Kessler replaced the receiver. The doorway was wide open now, and light outside had settled upon it. One of the bodyguards was shielding his eyes, another was talking into a radio. Flurries of brightly-lit snow drifted past them. Kessler waited, curious to see who had arrived.

As the beat of the chopper-blades began to recede, a figure with blond hair, a long overcoat hanging from his shoulders, walked into the building. He paused for a moment to take off his gloves and handed them, together with his coat and scarf, to one of the staff who appeared beside him. It was Pierre Lambert.

Kessler had no desire to speak to him, but now it was unavoidable. Lambert strode across the hallway in his direction, a smile on his suntanned face.

'Good evening, Doctor Kessler,' he said, clapping him on the shoulder. 'What have you been cooking up in that great laboratory of yours since my last visit here, hmm?'

Kessler cleared his throat.

'We have been at work on the same project as before, of course. And we have made significant progress.'

'I know all about that,' said Lambert. 'You don't need to convince *me*. Erixil is proving more successful than we could have hoped. Now we're taking on the European giants, and we're winning. It's very exciting.'

They began walking towards the salon.

'That isn't what I meant,' said Kessler. 'In research terms, Erixil is no more than a footnote, history. We're well beyond – '

'You're too modest, Doctor. We've only just begun with this thing. But you're right. We must start thinking about where we go from here. I've been meaning to talk to you about that. Perhaps when we have a quieter moment you could allow me to bounce some ideas off you.'

Kessler was surprised. He'd never reckoned Lambert as an ally in the battle for pure research.

'As you wish, Herr Lambert. But what kind of ideas?'

They were standing together on the threshold of the salon. Lambert took a glass of champagne from a waiter and raised it in response to someone in the room. Then he turned back to Kessler, lowering his voice.

'I think, in a word, Doctor, that it's time we did something for the gentlemen, don't you? Something to give them back some of their lost youth as we have the ladies?'

Kessler said nothing.

'And if we can regenerate skin, why not hair? For something that actually worked, even partially, I'm convinced the market would be even bigger than Erixil's. I've already sent some research to Oswald. The figures are very pretty.'

'You've sent a report?' said Kessler, swallowing a mouthful of champagne. 'When was that?'

'Three weeks ago. Oswald must know you're very busy, or he'd have asked you for an assessment by now. I know he's quite excited about it.'

'I haven't heard a thing about it.'

'With something like that we could completely drive the opposition from the field, across a whole range of products. This sort of thing acts cumulatively, you know.'

'I see.'

Lambert had caught someone else's eye. It was Frau Bruggman: a tall blonde woman in her late thirties – at least ten years younger than her husband, but still not too young for cosmetic surgery. Kessler recalled that her breasts had been remoulded by the surgeon's knife just eighteen months earlier, in that very clinic.

'Give the idea some thought,' said Lambert, 'and tell me what can be done. The existing products are quite derisory, you know.'

Kessler did not have to reply because Lambert was already greeting one of the UBG directors and his wife. Karl Moser, the Mendelhaus deputy chairman, was with them; he and Lambert shook hands warmly.

Looking around the room, Kessler caught sight of Edward Geiger at the other end of the room, a tall, erect figure, talking to two of the Japanese doctors. He wondered for a moment whether the Professor in fact spoke Japanese. He had never claimed that skill, but then he would never have bothered to mention it unless it was to some purpose. As for his many interviews with Hiraizumi, these had always been conducted alone.

Kessler went over towards him, but before he could get within earshot there came the sound of a small silver bell, which one of the waiters was ringing. The room fell silent and Oswald Hunziker began a short speech. For the benefit of the Asian visitors it was in English, but in the background Kessler could hear Japanese softly spoken in translation. He recognised the voice of the interpreter as Geiger's.

Still carrying a glass of champagne, Pierre Lambert left the reception and wandered slowly, almost aimlessly, into the hallway. The last of the guests had arrived half an hour since, and the bodyguards were all sitting in leather armchairs at the far end, smoking and talking in low voices. None of them saw the head of the Cosmetics Division go through the small door between the elevator and the entrance to the swimming pool. As the door closed again one of them did look up, but seeing nothing, went on with the joke he was telling about the Swiss, the Italian and the Jew. The other bodyguards were enjoying it.

On the other side of the door lay a narrow corridor. As he walked towards the shadows at the far end, Lambert covered his nose with a perfumed silk handkerchief to attenuate the smell of rotten eggs. As he went on the noise of the reception died away behind him, until the only discernible sound was the movement of air through the ventilation ducts overhead. At the large riveted door, he removed a plastic card from his wallet and slippcd it into the panel set into the wall on his right. There was a

461

satisfying click and he pushed the door open with one finger. Once inside he made his way briskly along the corridor until he came to a door on his left.

He went into what looked like a small kitchen, except that instead of a refrigerator there was a row of blank-faced electronic apparatus and, incongruously he always felt, a photocopying machine. He closed the door behind him and sat down at a desk on which a small IBM flickered silently. Then he reached into his jacket pocket and took out his wallet. Laying it open in front of him, he extracted a plastic card, a small steel blade inside a protective sleeve, and a small foil packet of cocaine. With the tip of his finger he put a smudge of the white powder on the end of his tongue: it was already very fine. Working quickly, concentrating, he worked it into two neat parallel lines on the back of the plastic card. He noticed, with some pleasure, that his hands were steady, like a young man's.

He picked up his wallet again and looked through the bank notes inside. He never carried much cash, but he found one 200 franc note crisp enough for his purpose. He was just rolling it up when his eyes came to rest on something else there: a small photograph of a woman. He took it out and looked at it. The woman was young and blonde and she had signed her name in one corner. It was not unusual for Lambert to put a girl's photograph in his wallet, but he had felt different about this one. Even among other models she could turn heads, and just to walk with her on his arm gave him a sense of power that his success at business, however great, could not. He had believed that she was different in other ways too. She was bored with the people she met in her work: they were shallow, unintelligent – whereas she had done a year at university and spoke four languages, three of them flu-ently. All they cared about was being famous, whereas she wanted the simple things, the things that had real value. Or so she had said.

Lambert flushed with anger at the thought of it. She had no time for him now. She had decided to go off with a television producer. He was making a feature film with some soap stars from the States, and he was going to get her a part. She had always wanted to get into films, and modelling was a kind of acting, as she had so often explained.

Keeping his eyes fixed on the photograph, Lambert rolled up the bank note and used it to sniff up the lines of white powder: one line through the right nostril, one line through the left. It only took a minute. When he was done he took a cigarette lighter from his pocket and burned the photograph, holding it in his hands until there was nothing left but the corner with the signature. He let the flame burn his fingers before blowing it out.

He could feel his pulse quickening as he walked out into the corridor. The rush of air through the ventilation ducts seemed louder; it blended with the sound of his breathing, a healthy sound, strong and regular. He stood for a moment, looking back the way he had come, listening. There was only silence. He turned his back and walked on.

As always, it was cooler near the back of the building, and the sound of the ventilation system was louder, the rush of air augmented by a distant, metallic vibration. Lambert went through the double fire doors, pushing them back like an opera singer making his entrance. He felt young, strong.

Only six people – the executive directors – had passes to all sections inside the mountain. Even Geiger and Kessler could not gain access to the area where the boardroom and other offices were located, without approval. By the same token it was not permitted to install locks or security devices anywhere that could keep directors out – a simple precaution against unauthorised work or concealment of data. For the medical staff, the researchers and the ancillary teams, special passes were issued which allowed them to move freely around their own work areas, but not beyond.

He had reached a part of the laboratory with which he was less familiar. The corridor in which he was standing seemed to narrow slightly and curved round to the left. On his right there was another fire door. Laughing softly, he approached the fire door and looked through the reinforced glass window. Another corridor stretched away into the distance. He imagined the other directors drinking their stupid cocktails in the clinic and shook his head. Then he pushed open the door and walked silently through. Perhaps it was the drug, but he thought he could hear music. A note was played, held for a long time, then it rose a semitone and was hardened. It was unbearably beautiful. Lambert leaned against the wall, squeezing the bridge of his nose with his right hand. Then it dawned on him where the music must be coming from. A smile spread across his lips. He walked forward, shuffling almost, like a sleepwalker.

Cathy's room was not hard to find. The others around it were unlocked, empty, as if in fear of some contagion. He opened the door quietly and was surprised to find himself in semi-darkness. It took a moment for his eyes to adjust and then he saw her. She was standing at the foot of the bed and turning the pages of a book of music. So Geiger had set up a magic mirror to watch his princess. Lambert could hardly suppress his laughter. He looked around the small observation room, noticing a camera which observed the observation room itself.

'Chinese puzzles,' said Lambert, shaking his head. Under the mirror there was a bank of recording equipment. He looked at the door to her room. It was smooth and looked heavy. Set in the frame was a slot for a pass. Lambert felt a twinge of fear. What if his pass would not open it? Breathing quickly now, he went to the door and put in his pass. Hearing the lock move, he pushed the door open an inch or two.

She did not seem to have heard at first. She was sitting on the far side of the double bed now with her back to him, her long dark hair spread over her shoulders. She seemed to be working at something, something in her lap. There was a faint smell of cologne which Lambert identified immediately as a Guerlain fragrance of which he was particularly fond. He sipped in the air as though tasting wine. As he approached he saw that she was tightening one of the strings of a violin. The bow lay across her pillow. He was about to speak when she said: 'What time is it, Professor?'

He hesitated.

'Twenty past eight.'

She looked round suddenly and stood up. She was wearing a night-dress, simple and white, that went down to her knees. Beneath it Lambert could see that she was naked, and for a moment he wondered at the familiarity of her greeting. Did Professor Geiger visit her often at night? Did he keep her there for his work or for his pleasure? What games did he play with his two-way mirrors and his cameras? Even men of science were made of flesh and blood.

'Pierre? What's happening? What are you . . . ?'

He put his finger to his lips to silence her, and then closed the door. She stood watching, holding the violin across her stomach as if it might protect her.

'I didn't know about all this, Cathy, or I'd have come earlier,' he said. 'They told me you'd returned to Zürich.'

She did not move, frightened by the expression on his face.

'What do you want?'

He resisted the temptation to get closer. Her eyes were wild and staring, like an animal's, but beautiful still.

465

'I thought we were friends, Cathy. You don't think I'm part of all this, do you?'

She hesitated for a moment, staring in disbelief. Then she flung the violin onto the bed and rushed towards him.

'Are you going to get me out of here? Can you get me out of here? You've got to . . .'

'Cathy, Cathy.' He put his arms around her shoulders, drawing her to him. She was shaking. 'Of course I am. Professor Geiger's antics have gone far enough.'

She stepped back from him.

'It isn't just Geiger. It's all of them. I thought you . . .'

'No, no, Cathy, not me. I've been kept in the dark and other directors have too. Don't worry. I'm going to put a stop . . .'

'Thank God.'

She put her arms around him. He felt the soft warmth of her form against his chest, breathed in the perfume of her hair. She was still as beautiful as he remembered her – more beautiful in fact. The models that he met in the course of his work were cold and proud, their occasional sweetness affected, no more than a ploy. He had always known that, and yet he had still fallen for it. But Cathy's beauty was an expression of her being. She was more desirable than they could ever be.

'Wait,' she said, pulling away from him, 'he may be watching us. He's always watching.'

She pointed to the TV camera high up on the opposite wall.

'Don't worry about the professor. He's in the clinic. I just left him. And even if he does see us he's too late.'

He reached inside his jacket and took out a slim automatic pistol. It felt alive in his hand, dense, mercurial. He blinked at the pleasure everything was giving him.

'Now,' he said, laying the barrel of the pistol against the palm of his left hand. 'You'd better get dressed. Do you still have your clothes?'

'Some of them,' she said.

'Well get changed. That way no one will bother to try and stop us. They'll think you're with me. Here.'

From his pocket he pulled out a small jewellery case. Inside it was a pair of diamond earrings. He had bought them two days earlier for the girl in the photograph, but since she had cancelled their last date he no longer had a use for them.

'You'll look more like a guest with these. You don't need make-up.'

She took them and went to her wardrobe. After ten days in the mountain Geiger had given her back some of the clothes she had come with. She had even gained the impression that he wanted her to wear them, as if that might mean she had accepted her position, that things were becoming normal again. For that reason she had never touched them. They had remained neatly folded in the drawers of the wardrobe.

Hastily now she reached for them. The style that she had once prized seemed ridiculous now – even when it came to her underwear: lacy, pointlessly intricate, trivial. But there was no time to think about that. She wanted only to escape. To leave the nightmare behind. At last someone had come to put a stop to it, just as she had prayed would happen day after day. In her dreams it had been Michael, but he was far away.

She took a skirt from its hanger, a black one with pleats, and pulled it up around her waist. She slid it around until the buttons were on her hips, and fastened them one after the other. Her haste made her clumsy: her nails caught on the material, and the buttons kept slipping from between her fingers. Then she took a bra from the drawer and, pulling the night-dress over her head, clipped it together beneath her breasts. As she slid the first strap over her shoulder she saw that Lambert was watching her, the pistol still in his hand. She turned her back on him and took out a silk blouse from the wardrobe.

She was stooping down to get a pair of shoes when Lambert said: 'Didn't Geiger leave you a coat?'

She shook her head.

'What about stockings? Your legs are bare. That might attract attention.'

'I have all that,' she said. 'I just need a few seconds.'

He didn't wait for her to put them on. As she turned back to the wardrobe he felt himself carried across the room towards her as if on a breaking wave. He pushed up hard against her so that her face was pressed against the mirror. She let out a single, astonished cry.

'Cathy, Cathy. I would never, never hurt . . .'

He could hardly control his breathing. He wanted to laugh, to shout. He pushed his fingers in between the buttons on her hip and pulled hard. Two buttons came away. He needed both hands. Momentarily he released her. As she spun around to face him he jabbed the gun against her throat, once more forcing his body against hers, pressing his knee into her groin. Her breath was hot against his face, clean and sweet. The gun was jammed so hard against her jaw she could not speak. As she stared at him there came only a single muted sob. Again he tugged at the skirt. This time it came away.

'No!'

Her big dark eyes were brimming. Lambert lunged at her face, licking at the salt tears.

'Never Cathy, I would never . . .'

He kissed her face and throat, the smell of her making him dizzy. Then he grabbed at the delicate stuff of her blouse and ripped. Keeping the gun pressed against her cheek he pushed his face into the abundant flesh of her exposed breasts. She was perfect. He would never let anyone hurt her. She was the woman he wanted, the woman that would complete his life. Both he and Cathy

468

were silent now, and the only sound was that of her rapid breathing, breathing through clenched teeth. As he moved his free hand down to her belly he noted how the breathing grew faster, more urgent. She swallowed as he pushed his hand into the abundant dry warmth of her crotch. He felt himself harden. Then he forced her to the foot of the bed.

It was then she screamed. The loudness of it surprised him, stabbing his head like a knife. He let go his grip, just long enough for her to free herself. The next moment he felt her clenched fist slam against his temple. Then she was on top of him, punching, clawing, her voice a torrent of rage and hatred. She was so strong. He staggered back towards the door, fending her off with his left arm. Then astonishment gave way to insane rage. He stabbed the gun out in front of him, and she froze, breathing in great hoarse gasps.

'You hurt me, Cathy. You shouldn't have done that.'

Still he held the gun out straight, his finger tight against the trigger. She had pulled up in front of him, standing suddenly erect as if ready to receive the bullet, to die. Her courage frightened him, releasing a high-pitched laugh which sounded effeminate, mad. It felt like a spring had given way in him; like something had broken in his head. He squeezed the trigger convulsively, screwing up his eyes against the anticipated explosion. But there was nothing. *The safety!* He fumbled with the gun as Cathy leapt towards him. He lashed out at her, cracking the barrel of the pistol against the side of her face. She spun around, staggered, and almost collapsed against him. He gripped her by the arms and held her away from him, afraid to let her get closer. Her head lolled against his chest. She looked up at him dumbly, her mouth open. She moaned again, pathetically this time, like a lost child.

Lambert let the gun fall to the floor and, catching her under the arms, dragged her to the bed. He no longer

469

felt any desire for her. He wanted to punish her now, to fuck her like a cheap whore. Using both hands, he tore the delicate lingerie apart.

'*Sale pute!*'

He unzipped himself, and then, gripping her under her knees, pushed her legs back violently, almost as far as her shoulders. She was still conscious, barely, but too weak now to struggle.

'*Sale putain!*'

The door to the room cracked back against the wall like a gunshot. Lambert's head snapped round, a fleck of saliva flying from his open mouth. Geiger was standing in the doorway, his face white, his eyes staring. Without saying a word he strode towards the bed and seized Lambert by the throat.

Lambert struggled to free himself, but Geiger's hands were powerful. He could feel the sinews cracking in his neck. With the strength of terror Lambert hauled himself to his feet and clawed at Geiger's hands. But Geiger did not move. He stared down at Lambert with the face of a madman.

'For God's sake, Edward! What are you doing?'

It was Kessler. He ran towards them, taking hold of Geiger's right arm with both of his own, struggling to break the grip round Lambert's neck.

'Edward!'

Geiger looked round at his colleague and then suddenly let go. Lambert fell to the floor and lay there coughing and choking. Kessler dragged Geiger back, as if afraid he would attack again.

'Get out of here!' shouted Geiger. 'Get out, you fucking, fucking scum!'

Lambert struggled to his feet, still unable to speak. Kessler went to Cathy's side and looked into her face, running his fingers along her jaw, opening her eyelids with his fingers.

'There's no fracture,' he said. 'She won't need anything for this.'

As he spoke he seemed to notice her nakedness for the first time.

'As for – ' he looked down towards her still exposed sex, 'I think the risk of fertilisation at this time is minimal.'

'I didn't get that far,' said Lambert hoarsely. 'Your precious concubine is still unsullied.'

'You scum,' said Geiger. 'I should have killed you.'

Lambert was slowly tucking in his shirt, adjusting his tie. There was a single spot of blood on his collar.

'Me?' he said. 'What have I done?'

'You have endangered this entire project!' rapped out Kessler, covering Cathy over with a sheet. 'Have you any idea how important this woman is?'

'You tried to rape her, you piece of shit,' said Geiger.

Lambert picked up his gun from the floor and put it back inside his jacket.

'I suppose you should know all about that, Professor,' he said, examining his neck in the mirror. There were faint bluish bruises. 'Isn't this whole thing a rape, albeit a more sophisticated kind, as befits the age?'

'What the hell are you talking about?' said Kessler. 'This is . . . this is . . .'

'The only difference is that I wanted this girl for a few minutes, whereas you want her forever. I'm content to borrow her body. You want all of her, body and soul, even, so I'm told, her unborn children. And you too will use force to get what you want.'

He looked Geiger full in the face.

'So tell me, Professor: who is the rapist?'

'You are as ignorant as you are degenerate,' said Geiger, getting control of himself now. 'If you ever come near this woman again I'll kill you.'

471

Lambert was already at the door. He was smiling now. 'You won't get the chance, Professor Geiger,' he said. 'You're already finished here. I'll see to that.'

7

The Phönixlager. March 4th, 1996.

He was standing at the drinks cabinet, a damp bathtowel around his middle when Katya Schindler rapped on the door. He ran through to the bedroom and slipped between the sheets. It was only when he had called out for her to come in that he realised he was still holding the unopened bottle of beer. He set it against his thigh under the blankets so that she wouldn't see anything suspicious.

'I hope you are feeling better, Mr Diaz?'

Her features worked hard to express concern, but he could see her eyes taking him in, questioning, puzzled, faintly annoyed.

'It's ridiculous,' said Mike, giving an involuntary shiver as the chilled bottle moved on his thigh, 'I just can't seem to shake off this cold. It seems to have gotten worse since I arrived.'

'Is that why you've been having heat treatment?'

Mike eased himself away from the bottle. It didn't take long for news to get round the clinic. He hoped she hadn't been speaking to the Japanese wrestler about his sniffing around on the first floor.

'Yes. I don't know. I just thought it might do me some good, but it seems to have worked the other way.'

The truth was that it had been the only way he could

473

justify going through into the one part of the clinic that really interested him. He had had two sessions of being smeared in sulphurous mud on the previous day, just so that he could get a look at the riveted door again. But he had learned nothing new, and could think of no way to get through it. The door on the left before the shelves was just another storage closet in which cleaning materials were stacked on shelves. He wanted to ask the girl at the desk what was behind the big door, but was afraid of arousing suspicion. The mud sessions had left him feeling drained, and faintly nauseous.

'The treatment is not recommended for someone with a fever, however slight.'

'I should have thought about that,' said Mike, trying to sound contrite.

Miss Schindler stood looking down at him, not speaking until he returned her gaze. He felt vulnerable, looking up like that. There was some deep coldness, some stone hardness about her that unnerved him. It occurred to him that she might have looked at Cathy with the same cold eyes.

'The problem is that we had organised the operation for yesterday, and now today it looks as though you are still not fit for the anaesthetic.'

Mike felt a knot of irritation form between his eyebrows. He thought about the astronomical sums he was paying to drink beers out of the drinks cabinet and look out the window at their dumb mountains, and they were treating him like he was on welfare.

'I'm sorry to be so insistent, Mr Diaz. It's just that we do have other clients and we have to keep to a fairly strict timetable for the theatre.'

Mike shrugged.

'Maybe if I stay in bed today I will be okay for tomorrow.'

474

Miss Schindler compressed her lips and sent out a little strangled sigh through her fine nostrils.

'Will you go without dinner tonight, so as to be ready for the theatre tomorrow morning?'

'What if I'm not better?'

Mike felt a flutter of nerves at the thought of the operation. He jumped, surprised to find the bottle against his skin again.

'If you are not better we will have to think about discussing other plans.'

And then she was gone.

Mike got out of bed and went through to the drinks cabinet. He returned the beer to its shelf, and then started to pace back and forth on the oriental rug, dabbing at his nose with a paper napkin.

At four o'clock in the afternoon there was another knock on the door. Mike turned from the window as the woman came in.

'Excuse me, I have to tidy a little. I come this morning but the room not free.'

'Sure, go ahead. If you don't mind cleaning up around me.'

He watched the woman as she moved about the room. She removed the flowers from the vase and replaced them with an identical bouquet. She was short and dark with a shadow of down on her upper lip. Portuguese, maybe, or Spanish, thought Mike.

'*Imagino que hay mucho trabajo a hacer aqui,*' he said.

The woman looked up, startled. Mike too was surprised. He hadn't planned to speak to her in Spanish. It had just come out. Maybe it was because he had been locked up on his own all day. Maybe it was because she reminded him of his mother – her work-reddened hand clenched in the yellow duster.

'*Prego?*'

Then he realised that she hadn't understood what he had said. She was Italian. Mike felt himself flush. He tried to think of the Italian words.

'*Lavorare molto*,' was the best he could do, making a gesture as if he were dusting. She stood up straight and put her hands on her hips. When she smiled he could see gold in the back of her mouth. She said something long and involved in Italian, the best part of which escaped him.

'Excuse me?'

She paused again. She smiled, nodding as if she had understood.

'I say it is truth what you say. We have lot of work to do, but worst is we not go home at the end of day.'

'You stay in the clinic?'

She pointed down at the ground.

'Upstairs,' she said.

Mike thought of the key in the lift. It was for the staff. They had rooms down below. It had to be below ground level, otherwise he would have seen something. The lift had to go down at least fifty feet. The place was like a rabbit warren.

She had gone on with her work, and was now dusting the glass table, having sprayed a little polish. Mike wanted to ask her more. Maybe she knew about what was behind the riveted metal door. He looked across towards the corridor. The door to his room was half open, her trolley of cleaning materials standing outside. He felt sure somebody was listening out there, Miss Schindler maybe, come to check up on his health. He had to take a chance on being overheard.

'So when do you go home?'

She continued to work as she spoke.

'Tomorrow I go back down. One week down, one week up.'

'I see,' said Mike. 'So they rotate the staff.'

476

'Rotay?' She was looking at him, her duster poised over the desk.

'They change the cleaning staff.'

'Change, yes. One week down, one week up.'

Mike tried to think how he could ask her about what went on behind the riveted door he had discovered. Maybe he would just bluff it; say something like – *so you just do the rooms and then you clean the laboratory?* But it seemed like a big risk. Maybe she had strict instructions about talking of what went on inside the mountain. If he wasn't supposed to know about that side of things, it would probably confuse her if he brought it up. She might mention it to someone else, someone more important, and then his cover would be gone. She had almost finished in the sitting room. She put the cleaning materials back on her trolley and then went through to the bathroom. He racked his brains trying to think of the right question.

'All finish very soon,' she said, her voice reverberating against the marble.

'You go upstairs now,' he said. 'And take a rest, yes?'

'Not so soon,' she called back, her voice accompanied by the sound of nylon scrubbing against enamel.

'In the back. One hour.'

She came to the doorway, the brush still in her hand.

'Five to six in the back,' she said, pointing at her watch. '*Then* I finish.'

She picked up her things and left, closing the door quietly as she went out.

Mike came away from the window and sat down. He closed his eyes like a man with vertigo. *In the back.* Did she mean through into the back of the clinic, inside the mountain? He looked at his watch, jerking his hand abruptly. *Five to six.* Did she mean she went through into the back at five to six or that she worked for an hour cleaning from five to six o'clock when she came back into the clinic?

It was twenty-five past four according to his watch. If she was going to go through the door at five he had to follow her. But how? He couldn't bribe her. And anyway she probably worked with a team of cleaners.

He stood up, jerked up onto his feet with his anger and frustration. Suddenly all the energy drained out of him, and he sat back down. He realised how futile the whole thing was. There was no way he could ever get to Cathy, if she was even there, if there *was* a laboratory. The thought that she might be hundreds of miles away or dead somewhere, her beautiful eyes closed forever, came to him with the full force of certain truth.

Here he was pretending to be a multimillionaire needing a nose job to save a woman who didn't even want to see him, if she were still alive at all. It was too grotesque. He brought his hands together, twisting them, searching in himself for something to sustain him, some kind of resource, but there was nothing. He was empty.

He sat like that for ten minutes, a quarter of an hour, his lips parted, his hands palms upward on his knees. Then he thought of the steam he had seen coming out of the rock. If there was ventilation maybe there were shafts. Maybe he could crawl through to the back. It was an idea he had been turning over in his mind all day. Now he felt it like something dead in his mouth. A dead, stupid idea, pressing down on his tongue like clay.

He stood up and went to the door of his room. He had no choice. Somehow he had to follow the woman through the metal door. That was where Cathy was. He had to believe it. He looked down at his hand on the door handle. It was no longer his hand. He clenched his eyes tight shut and opened the door.

Moving was easier than standing still. That was the first thing he realised when he was out in the corridor. In the distance he could see the woman's trolley with its cleaning materials. The door to one of the other rooms was open, and he could hear her voice. She was speaking Italian to one of the other cleaners. He looked at his watch as he walked. It was ten minutes to five. He knew he was going towards the metal door, but he had no other clear idea of what he was going to do.

In the reception area, a different girl was talking to one of the uniformed boys who was holding the fur coat which Mike had been given to keep himself warm. There was snow on the floor. A new arrival. Without questioning whether they would look up or ask themselves what he was doing, he went through the door into the corridor that led to the riveted entrance.

He walked past the heat treatment room, oblivious to the voices within, oblivious too to the smell. Then he turned the corner and was facing the door. Nothing had changed. Then, with perfect lucidity, but seemingly without thinking, he opened the door to the broom closet on his left and stepped inside.

The darkness brought him back to himself in a rush. It was as if he were coming round after having been unconscious. The smell of the cleaning materials was sharp in his head. He heard the blood throbbing in his ears. The thought of the risk he was taking made him tremble. He had to clench his fists to stop his hands shaking. What happened? It was unlike anything that had ever happened to him. Something had brought him to this dark space, and he knew it wasn't his own will. He couldn't have willed such a bold, lucid act.

He heard the door at the end of the corridor come open, and the voices of the women. He tensed, leaning forward, listening. It sounded as if there were only two of them. They were talking in Italian. As they came nearer he could hear the wheels of the women's trolley on the linoleum. As if to hide himself better, Mike stepped back in the dark, his hand knocking against some broom handles as he did so. Then the full danger of his situation became clear to him. *The women were coming to take things from the broom closet.* They would need polishes, cloths, maybe clean overalls for the laboratory. Each step brought them closer to discovering him. He saw the door open and the light falling on his terrified face as if it had already happened to someone else. The wheels of the trolley seemed to be running along his raw nerves. Then they stopped.

They were directly outside the door of the closet. When the woman spoke, her voice was loud. Mike shut his eyes. The other woman laughed softly, conspiratorially. Something brushed against the door. Then he heard the trolley move again. They were walking away from him. He heard them stop at the door, silent now. Something was happening, but he didn't dare look. There was a deep subterranean clunk, and the door opened. Mike reached forward for the handle and turned it noiselessly. He peered out through the crack and saw the second woman going in through the door. He could see how thick it was, and inside, he saw that the white walls were brilliantly lit with neon. The second woman moved out of sight and the door began to close. It moved slowly as though on a hydraulic hinge. Holding his breath, Mike stepped out in the passage unable to believe that his chance had come. He took a step forward to meet the closing door, but in that instant voices seemed to explode behind him. More women were coming in from the main building; probably cleaners from the same team. He just had time to get back in the closet as they came round the corner. The last thing he saw as he closed the door to the closet was the steel door coming to with a heavy clunk. One of the cleaners cursed.

8

The Phönixlager. March 5th, 1996.

Mike watched Katya Schindler's face as she spoke. They
were in a small, windowless room lined with white ceramic
tiles.

'I don't understand. Why should they . . .'

But whoever was speaking on the other end cut her
short. The voice droned on. As she listened Miss Schindler's transparent blue eyes focused on Mike's face. He
was sitting in a kind of dentist's chair, wrapped in a
starched green robe. His hair had been covered with a
tight-fitting green cap. He looked worried.

The morning had gone from bad to really bad. He
had woken up ravenous, having missed dinner the night
before. When he called through to room service they
asked him if he was the Mr Diaz who was going into the
operating theatre that morning. *Yes, I guess I am*, he
heard himself say, and had hung up. The realisation that
he had run out of time and would finally have to go
through with the operation sat against him like a heavy
weight. They were going to break his nose, maybe even
cut something out of his face with their sharp knives. It
scared him. He had gone into the bathroom to take a last
look at his nose.

Miss Schindler had come to his room almost immediately afterwards to explain that the operation would take

place at eleven o'clock. He wanted to make an excuse, to claim that his cold hadn't quite left him, but the expression on her face made this seem like an impossibility. Since then he had been in her capable hands.

'Well, of course. Yes. No, everything is ready.'

She listened for a moment longer, and then put the phone down. She frowned, her eyes fixed on his face.

'Is there a problem?'

She became aware suddenly of the impression she was making. A stiff smile opened under her finely modelled nose.

'There's no problem, just a slight change. Nothing to worry about. In fact you should be flattered.'

Mike searched her face, trying to guess what she was thinking.

'What change?'

'Well our cosmetic surgery specialist, that was him on the phone, our specialist for this kind of thing is not going to be carrying out the operation.'

Mike felt an ice-cold ribbon unwind along his spine. Someone knew. Someone had been telling stories about him. He blinked once, trying to control his face.

'I don't understand.'

Miss Schindler continued to smile.

'It's really nothing to worry about.'

She brought her hands together and sat next to him. 'It seems that two other surgeons expressed an interest in your case. This happens from time to time. When we have a particularly interesting case and – '

Mike cut her short.

'What's so interesting about my case?'

His voice came out louder than he had meant. For the first time Miss Schindler looked genuinely perplexed. She frowned at him for a moment, and then shook her head.

'It needn't be something that we, as laymen, would be able to see or understand. Nor is it necessarily a question of your being particularly interesting. It may be that something has been developed here in the Phönixlager, some new technique, surgical or biochemical' – she opened her hand and looked at the palm – 'and they want to take this opportunity to use it.'

Mike felt the sweat squeeze under his green cap.

'I'm not sure I like the idea of being a guinea pig for new – '

'Mr Diaz, I'm sure that when you spoke to Mr Bruggman he told you that what goes on here at the Phönixlager really is very special. We are talking about some of the world's leading surgeons. There is absolutely no question of trying out things which are not fully understood. It is simply that things developed in our research department feed through into our standard practice, and this may require the intervention of some of our leading people. But I assure you, if you were to look at our records for cosmetic treatments you will find them impeccable.'

'So who is going to be doing the cutting?'

Miss Schindler compressed her lips in an expression which was beginning to be familiar to him. Then her expression changed.

'Well, that's the extraordinary thing. I mean that is what surprised me. You see Mr Steffen – that's the surgeon I just spoke to – said that our director of research himself will be supervising the operation. His deputy Doctor Kessler will carry out the work.'

She looked at Mike again, trying to guess why the request had been made.

'Edward Geiger is a genius,' she said, as if repeating an incantation. 'You should be very flattered.'

Then she stood up and excused herself, going out through the swing doors.

Mike lifted his hands from the arm rests. His palms glistened with sweat. He did not know what to do. Was this something to do with his search for Cathy? Or was it

483

simply a novelty, some change in procedure which had put Miss Schindler off her stride? He wiped his hands on his sterile robes and gripped the arm rests. He had to think of what was best for Cathy. He could insist on being treated by Mr Steffen, whoever he was, but this would only give rise to more explanation from Miss Schindler, and anyway, by coming to the clinic he had put his faith in the whole set-up, not in any particular doctor. There was no argument for insisting on Steffen, and if Geiger was a genius and the Phönixlager was the best, where was the danger?

Miss Schindler came back through the swing doors, smiling. She was carrying a small glass tumbler which contained a pinkish fluid. She handed it to Mike.

'This will help you to relax,' she said. Mike looked into the glass as if to see whether it held life or death, and then swallowed it down, fixing his mind on Cathy.

'We can go through now,' she said, still smiling.

They walked along a tiled corridor. Then they were in the operating theatre and Miss Schindler led him to a padded chair, articulated in three places.

The theatre was dimly lit, although suspended over his head was a system of lights which had yet to be illuminated. He tried to concentrate on the chrome rim around one of the lamps. In spite of the drug Miss Schindler had given him, he felt scared. He heard footsteps. Someone had come into the room. He didn't want to look, but then the idea that it would be Cathy herself made him turn his head. A shadowy face appeared next to his own, he tried to focus on the eyes which was all he could see over the mask.

'Mr Diaz.'

The voice was warm and syrupy. Another voice was near to him, vibrating in the air which seemed to have become thick and sweet.

'I am going to fix this into your arm, Mr Diaz, and then I am going to put you to sleep.'

There was a faint stinging sensation in his left wrist, and he tried to move his arm, but it had become heavy, immovable.

'I want you to start counting . . .'

The second voice boomed in his ear, seeming to disintegrate into furry lumps of sound, and then he was drowning, black nothingness flowing into him like water into the mouth of a drowning man.

9

The Phönixlager. March 5th, 1996.

She put down the violin as soon as Geiger opened the door. She looked terrible. There were several bruises on her face, and a cut on her bottom lip. For a moment he could not speak.

It irritated her, the way he watched her now. In the month she had been a prisoner their relationship had changed. At first his fixed stare had frightened her. He had looked at her as if he were not implicated, as if he were invisible to her, and was not himself observed. She was sure he watched her from behind the mirror. She had tried to look through the glass when the light in her room was switched off, but there was nothing. She knew he recorded her music. She had heard him play back tapes. But now he was self-conscious of her. He still watched her, but when she looked back at him he lowered his eyes. Since Lambert it was even worse. What confused her most was that it wasn't just remorse he felt. There was something more.

'That's a beautiful piece you were playing,' he said. Cathy watched him. He looked as though he had something to say to her. 'I think I prefer the Amati to the Stradivarius in this reduced space.'

Still Cathy did not reply. She dropped the violin onto the bed as if it were nothing to her.

'Cathy I – '

'If you try to apologise to me for what happened I will, I will . . .' She collapsed against the wall, racked with sobs. It was too grotesque. He was apologising for Lambert as if he were innocent. He was crazy, mad. His voice close to her, low, reassuring, made her turn. His face was close to hers. He had a faint soapy smell.

'Cathy, I know you think I am no better than, than *that* person. But you must believe that I think I am. I want the best for you that is possible. Your freedom is incompatible with the needs of science but – '

'Incompatible!' Cathy could only stare.

Geiger nodded and attempted a smile.

'Just remember my promise, Cathy.'

'What promise?'

'I said that nothing that I will do to you cannot be undone. Remember that.'

Cathy frowned. Geiger looked at her mouth.

'How is your lip?' She said nothing. She saw that he was struggling for some kind of communication, some kind of link. 'As Proust says, the Stradivarius is for oratory whereas the Amati is for conversation,' he said after a moment.

'Oh yes,' said Cathy. 'The Amati is a much better instrument for a prison.'

He waited a moment longer. Cathy stood her ground. Then he turned and went out of the room.

She had never seen him so worked up. She stood for a long time in the centre of the room, trying to work out what was happening. Then she picked up the delicate Amati and set it against her pale throat.

10

The Phönixlager. March 5th, 1996.

Mike felt as though he were rising through water. There was a rushing sound in his ears and as he approached the swirling surface, the first pain. It felt like something had been driven hard into the centre of his face; a spike or peg. There was no burning, or stinging, just a dull ache, as if his face had been partially demolished and something heavy had been set into it. He tried to understand what had happened and wanted to lift his hand to the area where his nose had been, but his limbs were like lead. He shouted, or tried to shout, but the sound he made seemed to come to him from a great distance. Then he realised that his mouth was parched. He swallowed and his ears popped. Suddenly his head was full of real sound. An interior. Someone was talking. He heard a tap running into what sounded like a metal basin. The clarity of the sound was exquisite. Then his mind caught on the voices of the two men who were talking. He sensed that they were standing in front of him. He tried to open his eyes, but the lids were heavy. As he listened he realised that it was a voice he had heard before.

'The patient should come round in another twenty minutes.'

It was a woman's voice, Miss Schindler's perhaps. It

sounded close. He felt the pressure of a hand on his sleeve.

'That's fine, Katya, I will look after that. If you could just leave us alone now.'

Mike recognised the voice of the man. It was the thick voice that had asked him to count himself to sleep. There were footsteps and then a door closed. Immediately the two men in front of him began to speak in violent, suppressed whisperings. They were speaking in English.

'This is hardly the time or the place, Mr Krystal. You are not even properly dressed for the theatre.'

'I'm sorry, Professor, but I have instructions which I must – '

'Instructions!'

' – which I must follow. Yes Professor, instructions.'

Adrenalin and fear rushed through his drugged body and with an enormous effort Mike managed to lift his eyelids. His view of the room was partially obscured by a gauze dressing which had been wound around his head, across the bridge of his new nose. But above the frayed strands of gauze he could see the suntanned face of the man he knew to be Ernst Krystal, the man who had tried to have him killed.

'Ah, here we are.'

Suddenly his view was blocked by the face of another man, a third, the man with the deep voice. This man began to touch Mike's head. There was a rustling sound as his hands worked at the bandages around his head. Mike tried to concentrate on what was being said, by Krystal and the man he had called Professor.

'The problem is we are running out of time, Professor Geiger.'

The man who was attending to his bandages stepped back and again Mike could see Krystal's animated face. Would he be able to recognise him from their brief meeting at the airport? As if the killer could hear Mike's thoughts, he turned and looked at him. Mike lowered his eyes. His mouth felt like paper. Then he realised what the man standing directly in front of him was doing. Working very carefully, hardly touching his face, he was removing the bandages from his head. He passed his hands across his face, and the gauze which had obstructed his gaze was gone.

'I have always done everything possible to accommodate the imperatives of the board, Mr Krystal, but I am afraid that in this case I cannot back down.'

Mike raised his eyes, as another swathe of gauze was removed.

'But as long as she is here we are running a serious risk.'

Mike jerked back in his chair. The two men stopped talking and looked at him for a moment. They looked surprised that he should be awake.

'Careful of the dressing, Egon.'

The man working on his bandages looked into Mike's eyes.

'I'm nearly finished now, Mr Diaz. I'm going to leave the dressing on the nose. You are going to have to be very careful with that for a week or so.'

Mike stared at the friendly face, tensed for the moment in which it moved away revealing him to Krystal. What could he do? He tried to move but the drugs seemed to have filled him with lead. His heart started to pound. His breath came rasping through his mouth.

'The patient seems to be in some distress,' said the man closest to him. Mike felt more bandages come away. This was it. He would die now, and Cathy was so near! The *she* Krystal had spoken of had to be Cathy, it couldn't be anyone else.

The voice said: 'He's fighting against the anaesthetic.'

Then the face moved away, so that the bright overhead lights fell directly onto Mike's puffy face, and the pristine dressing which covered his nose. The man called Geiger had moved between Mike and Krystal. All Mike could see was Geiger's broad back.

'We had better carry on this conversation in another room,' said Geiger. Then Mike was alone with the doctor. He let his head roll back.

'That's better, just relax.'

11

Brig. March 6th, 1996.

The mortuary photographer wasn't more than thirty years old, with sandy-coloured hair, a thin moustache and glasses. He lived in a small apartment block overlooking the railway, with his wife, who looked older than he did by a few years, and a baby who cried a lot. His name was Greber. The furniture in his flat was cheap, and through the walls you could hear the neighbours talking, or the sound of their televisions, or more usually both at the same time. From this Waterman deduced that photographing stiffs was not a well-paid profession in Switzerland, at least not in a small town like Brig.

'Listen,' he said, leaning across the coffee table, upon which lay a heap of old wax crayons and several plastic farm animals. 'What I mean is, the photographs we have don't tell us very much. There's not enough detail. We need better prints.'

Greber sat listening on the edge of a small sofa, his hands locked together in front of him. Like most people on a tight budget confronted with something unusual like this, he was torn between the fear of getting into trouble and the hope of making some easy money.

'You think my pictures no good?' he said. 'You are going to complain?'

'Hell no, Mr Greber. We just need some more. Better ones.'

Greber nodded. The fear was still on top by the look of things.

'You not complain, *ja*?' he said again.

Waterman caught sight of Frau Greber. She was watching from the kitchen, the baby in her arms. Most of the kid's supper looked like it was dribbling down its face, but at least the sight of the stranger was enough to stop it yelling for a while.

'No, I'm not going to complain. I just need better pictures, better prints.'

'Have you asked the authorities? The police?'

Waterman shook his head.

'You haven't say my pictures no good?'

'I haven't said anything to anybody – and I won't – if I can get some more from you.'

He waited for the point to sink in and then added: 'I will pay for them, of course.'

'*Ja*,' said Greber, nodding. The hope was starting to come through at last. 'But what is wrong with the pictures? No one complain before. They say maybe I get job in Basle.'

Waterman took out the photographs he had been given at the American consulate and, clearing aside the crayons and farm animals, placed them on the coffee table.

'You see? No detail. All washed out.'

Greber picked up the prints and looked at them one after the other.

'*Ja*, these very bad. But I not print them.'

'Sure, I never meant to say that it was your fault personally. The point is . . .'

'But where you get these? These are not from my studio. I never pass these.'

Waterman looked puzzled.

493

'I got them from the US consulate, and they got them from the Police here.'

Greber shook his head again.

'These *not* from my studio. These are not the pictures I took.'

As he was speaking a big diesel went by outside, sounding its horn, making all the windows rattle. The baby started to cry again and its mother started jogging it up and down on her shoulder. Then she disappeared from view. In one of the next-door flats someone turned the television up louder.

'You mind if I smoke?' said Waterman, taking out a pack of cigarettes. 'You want one?'

Greber looked back towards the kitchen and nodded.

'Thanks.'

Waterman gave him a light.

'Let me get this clear,' he said, taking a drag. 'These are not the pictures you took of Matt McArthur?'

Greber shook his head again.

'Same *negatives*, different prints. I give both to morgue for their records. I not keep negatives.'

'And how many prints do you normally make?'

Greber shrugged.

'Depends. Maybe six. With the movie star, I think more – twelve maybe.'

'I see.'

Waterman thought for a moment. Then something occurred to him.

'Say, you didn't keep any of those prints for yourself, by any chance – just for the records, I mean.'

Greber exhaled slowly. Then he got up, opened the window a little, and sat down again.

'No. It's *verboten* – not allowed. I never do that. Only have contacts. Very small.'

Waterman tried looking Greber in the eye, but he suddenly seemed interested in arranging the wax crayons on the table.

'That's a shame,' he said. 'I mean, it can't be every day someone that famous gets wheeled into the morgue, can it? It sure would be something to show your grandchildren.'

'My wife not like pictures like that, with the baby and everything.'

Waterman sat back in his chair.

'Sure but it could be worth something. Hell, I know a cheap-shot journalist in LA who'd have just loved pictures like that for his story. You ever seen *Exclusive!* magazine?'

Greber shook his head.

'They pay big money for anything like that: dead actors, pop stars drying out some place, politicians at strip joints. It's their stock in trade.'

'How much they pay?' said Greber.

'Thousands of dollars – *tens* of thousands for someone big, like McArthur.'

Greber laughed. The fear was gone. Now there was only the hope. Waterman let the numbers sink in: ten thousand dollars could make a lot of difference to someone, especially if they didn't have it.

'Of course I don't have that kind of money myself,' he said. 'But then I only want to look at the pictures. I don't want to publish them.'

Greber was still toying with the crayons on the table, his eyes narrow to keep out the smoke. Waterman could tell he was enjoying the cigarette, probably because he'd been forced to give up – for the baby's sake was it, or just to save money? Waterman slid the packet towards him. Greber took a fresh cigarette and lit it from the old. Then he stood up.

'Okay, come,' he said.

He led Waterman out of the living room into what

looked like the only bedroom in the place. There were two single beds pushed together against the far wall and a cot just in front of the door. There were closets along one wall, but Greber had to move the cot to get them open. Through the window could be seen the very edge of the town with the steep wooded slopes beyond them, lit up brightly by the moon.

From the top-most cupboard Greber pulled down a cardboard box, full of screwed up pieces of newspaper. He put the box down on the ground and started sifting around inside. Finally he produced a fat plastic folder, full of black and white prints.

They weren't all stiffs by any means, even from the doorway Waterman could see that. There were a handful of straight portraits, and a whole lot of nudes too, mostly of the obscene variety; big white thighs encased in fishnet stockings, tongues curling salaciously towards upper lips, the usual ugly parody. He didn't reckon they could fetch much, judging not so much from the quality of the pictures as the quality of the women, but that wasn't his business. He waited for Greber to hand him what he wanted to see.

The light was bad by the door, and to get a better look he went to the little bedside table and switched on the reading light. These prints of McArthur were completely different from the ones the consulate had given him. They were slightly bigger, sharper and carefully exposed so that all the detail on the torso was visible, every mole and every freckle.

'Some lens you got there,' he said. 'You got a magnifying glass I could use?'

Greber went back to the cardboard box and produced one with a silver handle that looked as if it had started life as a piece of cutlery. Waterman took it and scanned the pictures again, first the one taken from the side, then

496

the other, taken from above. At first he saw nothing unusual, but then . . .

There it was as plain as day: a small white scar, barely an inch wide, just below the fifth rib. McArthur was skinny enough that you could count them. That was why the pictures given to the US authorities had been of poor quality. They had been doctored to conceal the evidence of surgery – surgery that was supposed never to have taken place.

'You seen now?' said Greber. 'I take very good pictures, *ja?* No complaints.'

Waterman reached for his wallet.

'No complaints at all, Mr Greber,' he said, 'none whatsoever.'

'How much someone pay for these?'

Waterman smiled.

'Could be a lot so long as you're careful. So long as you put them safely in one of those banks you got here.'

'In a bank? Why must I use a bank?'

'Because,' said Waterman, handing over a hundred and fifty francs, 'if anyone finds out you've got them, you may not even live to spend what I'm giving you.'

12

The Phönixlager. March 6th, 1996.

He watched the thread of saliva pull down into the milky vomit and breathed the sharp smell of disinfectant in the bowl. It was the third time he had vomited and there seemed to be nothing left to bring up. Another spasm gripped his stomach but all he could find was spittle. Katya Schindler had warned him about the after-effects of the anaesthetic, but he hadn't expected anything so dramatic. He leaned back from the toilet and rested his head against the open door. He had slept solidly for eighteen hours. Consciousness and a splitting headache had been exchanged for sleep at about eight o'clock when he had first rushed into the bathroom, his hand over his mouth. Now he was feeling slightly better. He just felt like he was going to die.

Gripping the sink, he raised himself up and looked in the mirror. A stranger with a meringue-sized lint dressing on his nose stared back through small red eyes. Mike looked down at the plug-hole and spat copiously. He tried to put his thoughts in order. The long night's sleep had been so full of violent nightmares, it was difficult to separate reality from dream. But what kept coming back were the words Krystal had spoken in the operating theatre – *as long as she is here we are all in danger.*

So Cathy was here. Somewhere near. Who else could

he have meant? It had to be her. He opened the faucet and splashed cold water on his eyes, avoiding the dressing. What he didn't understand was why Cathy should represent a danger to them. Had she come across something in her research like the guy on the stairs, Waterman, had said? Mike touched at the dressing on his nose. What did they intend to do with her? Why had they held her in the first place? Why wasn't she already dead? There were so many questions.

'Ouch.'

Lost in his thoughts he had touched a particularly sensitive part of the new nose. He looked in the mirror. What had they done to him? But there was no time to worry about that. Cathy was imprisoned somewhere in the clinic, probably through the door he had found, somewhere inside the mountain, and her time was running out. He knew how to get through that door, but even if he got through by following the last of the cleaners they would see him as soon as he was on the other side. He could try looking official, but his own cleaner would be bound to recognise him. Anyway, it was going to be pretty tough looking official with the meringue on his nose. He had to think of something else.

By early afternoon the anaesthetic had worked out of his system. He had managed to hold down his lunch and was ready to face Katya Schindler who was due to arrive at three o'clock.

He was lying on the bed, trying to decide whether to risk leaving a message for Tania at the ski school to let her know what he had discovered, when there was a knock on the door.

'How are you feeling?'

Miss Schindler was out of uniform for some reason and was wearing black. It brought out a sinister side in her symmetrical good looks that made her more attractive.

499

'No news is good news, I guess.'

She smiled at his expression, not understanding a word of what he had said.

'You will have to wear the dressing for a week or so.'

'How often will I have to change it?'

'You can't change it. It has to be kept as clean as possible. Nothing must disturb the epidermis for at least five days. There is a risk of infection.'

'Great.'

'All you have to do is rest and keep your nose clean.'

Mike's eyes cut across to her delicately curved mouth. There was no hint of a smile. Miss Schindler didn't make jokes.

After she had gone he went into the lounge and stood looking out at the mountains. The afternoon was sliding into five o'clock, the moment at which he had an opportunity to go into the mountain, and still he didn't know what he was going to do. He pictured himself standing before the steel door, but he couldn't imagine himself on the other side. The cleaners would go through the door which would slowly close on its hydraulic hinge. But if he followed they were bound to see him. He couldn't wait until they had gone ahead, unless . . .

Mike took a step towards the thick glass window. His breath came and went in a little round of mist on the cold glass. There was a moment, the moment in which the door was closing, in which he could step forward and block the door. If he put something in the door after the cleaners had gone through he would be able to wait for them to go on into the laboratory. They might notice that the door didn't click shut, but he would have to take a chance on that. And once inside . . . what was he supposed to do then? He brought his hand to the dressing on his nose, and lowered it again, thoughtfully. It was no use trying to see what would happen afterwards. He would have to somehow find Cathy. That was all there

500

was to it. Maybe he would get lucky. He looked down at his trousers. The least he could do would be to disguise himself a little. Maybe put on cleaner's overalls. He thought of the broom closet in the corridor where he had seen the overalls on the first day, and went immediately to the door of his room.

The corridor was empty. He walked quickly to the closet and opened the door. Using the faint light of the corridor he looked for the light switch. There was no sign of anything by the door. He could make out coats and overalls hanging up on the other side of the small room. He reached in and took a couple of coats. Then, checking that there was still no one in the corridor, he rushed back to his room.

In the light from the panoramic window, he saw that one of the coats was for a woman. The other was larger but also looked distinctly feminine. There were large grey buttons and a patch pocket on the left breast. He slipped on the coat and went into the bathroom to look at himself. He wished he hadn't.

At ten minutes to five he was in the closet outside the steel door. He had walked in from the main clinic, the work-coat wrapped in a towel, a copy of the *Wall Street Journal* in his left hand. No one seemed to pay him any attention. If the girl at the desk had noticed him she pretended not to.

He put the coat on in the dark and folded the newspaper into a wedge. He would wait for the last of the cleaners to go through – he was pretty sure there was a team of four – and then step forward to wedge the door. He stood in the total dark breathing the faint smell of eggs and newsprint through the antiseptic smell of the dressing.

Someone said something in the room behind him where a treatment was going on. He tried to control his breathing, but as the moment approached he felt his heart begin to race and his breath came in shorter gasps. It seemed that he stood like that for an hour, the sweat trickling down his temples. Then, at last, the door opened at the end of the corridor and he heard the voice of his cleaning lady. His pulse beating in his throat, he listened to them come on down the corridor. One, two, three, four, five, six paces and they came round the corner. They stopped outside the closet. Mike gripped the newspaper, praying that they would not discover him. There was a rustling sound and he heard the steel door clunk open. They pushed the trolley through. Mike checked the impulse to look. He had to wait for the next pair of cleaners. That would be the moment to make his move.

He listened hard in the silence which followed the closing of the steel door. Again someone said something in the room behind him. It sounded like German. There was the sound of a loud slap and then some laughter. He listened with his ear pressed against the door, but there was nothing. Maybe there were only two cleaners today. His hand was wet around the tightly rolled newspaper. The strain was giving him a headache. His nose hurt too. There was a dull throbbing pain in the centre of his face. Then he froze as he heard a door open, but it was only someone coming out of the mud room. Loud voices boomed in German and then faded as the door into the main clinic closed. The silence returned. Mike thought he was going to go crazy. He scratched wildly at his scalp which was damp with sweat.

After what seemed like ten minutes at least he opened the door of the broom closet and peered out. The light in the corridor had been switched off. It was pitch dark. He pushed the door open just a little more and stepped out. At that moment the light snapped on and he heard loud female voices speaking in urgent, staccato Italian. They were late. They came on down the corridor bustling,

502

pushing the trolley of cleaning materials. Mike just had time to get back in the closet.

'Ma yo, non ho fatto niente!'

'Ecco tua problema.'

Outside the closet they fell silent, and one of them leaned against the closet door. Mike could hear her breathing. Then there was the clunk of the heavy locks and they pushed the trolley through into the interior of the mountain. Mike counted one second and then opened the door a crack. The last woman was just moving out of sight. Holding his breath he stepped forward, the rolled newspaper extended in front of him. The door was closing. He wedged the paper between the door and the frame. It closed on the paper as though it had been a Kleenex. The bolts thumped into their sockets. Unable to believe his eyes, Mike looked at the piece of newspaper which was still sticking out of the door. Someone would see it! He pulled at the paper and half of it came away in his hand. Suddenly there were voices behind him. He stumbled back into the closet, his head pounding.

'So even if the results aren't ready by the weekend we can set up the second stage on the basis of the computer models.'

It was a man's voice. Mike waited for the moment in which they would discover the newspaper. There was a moment's silence and then the door opened. The man walked through without another word. After they had gone Mike peered out of the closet. There was no sign of anything on the floor.

He looked down at himself. He was still wearing the work-coat. He stripped it off and bundled it into the closet. Then he made his way back along the corridor to his own room.

Once inside, he filled a tumbler with scotch and took a long drink. His head felt like it was about to explode.

'Fuck.'

He walked across to the window and looked out at the darkness. He finished the scotch, and swore again, softly this time.

'I'm screwing this up, Cathy.'

He put his hand into his mouth and bit the fingers. The pain was soothing. There were tears in his eyes.

'Cathy.'

He walked back and forth across the room, touching lightly at his nose, which, now that his head was hurting less, had started to ache. Eventually he sat down in one of the plush armchairs, exhausted.

When he woke up it was half past seven. He looked at his watch in disbelief, and stood up as if he had somewhere to go. But where was he to go? He looked out at the dark mountains. There was only one place left to try.

As far as he could remember, the jet of vapour he had seen when the helicopter was landing had appeared more or less directly over the central block of the clinic. It seemed to him that the only way of getting to the vent – if that was what it was – the only way to get to it was by climbing up the mountain. But how was he supposed to get outside? There was no way he could just walk past the girl at the reception desk. Maybe he could create a diversion, get her to leave her desk for a moment. He thought hard. Nothing came. Then he thought of the terrace on the first floor. If he could get out onto the terrace he might find a way up onto the rock. The Japanese wrestlers might see him, but that was a risk he had to take. And there was the girl. How was he going to get past her? She always seemed to have her nose buried in her magazine, but what if she looked up?

Mike stamped his foot hard. It was hardly audible in the thick carpet. He was procrastinating again. The only way to do this thing was to do it. Fuck the receptionist!

If she asked him what he was doing he'd just say he wanted a change of scenery.

Approaching the reception area, his doubts returned and he began to slow down. He was wearing a roll-neck sweater and pants. It was going to be pretty cold out on the mountain. He almost came to a halt, but then he urged himself on. Without looking over at the girl he walked towards the elevator door and pressed the button. It seemed to take forever to come down. He felt sure the girl was looking across at him – could feel her eyes on the back of his neck. His scalp crept and he gave an involuntary shiver. But the door opened, and there was no voice calling him to account for himself. He stepped forward into the illuminated box. The door closed behind him.

On the first floor he looked left expecting to see the Jap bodyguards. There was nothing. Just silence, and the corridor funnelling away to darkness. The door to the terrace was just next to the lift. There was an aluminium handle and an old-fashioned keyhole. He gripped the handle which was surprisingly cold and pushed down. It didn't move.

'Shit.'

It was locked. He looked through the glass door at the terrace, but it was difficult to see beyond his own reflection. The dressing on his nose looked huge, comical. Then he noticed the snow and ice all around the edge of the glass panel. Maybe it was just frozen. He put his hand on the handle again and pushed down, slowly increasing the pressure. When it gave, he let out a cry which sounded deafening in the silence. He bit his tongue, looking along the corridor to where the bodyguards would emerge. There was nothing. Then he pushed the door. It didn't move. He pulled it towards him, but it clearly didn't open inwards. Then he leaned back and threw his shoulder against it.

He couldn't believe how cold the air was. It cut through his sweater like a knife. The wind, which had been completely inaudible inside, howled across the face of the mountain throwing a fine grit of ice particles against his face. Fearing for his dressing, he advanced with one hand over his nose, the other clamped under his armpit for warmth. There was a thin sliver of moon which illuminated the virgin snow on the terrace. Sun-loungers were stacked ready for the better weather. He walked forward slowly, bracing himself against the wind, until he came to a balustrade.

He could see the empty helipad and the faint glow from the reception area of the clinic. His teeth were chattering uncontrollably and the left side of his face had already gone numb. He put his back to the balustrade and looked up at the face of the mountain to the place where he thought he had seen the vent. The mountain was all ribbed and notched. Weak shadows from the moonlight suggested depressions or maybe even caves, but he could see nothing that looked vaguely like an artificial hole. A strong gust of wind threw more ice against his face, and he looked back at the entrance to the terrace. The weak light of the corridor looked inviting and warm, but he knew he couldn't go back. Once he had started he knew that there was no way of stopping. Inaction was torture. He had to go on.

He looked for a place where he could get onto the rock. At one point on the terrace the balustrade disappeared into the mountain and there was a crevice running diagonally away from a cement upright. Urging himself forward, he staggered back across the terrace. A blast of ice particles lashed his face making his ear sting with the cold. He tried to cover the dressing on his nose. It was wet and felt like it was coming away in one place. He pressed himself against the cement upright which provided a little shelter for a moment. Yes, one of the strips of plaster which held the dressing in place had come away. He tried to press it back but his nose was too painful. *All you have to do is keep your nose clean.*

He shook his head and looked up at the crevice which ran upwards away from the terrace. The rock looked dark, hostile. It was black where the drifting snow hadn't taken a grip. He shouted out as he urged himself up onto the edge of the balustrade, but his voice was whipped away by the wind.

Another blast threatened to push him over the edge of the balustrade. It wasn't a long drop but he knew that if he fell it would all be finished. If he didn't break something he knew he wouldn't have the strength to climb back up, and he couldn't just walk in through the front door. If he knocked himself out he would freeze to death in five minutes. He squinted against the biting wind and looked for a place to grip. About a foot from where he stood there was a little foothold. Mike reached forward with his foot, but it was too far. Then, blindly, no longer really conscious of what he was going, he threw himself across the gap.

He had struck his head. It had made him dizzy for a moment. Now the blood was trickling down his forehead and into his eyes. But surprisingly the wind had dropped. He was squeezed into the crevice, the black rock pressing against his shoulders. It was uncomfortable, but it gave a little shelter. He looked up to where he wanted to go. But where was he going? He realised for a moment that he had abandoned any plans other than the simple idea of going up. It was a dangerous way to think. The cold was making him euphoric, crazy. He had to keep control. He would work his way up the mountain, looking down, using the terrace to keep his bearings, and he would look for the air vent in the area he remembered having seen it. That was a plan. He blinked hard. His face was numb. There was no pain from the cut on his forehead. Lifting his left leg, he looked for a toe hold and then raised himself up.

'Don't worry, Cathy. I'm coming to get you.'

He continued to climb, saying Cathy's name. It reassured him to speak, even though he could hardly hear his own voice in the howling wind. He told her how he loved her, how he loved her hair and eyes, how she had misunderstood him, how he was going to make it up to her. After about ten minutes of slow climbing he rested against the sheltering rock. He breathed hard, pressing his frozen hands into his armpits. Ahead of him there was an exposed slope which was covered in snow. He felt the warmth of hope dying inside him. He had to check how far across he had come. He lifted himself out of the crevice and looked down. The wind struck against him, almost like a blow in the face. He covered his nose and squinted down at the rocks below.

There was nothing. All he could see was the rock face. Panic expanded in him. Then he saw the faint glow thrown across the snow by the reception area. It was away over to his right. He would have to re-traverse the rock if he was going to be anywhere near the vent. Then there was a strange noise. And he felt himself being shaken. He was laughing, laughing hysterically, the hot tears streaming from his eyes. He crept back into the cover of the crevice and tried to control his breathing. He looked back across the rock face. It looked very rough and broken. Higher up there were steel barriers to stop avalanches. A large boulder, capped with snow, jutted out of the steep slope.

Then he saw something else. He blinked hard, and pressed the water from his eyes with his numbed finger tips. It was a trail of some kind. Like a goat or sheep trail which had been widened by people. But then that was logical. If a vent had been pierced in the mountain, a certain amount of work would have been done from the outside. Men would have come up here to maintain it, to clear away snow during particularly heavy falls. Mike felt the adrenalin surge through him. He stumbled forward towards the trail.

It was easier going now, though he was less sheltered. The wind pressed against his back, and occasional blasts of ice whipped against him. But the movement helped, and he felt more alert, more in control. From time to time he looked down to where the clinic threw its ghostly light onto the snow. After what seemed like ten minutes he stopped. His breath came in short gasps, and his feet and hands were completely without feeling, like dead weights on the ends of his limbs. He looked down at himself. There was a crust of ice and snow on his left side and it felt as if it went right around his back. He had seen nothing that looked vaguely like an air vent. Standing still, he started to freeze up. He tried to say Cathy's name but his mouth wouldn't move. His lips hurt. A blast of snow and ice closed his eyes, and he felt himself falling backwards.

It was remarkable. Now that he was lying down, he felt relaxed and warm, as if he were back in the bedroom, back in Cathy's apartment in New York, her music on the stereo, a Bach violin partita. He saw the pictures on her walls and the piles of books and compact discs threatening to topple over at any minute. Then he saw Cathy's face, but it was strange somehow. Her eyes looked blank, and she had a tube going into her nose. He reached forward with both his hands to kiss her fore-head. He pushed the thick dark hair away to kiss her forehead, but it came away in his hands and he saw that she was bald and that there were metal tubes fixed into her head like the photographs of the cat he had seen at Anna's house. His eyes snapped open. For a moment he couldn't see. His face was covered with snow. He cleared his eyes with hands that were curved and hard like claws.

509

Lose consciousness and you'll die here. The thought dropped into his consciousness like a stone into a still pond. He felt the ripples of understanding expand. He pushed his tongue between frozen lips and bit hard.

The pain seemed to reach him from a distance. He drew his lower lip into his mouth. It felt like cold, dead meat, and he bit again, furious with himself, with his failure, his stupidity. There was a taste of blood and surprising heat in his mouth. He rocked his head from side to side and then jerked up as if he had been pulled by a wire. Sitting upright and blinking away the ice and snow, he saw the form drifting towards him. It was taller than a man, and translucent somehow, like a ghost. It was coming towards him quickly and he was sure he was about to die. Then it enveloped him completely and he was surprised to feel not the freezing dead cold he had expected, but warmth . . . and then it was gone, and he was still sitting there, blood oozing from his lip. Then, as he looked and blinked, another form rose out of the rock face about twenty feet below where he was sitting and he knew what it was. He had found the vent.

He staggered to his feet and started to move forward, but the ice, the steep slope and his complete exhaustion overcame him. He tripped and fell headlong, sliding down on his back, bumping against jutting rock. He came to rest about three feet from the hole. He crawled forward on his hands and knees, staring at the perfect black round. A thick steel grill covered the entrance. As he stared, more warmth rushed up, condensing in the freezing air over his head. He pushed his fingers into the mesh of the grill and pulled. It didn't move. He felt around the rim with his stiff fingers, looking for screws or clips, but it was round and smooth. Then he pushed as hard as he could. Still it didn't give. He sat back and looked at it for a moment. It seemed impossible that he could be defeated in the very last moment. The wind howled across the face of the mountain filling his ear with particles of ice. Then it was suddenly calm, as if someone had switched off the wind machine. He set his feet against the grill and kicked as hard as he could. Immediately the grill popped out of its frame and was gone, clattering down inside the ventilation shaft. Mike blinked, unable to move for a moment. Then, feet first, he worked his way into the black hole.

Inside the shaft there were ribs every couple of metres which were riveted in the same way the steel door had been. It felt like old, sturdy equipment from the fifties maybe. It sloped down fairly steeply, and he had to grip the ribs with his numbed hands to stop himself falling. After about five minutes he came up against the grill. It had lodged sideways in the shaft and he had to squeeze past. He stopped and looked up. There was the faintest suggestion of light in a distant round the size of a silver dollar. He breathed the warm air, and waited for the feeling to come back in his hands. He touched at the cut on his head which had started to throb, and he sucked at his lower lip which was bitten quite badly. But he was not going to die. He knew that he was not going to freeze to death, and he was at last inside the mountain. He couldn't be sure that the shaft would take him to where he wanted to go, but if the ventilation system also served the laboratories there was a good chance that he would be able to smell the difference and make his choice. Labs smelt like labs, didn't they? And the clinic smell, well he could recognise that.

He sat for a long time, letting the warmth creep back into his body. Then, taking a deep breath he reached down to the next ribbed join with his foot. After five minutes of slow descent the shaft started to level out. He turned, having to bend himself almost double to get round, until his head was facing forwards. Then he went forward on his hands and knees.

It was pitch black ahead of him. The air in the shaft kept changing. Sometimes it rushed past him in a light breeze smelling faintly antiseptic, then it seemed to drop a couple of degrees and slow down. It was hard work moving forward across the ribbed joins and his knees started to hurt.

After what seemed like a long time he stopped and listened. Apart from the air moving past his ears it was completely silent. If he turned his head he could hear the silence perfectly. The idea of the tons of rock pressing against the steel shaft was unnerving. He started to feel claustrophobic. He blinked as he went forward as if to get the blackness out of his eyes. He said Cathy's name between breaths, but the idea of arriving in the brightly lit laboratory was more frightening than being trapped in the dark, so he tried not to think, just to act.

The pain in his knees was unbearable. He stopped crawling and lay flat on his stomach, listening to his own deep-drawn breath. But there was something else. It sounded like tapping. He held his breath and listened: silence, the faint rush of air moving along the shaft. Then there was a distinct click, like the blades of a pair of scissors or shears coming together. It sounded close. He tried to identify where it was coming from. It was up ahead. Then there was silence again. What had made the sound? It could be some piece of machinery. A thermostat or something clicking on. But it had been a loud click, like something cutting through wire. Again he listened, but there was nothing.

He raised himself up on his knees, clenching his teeth against the pain. He moved forward a couple of feet and then reaching out with his left hand, almost fell headlong into the black emptiness. He caught his breath, and very carefully felt along the edge of the hole. There was another shaft which rose vertically into the one in which he found himself. It was smaller and the air smelt different, moister. He reached forward and felt inside the shaft. On one side there was a ladder. Once again he turned around so that his feet were facing forward. He rubbed his knees for a moment. Then he put his foot on the first rung of the ladder and tested its strength. He lowered himself a couple of feet and rested, leaning back against the other side of the shaft which was narrower than the one above. What was he supposed to do now? He had no idea of how far down he had come. For all he knew he might be below the clinic, moving down towards the lower floors where the cleaning staff had their rooms . . .

Click.

This time the noise cracked like a pistol shot. Mike almost lost his foothold, he was so startled. He had the distinct impression that the sound came from his left. Not directly ahead as he had first thought. He reached forward to what should have been the side of the larger shaft and found that there was nothing there. A hole corresponding in size to the one in which he was standing had been let into the side of the larger shaft. The same was true of the other side. He had reached some kind of junction.

He looked along the shaft from which the noise had come. Then he came up the ladder and went into the narrow shaft towards the noise. As he moved forward he breathed the antiseptic smell. It was quite powerful now. He stopped moving. Somewhere up ahead someone was moving around. He listened for the clicking sound again, and to his surprise heard what sounded like a voice. It was humming something. A tune that was familiar to him somehow, but which he couldn't for the moment place. Then there was the loud click again and a distinct sigh. Mike listened, his heart thumping like a hammer against the round floor of the shaft. Then, to his alarm, whoever it was in the shaft up ahead started to move towards him. He could hear the grunts of the person as he came forward, and the noise of his knees or elbows knocking

513

against the walls of the shaft. Mike started to retreat as quietly as possible. If he could climb down into the vertical shaft he would be out of sight. He began to move . . .

The shaft in which he was crawling was suddenly filled with light. It was like the light from a hand-held flashlight. It threw shadows in all directions. Mike saw the ribbed interior of the shaft receding towards the source of illumination. Then, as he watched, a figure carrying the flashlight moved across the hole at the end of the shaft and was gone.

The darkness returned. Mike could still see a faint flickering light at the end of his shaft. He moved forward as quickly as he could, hoping his own noise would be covered by the movement of the other man.

When he got to the end of the shaft he looked to his left in the direction the stranger had gone. He could see stray beams from the flashlight, and once again there was the loud click. Then he looked right and was surprised to see a more constant, though much dimmer light. An entrance? It was coming from the end of the shaft along which the other man had crawled. Where did it lead? Mike tried to work out what the other man had been doing. Some kind of maintenance work maybe. The air which drifted towards him along the shaft smelt like a laboratory. Then, as he hesitated at the end of the shaft, he heard music. It was barely audible, and at first he thought it was the stranger humming, it was certainly the same tune, but then, as he listened, he could hear that it wasn't made by a human voice. It was a violin. *It was Cathy, Cathy playing a violin*. He tried to climb to his feet and banged his head on the roof of the shaft. Then he started to crawl towards the sound.

There was a chance that the maintenance man would come back along the shaft and find him there; he had to move as fast as possible. He clenched his teeth against the stabbing pains in his knees, and fixed his thoughts on

Cathy. As he approached the source of light he slowed down. He stopped for a moment and listened. He could still hear the music, but it had been a while since he had heard the click of the shears. There was a sharp turn in the shaft and then he was in an even narrower stretch. There was hardly enough room for his shoulders. He crawled forward, blinking the sweat out of his eyes. Then he saw the hole.

It looked as if someone had removed the grill from a ventilation duct. There was a rectangular metal frame with some kind of clip on the bottom. He moved forward trying not to make a noise. Then he was at the hole and looking down at the grey linoleum on the floor of a corridor. The music stopped and he listened to the silence. Then the same piece started again. It sounded as if it might be a recording but it was difficult to be sure because it was so faint. He leaned into the hole and looked along the corridor to his left, the direction the music was coming from.

There was no other sound. The corridor was empty. He moved a little further along the shaft and then pushed his legs through the hole. He dropped to the linoleum floor, falling back against the wall. For a moment, he listened hard, crouching down. Then, as he slowly stood up he noticed the state his clothes were in. His pants were covered in black dirt which he had picked up inside the ventilation shafts. There were holes in both knees and dark stains where he had grazed himself. There was more blood on the sleeve of his sweater. The face of his watch was shattered, the hands fixed on a quarter past. His lower lip felt like an inflated rubber tube. He brought his hand to his nose and felt at the dressing. Miraculously it was still in place though some of the adhesive tape had come loose. How was he going to explain his appearance? He smiled at himself, pain lancing through his bottom lip. If he was found inside the laboratory, if that was where

515

he was, it wouldn't matter what he looked like: it would be the end.

Walking slowly, tensed for any other sound, he walked towards the music. It brought him to the end of the corridor and to double swing doors which opened onto a long tunnel-like corridor which was brightly lit with neon. Through the swing doors the music was louder. He moved swiftly, sliding along the wall as if that way he was less conspicuous.

With every step, he had a growing sense that he was walking into a trap. But nobody could know he was going to come down through the air duct, and anyway nobody knew he was in the clinic to look for Cathy. They had operated on him, and now he was waiting for the green light from Miss Schindler to leave. Yet, in spite of all the arguments, it felt like he was being set up. It seemed too good to be true. The music seemed to be leading him towards his lover. It was more like Walt Disney than real life.

He had come to a door, had almost gone past it, he was so lost in thought. Now he stopped. The music seemed to be coming from inside. This was it. Behind the door Cathy was playing a violin, or it was a trick and Krystal or one of his hoods was waiting to put an end to him. He looked down at his empty hands, and made fists. He would have liked a weapon, even if it was only a piece of wood, or a knife. The music came to a stop. Mike crouched at the door, every muscle in his body tensed. There was water on the floor. He noticed in a vague, abstracted way that it came from his clothing, from the melted ice and snow. The music began again as he burst into the room, unaware of a small security camera which clicked on as he opened the door.

A digital tape recorder stood on top of a cabinet in an empty room, which was unlit except for a screen set in the wall, some kind of window into . . . but before Mike could come to terms with what the panel was he saw a dark-haired woman lying on top of a hospital bed. Her face was almost as white as the pillow. There was a dark contusion on the left side of her face which shaded to deep indigo in the eye. The mouth was puffy and swollen and there was a little vertical cut in the lower lip. It was Cathy.

He rushed against the glass as if to break through. Like the window in his room it was so thick there was no resonance. He hammered with his fist and shouted her name. Then he was silent. He could hardly bear to watch her as she came awake. Her bruised eyes flickered and she swallowed painfully. Then, slowly, as if every movement required total concentration, she rolled her head across and looked at him.

'Cathy!'

Her big Egyptian eyes looked like black stones. They fixed on him without blinking. It frightened him, the way she looked. He thought she must be drugged, unaware of what was happening, unable to focus. Slowly she climbed from the bed. He was surprised by the rustle of the sheets. Sounds from inside the room seemed to come to him electronically amplified. She walked across the room and stared straight at him, unseeing. What had they done to her? She no longer recognised him. It sent him frantic. He shouted her name, no longer conscious of the danger.

'Cathy! Cathy! I'm here, here!'

She frowned slightly, but was otherwise quite unaware of him. Still her eyes held him and it seemed to him that she was looking out at him from behind her eyes; looking out from some dark place inside her. She stared hard and then brought her face close to the glass, shading her eyes as though trying to see through. *A mirror.* Mike almost laughed as the realisation dawned. She couldn't see him because there was some kind of mirror. As long as there

517

was more light in her room than his she wouldn't be able to see.

'Hold on, Cathy, I'm going to try to find a light.' He rushed back to the outer door and fumbled around the frame. A neon tube fixed in the ceiling flickered on as he rushed back to the mirror.

'Cathy!'

Her mouth dropped open and she stepped back sharply. His eyes filled with tears as her expression changed from astonishment to delight. She brought her hand to her mouth. Her smile had opened the cut in her lower lip.

'Michael!'

Her voice boomed in the room. Suddenly he was aware of the danger they were both in.

'Cathy, how do I get to you? Tell me how to get in.'

Her mouth was bleeding. She was blinking away tears now, and shaking her head in disbelief. 'Cathy, you've got to – '

'I can't believe it. I've so often thought about you, Michael, so often regretted what happened.' She rushed against the glass. 'But what happened to your face?'

'Never mind that. Look you've got to – '

She shook her head.

'I can't hear you, Michael. The room must be sound-proofed.'

He looked down at the recording apparatus. Maybe there was some switch that would let her hear him. But there was no time for that. He started to look around for a way into her room. There was a door to his left which looked as though it went through but it was perfectly smooth. There was a slot for a security pass. The frustration sent him crazy. He ran against it, almost breaking his collar bone. It felt like a block of solid steel. He rushed back to the window. Cathy was crying, a hand pressed to her forehead. Blood from her cut lip ran down her chin.

'Michael.'

Her voice, magnified by the recording equipment, was unbearable.

'I'm here, Cathy. I'm here. How can I get . . .'

'Michael, I can't hear you. But I know you can hear me.'

Mike stopped in mid-sentence. He watched her, waiting for her to go on. But something seemed to relax in her. Her dark eyes seemed to go dead.

'He records me playing. He likes the way I play.'

She was no longer talking to him. Her voice sounded distant.

'Cathy!' He shouted her name. But she couldn't hear him. He watched her go over to the bed. She picked up a violin by the neck. She raised it above her head. For a split second it was poised above her, her thin white arm, pale and trembling. Then she brought it down with a deafening crack against the floor. She looked at him through the window, holding the neck of the violin which was all that was left apart from a wreck of strings and splintered wood. She laughed, her whole body shaken by spasms as she laughed at the broken instrument.

'A violated violin. That was an Amati, Michael. Good for conversation but not for oratory.'

'Cathy.' He banged against the glass. 'What have they done to you?'

She looked at him and seemed to see him again. She rushed across to the glass.

'What happened to your face, Michael? What happened to your nose?'

'Cathy, I've already said – ' But then he broke off, realising she couldn't hear him anyway. He pointed furiously at the floor, indicating that it had happened to him in the clinic.

'Here? In the Phönixlager?'

He nodded vigorously.

519

'You are here as a patient?'

'Yes!'

She dropped the remains of the violin and came up against the glass.

'Oh Michael. I've missed you so much.'

He touched the cold glass where she pressed her swollen face. He spoke her name over and over.

She was watching him again. In spite of the bruising the whiteness of her face made her eyes look all the blacker. They seemed huge, full of pain.

'He's watching us, Michael.'

Mike felt the hair rise on the back of his neck. He span round ready to defend Cathy from anyone who came near. The room was empty. Mike looked for hidden cameras. There was nothing.

'It's no use looking for him, Michael. You don't see him unless he wants you to.'

He turned back and looked at her again. She had become deadly serious.

'They are taking my children, Michael; my unborn children. All this' – she indicated the bruises on her face – 'all this was an accident. They are not treating me badly. I am their prize laboratory rat, sleek and white and clean with my little pink hands.'

She blinked, and gave a little shake, as if trying to wake from a dream. Mike raised a finger.

'Cathy. Cathy, wait. I'm going to find a way into the room.'

He started to move towards the outer door, but Cathy's voice boomed in the microphone.

'No! No, Michael. Don't leave me again.'

He gestured with his hands. He showed her he was coming in to find her. She shook her head and leaned against the glass.

Out in the corridor there was a door a little further along. When he came to it he saw that it was similar to the entrance by the mud room. You needed a card to get through. There were other doors on the opposite side of the corridor but that would take him further away from Cathy.

He went back into the recording room. Immediately Cathy spoke. She was lucid now. Full of urgency.

'Listen to me, Michael. The door you see there to your left. It's the only way in. You can't open it. Don't even try. Now look, I'm safe as long as they need me. They will do anything to keep me safe until I ovulate again. After that, after that I don't know. Now. I've worked it out. I am going to ovulate in about a week's time. I have another week. All you have to do, Michael, is check out of the clinic and get the police, get the American embassy, I don't know. Just get some help. What they are doing here is illegal, all of it. Not just what they are doing to me.'

She looked down at her feet. Mike could see she was exhausted.

'Cathy.'

She looked up, and for a moment he had the impression that she had heard him. But that was impossible. She continued to stare at him, looking more drawn and exhausted than ever.

Michael pressed up against the glass. It was cold under his fingers.

'I love you, Cathy.'

He mouthed the words and for the first time he had the impression he was looking at the girl he had known in New York. But the smile was gone almost immediately.

'Get help, Michael, or I'm going to die in here.'

He had to go now. He had to get back, to get help. But it seemed impossible to leave her. He put his hands against hers on the other side of the glass.

'Go, Michael!'

He shut his eyes and turned away.

He closed the door behind him and made his way back along the corridor to the ventilation duct. He wiped the tears from his face as he went along saying Cathy's name over and over to himself, the image of her bruised face, her black hypnotic eyes, fixed in his mind.

Then he was standing under the rectangular hole. Standing on tiptoe he reached up and was just able to get his fingers over the bottom edge of the frame. He took a deep breath and pulled. But there was nothing left. He was utterly exhausted. He collapsed, slowly sinking to his knees. Climbing back through the maze of pitch-black shafts seemed an impossibility. Now that he had found Cathy, half of what he had wanted to do was done, but it had taken all his energy, and all his desperation to do it. Now he had to save her. He had to follow her instructions. He was responsible for her life. He looked along the corridor. Everything looked different now that he knew Cathy was there. He took a deep breath and climbed to his feet. He had to find another way out.

There was no way of orientating himself. He walked around for almost half an hour, going around in circles, walking into dead-ends, opening doors into empty rooms, or rooms filled with humming apparatus. Then, as he walked into a brightly lit corridor he noticed that the linoleum was blue, not grey as it was everywhere else. He backtracked until he was back on the grey linoleum. Then he hurried forward. He had a distinct recollection of having seen a blue linoleum floor when he had watched the cleaners go through into the lab. There was a slim chance that this was the only part of the lab complex where the flooring was blue. Then suddenly he was standing before the main entrance.

He recognised the door at once. It was unlike any other in the laboratory, bigger, heavier, perhaps part of some older installation. And there was another difference: you needed a security card to get out as well as to get in.

Almost asleep on his feet, he ran his finger over the slot where the card had to go in. There was no way of tricking the machine and the door was at least six inches thick. He sat back against the wall and looked up at the massive steel door.

'Rest a little. Then go back to the ventilation shaft.'

He spoke to encourage himself in the oppressive silence, but he could hardly form the sentences he was so tired. He looked at his shattered wristwatch. *Must have broken it when I fell.* He had no idea of the time. He could feel his head swimming.

He straightened up with a start. He was falling unconscious, sprawled against the wall by the steel door, a prisoner. Soon, maybe in a couple more hours, the first staff would come in and find him there. He had to get back to the shaft. That was the only way out. He climbed to his feet.

The pain in his knees was unbelievable. He tried to walk, but each step was agony. How was he going to crawl through ribbed shafts out onto the mountain?

'Fuck it. *Fuck it!*'

His anger welled up and surged out in a stream of obscenities. He staggered against the door, and breathed for a moment. It was cold on his hands; cold, immovable. He turned and faced it, as though it had insulted him. His mouth was dry, but he managed to get enough moisture to spit.

'Fucking, *fucking* door!'

He struck it with his fist. The new pain in his hand surprised him, but he refused to be beaten, and he struck it again with his open hands now.

His breath came in short gasps. He leaned forward against the door, his hands burning with the blows he had rained on it. Then, leaning backwards, he pulled on a transverse bar, part of an older lock mechanism. The door rode open, silently, smoothly, and he was looking at the door to the closet in which he had hidden.

He couldn't believe it. He stepped forward jerkily like a marionette. It made no sense. On the other side of the door he turned and watched, stupefied, as the door came to on its hydraulic hinges. On both sides the locking mechanism had been switched off.

13

The Phönixlager. March 7th, 1996.

When he woke up the water in the bath was stone cold.
For a moment he couldn't think where he was. He stood
up in the tub and looked across at the mirror. He hardly
recognised the figure squinting back at him in the harsh
electric light. His hair was matted against his forehead
and on his left temple there was a dark bruise. Blood
from a cut had dried on his cheek. Somehow the dressing
on his nose was still in place, though several of the transverse strips of plaster had come away. His bottom lip was
swollen and felt painful when he touched it with his
tongue. Automatically he raised his arm to look at his
watch. The glass was cracked and it was full of water.
Looking down he saw that his knees were swollen. There
was a series of small cuts on his left knee which were
puckered and white from soaking in the water.

He stepped out of the tub and went through to the
lounge, walking slowly, his knees stiff and painful. The
first light of day showed the brooding forms of the surrounding mountains. He had very little time before room
service showed up with breakfast, and then there was
Miss Schindler to deal with. What was he going to say?
If he got dressed all he would have to do would be to
explain the cuts on his face. He would say he had gotten
drunk and then fallen against something. *I just got so*

depressed. All of a sudden I was looking at an empty bottle of whisky. Then I fell. Cut my head. Must have bitten my lip. He looked around the room. It was too tidy. He went across to the drinks cabinet and took out a few bottles. He took a bottle of Black and White and went through to the bathroom where he poured it into the sink. Miss Schindler was going to be very disappointed in him.

Back in the lounge he looked around at the neatly arranged furniture. What had he fallen against to hurt his head and to bite his lip so badly? The desk, the coffee table? Maybe he should break something. It would be more convincing. It couldn't make much difference to the bill. He wrapped a heavy crystal ashtray in a towel and brought it down hard against the corner of the glass coffee table. A brilliant fissure split the table top and a satisfying chunk came off the corner. There would be no blood, but it would have to do.

He went back into the bathroom where he washed and shaved. He put on some clean clothes, hiding the blood and oil-stained trousers and the torn sweater in his suit-case. When Miss Schindler came in he was holding his head like W. C. Fields after an all-nighter.

'Mr Diaz, you look terrible.'

'I feel terrible.'

And he explained what had happened. All in all Miss Schindler was surprisingly understanding. She said there was often a post-surgery depression. He got the impression that Miss Schindler had already seen rich clients with alcohol problems. Mike found himself cheering up under the influence of so much sympathy. She seemed to have bought the whole story. She looked at the dressing on his nose and replaced some of the strips of band aid.

'The most important thing is to keep this clean,' she said. 'The skin is particularly sensitive now. Contamination or any other disturbance could seriously compromise the end result.'

Mike nodded soberly, the model student.

When the door had closed he stood up and went to the window. Things had fallen into place incredibly well. Still the open door to the laboratory puzzled him. But gift horses were not to be examined too closely. After all, it was about time he had a little luck. The most important thing now was to get help. If Cathy was right they still had a little time to play with. She wouldn't be fertile for another week. Until then she was safe. But who was going to believe his story? As far as the Swiss authorities were concerned he was a drug pusher and possible murderer, and the American consulate was unlikely to believe his version of events. Once off the mountain he was a hunted man. Tania was the only person who could help. If she were to go to the consulate with his story, they might take her more seriously.

He looked across to the telephone. There was no line to Tania's chalet, but he could leave a message at the ski-school. He took his address book from the desk and sat down by the phone. Under T he found her round, girlish handwriting in the green ink she always used. He took up the phone and then paused. What was he going to tell her? He would have to be careful. Maybe the girl on the switchboard listened in to the calls. *I found exactly what I have been looking for all this time* – something like that, something cryptic? Or should he just ask her to visit him? That would be safer. *Tell Tania I would really appreciate a visit*. He dialled the number and waited.

14

The Phönixlager. March 7th, 1996.

When Geiger saw the debris of the violin his mouth dropped open. Cathy almost laughed, but she was so intent on watching his every move that she controlled the muscles of her face. He walked across the room and picked up the pieces of varnished wood. She thought he was going to lose control for a moment, something she had never seen.

'What happened, Cathy?'

His voice was constricted, strangled, pushed out under the sudden weight of his anger. Strange white blotches had appeared around his mouth. His face was otherwise dark, congested. He breathed for a moment. 'Do you realise how rare this instrument is?'

'Was.'

The vehemence of her single syllable made him blink as though she had slapped his face.

'You won't have the Stradivarius, Cathy. I won't let you play the Stradivarius.'

'Shove the Stradivarius.'

Geiger stared into her face. He looked so pained, for a moment Cathy wanted to console him, to co-operate. She drew her lower lip into her mouth and bit on it. She would *not* co-operate.

He handled her roughly as they went through the routine examination. He took her blood pressure, pumping up the armband until it hurt. Then he took her temperature and looked into her eyes and ears. Finally, looking away as usual, he felt her breasts. She gave a start as he squeezed, surprised to find her left breast sensitive, swollen. He turned immediately.

'What is it?'

She looked back at his questioning face, trying to work out what was happening.

'Nothing,' she said. Then: 'Your hands are cold.'

Geiger lowered her smock, looking into her eyes. He worked on as if nothing had happened. He took a sample of blood from her left arm. Another couple of minutes and he was finished. Then he closed his bag and stood up.

In every way the examination had been the same as every other day, except for one thing. He had not administered the hormone injection. She had never seen him look so cold, indifferent.

'So what about my hormone shot?'

She tried to make her voice sound challenging, authoritative. She felt scared.

'Not today, Cathy.'

He left the room without another word.

She sat for a while, touching her sensitive left breast. On the right too, yes. Her breasts felt swollen. A terrifying thought flashed through her mind. *She was starting to ovulate.* She went across to the desk and looked at the marks she had made on the inside of the drawer. She counted and recounted three times. According to her judgement, she had at least another seven days before she ovulated. Could she have lost sense of the diurnal cycle, and started to live a longer day and night rhythm? She had no way of telling whether it was light or dark. All she had to go by were her feelings of hunger, her digestive cycle, her tiredness. She knew she was sleeping more because of boredom, because of inaction, but she didn't believe her calculations could be so far wrong.

She put her hands to her face and screwed up her eyes. Her first fear was hardening into certainty. Geiger had withheld the injection because he knew she had started to ovulate. Soon they would come. It would be like the last time. She would fall asleep and when she woke up they would have stolen her treasure again. Except, and now she removed her hands from her face and looked at the blank wall, except this time she wasn't going to wake up.

15

The Phönixlager. March 7th, 1996.

The covering was removed from his eyes, and for a few moments Mike lay there blinking up at the bright lights above the couch. They were alone in the room, Kessler standing beside him, looking down at him, silent. The check-up had only taken a couple of minutes.

'So what's the news, Doctor? Everything shaping up okay?'

Kessler gathered up the wrappings which had contained the new bandages and threw them into a steel bin.

'You were lucky, Mr Diaz. You could have done yourself some serious harm. Fortunately there is no sign of subcutaneous damage. Nevertheless we shall have to keep you here for a few more days at least. The risk of infection is still very high.'

Mike sat up.

'I'd planned on recuperating somewhere else. Surely any place where . . .'

'Out of the question, I'm afraid,' said Kessler. 'We performed the operation and only we can be sure it is working out as planned. You don't want to end up deformed for life do you, Mr Diaz?'

'No, of course not, but . . .'

'Then you must stay for three or four more days. If we

find everything is satisfactory at that stage *then* you can go.'

Mike slung his feet over the side of the couch and stood up.

'Well, I'll have to make a few calls,' he said. 'Maybe I can rearrange my affairs a little.'

Krystal took off his glasses and placed them in his top pocket.

'Make all the calls you like, Mr Diaz,' he said. 'But you must stay in the Phönixlager.'

Cathy's words flashed through Mike's head: *just check out of the clinic and get the police.* He couldn't risk calling them from inside. They might be monitoring all the lines, in case one of the staff decided to inform on them. They wouldn't leave something like that to chance. It was probably just as well that he hadn't managed to get through to Tania earlier that day.

'Okay,' he said, 'if it's doctor's orders.'

Kessler opened the door for him.

'Yes,' he said. 'Let's call it doctor's orders.'

Miss Schindler was standing outside, her clip-board at the ready. She escorted Mike back to his suite.

'Look's like I'm gonna be okay,' he said after they had gone most of the way in silence, 'in spite of my little fall.'

'You need have no doubt on that score,' she said. 'Dr Kessler is one of the finest surgeons in Europe. It is rare indeed to see him take such interest in a routine operation. You are very fortunate, Mr Diaz, very fortunate.'

She smiled her tight, cursory smile, and left. Mike slouched down into one of the big armchairs. It was crazy, but something told him he wasn't very fortunate at all.

16

Brig. March 8th, 1996.

Waterman was just finishing breakfast when the waiter came up to his table.

'Room thirty-one?'

Waterman looked up. The waiter was a young man, Italian like most of them, with shoulder-length hair that needed washing.

'Yes?'

The waiter gestured towards the kitchens.

'There is a call. Thirty-one, please.'

'A phone call for me?'

'*Si. Per favore.*'

Waterman stood up and followed the waiter to an alcove just behind the big tables where the morning buffet was set out. A large German man wearing a white polo-neck shirt stood pondering the selection of breakfast cereals on offer. Waterman squeezed past him.

'Hello,' he said picking up the receiver.

'Mister Waterman, this is Amalie. Anna's friend.'

Her voice was faint and she sounded nervous.

'Of course. How are you?'

'I'm okay. Did I call too early?'

'Hell no, I was up ages ago. I got things to do.'

He suddenly realised that his voice could be heard right across the room. An old couple who never seemed to speak a word to each other were both staring at him from the far corner.

'Is something up?'

'Well, you asked me to call if the police found my van, the Volkswagen.'

'And have they?'

'Yes. They called me this morning.'

Waterman brought the phone closer to his mouth, turning away from the other people in the dining room.

'Where was it?'

'They said it was in a parking lot outside Alleinmatt. It was standing there for about two weeks, so the attendant got suspicious and reported it.'

'Alleinmatt? Isn't that a ski resort?'

'Yes. It's in the Valais – where you are now. They don't allow cars there, so you have to park outside the village and use taxis.'

Waterman picked up a pencil and wrote the name of the resort across one of the scraps of paper the waiters used for taking orders.

'They got any better ideas who took it now? Was there anything inside the van?'

'They didn't say. I'm sorry.'

Waterman thought for a moment. The kitchen doors swung open beside him and a trolley rattling with clean plates was wheeled out by one of the kitchen staff. The old couple in the corner were still watching everything.

'Listen, Amalie. The American guy who stayed with Anna, the one the police are looking for . . .'

'His name was Michael Varela.'

'Right. Did they tell you that?'

'No, some of Anna's friends did. They met him.'

'Okay. Well Anna must have trusted him, right? I mean she put him up, she hid him from the police, maybe she even lent him your van.'

Waterman could hear Amalie strike a match. She was lighting a cigarette.

'Like I told you,' she said. 'That's the way she was. She trusted people even when she had no reason to. She felt sorry for almost anyone who was in trouble. Here most people – they just don't want to know. You get into trouble and they treat you like you're some crazy animal. Anna was . . .'

Her voice trailed away. She still sounded upset.

'I understand,' said Waterman. 'What I meant was, maybe they were actually working on something together.'

'What do you mean?'

'Look, it's a little complicated to explain right now, and I'm not sure how it fits, but can you think of any reason why this Varela character should want to go to Alleinmatt?'

Waterman could hear the girl breathing. She was drawing deep on her cigarette. He wanted one too.

'People go to Alleinmatt to ski, to have holidays,' she said.

'I don't think Varela was looking for a holiday somehow.'

'Well maybe he wanted to ski into Italy. I think you can do it from there. Maybe he wanted to avoid going over the border by road.'

'Maybe, only . . . You're sure Anna never said anything about the place? Did she have any connections there?'

'She had a friend in the ski school. A girl called Tania – Tania Schaffner, I think. I never met her, but Anna talked about her sometimes.'

Waterman wrote the name down. Over on his table one of the other waiters was clearing away the breakfast things.

'Do you have her number up there?' he asked.

'Let me look.'

Waterman waited while she checked the numbers Anna had written up beside the phone. It seemed to take her a long time.

'No, it's not here,' she said. 'But I'm sure one of her friends would have it. Have you talked to Hans Fleischman yet?'

'I've been in too much of a hurry. But I've still got his number in Zürich.'

'I spoke with him a couple of days ago, and I told him about you. He was very interested.'

Waterman felt a twinge of concern. Since he'd been in Switzerland he'd told so many off-the-cuff lies about himself he was having trouble keeping track of them all. That was the trouble with working in a hurry. He couldn't help thinking of what happened to Sam Chaney. He'd gotten careless, and the next moment his brains had been splattered all over the table-cloths of some Wall Street restaurant – a restaurant full of people . . .

Instinctively Waterman spun around. One of the waiters smiled at him. The old couple in the corner stared. There was no assassin. But then Chaney probably never saw him coming either.

'Anyway,' said Amalie, 'he said he'd be happy to help out if he can. The only thing was, he asked me what paper you worked for and I didn't know.'

'Well,' said Waterman, 'I'm freelance. I sell the story to whoever pays, you know.'

'Yes, I know. Anyway, if you want to talk to him, he may have Tania's number.'

'All right, I will, Amalie. Thanks. I'm glad you got your van back.'

'Thank you,' said Amalie. 'Goodbye.'

Waterman was about to hang up when he heard her call his name.

'Yes?'

'Are you going to find the man who killed Anna? Are you going to get him?'

'You bet I am,' he said. 'You bet I am.'

Back in his room Waterman dialled Hans Fleischman's number. The phone at the other end rang three or four times and then there came a click followed by the hiss of an answering machine. The outgoing message was very brief, just a few words in German, and no name was given. Waterman waited for the electronic tone and then started speaking.

'This is a message for Hans Fleischman,' he said. 'My name is Harry Waterman, and I'd like to talk to you about Anna Norden. I believe you already know why. You can reach me . . .'

He was interrupted by a click. Then a man's voice said: 'Hello, this is Hans Fleischman. Sorry. I just got in.'

'Mr Fleischman. This is Harry Waterman. I believe Amalie told you something about me.'

'Yes, of course. You're the reporter, right?'

The voice sounded young, but confident – and the English was good. Waterman couldn't visualise the kind of drop-out he had been expecting.

'Yes, that's right. I'm really just calling to get a telephone number of one of Anna's friends. Her name's – '

The voice broke in: 'You're trying to find out about Anna's death, right?'

'Yes, well kind of. I mean my story is – '

'Why do you think it's so interesting? Is it the political thing?'

Waterman had thought all this through before, but since no one had really asked him very much about his 'story', he'd almost forgotten what he meant to say.

'Kind of,' he said. 'I'm trying to look at the whole spectrum. People in the US are pretty ignorant about this

537

country, you see? They think it's all cuckoo clocks and milk chocolate.'

He thought he'd done pretty well there, but Fleischman persisted.

'But what do you think about the murder? Do you think it was anarchists, like the police say?'

Waterman squirmed.

'I don't know. I mean I doubt it, I guess. Anyway, the number I'm – '

'I can tell your American readers a lot about this country if you like. We can meet. Where are you now, in Zürich?'

'No,' said Waterman, grateful for an excuse, 'I'm in Brig.'

'Brig? You think that's where the killer went?'

'No,' said Waterman. This guy was really getting to him. 'I mean, maybe. It's too complicated to explain right now. I just want the number of a woman called Tania Schaffner. Have you got it?'

'Tania Schaffner? She was a friend of Anna's, right? A ski instructor or something.'

'That's right. At a place called Alleinmatt.'

There was a pause.

'*Ja*, I think that's right.'

'Do you know the number?'

'In Alleinmatt? No. I think I only met this girl once, about a year ago. She wasn't very . . . mature, politically. You think she can help you?'

'Maybe,' said Waterman. 'I guess I'll just have to try one of Anna's other friends. Or the ski school maybe.'

'Good idea,' said Fleischman. 'But give me your number and I'll call you if I find out.'

'Thanks,' said Waterman. 'That sure would be a help.'

17

The Phönixlager. March 8th, 1996.

She was breathing deeply. They had taken her from her bed and wheeled her through to the operating theatre. Only now did Geiger take his eyes off her face. The harsh overhead light only emphasised the perfection of her beauty. Her rich colouring, the black glossy hair, and her red lips, held him for a moment in the silence, a silence broken only by the electronic blip following her heart. There was a tiny beauty spot on her left earlobe. He had never noticed it before. In spite of the weeks of intimate contact there were still things he had not seen. He felt an urgent need to know everything before she was gone. The thought that she was about to disappear from his life brought a cold, dead feeling into him. He shuddered in spite of the heat of the lamps.

'I am ready to proceed, Professor.'

Kessler's voice brought him back to the present business. Kessler was sweating profusely over his mask. He held the ultrasound scanner on the exposed abdomen of the sleeping woman.

'Yes. We will proceed with the aspiration.'

Geiger took up the sterile needle and leaned forward. Hardly hesitating, watching the ultrasound screen all the time, Geiger inserted the needle into the anterior abdominal wall. The graffian follicles were fuzzily visible on the monitor screen. Several of them bulged slightly with ripe oocytes, unfertilised buds of humanity. Geiger frowned, leaning forward slightly, his hand steady. He had expected five eggs, no more. Here there were eight. Aware that it was because of his efforts that the woman's body had given up these treasures, and given them up earlier than was natural, he nevertheless could not suppress a feeling of gratitude and wonder at the generosity of the organism.

The fine point of the needle slowly approached the first follicle. With meticulous care he aspirated the first oocyte. Then he slowly withdrew the needle and deposited it in a deep cell cooled with liquid nitrogen. Cathy's egg froze instantly. The process was repeated eight times.

After two hours Geiger walked away from the table and removed his mask. Kessler wiped an antiseptic swab across the woman's abdomen and then pulled down her green smock.

'It's done, Egon.'

Kessler looked up, surprised by the tone of the other man's voice. Geiger was pale, his face glistening with sweat.

'We have done it. We now have a stock sufficient for our work.'

He gave a deep sigh and then came back across the room to the table. He closed the lid on the metal box the size of a suitcase in which the eggs were stored. Then he looked at the woman's face.

'We no longer need her.'

Kessler sniffed.

'Then let us not waste any more time,' he said.

He withdrew the cloth covering a tray on which there was a variety of surgical instruments, and a disposable syringe.

18

The Phönixlager. March 9th, 1996.

The sound of his own scream brought Mike to consciousness. At first he thought he had reached another part of his dream, but the faint blue light behind the curtains and the red digits of the electric clock told him that the room was real. He swallowed hard, breathing more regularly. What was it? He tried to remember the terrible thing he had seen. Then it came to him. He struggled out of the sheets and went across to the light switch, staring back at the bed. But the dampness he had felt was only sweat. He sat down again and held his throbbing head. *Cathy, Cathy, Cathy . . .*

He had returned to her room, to the side of her bed, but when he had drawn back the covers there had been nothing there, nothing but the sheets, heavy with her blood. And she was gone. He stood up and looked at the dead light of the room. Then he went through to the bathroom and splashed his face with cold water. He had to get a grip on himself. He was falling apart.

For the hundredth time he went through the reasons for waiting, for *not* leaving the clinic to get help. In the first place, he had time. Cathy was safe for another week. She had said so herself. So there was no reason to go against Doctor Kessler's express demand that he stay for a few more days. If he checked out against Dr Kessler's

541

advice he might arouse their suspicion. At the same time, he had no idea what to expect once he was away. If the police were really determined to nail him as Anna's murderer they could have got hold of photographs by now. Maybe his picture was in all the papers. No. Without Tania's help, without her ears and eyes, the outside was too dangerous. And he still hadn't heard back from her.

But if he had good reasons for staying put, it didn't make it any easier to do. After two days he felt close to breaking point. He could think only of Cathy, of what they might have done to her. He slept only fitfully, one hour at a time, and folded in the heart of each hour's sleep was a new picture of her death. Sometimes, as he lay there, half awake, he would begin to wonder if he had ever found Cathy at all, if he had not dreamt everything. His swollen lip and the bruises on his knees were his greatest comfort. It was they alone that told him that it had all been real. Standing before the mirror he checked the lip for the hundredth time. The swelling had gone down, but there was still a clear, thick line of clotted blood.

Keep calm, Mike, she's still there . . .

His eyes ached. He stumbled back to the bed and switched out the light.

He awoke to find Kessler standing in the door to the bedroom. He had never come into Mike's room without knocking. Mike looked down at his exposed legs. He covered them with the sheet.

'Good morning, Mr Diaz. You are sleeping late today.'

Mike reached for the light switch, but Kessler was already moving towards the window. The room was bathed in the white light of an overcast morning. Mike shaded his eyes. He could see the clouds moving away towards the south, driven by a strong wind. He checked the time. It was just after nine o'clock.

542

'Good morning,' Kessler repeated, still holding the bag. 'I hope you will forgive me for disturbing you like this, but it is important that you be checked at this stage, to make sure there is no infection. I'm sure you would not want to risk that for the sake of an hour's sleep.'

Mike took a robe from the bathroom and tied it around him. Miss Schindler had not said anything about a check-up that morning, but maybe Miss Schindler had lost interest in him now that he was no longer getting drunk and smashing up the furniture.

'So does that mean I'm gonna get to see your handi-work, then, doctor?' said Mike.

'I would advise strongly against that,' said Kessler. 'It will be at least another week before your nose will have recovered sufficiently to yield a pleasing result. For the present it will remain swollen and somewhat disfigured.'

'No kidding?'

'I'm afraid so. It would be much better if you were to wait. There have been cases of trauma caused by such premature curiosity.'

'So are we going back to the clinic?'

Kessler smiled tightly.

'That will not be necessary, Mr Diaz. I can see as well in here, and I have all the necessary materials with me. Please.'

He indicated an armchair in the corner of the room. Mike sat down, his eyes following Kessler's busy white hands. After a moment's preparation Kessler began to unpeel the tape from around the bandages. Mike felt his nose tingle as the lint was slowly pulled away. For a few moments neither man spoke. Mike tried to squint at the sides of his nose. They looked red and swollen, painful.

'How does it look?' Mike asked, trying to keep the anxiety out of his voice. The thought that maybe some-thing had gone wrong had set his heart thumping. Climb-ing around on the mountain in freezing cold hadn't exactly been doctor's orders. The tingle in his nose had already become a faint throb.

Kessle hummed positively.

'I don't think we have any problems here, Mr Diaz,' he said. 'I see no sign of inflammation. The scars are healing nicely. I think we can say it is a good job. A little more time and you will have a nose that is entirely satisfactory. Just like the one you chose, in fact.'

Mike couldn't help feeling a spasm of relief. And yet the thought of possessing this beautiful new feature gave him no pleasure. His old nose hadn't been the kind models paraded around on the pages of *Esquire*, but at least it had been *his*. And if it was good enough for Cathy then it was good enough for anyone.

'Well that's great, Doctor Kessler,' he said, trying to sound enthusiastic. 'That's what I came for.'

'And if you decide that the result of our work is not so pleasing after all,' Kessler added, 'you may of course return to us for further alterations. You will be guaranteed priority in that event.'

He prepared a new dressing – a lighter one, it felt like – and taped it on.

'Thank you. So when can I go?' Mike said. 'I really should get back as soon as possible.'

'We have a helicopter leaving in about an hour. The flying conditions are not ideal, but nothing to worry about.'

Mike looked up at Kessler's face.

'You meant that's it? No more check-ups?'

'Nothing that requires you to stay here. If any complications or discomfort set in, you can of course get in touch with us. I have prepared these for you.'

He handed Mike a small jar containing white pills.

'Simple pain-killers. Not more than two in twenty-four hours. But they might be useful.'

544

Mike looked at the jar, Kessler standing over him smiling.

'But apart from that, all you need do is continue to take care, avoid sports of any kind – for the next four or five weeks ideally – or any violent physical activity that might result in your taking a knock. I will tell the pilot to expect you. Will you be returning to Zürich?'

'Not immediately,' said Mike. 'I have some things to pick up at Alleinmatt.'

'Very good,' said Kessler. 'I shall instruct him accordingly.'

He held out his hand.

'It has been a pleasure, Mr Diaz.'

They shook. Mike thought he could detect a faint look of triumph in the doctor's face.

'The pleasure's been all mine,' he heard himself saying. 'Thank you.'

He hoped Tania would be waiting for him at the heliport, but there was no sign of her as he crossed the tarmac and headed towards the small grey building that served as a terminal. He had left another message for her at the ski school, but that was only an hour earlier, and the chances were she was still at home or maybe taking a Saturday morning class.

Approaching the door, the sound of the Mendelhaus chopper taking off again behind him, he found it difficult not to break into a run. There was something in the way things had happened, the way Kessler had come to see him, something in that faint smile of his, that scared him. It had all been so easy. Even the cost of his stay, the size of which he hadn't dared to enquire about for fear of seeming concerned about it, had barely been mentioned. The girl behind the reception desk had said that they would send him a bill in due course, and that was that.

He had not even seen Miss Schindler again. It was as if they had suddenly decided to get rid of him.

And now he was away from Cathy again. She was trapped, alone, under sentence of death. She had said they had a week, but what if she were wrong? At that moment he had the distinct impression that someone was looking at him. *Maybe they had recognised him from the papers*. He glanced across the room and saw an old woman staring at him. She turned away as he looked up. He lifted the lapels of his coat and quickened his pace. He told himself that she was probably just looking at the dressing on his nose. He had to get Tania. Only she could help him. He pushed open the door and hurried towards the exit on the other side.

'You want taxi, mister?'

A man in a leather jacket with a thick brown moustache was calling to him.

'Yes!'

'Lucky, I just leave someone here,' said the man, studying Mike's bandaged nose for a moment. 'Where you going?'

'Up the side of the valley,' said Mike, pointing beyond the village towards the western slopes. 'There's a road that goes towards the Höllenspitze, under the gondola lift.'

'*Ja*. I know the road,' said the driver unhappily, 'but there's a lot of snow still.'

'Can you get me there?'

The driver shrugged.

'Maybe with chains, but it can be closed . . .'

'Can you do it or not?'

'Okay mister, okay. We go.'

The driver shook his head and put Mike's suitcase into the trunk of his taxi, which was a big old-fashioned Mercedes with an upright grille and cream-coloured paintwork. They had to take the long way round the village where cars were not allowed, but they were soon climbing into the mountains. As they climbed away from the village through forests of tall pine trees, the road became narrower, its surface more treacherous. At each hair-pin bend the driver went down into first gear to keep from skidding on the hard-packed snow. Looking back up the valley Mike could see the distant outline of the Heulendthorn, and just beyond it, almost completely out of sight, the uppermost crags of the Phönixlager.

The last section of the climb was the worst. The driver swore and complained as his taxi skidded on the corners. There were steep, vertiginous drops on the valley side, against which the only protection was a series of stout wooden posts painted red. A plough had evened out the surface of the road, but a dusting of fresh snow in the night had left it thick enough for chains to be necessary. The last time Mike had travelled that way in Tania's Opel Corsa, the road had been given a sprinkling of grit, but that had been buried long since. Travelling only in the bottom gears, it took them more than twenty minutes to reach their destination.

The chalet was some fifty yards from the road at the end of a narrow track. From the back of the Mercedes Mike could see a plume of grey smoke rising from the stone chimney and Tania's car parked outside. She had to be in. He climbed out of the cab and gave the driver forty francs.

'You want I come back some time?' he said. 'Maybe later?'

'That's okay,' said Mike, taking his suitcase from the trunk. 'I'll manage, thanks.'

The old Mercedes turned around and headed back down towards the village. Mike walked slowly towards the chalet, his tooled leather shoes slipping on the snow. He had to grab hold of the ramshackle fence that stood beside the track, the only protection from a steep fall into the pine woods below the house. A freezing wind was driving up the valley, shaking clouds of snow from the pine trees, scattering the smoke from the chimney as soon as it appeared. It was just as well Tania had lit a fire.

He knocked three times on the door and waited. The wind blew icy snow into his face. He knocked again. There was no answer.

'Tania?'

The sound of his own voice gave him a bad feeling of *déjà vu*. He set his jaw and tried the handle, but the door was locked. She *had* to be there. He put his face close to the edge of the door and shouted again. For a moment he thought he caught the smell of smoke from inside. It smelt like she had lit the fire with an old fur coat. There was an acrid smell. He shouted a third time and slammed his palm against the door.

The shutters on the near window were closed, but through a hole in the wood Mike could see flames flickering in the fireplace, just the same as when he had first seen it. But the burning smell was unmistakable this time, strong . . . too strong!

He scrambled back to the door and slammed his shoulder against it. But it was rock solid, and it was difficult to grip against the hard-packed snow. He shouted again, and a third time, the panic rising. Then he took a step back and slammed his foot against the lock. There was a splintering sound as the frame gave way. Another kick and the door flew open. A grey wall of smoke loomed out towards him. He covered his face with his sleeve and ran inside. There were flames around the fireplace, but the rest of the room was in darkness. He flung open the windows, first in the main room, then in the kitchen, knocking against the oak buffet as he passed. Two silver trophies crashed to the floor.

'Tania?'

He shouted her name again, choking as the fumes filled

548

his lungs. He flung open the door of the bedroom. It was empty.

From the kitchen sink he grabbed a washing-up bowl, emptying dirty plates onto the floor. He opened both faucets and filled the bowl with water. The flames had spilled beyond the grate and ignited a pile of old newspapers and twigs that lay in front of it. The rug too was beginning to burn. At the foot of the fire what looked like the remains of a big feather cushion gave off clouds of acrid brown smoke. A few more minutes and the whole place would be ablaze.

As he flung the second bowl of water over the flames he saw her. She lay on her front a few feet from the sofa, her blonde hair covering her face, one hand outstretched towards the flames.

'Tania!'

He ran to her, rolling her over. Her body was limp, heavy. He looked into her face and saw traces of blood around her nose and mouth. Her eyes were barely closed, the eyes of a drug addict or a drunk. He seized her under the arms and dragged her towards the door. As he reached the threshold he noticed that there was more blood on her hands. Two of the nails were broken. He lay her down in the snow and looked again for some trace of life in her expressionless face . . .

'Tania, wake up!' he shouted. 'Tania!'

The door of the chalet suddenly slammed shut, pushed by the wind. Mike looked up to see a man coming round the side of the chalet, a stocky man with a beard. It was Hans Fleischman, Anna's friend. At the bottom of the path Mike could see his white hatchback.

'Hans?'

Fleischman ran towards him.

'Mike, what are you doing here? What's happened?'

'We have to get Tania to a hospital. There's been a fire.'

Hans stood looking at him for a moment. He seemed unsure what to do. Mike knew he was suspicious.

'There's no time to explain!' he shouted. 'Get the car! Just get the car!'

'Okay,' said Hans. 'But what . . . ? Okay.'

He ran back around the side of the house. Mike waited with Tania, no longer able to look into her face, trying to shut out the growing certainty that she was already dead. The north wind whipped tears into his eyes.

'I should never have dragged you into this.'

He heard the car starting. It reversed and then moved around towards him, its yellow headlights blazing. A Fiat Tipo. For the first time Mike wondered what Fleischman was doing there. Had Tania called him for help? Or had Fleischman come after him, for his own reasons? *A Fiat Tipo* . . . Mike held his breath, staring at the oncoming car. He had seen that car before, and now he knew where: he had followed it from Ernst Krystal's house and lost it in the Zürich rush hour, the night Anna was killed. *We worry a lot about infiltrators*, she'd said. *To a lot of big businesses we're a real threat.*

In an instant everything became clear to him: the Fiat would have led him straight to Anna's house if he hadn't lost it in the traffic, because that was where Fleischman had been going. Anna's last words to him: *Mike, there's someone at the door.* Tania too must have welcomed him as a friend. Mike saw the broken fingernails, the cushion in the fire, *the cushion he had used to smother her.* Tania was stronger than her friend. She must have struggled. She must have fought to stay alive . . . In his head the rage broke loose.

'SON OF A BITCH!'

Fleischman was half way out of the car when Mike threw himself against the door. The German screamed as his chest and leg were crushed against the frame. He

550

looked into Mike's eyes, and in spite of the pain, he smiled.

'I'm gonna kill you! I'm gonna kill you, you son of a bitch!'

Mike wrenched open the door and then slammed against it again. There was a sound like a muffled gunshot and Fleischman stared in astonishment as he felt his ribs breaking. The smile was gone now. He twisted and tried to free himself. Mike wanted him to scream some more. He threw his shoulder against the door, struggling to keep his grip on the snow, once, twice . . .

'You son of a – '

The blow to his midriff almost lifted him off the ground. He staggered backwards, struggling to draw breath. Fleischman, holding his ribs with his free hand, reached back inside the car for a gun which lay on the passenger seat. Still bent double, Mike lunged at him again, but this time Fleischman was ready. His feet squared like a boxer's, he struck down with the edge of his hand into the other man's collarbone. To Mike it felt as if a spike had been driven into his shoulder. Clenching his teeth, Fleischman took Mike by the throat and flung him down onto the driver's seat, the barrel of the silencer pressed hard into his left eye. He was laughing, gasping for breath, and laughing.

'You really hurt me, my friend,' he said, struggling to articulate his words through the pain which seared his left side. 'Yes. But I will pull through, as you say. And you look so foolish with your clown's nose and your one scared eye.'

He removed the gun from Mike's eye and aimed it directly at the centre of his forehead.

'You've saved me so much trouble by coming here.'

There was a moment in which the two men looked at each other. The mountain wind blew the hair across Fleischman's forehead, and Mike saw two deep scratch marks lost in the hair-line. The sound of a car door slamming made the German look up. Closing his eyes against the pain and fear, Mike knocked the gun sideways from his face. There was a deafening roar as Fleischman fired into the passenger seat. He struggled to regain his balance. Mike jerked his right knee up with all his strength into his groin. Fleischman fell forward against him, groaning in pain. Mike heaved himself sideways and pushed the German's face down against the gear lever. He blinked, trying to clear his head of the pain in his left shoulder. Then, struggling up from the seat, he grabbed Fleischman by the belt and pulled him backwards out of the car.

'Now, now – ' he gasped.

He reached forward for the gun which was still on the passenger seat. At that moment there was a crack, like someone cracking a whip, and the windscreen exploded into a thousand pieces. Mike's head snapped round. Halfway up the track that led to the road stood the upright figure of Ernst Krystal. He was dressed in a dark blue coat. In his gloved hand he was aiming a pistol with an elongated barrel. There was another flash and a crack. As Mike dived back into the car a third bullet hit the door, punching a single neat hole.

He could see Krystal's green Mercedes parked halfway across the entrance to the track. He felt no fear, only a burning desire to kill them, to destroy them all, to run them down. He put the car into gear, ducking low behind the dashboard, and moved off down the track, pushing out the remains of the shattered windscreen with his fist. The wheels skidded wildly on the snow, then seemed suddenly to bite. Mike looked up, hoping to find Krystal in his path, but he was gone. Then he saw him, standing below the track among the trees, the gun pointing straight out, his hand steady. Mike changed up into second gear, throwing himself almost flat against the passenger seat, expecting Krystal to try and shoot through the doors. There were two sharp cracks, but Mike was not hit.

He looked up in time to see the Mercedes directly in front of him. Swerving to the left, he struck it forward of the wheel arch, crumpling the right wing of the Fiat, sending the whole car skidding out onto the road. In the impact Mike's whole body was thrown against the steering wheel, knocking the wind out of him. The pain in his shoulder had spread now. He could hardly move the fingers of his left hand. Looking over his shoulder he saw Fleischman and Krystal running towards him, their breath condensing in the bright air.

The engine was still running. Mike struggled frantically to get it into reverse. Then he let out the clutch with a jerk, sending the car back hard against the Mercedes. Then he thrust it into first and headed off down the mountain. A bullet slammed into the dashboard.

One of his front wheels was scraping against the crumpled bodywork, and there was a whining sound coming from the engine. As he hit second gear he checked his mirror. Without snow chains the Fiat was almost uncontrollable above walking pace. He coaxed the swaying car up to twenty-five miles an hour, almost losing control on the first bend. Steering into the skid, he hit a post which seemed to deflect the car back into the middle of the road.

Mike gripped the steering wheel harder, willing the car to stay straight. He took the next three corners in second, looking back over his shoulder for his pursuers. There was nothing. He started to breathe more easily, and felt gingerly at his collarbone.

Maybe they gave up. Maybe they think it's too risky.

The road was getting steeper. One bend led almost straight into another, and the falls seemed steeper than they had on the way up. Sometimes he couldn't even see where a fall would end.

Then a straight stretch of road opened up in front of him, cut into the face of the rock, descending gently. Mike moved the car up to third gear, hitting twenty-five, thirty, screwing up his eyes against the blast of the freezing air.

Just a little while now.

Then he saw it! It was moving around the corner behind him, maybe two hundred yards back. Fleischman was at the wheel, and Krystal was leaning out on the other side with the gun. It was coming on straight and true and Mike could see the lumps of snow thrown up by the snow chains.

Instinctively he hit the accelerator. The Fiat did a crazy kind of dance on the ice, slewing back and forth across the road. The door beside him suddenly swung open. He pulled it shut, hanging onto the wheel to keep from falling out. He changed down before the next corner, but his speed was still too high. The back of the car slid out towards the valley floor, the rear wheels spinning, knocking down a warning sign by the side of the road. A broken wall of granite loomed up in front of him . . . he swung the wheel back towards the precipice, holding off the brakes. The car regained its grip long enough for him to look in the mirror. The nose of the Mercedes edged into sight, its snow chains audible now, rumbling against the surface of the road, holding it steady. Now it was only a hundred and fifty yards behind, rolling on as relentlessly as if on rails . . .

It was too far to the village. Too far. There was no way he could escape. As he forced his car round each corner, the wheels skidding, the certainty arose that he was going to die. He had never had a chance from the start. They had always been in control of everything. They had everything covered. He had thrown his life away, and others' too because he refused to see what was obvious. In the mirror he saw the Mercedes again, closer still, moving up on him slowly, almost casually. They had the whole thing worked out . . .

He urged the car forward for the last time. It responded with a sudden burst of speed that forced him against the back of his seat. In the mirror he saw Krystal take aim and fire. He ducked forward. The back window of the Fiat burst, showering him with glass.

He saw the warning sign too late. Bracing himself against the wheel, he stamped on the brakes. The car spun out of control, the back smashing against the low concrete blocks on the outside of the road. He tried turning into the skid, but the tyres had no grip. A chasm opened up below him. He caught sight of the church spire, the Heulendthorn, the distant rim of the Phönixlager . . . *Cathy, forgive me* . . . He let go of the wheel to cover his face.

The Fiat slammed sideways-on into the trunk of a fir tree that clung precariously to the side of the mountain. The body buckled around it, stopping the car dead, the front wheels on the road, the back wheels over the edge still spinning. Mike tasted blood in his mouth. Barely conscious, he opened his eyes in time to see the Mercedes high up on the road above. He fought to push open the door but it wouldn't open, twisted by the crash. He had no strength, no strength in his legs. With his last ounce of effort he hauled himself out of the driver's seat, trying to reach the passenger door. As he dragged himself out onto the road, hands first, unable to raise himself, he could hear the noise of the Mercedes approaching, the noise of the engine and the chains chewing up the road . . .

The Mercedes was just above the corner when Krystal caught sight of the mountain rescue helicopter in his wing mirror. It was barely fifty yards behind him, and falling like a stone. Someone was leaning out of the cockpit and pointing a gun.

'*Blüter Hund! Was ist . . . ?*'

There was a flash and a flare zipped towards him. It burst in through the back window, landing just behind Krystal's seat. Frantically he scrambled to recover it as the interior of the car filled with choking purple smoke. Blinded, screaming, Fleischman hit the brakes, taking the hairpin bend too soon. The Mercedes plunged down the short, steep slope on his right and then out into space. It turned slowly once in the air trailing a plume of purple smoke. Then, striking a spur of rock, it went end over end before smashing flat on the road below.

Harry Waterman looked back over his shoulder, shouting over the noise of the chopper blades.

'You got a gun, Mr Varela?'

Mike, huddled in the rear seat, shook his head.

'Okay. Take mine. I'm getting pretty handy with this thing anyhow.'

He held up the flare gun and grinned. Mike tried to grin back, but the effort was too much for him. He was still concussed from the crash and at the other end of consciousness he knew there was the terrible pain in his shoulder. His nose hurt too. Remembering the jar of pills Kessler had given him, he slipped a couple into his mouth. But he couldn't swallow. He had no spit. He crunched them up and got them down that way. Waterman handed him a revolver and faced front again. Beside him the pilot, Wolfgang, sat silent, grim-faced.

'I still can't believe you did all this on your own,' shouted Waterman, shaking his head. 'I had you down as part of a team for sure.'

Mike leaned forward. He couldn't let it pass.

'I wasn't alone. I had Tania, Anna, her friends.'

Waterman nodded slowly.

'Yeah, I'm real sorry about her. Fleischman got a head start on me. He must have taken off for this place the moment I called him. I'd no idea how he really fitted in to all this. Son of a bitch must have been the company's main man on the inside – although you can bet there are others. They don't leave anything to chance in this little country. They probably got infiltrators in the boy scouts.'

Mike tried to concentrate. Eveything since the crash had been a daze.

'How did you find out about Fleischman?'

'I never did till it was too late. When I got to the ski school, they told me someone else had come looking for Tania Schaffner about half an hour before. That gave me a very bad feeling. Lucky for you Wolfgang was there to help me out.'

The pilot started talking on the radio. The police had already been alerted, but they would have to come all the way up from Brig. Meanwhile a pair of ambulances struggled up the winding road towards Tania's chalet. The red chopper flew on, high above the roofs of the village, heading south-east towards the Italian border.

'You sure you wanna do this, Mr Varela? Look's like you've had enough action for – '

'I'm sure. There's no time left. If they hear what's happened . . . they may know already.'

Wolfgang looked round at him and nodded grimly.

'We make them pay right now, *ja*?'

'*Ja*,' Mike said. But his anger was all but gone. He only wanted to see Cathy alive again, to set her free. If he couldn't do that, it would all have been for nothing.

'Okay,' said Waterman. 'I just hope the cavalry ain't too long in coming. These guys don't fuck around.'

He looked back at Mike again, scarcd by the expression on his pale face.

'But then neither do we, right?'

They were climbing up the eastern slopes of the valley. Down one of the steep trails a group of skiers wound their way, braving the harsh wind. A minute later they were in the next valley, the floor of which was at a higher altitude than Alleinmatt, an unsettled expanse of sparse woodland, strewn with vast boulders deposited by a retreating glacier. Mike caught sight of the narrow road that crossed a neck of Italian territory, passing just below the Phönixlager, before finally leaving Switzerland for good. Beside it ran Mendelhaus's dedicated telephone lines.

'I go in low,' said Wolfgang. 'We surprise them.'

He brought the chopper down almost to the level of the valley floor, following a stream that cut a jagged course through the rocky landscape. Waterman braced himself against his seat every time they swung round a bend, the blades almost touching the ground. Up ahead, over the tops of the trees, Mike caught a glimpse of the granite spines that crowned the Phönixlager.

'Up there!' he shouted. 'On the south side, remember?'

Wolfgang nodded.

The stream was getting narrower, the fir trees closing in on either side. They climbed free of them, passing over the road which now looped back and forward as it too climbed towards the top of the valley.

'Maybe they see us, maybe not,' said Wolfgang.

Ahead, the great horseshoe of rock was drawing closer, a deep forbidding grey, rising from out of a shadowy white wilderness. As they followed it around to the south the great granite cliff rose up above them, hiding from view the Heulendthorn which lay just a mile or two beyond it. Wolfgang kept the chopper close, hugging the contours of the cliff.

'Say, Wolfgang,' Waterman said, trying to sound calm, 'you sure we shouldn't give this thing a wider berth, I mean . . . Jesus, that's close!'

'We surprise them!' shouted Wolfgang again. 'Okay?'

He put the chopper into a steep left turn to avoid a sharp outcrop of rock. As he did so the grounds below the clinic suddenly came into view. There was another chopper waiting on the helipad, its blades slowly turning.

Immediately a voice came over the radio: *'Hier spricht Phönix eins. Identifizieren sie sich!'*

Wolfgang brought them swooping down towards the front of the clinic.

'Hallo, Phönix eins,' he said. *'Hier spricht der Engel aus Tod!'*

'Was haben sie . . . ?'

The controller never finished his sentence. There was a thunderous, titanic boom, like the eruption of a volcano. A pressure wave threw the chopper up like a shuttlecock. All three men were thrown down against their seats. Then the chopper spun towards the ground, the tail rotating.

'JESUS CHRIST!'

Waterman spat out the words as Wolfgang fought with the controls, throwing the fragile aircraft up through a cloud of smoke. Splinters of rock struck the underbelly and the windscreen. Above the roof of the clinic a vast black cloud flecked with orange flame spewed out from inside the cliff, hurling rock and debris far into the air, engulfing the whole complex in a maelstrom of dust and smoke. As they climbed, a second great explosion seemed to tear the heart from the mountain, throwing a tongue of flame outwards towards the valley. The chopper jolted again, but they were high enough now to be clear of the main blast. But they still climbed until the uppermost crags of the Phönixlager lay below them.

Then they were flying through clean air, beyond the explosion. There was sun on the mountains further down the valley.

'Cathy!' Mike shouted her name as the realisation hit him that it was the lab that had been destroyed, the lab and everyone in it. He threw himself against the window, staring down at the scene below and behind them, still obscured by the drifting clouds of smoke.

She was gone.

Hans threw the chopper round in a steep turn and they went back. They hung there, hovering high above the scene, watching, the wind swaying them slowly back and forth. No one spoke, except for Wolfgang putting out a distress call on the radio. Mike leaned back against his harness. It was all over for him now. There was nothing left. In his mind Cathy appeared as he had seen her for the last time, through the sound-proof glass of her cell. *Get help, Michael, or I'm going to die here.* He let the pain take him now.

Waterman couldn't bring himself to look round. He tried saying: *I'm sorry, Mr Varela*, but the words just wouldn't come out. He was surprised to find blood oozing from a wound on his scalp. It ran down his left temple and into his ear.

'I guess they – '

Then he saw something, away to the right, beyond the other side of the ridge, something bright and shining, like a brilliant star rising into the sky, a thin red tail of smoke behind it. For a moment he looked at it stupidly, lulled by the rhythmic thwack-thwack-thwack of the rotor. Then he pointed.

'There's a flare down there,' he said.

Wolfgang moved the chopper towards the star, which hung motionless in the air before beginning a slow, drifting descent. It had been fired from the frozen wasteland which the walls of the Phönixlager all but enclosed. As they drew closer they could make out a solitary figure waving at them with both arms. They could see tracks in the snow leading to what looked like a small door in the side of the mountain. The figure was still waving as they put down on the snow fifty yards away – not waves of urgency this time, waves of joy.

Mike ran towards her, his legs sinking deep into the snow. He stumbled and staggered, not looking where his feet were going. He wanted to fly to her. She had pulled back the hood of her jacket so that her black hair blew wildly in the wind. Before he could embrace her he fell forward, tripping in his eagerness, burying himself face down. She came and bent towards him, laughing as she helped him up to his knees.

He looked at her, framed in the perfect whiteness all around them. There were still marks of violence on her face, but she was smiling.

'Cathy,' was all he could say. 'Cathy.'

And he would have said it again if she hadn't kissed him, pressing her smiling mouth against his. Harry came stumbling up in the deep snow, a checked handkerchief pressed to the wound on his head. Mike frowned, trying to take everything in.

'But how did you . . .'

She pointed back towards the door high up in the face of the rock.

'There's a door,' she said. 'A big steel door that's normally sealed, and a path cut into the rock. They took me out that way.'

'They?'

'Geiger and Kessler. They gave me the flare-gun and the clothes and told me to wait. They said someone would come.'

She smiled.

'I didn't know it would be you.'

She kissed him again, her arms tight around his neck.

'But what have they done to you?' she said, laughing. 'You look terrible.'

Mike lifted a hand to his face. He could feel a large lump on his forehead and the bandage over his nose was hanging off.

'You don't wanna see it now,' he said. 'It'll be swollen and disfigured, they said, for at least another week. Then I'll have a real wasp nose. You'll be ashamed of me.'

'Let me see,' she said and, reaching forward, took hold of the curled-up end of the bandage. It came away in her hand. She didn't even pull. Mike tried to judge her reaction, his eyes searching her face.

'Well?' he said. 'What do you think? I haven't even seen it myself yet. They wouldn't let me.'

Cathy said nothing. She just nodded. Mike's heart sank. This was what he had feared.

'It's not that bad, is it? I mean it's still got to heal a lot. It will get better.'

'Mike,' she said. 'It's exactly the same. They didn't touch your nose.'

'What? But that's . . . I mean . . .'

'They knew all along, Michael. They knew who you were. And they knew why you had come. They didn't need to operate, don't you see? They just went along with your plans as far as it suited them.'

'But the *pain!*'

'That would be easy for them; an injection, a drug. They let you find me, Michael. For a while, you were their laboratory rat too.'

Mike looked down at the snow, struggling to understand.

'So the door was open for me. The door to the lab.' Mike shook his head in disbelief. 'It's all so – '

'Geiger,' said Waterman. 'That's the only word for it.'

He gave a cough and felt in his pockets for cigarettes. His raincoat was flapping about him. In the rapidly clearing sky above them a succession of police helicopters appeared, heading for the Mendelhaus complex. A shout from behind made them turn. Wolfgang jumped out of the chopper, and came crunching towards them through the snow.

'I got news,' he shouted. 'Tania, she is going to be all right. She is going to be fine.'

Mike let out a whoop of joy. Harry lit a cigarette.

'I guess Fleischman wanted the fire to finish her off –
look more accidental,' he said, 'that sick son of a bitch.'

He dabbed at the cut on his head. It looked like it hurt.
Mike smiled at the man he had just got to know. With a
flourish he produced the jar of pills.

'Here, I'm feeling generous. Have a pain-killer.'

Harry shook his head, and started to laugh, trying to
find a clean spot on his handkerchief.

'The way I'm feeling, Mikey,' he said, 'forget the pain.
Just gimme the killers.'

19

The Italian border. March 9th, 1996.

The steel-grey Mercedes nosed down through the rising fog, snow chains rumbling on the packed snow and ice. The mountain road was narrow here, twisting and turning in the shadow of great spurs of rock. The man at the wheel peered forward occasionally, trying to make out what was coming up the road.

'Relax,' said the man in the passenger seat. 'There's nobody on this stretch of road at this time of year.'

The two men drove in silence for a while. They both looked exhausted, although content. They looked as if they had just finished a hard day's work.

Then the driver glanced across at his companion.

'What time is the flight again?'

The other man laughed. He glanced back at what looked like a steel suitcase on the back seat.

'There's plenty of time,' he said. 'Just get us out of the mountains. We should reach Linate airport by six.' A broad smile opened in his otherwise severe face. 'We might even have time for a bite to eat.'

Once again he looked back at the steel case. Then breathing a deep sigh he leaned forward and pressed a button in the instrument panel. The car was instantly filled with the tumbling notes of a Bach violin partita.

Epilogue

Extract from Exclusive! *magazine. May 2nd, 1996.*

The plot continues to thicken with regard to the destruction of the Mendelhaus research laboratories reported last month by your correspondent. Originally thought to have been the work of anti-vivisection extremists, it now seems that at least one Mendelhaus employee was involved. According to Paul Ackermann, a spokesman for the Brig authorities, the explosion in the main laboratories would have required at least a hundred kilos of Semtex: 'There is no way that such a charge could have been placed without inside help,' he said.

Police investigators believe the explosives were placed inside the main ventilation shafts and were ignited by a timing device.

The death of more than half of the Mendelhaus board, many of whom were visiting the laboratory at the time of the explosion, has also raised a few eyebrows. In spite of meticulous policework two bodies remain unaccounted for: that of Edward Geiger, head of the research program at Mendelhaus, and considered to be the brains behind the Erixil cosmetics product range, and Egon Kessler his assistant. According to Ackermann, the fire caused by the explosion was so intense that the missing bodies may simply have been incinerated. For the time being the search continues in the hope of finding less combustible remains such as teeth.

It is estimated that around $100 million's worth of equipment was lost in the explosion and subsequent fire which occurred in the early afternoon of March 9th. But the biggest loss is certainly the research material accumulated over years of hard work. So far we have no idea of the exact nature of Professor Geiger's work although it is thought to have had some bearing on genetic engineering.

If the remains of the missing men are not found, their complicity in the explosion may become an issue. A case of industrial espionage? *Exclusive!* thinks so and will keep its readers informed.

New York. January 4th, 1997.

It was raining when they left the hospital. Cathy looked tired and pale. Mike led her to the parked car and opened the door. She looked up at his face for the first time since the examination. A gust of wind blew a dark curl across her mouth.

'I'm sorry, Michael . . .'

Before she could go on Michael drew her against him, burying his face in her hair.

'Don't say that, Cathy.'

He tried to find the words to comfort her, but no words came. After a moment she pulled away from him. Mike tried to smile.

'We're going to stop all this now, honey. No more tests.' He lifted her chin and kissed her on the mouth. 'If you want a child we can adopt one. A nice little brown-eyed Mex just like daddy.'

Cathy nodded.

'That would be nice,' she said. Then her face looked desolate again.

'It was something they did to me in that place. I know it. So I wouldn't be any use to anyone else. But Geiger said nothing would be irreversible. He promised me that.'

'But there's nothing really wrong with you, Cathy. There's nothing wrong at all. What *could* they have done?'

Cathy looked away towards the grey hospital building. Then she lowered herself into the car. Mike walked round to the other side and got behind the wheel. In three months she had been to six specialists and none of them could see anything wrong with her. She no longer ovulated, and none of them could see why. Once more she found herself being told she was a unique case. The doctor had shaken his head, frowning down at a sheet of figures. *It looks like some kind of genetic disorder, Mrs Varela*. That was all he could say.